Who'd Have Thought It?

by

CHRISTINE WEBBER

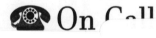 

On Call

With much love to Dashing Doc D –
without whom I might have been a SWOFTY

First published in Great Britain in 2016

Copyright © 2016 Christine Webber

A CIP catalogue record for this book is available from the British Library.

Cover design by www.jdsmith-design.com

Published by On Call

Printed and bound in Great Britain by Clays Ltd, St Ives plc

Typeset by the BORN Group

ISBN 978-0-9954540-0-2

Acknowledgements

Many people have helped me to make this book happen, and I am enormously appreciative of all their support and advice.

I want to thank Helen Baggott for her brilliant editing and proofreading; her expertise, efficiency and wisdom greatly improved my manuscript. I also want to thank Jane Dixon-Smith for designing my gorgeous cover – as well as for her patience and understanding.

I am deeply indebted to Dr Dawn Harper and Julie Peasgood for their generous and lovely cover quotes.

Thanks also to Daniel Knight and Mark Williams of the Born Group for their typesetting skills; I could not be more pleased to have found them. And I am hugely grateful to my printers, Clays, who have held my hand tightly during this venture! Clays printed several of my self-help books when I was published by Hodder, but with this novel I have had the chance to work more closely with the company – notably with Rebecca Souster and Georgina Aldridge – and it has been an exciting and rewarding experience.

I also want to extend my personal thanks to two amazingly supportive organisations – the Society of Authors and the Alliance of Independent Authors.

A special mention must go to my friend Dr Carol Cooper who became a 'hybrid' author long before I did, and who has served as my mentor and inspiration.

I also want to thank other independent authors who have helped me – especially Anne Stormont and Jane Davis.

My great friend Fiona Harris has loved this book since I first had the idea back in 2010 and her encouragement has been unwavering for all of that time; I am more thankful than I can say. Another Fiona – my second cousin and friend, Fiona Stevenson – read the manuscript and praised it extravagantly at a time when her affirmation was particularly appreciated. I also want to thank Dr Max Pemberton, who is not only a great mate and support, but who knows everyone and can always come up with a name and contact details when I need it! Thanks too to Sue Gibbs and Neil Monaghan who have cheered me on from the sidelines.

Finally, heartfelt thanks to my wonderful husband David Delvin, who kept me going with endless cups of tea, and provided expert advice on both commas and medical matters.

Prologue

'Put your clothes on, Anne. We need to talk.'

Only he, out of everyone she knew, refused to call her 'Annie'.

'Sounds ominous.' She attempted a smile, which was not returned.

They were in Venice to celebrate the thirtieth anniversary of their first meeting.

Despite the glorious spring weather, the luxury of the Hotel Danieli, and the joy of feeling as though she were a tiny figure in a Canaletto masterpiece, the trip had not been a success.

She had attempted to fill the uncomfortable silences with chatter. His irritation had been palpable.

Tomorrow, they would fly back to Cambridge; she to her hectic schedule as a GP and he to his long days as an orthopaedic surgeon. Once home, they would barely see each other. Hardly talk.

Annie was lying on the huge bed, dressed only in her lingerie. She might as well have been wearing a sack. For the past hour, her husband had been absorbed in his huge tome by Max Hastings – except when he had been reading, or responding to, the absurd number of texts coming his way.

Why did he want to talk now? He could save whatever it was till they went out for dinner. It would make a change to chat while they ate.

'Please, Anne.'

She walked to the wardrobe and extracted high heeled shoes and the black dress which made her look a size smaller. He did not help with the zip.

'It's not easy to know where to start,' he began.

But then the words tumbled out of him as he detailed the depressing state of their marriage.

A burst of laughter drifted through the open window from the gondolier station below, and in the distance, there was the sound of a violin tuning up. She had suggested going to a concert; there were posters everywhere advertising performances of Vivaldi's *Four Seasons*. He had been loftily dismissive. Surely, he had said, they were above such 'touristy' offerings?

Tears were running down her face now. She brushed them away impatiently.

'So,' he stated, dramatically. 'This is the end of the road.'

'We can try again,' she wailed. 'Perhaps it's my fault …' Suddenly, all dignity gone, she flung herself on the floor and started to crawl towards him.

Apparently unmoved by her distress, he strode to the other end of the room, and insisted that he must finish what he had to say.

His coldness demolished her, so she remained in a heap on the carpet, and listened.

'Perhaps it's inevitable that the magic goes out of a marriage.'

Inevitable? Was it?

'I'm afraid it's not just that our relationship is redundant. There's someone special …'

Her heart froze.

'… and I am so incandescently in love with her that I cannot live a lie any longer, which is one reason I cannot bring myself to have any action with you in the bedroom department.'

Suddenly angry, she pushed herself to her feet, then walked over to the dressing table and sat down in front of the mirror.

Bedroom department! Did he think he was in Selfridges?

'I'm sorry, Anne,' he continued. 'I realise this is hard, but I want a divorce. I apologise if I've been rude.'

She shrugged.

'I'll make it as easy for you as I can. We can discuss what to do about the house.'

She reached for cleansing cream and cotton wool and started to wipe the damaged make-up from her fifty-four-year-old face. In the mirror, she could see him watching her.

'Do I know her, Edward?'

She hated how formal she sounded, but he was just as opposed to the shortening of *his* name as he was to the lengthening of hers.

She saw him smile at the thought of his beloved.

'It's Suzie,' he answered proudly. 'From the tennis club.'

Her mind was blank.

'You know, pretty, blonde, runs a bridal shop.'

After a moment, it dawned on her who he meant. That forty-ish woman with a bottom that was far too near the ground; the one with the squeaky voice … who had had chlamydia last year, as Annie knew because *she* had treated it.

'Susan Hatfield?'

'Yup.' He blushed at the sound of her name.

'Oh dear God. I bet she calls you something cute. "Eddie", is it?'

'Teddy, actually.'

'I suppose all those texts have been from her?'

'Yes. She's been torturing herself by imagining that you and I might rekindle our marriage here in Venice.'

'What a coincidence! I'd been imagining the same thing.'

'Anne …' He walked over and attempted to put a conciliatory arm round her shoulders.

She shrank from his touch.

'I feel so relieved that it's no longer a secret.'

'Oh, jolly good,' she jeered. But her sarcasm was wasted on him.

He smiled. His evident uplift in mood now that he had made his confession was the biggest insult of all.

3

There could be no question of them dining together – she would probably weep, drink too much and disgrace herself. Anyway, she might never want to eat again.

He probably did not want to spend the evening together either. What he did want, obviously, was to speak to that scheming hussy. His eyes kept darting to the bedside table where he had left his mobile phone.

She would go out. Maybe hear the *Four Seasons* after all.

'Why don't you ring her?' she suggested.

'Can I? That would be wonderful.'

Biting her lip in an attempt to stem further tears, she scooped up her handbag and rose unsteadily to her feet.

'I think,' her quavery voice announced, 'that I'll go to a concert.'

Surely, he would try to stop her, or at least express anxiety that she should not be alone after such a shock? She paused, to give him one last chance to be kind, but he had already picked up his mobile phone.

The room swam before her eyes, so she left it.

Leaning against the door she had just shut on her marriage, she breathed deeply. 'Well,' she murmured to the long and empty corridor. 'Who'd have thought it?'

Chapter One

Annie felt different, but was not sure why.

The alarm had gone off as usual, at 6.30, and she wished – as she invariably did – that she could stay in bed a while longer.

Rolling on to her back, she looked up at the ceiling, then down to the floor, then to the left, and right. Everything in her bedroom appeared normal; in fact, exactly the same as it had when she had returned from Venice one year and thirteen days ago.

She stretched further down the bed, trying to capture and identify this elusive sense that something had changed.

Then, she blushed as she remembered her dream. She had been in her surgery, seeing a stream of well-spoken men in beautiful suits. It was hard to remember who they were exactly, but as she had rather a penchant for television journalists, perhaps one of them had been Dermot Murnaghan or Gavin Esler. But when she had buzzed in her next patient, instead of undressing himself, he had begun to remove *her* clothes. Her pulse quickened as she recalled the agreeable encounter she had enjoyed with her long-term hero and fantasy figure, Patrick Pace.

So, *that* was different. And there was something else; she had woken with no sense of regret about the past. Instead, for the first time since Edward had rejected her, she felt that her future was promising.

Janey would be pleased. Her best friend had been telling her for months how it was so trendy to be single in mid-life that the Department for Work and Pensions had created an acronym, SWOFTY, meaning Single Women Over Fifty. According to Janey, who had seen an item on BBC's *Breakfast*, SWOFTIES were all 'out there' and 'living for today' and 'having a ball'. Suddenly, Annie liked the idea of being one of them.

She climbed out of bed and padded over to the windows, before drawing back the curtains to reveal a grey and drizzly day.

A lone cyclist rode by on the village street below. Despite his waterproofs, Annie was able to make out the tall, fit outline of Rupert, the husband of her friend Diana. He biked to the station every morning en route to his desk in Whitehall.

Rather him than me, she thought as she decided that her own cycle would remain in the garage today.

The phone rang. She reached for the handset from the small table beside her.

'Hello!'

'How are you, Mum?'

Alice, the elder of her two daughters, had never actually spelled out that she liked to check up on Annie, now that she was alone. But that is what she did, most mornings, before her own day as a junior doctor began. She was a kind young woman, and the sound of her voice on the phone was almost as comforting as a cuddle.

Alice had been a very 'huggy' little girl and Annie could always cheer herself up by summoning the memory of the pleasure she had felt when her small daughter had wrapped her thin arms around her neck, and whispered, 'I love you, Mummy,' into her ear.

'I'm great,' Annie answered.

'Really?'

Annie could hear the relief in her daughter's voice.

It had been no surprise to Annie that Alice had chosen to become a doctor. However, she had been amazed that her petite daughter had picked orthopaedics, Edward's specialty. She suspected that,

6

deep down, Alice was seeking his approval. After all, she had been trying to please him since birth.

Edward had been so sure that she was going to be a son. Had Alice ever picked up on his disappointment? Annie hoped not.

'Mum!' Alice was saying. 'Are you listening? I'm trying to tell you that I saw Dad last night.'

Alice had refused to see her father for nine months after he had split from Annie. Their eventual first meeting had not been a success. But now she had obviously bowed to pressure and seen him again.

'It was awful,' Alice continued. 'He told me that I'd had plenty of time to get over him leaving you, and insisted I meet Suzie. She was sitting in the car outside the restaurant, so I felt I had to agree to us all having dinner together. She's nauseating. I'm sure that Grandma would have called her "rather common".'

Annie was overjoyed at the venom in her daughter's voice. But she struggled to be fair.

'She can't be all bad.'

Alice snorted in a very derisory way. 'The other thing,' she went on, 'is that Dad's bought a new car. A two-seater sporty thing, a BMW. Tony says he must be having a male menopause!'

Annie giggled and considered an even more unkind comment about her ex-husband, but decided against it. 'Who's Tony?' she asked.

'Oh, the Specialist Registrar on our firm.'

'Mmmn. What's he like?'

'Old and married.'

Alice sounded rather snappy and Annie found herself wishing, not for the first time, that her daughter would work less hard, be jollier and find a boyfriend, but she resisted the impulse to say so.

'You know, Alice,' she ventured, 'I don't think you should be too hard on your father.'

'Mum, you're too nice for your own good.'

Annie wondered if she should admit to her real feelings about Edward and his 'amour' from the tennis club.

7

'No, I'm not,' she responded.

'Yes you are, Mum – and he's a total wanker at the moment.'

Annie tried to suppress a giggle. She knew she should stand up for Edward even if she was not prepared to do the same for Sultry Suzie. But somehow the moment came and went.

'What's your agenda today?'

'Knees and more knees. There are two double replacements on the list. And then there's a trauma case – a young guy who crashed his motorbike. I'm going to speak to him in a moment; I don't think he's realised that he might never walk properly again.'

'That sounds like a difficult conversation.'

'I know. But Tony wants me to deal with it, so …'

'Alice – your dad means well, you know. And he must have wanted to see you a lot last night to have driven down to London to have dinner with you. After all, I bet he had to be back in Cambridge to operate this morning early, as usual.'

'Yeah, well. He needs to make an effort, doesn't he – after breaking up our family?'

'Mmmn. Still, I'm beginning to think there's life post-divorce after all. Perhaps I'll find some young hunk like Janey's?'

'Oh my God! You've changed all of a sudden, which is good, but – slightly weird. Gotta go, Mum. Love you.'

Annie kept thinking about her daughter as she worked through her morning surgery. There had been a marathon in Cambridge at the weekend, so several of the patients had sprained ankles, blisters, backaches or groin injuries as a result. Other than that, the session was pretty dull with an endless crocodile of individuals presenting with the sort of coughs and colds that would clear up on their own if only people would stay home and take an aspirin.

'No wonder Alice didn't want to be a GP,' she murmured to herself after a patient who had just spent ten minutes sneezing all over her finally left the room.

Still, her job had many good moments. It was always terrific to reassure nice, decent individuals that some lump they had found would not kill them. The downside, obviously, was when she had to tell them that it might.

She handled all the contraception in the practice too, which she enjoyed, so her spirits rose when she saw that the next patient – a woman who had had her second child just three months ago – was coming to have a coil fitted.

Annie could not help noticing that this young mum was immaculately waxed, despite having a baby and a young toddler. It must be a priority for her.

Now she came to think about it, she realised that she could virtually judge a woman's age by her depilatory habits.

The mid-lifers, like herself, had mostly stuck to shaving – with the odd application of Veet or Nair for special occasions – but practically everyone under thirty-five had little or no pubic hair.

Annie found herself thinking about the young patient again during the weekly staff meeting that afternoon. Then she allowed herself to revisit her dream, which led to her wondering whether such an elegant lover would expect a waxed-woman, or whether one could get away with a bit of fuzz here and there.

Suddenly, she caught the eye of Dr Jonathan Williams, her partner in the practice. He was staring at her rather quizzically, which probably meant he realised that her attention was wandering. She looked away quickly.

It was half past four before the meeting finally finished. She could have gone home then, as Jonathan was taking the late surgery, but since Edward had left she had had little inclination to rush back to an empty house. Her evenings as a single woman tended to feel as though they were in an oddly elongated time-zone. She would catch up on emails, phone a friend, have a meal and wash her hair, and find that there were still several hours to get through before bedtime.

But as she sat in her consulting room, completing her patients' notes for the day, it occurred to her that she might start to enjoy her 'after-work' hours now that she was feeling more optimistic about the future.

She was about to drive home to find out, when Carole, the practice manager, rang through to say that Janey had just walked in. She leapt out of her chair and practically collided with her best friend in the doorway. Immediately, she felt that huge rush of gladness she always enjoyed when they were together.

'So pleased you're still here!' Janey dropped everything she was carrying and swept Annie into a bear hug, before stepping back and looking her up and down. 'You look cheerful,' she concluded.

'I am. In fact, I was going to email you to ask if I'm in a new phase of the grief process, or whether I've got to the end and made you redundant! Come and have some tea in the staff room, and tell me why you're in Cambridge.'

Together they gathered up Janey's laptop and other belongings and wandered along the corridor, chatting as they went.

'I'm writing a story on some new university research. Rather boring, and not much money, but needs must. I've been interviewing professors all day and I'm knackered, so I just stopped on the way to the station in the hope you might still be working.'

She threw her bags on the staff room floor and stood watching Annie as she switched on the kettle.

'You seem so much better,' she decided.

'Do I? In what way?'

'You're kind of "jaunty" – and you haven't been that for a while.'

'It's probably because I had a saucy dream last night about Patrick Pace and have been thinking rude thoughts all day!'

'I thought you'd given up men for ever?'

Annie grinned but said nothing as she dropped teabags into two mugs and poured boiling water over them. It was only after she had added milk and handed the hot drink to her friend that she noticed how extraordinarily exhausted Janey looked. And thinner.

'Are they awfully well-cut trousers or have you lost weight?'

'Both, I expect,' Janey giggled as she kicked off her shoes and settled herself in one of the old, saggy sofas that hugged the walls of the room.

After a stream of catastrophic affairs with married men, Janey had finally struck gold with Miguel, a Spanish salsa teacher who – at thirty-eight – was some fifteen years her junior.

But was it all as wonderful as it seemed? Suddenly, something about Janey accepting an assignment that took all day for an inadequate fee, plus her tired appearance, caused Annie to wonder if life with the Mediterranean Dreamboat was quite as idyllic as Janey implied.

'He is *good* to you, isn't he?' Annie asked as she sat beside her.

'Brilliant!' Janey emphasised the word with a decisive nod of the head. 'And, quite apart from his other talents, he cooks marvellously. I just wish I had more appetite. He says I don't eat enough to keep a fly alive, but I always feel so full these days.'

'Must be true love!'

'But will it last? I used to think that you and Edward were the perfect couple.'

'So did I – how wrong can you be? Obviously, now I look back, things had become pretty unexciting. Still, I hadn't realised how desperate they were till Venice. I only wish he hadn't dumped me while we were supposed to be having a romantic anniversary.'

'Yes, very inconsiderate – especially when you paid for it.'

'I suppose my attempts to seduce him by lying around in my undies forced his hand. The funny thing – though of course I didn't laugh at the time – was that he kept saying "I've started, so I'll finish …" as if he were presenting *Mastermind*.'

Gratifyingly, Janey dissolved into giggles.

Had it actually happened quite like that? Probably not. But it was near enough.

'I did sometimes think that he was a pompous twit,' Janey remembered. 'So, are you really over him now?'

'I hope so, and most of the credit must go to you. You've been marvellous and better than any therapist.'

Janey drained her mug and jumped up. 'I must go. But I'm so glad you've started fantasising about Mr P again; you and your broadcasters! Shows you're back to normal. Let's start thinking about internet dating. I'll email you tomorrow.'

With that, she stepped back into her four inch heels, swept up her bags, hugged Annie again, and left.

Annie straightened out the throw on the sofa and meandered back to her consulting room, surprised to find herself suddenly tearful. But her eyes were moist with gratitude, not sadness. Janey was the best possible friend. And her support had been supremely reliable through the bad times, even if she had kept going on about phases of grief because she had once written an article on them.

The thing was though, that apart from all those 'anger' and 'denial' periods that health writers know far more about than doctors, there were lots of other phases. Like the one when you stand at the freezer door devouring ice cream straight from the tub. Or the one where your sister-in-law invites you for dinner and you are pathetically grateful when her neighbour sneaks his hand on to your knee under the table. Or the make-over stage where you lose half a stone, get a new haircut and colour, join a French class and enrol at a gym. Annie winced at the memory, knowing all too well that every other mid-life, middle-class dumpee deals with rejection in a similar way. How awful to be so unoriginal!

'Are you off?' Carole was tapping away at her keyboard as Annie passed her doorway on the way to the car park.

'I think so.'

'How's that empty-house-feeling coming along?'

Carole rarely chatted about personal issues, but when she did, it generally hit the spot.

'Funny you should ask. Better, I think. How are things in your full house?'

Carole had an out-of-work husband and twin teenagers.

'Gruesome. That's why I prefer working late to going home!'

Annie smiled ruefully. 'See you tomorrow.'

The Cambridge rush-hour was in full swing, which meant that the drive back to Little Trumpford would be slow. Still, there was nothing to hurry for. Perhaps she would break the journey at Waitrose.

At least she no longer had to shop for all the products that Edward had been unable to live without. No need to heft a box of Stella Artois into the boot, or a case of burgundy. She could just pick up the odd bottle of red or white wine on special offer. And of course she no longer had a reason to buy the thick-cut marmalade that he adored and she loathed.

In fact, there was still an unopened jar of it in the kitchen. She should have thrown it out ages ago, especially since it had often reduced her to tears as it sat there, silently reproaching her for having lost her husband to another.

She glanced at her watch. Janey would be on the train back to London now, excited about returning to her swivel-hipped lover. What was that she had said about internet dating? Surely that would be very scary? But Janey would know all about it. She was what Annie's daughters called a 'cool' friend; she always had been, ever since they had first met in 1983.

Janey had been a young reporter on the *Harrow Observer* and her boss had sent her out to do a story about junior doctors and their long working hours. So, she had hung around the entrance of Northwick Park hospital, waylaying anyone in a white coat who looked tired.

'Are you a doctor and are you exhausted?'

'Yes, and yes,' Annie had answered. 'But at least I'm dry, which you're not.'

'I know. It hasn't stopped raining all day.'

They stood there, Annie remembered, summing each other up, two twenty-somethings desperate to make good in a world that still seemed very male-dominated despite the women's lib movement and the fact that there had been a female prime minister for four years.

She smiled as she pictured her friend at that first meeting, with her gloriously 'big' auburn hair, modelled on one of the actresses

13

in *Dynasty*. Even having been rained upon, she looked fabulous and fashionable. Annie's own hair had been treated to one of those wash-and-wear perms of the period – which was not very 'her' but was at least easy to manage while she struggled with a schedule that frequently involved working a hundred hours a week.

It had been a strange time for them both. Annie had recently returned to London, after training in Edinburgh, having realised that she did not love her boyfriend enough to marry him. And Janey was in lust with a married man who kept promising to leave his wife but never did.

On an impulse that they both loved to recount, they had elected to have a drink at a local pub. One white wine spritzer became three, and dinner took the form of several packets of dry roasted peanuts.

At some point she had introduced herself as 'Anne', and had been thoroughly taken aback when Janey decided that from now on she should be called 'Annie'.

'But …' she had protested.

'Trust me. "Anne" is far too dull for you. You're an "Annie" – no doubt about it.'

And, as she had chatted, munched nuts and considered her new name, she had realised that Janey was right. And that, as Annie, she immediately felt livelier and more the sort of person she thought she wanted to be. Whether it was the new name that did it, or the emboldening effects of the spritzers, once she had secured a promise that Janey would not reveal her identity, she had regaled her new friend with stories about mishaps and tiredness, and about how important it was to get the nurses on your side or else you were really done for, and how this was awfully hard because most of them were much nicer to the male juniors, as they were potential marriage material.

'And today,' Annie had confided, 'I've done something absolutely awful.'

Janey's eyes had widened. 'Have you killed somebody?'

'Not quite that bad.'

And then Annie had told Janey about the elderly gent who had been admitted with abdominal pains, and how she had had to feel inside his rectum – which is a way of checking for appendicitis. Unfortunately, she had made the fatal mistake of sitting down on the edge of his bed while examining him, and had fallen asleep.

'I was probably only "gone" for a couple of minutes,' she said. 'But when I woke up, my finger was still wedged right up inside his bottom. I was appalled, but the old boy said he hadn't liked to wake me, and anyway, he had quite enjoyed it!'

They had laughed themselves through that first evening, and – despite all the various ups and downs of their respective lives – they had been laughing together ever since.

With a start, Annie realised that her reminiscences had almost made her miss the filter-lane that would take her into the super-market car park. She eased her Fiat into it, waving apologetically to the driver behind.

Inside the store, she wandered up and down the aisles, chiding herself about the 'convenience-food' rut she had got into. She had always found the time and energy to cook properly when the girls lived at home. But now she was content to opt for a pack of smoked salmon, a bag of ready-washed lettuce, a jar of sun-dried tomatoes, a lemon and a small granary loaf. Dinner in a jiffy; that was what she wanted, and she liked to eat it off a tray while reading or watching TV.

The man ahead of her at the checkout also appeared to be shopping for one. His basket contained oven chips, a steak pie, a small pack of prepared green beans and a bottle of claret. He smiled as he noticed her sizing up his shopping.

He was attractive, with plenty of hair – greying rather attrac-tively round the temples – and his suit and shoes were immaculate. If only she could think of something to say. Janey would have given him half her life story by now, and doubtless been invited for a drink at the nearest pub.

He glanced back at her as he extracted his debit card from the machine. Annie felt herself redden. She should seize the moment, but her mind and body froze.

'Sorry to keep you waiting.' The woman at the check-out was talking. The man left. She quickly packed and paid for her items and walked back to the car.

Attractive Man's vehicle was parked near her own. He caught her eye as he shut his boot. Was he going to speak to her?

'Annie!'

She turned, reluctantly, in the direction of the voice.

Her friend Diana was sitting in her Range Rover and leaning out of the window, waving. Annie could see immediately that something was amiss. Diana was a physiotherapist. She was also immensely fit, despite being grey-haired and almost sixty. She could be quite intimidating – her father was a baronet, and her husband, the bicycling Rupert, was something incredibly high-up in the civil service – but she was a fascinating and lovely woman. Capable too; she ran highly profitable charity coffee mornings, and she regularly hosted convivial drinks parties where all her canapés were not just exquisite, but homemade. Despite the differences in their backgrounds and their attitudes to catering, Annie and Diana had become genuine friends over the years.

'Are you OK?'

Diana sighed. 'I've had better days.'

Annie gazed at the other woman, who, most unusually, looked somewhat wispy and old. 'Do you want to talk about it?'

Diana nodded. And then, completely out of character for her, she asked, 'Can you drive me home? I'll pick up my car tomorrow.'

Annie helped her from the Range Rover, took her arm and installed her in her own small vehicle.

She started the engine, and headed out of the car park on to the road that would take them back to Little Trumpford.

Diana stared ahead and said nothing for almost a mile. Then, as if waking from a dream, she shook herself slightly before speaking.

16

'I'm sorry to have hijacked you. I was parked, just thinking about going into the store, when I saw you draw up. I moved my car to be near yours so I could attract your attention when you came out. Pitiful, really, but I was afraid you wouldn't see me.'

'It's all OK. I'll get you home. Are you poorly?'

'Not in the way you mean. I'm just hugely grateful that you, of all people, turned up – because after what Edward did to you, you'll know only too well how I feel.'

'Rupert isn't leaving you is he?'

'No. But last night he confessed something that makes me wonder if I've ever really known him.'

'Sounds serious. Do you want to talk now, or wait till we're home and do it over a cup of tea?'

'Now would be fine. I've been mulling over things on my own all day and my head feels as if it's about to explode.'

'Mmmn … I know that feeling.'

Diana took a deep breath and exhaled sharply. 'Here goes,' she said. 'And try not to be shocked.'

'Doctors are unshockable.'

'I hope so. I have to tell you some history to make sense of what's happened now. I wouldn't normally discuss … you know … intimacy and such like, but I have to. So, Rupert and I have always been sexually incompatible. We've loved and liked each other very much, and been good companions. But … well … it just never worked in bed – for either of us. And I don't think that was too much to do with me, because, before I met him, I was in a relationship where I was like a bitch on heat. Unfortunately, that particular male was totally unsuitable. Rupert, on the other hand, was perfect marriage material. My parents were pleased. His were delighted. We had our children – God knows how, because he was not, to be honest, very … potent. So, after I'd produced the heir and spare, we never bothered with sex again. And one night when Rupert had a cold, he moved into his dressing room, and never moved back.'

'Sounds lonely.'

17

Diana shrugged. 'In a way it was easier for us both. Awfully English isn't it? We never talked about it, till last night.'

'And what changed?'

'His dominatrix has moved from Streatham to Cardiff.'

Annie felt her jaw drop.

'I told you you'd be shocked.'

'Well, that is something of a show-stopper. So, you mean he goes to prostitutes?'

'Yes. Apparently, he has done for twenty years or so – but only the sadomasochistic types.'

Annie was wondering how to respond when the traffic ground to a halt at the level crossing near the village. Playing for time, and hoping for inspiration, she put the car into neutral and pulled on the handbrake. Then she turned to look at Diana.

'How do you feel about that?'

'I wish I knew. Do you mind if I get some of the more lurid details off my chest?'

'Of course not.'

'Well, it seems that the woman he's been going to for three years is perfect for him. And he's been able to see her without too much effort. I get the feeling that he would just take an extended lunch break every couple of weeks and nip out to see her – Streatham not being too far from his office. But she's now told him that she was struggling to make a living, because south London's awash with S and M sex-workers. So she's relocated to Wales, where she's more of a rarity.'

'Who'd have thought it?'

'I know. Bizarre. He says that he arrives, and they have a cup of tea and a chat, and then she orders him to wash up and clean her oven and so on while she bellows at him that he's doing it all wrong.'

'He could come round to me. I'd love a kitchen slave.'

'You wouldn't like the next bit though,' Diana continued. 'After he's finished, he's allowed a treat, which involves her spanking him while she … um … criticises his equipment.'

'Oh my!'

'Quite. Then he gives her a hell of a lot of money and they have a glass of wine before he leaves.'

'Surely though he could get all that if he switched to someone else based in London?'

'He won't hear of it. He's really keen on her, so he's going to have to go to Cardiff from now on – and obviously he'll have to take a whole day off to do that, which is why he had to own up to me.'

Annie was sure she should say something wise and doctorly, but suddenly, the vision of Posh Rupert hurtling over the Severn Bridge to don Marigolds and be berated and thrashed struck her as so hilarious that she began to giggle. Fortunately, Diana started laughing too, and soon tears were streaming down her face, though whether they were entirely mirthful, Annie couldn't tell.

Suddenly, Diana stopped laughing. 'Bloody hell!'

'Are you OK? I'm sorry, we're stuck here. The train must arrive soon and then I'll get you home.'

'Don't look out the window,' Diana hissed. 'It's that ghastly woman who keeps trying to corner us about the church. Freda something. She's seen us. Oh Lord!'

One look at Diana's face convinced Annie that a confrontation with Freda would be a bad idea. So, she put on the hazard lights and made a U-turn, contriving at the same time to wave and shout out of the window. 'Sorry – emergency – home birth.'

They sped off, then used the alternative route via a bridge in the next village.

'Thanks,' said Diana. 'You're a pal. I can't stand that woman. Since St James's Church was taken over by the happy-clappy brigade I haven't crossed its threshold. Well, actually, that's not quite true. I went the first week when the new vicar arrived. But that bitch Freda – who doesn't even live in the village – was blocking the front door, handing out song sheets, and when I came in, she actually said to me: "Welcome, sister." Can you imagine her blasted cheek? I'd been going to that church for twenty-five years. And there she was, welcoming *me* when she was the stranger!'

'I hadn't realised how upset you were about St James's.'

Diana sighed. 'Sorry. Thanks for saving me from Freda. I might have hit her.'

As Annie drew to a halt in Diana's driveway, she wondered whether to suggest that her friend's fury was rather more to do with Rupert than Freda. She recalled how, when Edward had not long gone, she would fly into a rage at minor irritations which normally she would have ignored. But maybe now was not the time. 'Diana,' she suggested. 'Come over to me and have a drink and some supper. It'll just be a cold snack but …'

'You're a pet, but no thanks. I was awake all last night. I need to do some thinking, and then try to get some sleep.'

Annie touched the other woman's arm as Diana opened the car door. 'Is there anything at all I can do?'

'Not at the moment. I just have to get my head round Rupert's assumption that as we haven't had sex for a hundred years, I'll just accept his antics, and continue to be the perfect wife in all ways other than in bed.'

'And will you?'

'I really don't know.' Diana turned away quickly but not before Annie had seen the glint of fresh tears in her eyes.

Back home, Annie was contemplating what she might do with her evening when her mobile vibrated with a text from her younger daughter, Lucy, which simply said: *Call Me!*

Annie grinned. Lucy, who was in her second year at Sussex University, loved to chat, but there was no way that Annie was going to embark upon one of her 'marathons' before she had made a pot of tea and settled herself on the sofa. She would use the landline too – as not only was she unconvinced of the safety of mobiles, but she could hear more clearly on a 'proper' phone.

'Mum! Thanks for ringing. You remember Dave?'

Annie's mind was still on Rupert and his secrets.

'Not really,' she admitted.

'No worries. He packed me in last night.'

'I'm sorry.'

'It's cool, Mum. I was, like, thinking of dumping him anyway because there's this hunky lecturer who's very flirty, and really hot.'

'Lucy, this might not be the best idea. Why did Dave … um …?'

'Basically, I'd had, like, too much to drink, and while I was making out with him, I accidentally parked my chewing gum in his pubic hair. He said that was gross, and the next moment we were, like, breaking up.'

Sometimes Annie was so taken aback by what her daughter was prepared to divulge that she did not know what to say. Not that it mattered because Lucy could talk for England.

When finally there was a pause, Annie asked, 'What's that squeaky door I can hear?'

'It's not a door, Mum. It's seagulls! They're going mad. Someone's just thrown them some pizza.'

'Where are you?'

'I'm in a queue on Brighton seafront – a whole bunch of us are waiting to get into a club.'

It was typical of Lucy that she was having such a personal conversation with a crowd of friends around her and the public passing by. But, knowing Lucy, no one would take offence.

For a start, she was not only very pleasing on the eye, but she had always exuded such a sense of fun and high spirits that most people were captivated by her.

Edward's late mother had been fond of saying: 'You've got one bright daughter, and one beautiful one.'

Annie had never cared for this observation, but she did find it strange that two children born just a few years apart, to the same parents, could be so different.

Alice had emerged from the womb looking around her with an enquiring expression, and grew into a serious little soul with dead straight hair and a desperate need to learn about things, while Lucy just gurgled and smiled and loved life, had wondrously curly hair, and somehow managed to brighten everyone's day simply because she was there.

'So,' Lucy was saying, 'I'll see you down here on Friday. Thanks for taking the day off. I've booked a cool restaurant. Italian.'

'And what are you doing on Saturday, on your birthday?'

'Oh, you know. Party with friends. Lots of mates coming from different unis. Probably be mad! So it'll be fab that you and Alice and I can just have a quiet dinner the night before … Oh, gotta go. The doors are opening.'

Annie looked at her watch. It was well past ten o'clock. Time had flown.

She wandered through to the kitchen and poured herself a large glass of chilled Chablis while she assembled her cold buffet. She smiled as she remembered the attractive man in the supermarket. Had he eaten yet? Or thought about her?

Internet dating – that's what Janey had said was next on the agenda. She could feel another of her friend's projects coming on.

But what if you linked up with someone unsuitable? Still, look at Diana – married to someone for over thirty years without suspecting anything of his clandestine activities. Do people, she pondered, ever really know their partners? She often reflected on what had driven Edward into Suzie's arms. It was understandable, she supposed, that he might have been flattered by a younger woman's attention. But he had always been such a snob – forever mocking accents that were downmarket of his own.

'God, I'm getting like Edward's mother used to be,' she said aloud. 'Judgemental and middle-aged!'

As she shredded some lettuce, her thoughts returned to her own life. How, she wondered, would she deal with her nerves when she finally came to make love with someone new? What if he wanted anything athletic? It had been years since she had 'performed' in anything other than the missionary position. Suppose she had to go on top. That would expose the sorry fact that her fifty-five-year-old breasts were no longer as pert as they had been. Maybe she should advertise for a partially-sighted lover!

She laid out her supper on a tray, then took it through to the sitting room where she switched on the television to watch *Newsnight*.

Just as she was sitting down, a sudden urge came over her, which propelled her back to the kitchen.

Opening a cupboard, she grabbed the unopened jar of marmalade which had been the catalyst for so many of her tear-stained evenings. Edward was never coming home. But she no longer cared. And with that thought, she hurled his favourite breakfast treat into the bin.

Chapter Two

Was this the morning she was finally going to use the new yoga mat which had been lying under her bed for months – and watch the accompanying DVD, which was still in its cellophane wrapper? Probably not. Why on earth had she bought them? Online shopping – especially after two glasses of Chardonnay – had a lot to answer for!

But she ought to be exercising more. The pounds which had dropped off her a year ago were making a come-back. Of course, tennis was now out of the question; the idea of bumping into Edward and Suzie was so horrific that she had cancelled her subscription to the club. Still, she would cycle to work this morning. That would be something.

She threw on her dressing gown and headed for what had been Edward's study. It was a small room, along the landing at the back of the house, with a view of the garden. He had shut himself away here for hours at a time, but it was her space now.

Once the computer had warmed up, she checked her emails. There was one from Janey.

Thrilled you're going to start seeing men again. Got lots of ideas about internet dating. If you want a laugh, look at Toyboy.com – just in case you want a younger lover like mine!
Speak later. Lots. J x

She should be getting ready, but could not resist taking a peek at Janey's suggestion. The young men on the site looked about the same age as her daughters. How could she possibly contemplate a liaison with them?

She tapped out a rapid reply.

Will have a think. Do younger men expect you to have a bikini wax? Sorry to be so ignorant. A x

Was there time to make porridge? Probably – so long as she had a quick shower rather than a bath.

Twenty minutes later, she was deliberating over which of three pairs of black trousers she should wear and reaching for one of her many white shirts, when she heard the sound of a new email arriving in her inbox, so she sprinted back to the study.

Waxing essential. Young men get all their sex education from internet porn and don't know what a natural woman looks like. Must have a Brazilian at the very least. Some expect a Hollywood. Ouch! Will tell all at some point. But need first to talk about your clothes and hair. J x

Clothes and hair! What did *that* mean? Was her friend suggesting that she would be unlikely to meet anyone unless she had a massive make-over? That was dispiriting.

She dwelt on Janey's remarks for the whole of her bike ride to the surgery. Carole was in reception when she arrived.

'Oh, Annie … Your sister-in-law called. Can you ring her when you get a moment?'

'Thanks. How are you today?'

'Not sure. Last night, Gary suggested we move to Australia. He thinks he'd get better job security.'

'Oh!'

'Might be a solution, I suppose.'

25

Annie wandered into the staff room to make a mug of instant coffee. She had more to worry about now than Janey's earlier comments. It would be horrendous if Carole left.

Cradling her coffee and a Hobnob, she ambled along the corridor, deep in thought, and almost bumped into Dr Jonathan.

'Don't you look well,' beamed her partner. 'I thought yesterday that you suddenly … well … you're obviously … you know … getting …' He blushed slightly.

'You're right,' Annie smiled at him. 'I *am* getting back to normal. At last.'

'Good show!' he said. 'Uh. Have you got a minute?'

'Of course. Come in.' Annie pushed open the door to her consulting room with her bottom.

She sat down at her desk and watched as Jonathan threw his six foot two body into the patient's chair in front of her.

'So,' she said encouragingly, 'what's up?' She took a sip of her coffee, which, annoyingly, she had made too weak.

Jonathan jumped slightly in his chair. 'Sorry, I was thinking … about something else … yes, uh … I was wondering if we should extend our practice hours to accommodate more patients – especially those who commute to London. You know how the government's always going on about weekend-working. So, how would you feel if we offered a morning and afternoon surgery on Saturdays? And maybe do one late-evening session a week? Obviously we'd get time off on other days if we worked weekends.'

Annie considered the suggestion. Friends were always telling her how difficult it was to make doctors' appointments. 'Yes, fine with me.'

He smiled broadly. 'I knew you'd agree. The other thing is I wondered if you could do me a favour and see my eleven o'clock patient? I find her difficult at the best of times, but she's got some domestic crisis, and I won't have a clue what to say.'

'Of course I'll see her. But you're not quite the emotionally-stunted animal you make yourself out to be!'

He did not respond. Had she upset him? That was the last thing she wanted.

She looked across at him. He was wearing a green shirt and darker green corduroy trousers. And, for the first time she noticed that his black, curly hair was sporting the odd fleck of grey. They had worked together since Annie had joined the practice thirteen years ago. But they did not socialise outside of the practice. This was not her choice; she had invited him to parties during what she now regarded as 'The Edward Era', but he had never come. He was a quiet, bookish individual. She was aware that he had once been married, but had not had children, and that his main hobby was walking. She also knew that he was four years younger than her, and a very good doctor. That was all.

Before her arrival, he had worked in tandem with their highly idiosyncratic senior partner, Dr Margaret Beeching. And he had been mightily relieved to have Annie join him. Dr Margaret had grown even more eccentric with age. She refused to use a computer – despite having an IQ so high that it was virtually off the scale. And she always ran late, so that her patients clogged up the waiting room. Then there was the problem of her knickers. Margaret lived alone, and at the surgery she often appeared to forget that there were other people around, and would lift her skirt and start pulling down her pants on the way to the Ladies, which was just off the staff room.

Fortunately, the ever-constant restructuring of the NHS was a source of huge irritation for the older doctor, and she had been too stressed to work for the past three months. With luck, she would opt to retire soon. Of course, as the only two remaining doctors, Annie and Jonathan would have to decide whether to carry on as a two-handed practice – with locums to help here and there – or to bring in a new partner. And that might become more of an urgent decision if they did extend their working hours.

'No, I'm not,' he agreed.

'Sorry? Oh, my mind's been wandering. How rude. I was thinking about Mad Margaret. What were we saying?'

'I was trying to say that I'm not *quite* emotionally illiterate. In fact ...' He paused, apparently lost for words.

Annie looked at her watch. 'Come on, we've got a waiting room packed with ill people! Catch you later.'

Throughout the morning, her thoughts kept returning to the woman Jonathan wanted her to see. It sounded as if she was one of their 'heart-sink patients', so Annie wanted to be on form for the consultation, and on time.

It was a worry then when two appointments overran. One was with an old gentleman who was frail, and took ages to remove enough clothes for her to examine him. And the other was with a mother who wanted tranquillisers to help her seventeen-year-old daughter pass her driving test.

Are you completely mad?

With some effort, Annie resisted saying the words that sprang to mind.

How could anyone think it would be responsible to give a teenager – or anyone else for that matter – a powerful sedative when she was going out on the road?

'The test is a week away.' The mother pressed her. 'So she could take a pill today and see how it goes.'

What sort of parent, Annie wondered, would casually give her child seriously mind-altering drugs? And this woman was well-spoken and apparently intelligent. Astonishing!

Getting rid of her took ages, because she would not accept that 'No' meant 'No'. It was a relief therefore when Annie saw on her monitor that the next two patients had not turned up.

She made herself another coffee – this time extra strong – before quickly calling Diana to see how she was faring. Her friend was either not in or not picking up the phone, so she left a message; then, with five minutes to spare before 'Heart-Sink', she texted her ex sister-in-law.

Busy surgery. But so glad you got in touch. Are you working? Things good. Girls fine. No longer upset re Edward. Perhaps shouldn't say this to you, but may have had lucky escape! A x

Arabella's response was swift.

Gr8 u r ok. V short notice, but can you have supper with me, Covent Garden area 2morrow, and come to War Horse*? It's finishing soon and I've never seen it but someone I know is in it. Do come. Bella x*

Annie smiled. There were few things she would sooner do than meet with her former sister-in-law, who was a flamboyant, delight-fully gossipy character, and quite unlike her brother Edward.

Would love that. Have to see if I can get cover so can leave here early. Will come back to you.

It was eleven. She buzzed in Jonathan's patient.

Anxious to be friendly and accessible, Annie positioned herself by the door and grasped the woman's hand as she entered. Having got her seated, Annie perched herself on the corner of her desk in a bid to be 'collaborative', which was a technique that she had learned recently on a course.

The patient was forty-five and looked as though life had done her no favours. Her hair was messy and she was wearing a shape-less, grubby tracksuit.

'Hello, Mrs Hammond. I'm Dr Templeton. What seems to be the trouble?'

'There's no "seems" about it. My bastard of a husband walked out on Friday – after all I've done for him. Given him four chil-dren. Looked after his bloody awful mother till she died. God knows, that was purgatory. And now he's gone. Got some floozy from work. In love he says. What the hell does that mean? I can't stand the pain. You'll have to give me Prozac. Or Valium. Or both.'

'OK, let's just talk about this, Mrs Hammond. This is awful for you, I know …'

'You say that – but how d'you know? It's all right for you!'

'Well, the thing is that I do have some idea, because my own husband left me for someone else. And it's taken a while for me to get over it – about a year, actually and of course you're just at the beginning of that and it's very shocking and difficult.' Annie smiled encouragingly.

'Are you *laughing* at me? I can't go on like this for a year! I can't get through *today*. As it is I've had to get drunk all weekend, and it's costing me a fortune.'

'I'm definitely not laughing. I'm only trying to say that people feel very sad when a relationship has just ended, and that's natural.'

'I don't just feel sad. I'm devastated – and seriously depressed.'

Feeling that she needed to be rather more in control and authoritative, Annie edged off the desk, walked round to her own chair and sat down in front of her computer.

'I don't doubt,' she countered, 'that you're feeling awful. Really, really bad. But in fact that is not quite the same as being depressed. I mean, it would be odd, actually, if you *weren't* feeling diabolical. Wouldn't it? It wouldn't say much about what a marriage means if you could just shrug it off.'

'I don't know what the fuck you're talking about.'

'Mrs Hammond, please don't swear at me. I'm trying to help.'

'Are you going to give me Prozac and Valium or not?'

'Uh, I don't want to decide about that yet, because I think there are other ways of dealing with this.'

Mrs Hammond jumped to her feet. Then she pointed at Annie, which Annie knew from long experience is never a good sign.

'No wonder your husband left you, you stuck-up cow. God, you make me sick. Will you give me those pills?'

'Can we just talk about some other …?'

'Fuck off!' Annie felt a fleck of spit land on her cheek. She resisted the impulse to wipe it off as Mrs Hammond grabbed her bag, wrenched open the door and slammed it behind her.

'Mmmn. That went well then, didn't it, Doctor?' Annie murmured to herself as she reached for a tissue.

'How was my patient?' Jonathan asked at lunchtime. He had been out to the local deli and brought back Annie's favourite order of focaccia with mozzarella cheese and sun-dried tomatoes.

'I failed miserably. So much for that course I went on!'

Jonathan, who was sprawled out on the sofa, laughed.

'I'm really sorry,' she went on. 'I feel I've let you down, which makes it rather inappropriate that I'm going to ask if you could possibly add my last two patients to your list tomorrow. Edward's sister wants to meet me in London. And it means I could get an earlier train.'

'No problem,' he agreed, as he tore open a family-sized bag of salt and vinegar crisps. 'Is she the actress? Arabella something?'

'Yup. She's quite famous – because she was in *Holby City* for ages.'

'What's that?'

'It's a TV medical drama, which obviously you don't watch.'

He grinned. 'I get all the medical drama I want! But, yes, go early tomorrow. That's fine. And then you're off anyway on Friday, aren't you? And that's the day we're going to try out Gareth, the new locum. If he's good, I was wondering if we should consider him as a future partner.'

'He *must* have impressed you when you met.'

'Yes, nice fellow. He's trying to have a fresh start away from Wales, for some reason.'

'Have you checked that the reason doesn't involve the GMC?'

Jonathan grimaced. 'Well, no …'

'Only joking! I think that his original email mentioned "personal problems". Maybe he's leaving some broken-hearted damsel behind.'

'Tea?' Jonathan jumped up and flicked on the kettle.

'Please.'

'Annie – I was wondering …'

'What?'

'... well, whether, now you feel happier and so on, you'd like to have some proper time off? Particularly if Gareth works out. Of course, you must meet him before we decide anything. But it's just that I think you've been overworking. You've done extra shifts, several courses, out of hours cover. I checked, and you haven't had any leave since Mr Templeton went.'

'Is this suggestion because I didn't handle Heart-Sink Patient very well?'

'N-no.'

'You think I need a holiday?'

'Yes ... no. Look, Annie, I'm not good at these things. But sometimes people get over a crisis and *then* they get ill, or realise just how exhausted they are.'

'You're right. But I'm fine.'

'Don't be too hasty. Perhaps now you're feeling better, you want to reappraise ... I'm making a mess of this.'

'Not at all,' she reassured him. 'But we've never had this sort of conversation before. I mean you were sympathetic when Edward left, but we never spoke about it in detail.'

He ran his hands through his bushy hair. 'And that's my fault. Because I'm so hopeless at this kind of thing. So, I'm trying to put it right. And I can't help feeling that you ought to work less, or take some leave. Just think about it.'

So she did – on and off – throughout the afternoon. And the idea of real time off, substantial and significant time to do – whatever – began to take on a surprising appeal.

After her afternoon surgery, Annie tried again, without success, to speak to Diana on the phone. So she logged on to her personal emails to see if by any chance her friend had sent her a message.

She had not. But there was plenty of advice from Janey on how Annie might turn herself into a sex siren.

One email read:

You should definitely get a toy boy. They knock years off you.

32

Annie deleted that one. She was unable to summon much enthusiasm for dating very young men. Even if the sex was good, what on earth would they talk about in the morning?

A later email from Janey said:

I recently wrote an article for Red, *all about mid-life women and dating. And I interviewed this terrifying grande dame who runs one of those expensive introduction agencies. And she said that most older women need to grow their hair, lose weight and update their wardrobe, if they're to attract the right kind of man. I'm not saying you don't look lovely in your 'uniform' of Thomas Pink shirts and Joseph trousers, but I think you should maximise your opportunities – even at work – by wearing a skirt once in a while. And high heels. J x*

Annie replied: **I bike to the surgery. A x**

Not every day. Then, there's your hair. You've had a shortish bob for ever. Why don't you grow it a bit? You could even try an auburn rinse or something. J x

That's your colour. A x

Have you looked at me recently?! J x

Well, maybe your hair's a bit paler than it used to be. A x

Sweetie, I'm grey! That's just a strawberry-blonde rinse to hide it. Still, it's very kind of you to picture me as I once was. Especially when your colour hasn't changed in the past 30 years! J x

That's down to genes. My dad's eighty-four now and isn't even quite grey yet. But I expect you're right. I should experiment a bit – at least with clothes. Perhaps I'll buy myself something later. Any advice? A x

Go for pastels. With your fairish colouring – so long as you wear plenty of blusher and mascara – you'll look fantastic. J x

Annie laughed out loud at Janey's not very disguised encouragement to apply far more make-up than usual. But once she had finished work, she did go shopping. And, bearing in mind Janey's comments, she did something completely untypical and walked into Zara – which she had always assumed was only for young women. To her surprise, she loved the clothes and in the space of ten minutes she bought a layered pale pink skirt, beige-cream top and matching linen jacket. Next, she went into Russell & Bromley where she found really high, nude-coloured patent shoes, and then to Marks & Spencer where she purchased the palest tights she could find.

After finishing work the following afternoon, which was surprisingly warm and sunny for mid-May, she changed into her new outfit. Annie viewed this strange version of herself in the cloakroom mirror and decided that – on the whole – she liked what she saw.

Carole did too. 'What a transformation!'

Clearly, Annie realised, Janey was right. She must have been in a serious clothes-rut.

On the train to London, she noticed that the old gentleman sitting opposite her gave her legs quite an approving glance. And, as the journey progressed, and passengers came and went, one or two other males looked her up and down. It was a rewarding if rather strange feeling. Maybe this SWOFTY thing was going to be fun.

But then, on the packed Underground, a young Polish man leapt to his feet and offered Annie his seat. She was mortified. So much for Janey advising her to date a toy boy; how could that ever happen if she looked too doddery to stand between King's Cross and Covent Garden?

The restaurant, which was packed with pre-theatre diners was hot and crowded. It was also very noisy, as the sound of chatter and glasses and muzak bounced off the wood floor and unadorned walls.

Arabella was already at the table, sipping white wine. She looked her usual glamorous self – curvy, perfectly made up and with hair that was still a rich deep brown in colour. She got to her feet with difficulty in the tiny available space and leant over to give Annie a squeeze.

'I'm drinking Chardonnay. Are you happy with that?'

'I'll say.'

Arabella poured from the bottle nestling in the silver bucket beside her. 'Single life obviously suits you. You look great!'

'It's taken a while.' Annie unfolded a giant white napkin and used it to cover as much as possible of her new pale-coloured clothes, before dipping some bread into a mixture of oil and balsamic vinegar.

'Edward's a bastard,' said Arabella. 'Thank heavens our mother was dead by the time he left you. The shock would have killed her!'

Annie laughed. 'Your poor Ma. But she might not have minded. I was never good enough for her. By the way, Alice thinks that she'd have found Suzie "rather common".'

'Alice is spot on! Mother would have had a fit. You're not right about *you* though. She liked you. She thought you were bright and lively – and she adored your girls, and thought their genes were much improved by your input!'

'She had a funny way of showing it, then. Anyway, how is everything? Are you rehearsing? Any telly?'

'No, but there may be something in the pipeline.'

'And how's your love-life?'

'Much as usual. Jeremy's working … in the Coward play at the Duke of York's.'

'So, I suppose he drives back home to Henley every night?'

'Yeah, so no rest for me! He wants even more nookie than normal when he's treading the boards. He says it's the stimulus of having an audience. He may feel stimulated, but I feel knackered.

It's awful really, but I enjoyed the period when he was away on the pre-London tour and I could have a break.'

Annie giggled. 'Janey was suggesting I might want to try younger men.'

'I wouldn't go there if I were you. They're so obsessed with their strike rate and how often their favourite bit sparks into life.'

An Italian waiter was hovering. Both women plumped for pasta and a salad. He winked at Annie. She felt herself blush.

'Of course,' Arabella went on, 'you don't notice when you're young yourself, do you? When you're doing it every night and twice on Sundays.'

'I don't think Edward and I ever did it that much. But I bet he's swinging from the chandeliers twice nightly with sultry Suzie.'

'It's probably all she's good for, darling. He certainly didn't pick her for her brilliant mind or sparkling conversation!'

The Italian waiter was back again. He lingered over the absurd pepper mill ritual. How good was his English, Annie wondered? Probably good enough; he certainly seemed fascinated by their conversation.

Playing with her fork, and trying not to sound too interested, Annie asked, 'Do you see much of Edward and Suzie?'

'No.' Arabella wrinkled her nose. 'To be honest, though he's my brother, I never had much in common with him, and there's even less now he's with that ghastly tart. Jeremy thinks she's appalling – and of course he does have very good taste in women!'

The two friends laughed and simultaneously picked up their glasses and clinked them.

'So,' said Arabella, 'how are your girls?'

'Fine. Well, Alice works too hard, but despite how tough it is, she still seems to be determined to follow her dad into ortho-paedics. And Lucy continues to love being in Brighton. She's man-mad, but delightful. And she's excited about her twenty-first on Saturday.'

'Are you worried about Saturday? How will you all get on?'

'Oh, I won't see her on the day. She's just having some sort of informal gathering with her mates.'

'Really? I thought … ah well, maybe that's best.'

'Yes, she probably doesn't want any "oldies" there. So, I'm having dinner with her and Alice – in Brighton – tomorrow instead. And I'll visit my dad on the way down.'

'How is he?'

'Well, I know you still have grim memories of your father's dementia.'

Arabella sighed and nodded.

'So you don't need me to tell you how horrendous it all is.'

'No. So he won't be at Lucy's dinner?'

'Not a chance.'

'Surely Edward will be seeing her at some point?'

'I suppose.' Annie sipped from her wine glass, and looked away for a moment.

'Are you OK?'

'Yes,' Annie forced a smile. 'I … I'm pretty good about Edward having gone now. But I don't seem to be happy about sharing the girls with him. And I positively loathe the idea of them getting close to Suzie.'

'Thank heavens you're human. That's the nearest you've got to bitchiness in the past year. I'd almost given up hope!'

'You should have heard me ranting round the house in private.'

'Listen, of course you feel like that. So would anyone. When I broke up with Hugh – a million years ago – I wanted to keep my son all to myself. And, let's face it, I was the "guilty party"! Of course, that didn't quite work …'

They both fell silent. Arabella rarely mentioned her only child. He had sided with his father, and broken off all contact with her after the divorce. It was years since she had seen him.

Arabella looked at her watch. 'Ooh, curtain up in ten minutes, let's go. My friend Geraldine, the one who's in it, has X-ray eyes and will definitely notice if we're not there at the start!'

The play was every bit as spectacular and heart-wrenching as Annie had heard. But it was the 'puppet' horses that fascinated her most.

She was not alone.

'What can I say to Geraldine?' Arabella begged Annie afterwards as they stood outside the New London Theatre, being jostled by the departing audience. 'The harsh truth is that all the actors are completely eclipsed by the animals!'

'No idea, I'm afraid … but thanks for taking me. I really enjoyed it. I had worried that we might lose touch after Edward left.'

'Annie, you're the sister I never had. Now, go! Or you'll make me cry. Meanwhile, I must see my poor mate, and tell her she's "marvellous".'

On the train home to Cambridge, Annie found herself wondering about Arabella and her forty-one-year-old boyfriend, Jeremy. Was she as weary as she had sounded about his demands? Or had she just been playing for laughs? One never quite knew. They had been together for eight years. Maybe it had run its course.

Her thoughts turned to Diana. Would she remain with Rupert despite him having a dominatrix in Wales? It would be decades of history to walk out on.

Then Janey came into her mind. But surely she was fine?

Annie had, she realised, a niggling worry about her closest friend. But it was so vague and inchoate that she could not identify it.

The journey back to Cambridge seemed to be taking for ever. So, to speed it up, she played a game where she assessed all the men she could see in the carriage, and decided which ones she could imagine dating.

She gave a 'yes' to several. What on earth had got into her in the last day or so?

At last the train dawdled into the station and she ran for a taxi. Back in the village, she noticed that, despite it being past midnight, the lights were on in Diana's house. Annie considered asking the driver to stop; then she wondered if Diana was having a heart to heart with Rupert that she should not interrupt. But indoors, she found a note in Diana's handwriting on the doormat.

Thanks for trying to contact me. Sorry – been out walking a lot. I've decided to go away tomorrow. Rupert isn't here. I made him stay at his London club. I'll probably be packing most of the night, so whatever time you come in, please pop round and have a glass of wine, if you've got the energy.

Annie had been eagerly anticipating the comfort of her bed, but she knew that Diana would never have extended such a persuasive invitation had she not been keen to talk.

'You look beautiful,' Diana said, when she opened the door.

She was wearing a T-shirt and walking-trousers, and her face was streaked with dried tears.

'Well, *you* look as if everything is just too much,' Annie said quietly. 'And I know what that feels like.'

Diana wept then. And Annie took her in her arms and stood there, in the hall, holding her friend, and feeling her sobs vibrating through her own body.

Eventually Diana was all cried out, and she immediately swung into her customarily capable mode.

'Sorry about that. Red wine? White wine? Coffee? Hot chocolate?'

'Hot chocolate sounds great.'

'Good. But have some wine while you're waiting,' said Diana as she upended an already opened bottle of red into a glass.

'Are you having any?'

'Trust me,' Diana smiled wryly, 'I've had my fill. And if I'm to drive safely in the morning, I'd better stop now. Go on through.'

Annie wandered into the large, eau de Nil-coloured sitting room, which had been the location for so many happy gatherings. The top of the grand piano was crowded with photos chronicling several decades. A young Diana and Rupert on their wedding day. The christenings and graduations of their children, Sebastian and

Max. Rupert, with his smiling wife beside him, on the day he had been awarded his CMG.

Annie felt Diana standing behind her.

'It's hard to think that it's all over now,' her friend murmured, as she handed Annie a mug of hot chocolate.

They sat down together.

'*Is* it over, though?'

'I don't know. That's why I'm going away. I'm off to my brother's place in the Borders to think it out. I'm going to run and walk and cycle and play tennis.'

Annie nodded.

'Marshmallows!' Diana cried suddenly, and she sprinted off to the kitchen, returning with a packet of the squashy sweets – from Fortnum and Mason – which both women dunked into the chocolate.

'You look much like a marshmallow yourself,' Diana laughed. 'Those colours suit you.'

'Do you think so?'

'I wouldn't say so if I didn't. You must know you look good.'

'Well, I know I look different! And I suppose I feel different too. It's rather poor timing though that I'm suddenly happier – and even excited about my future – just when your life has fallen apart.'

'Well, from a selfish point of view, I'm pleased that you know what it's like to have your whole world rocked back on its axis – and also that you're now feeling strong enough to support me!'

'It's odd,' Annie reflected, 'just how volatile and ever-changing life is now. I never thought I'd get divorced. But once you are, you notice just how up and down most people's lives are. I've just done dinner and a show with my ex sister-in-law. It sounds like her current relationship may be heading towards its final curtain. Out of my close friends, it's only Janey who seems to be settled in a relationship – and hers of course is very new.'

'I like Janey. Whenever we've met at your house, I've always thought how bright she is, and how energising.'

'I know.'

40

'What's wrong?'

'Sorry?'

'I just thought,' Diana observed, 'that you looked worried about her for a moment.'

'How odd. No. Still, I do wonder if these relationships with much younger males are all they're cracked up to be. Arabella says it's exhausting because all that young men think of is sex.'

'Well, when Rupert was young, he never thought about it at all – or if he did, he wasn't thinking of doing it with me!'

'That must hurt a lot.'

'More than I ever realised.'

'Will you be OK driving all that way to Scotland tomorrow?'

'Yup. Don't worry about me. I'm a tough old boot.'

Something about the way she said it gave them a fit of the giggles.

'Will you be able to sleep now?' Annie asked as their mirth subsided.

'Hopefully. Thanks for coming round. It's been the best part of the day.'

Back home, Annie felt restless, despite the lateness of the hour. Part of her envied Diana her decision to stop working and disappear.

She recalled how, when Edward had first left, she used to have a fantasy of driving to the south coast, and then taking a ferry to France and motoring south until she found somewhere she wanted to be. But in reality, she had always known that she would deal with her pain better if she was busy. However, maybe she should have some time to herself now.

Did she even want to continue to live here? In this house? In this city?

And could she ever feel comfortable about sharing her bedroom with someone other than Edward? Since he had left, she had changed nothing in that room. She had even – despite reading Joan Bakewell's book *Centre of the Bed* – continued to sleep on her own side.

41

Maybe if she did take some sort of sabbatical, as Jonathan had suggested, she could go and live in London for while – or in her father's house in Teddington. Perhaps it was time to dip her toe into the possibility of a new life, just to test out some options of who she might become.

Chapter Three

'What *was* I thinking last night? I could *never* live here again.'

Annie spoke aloud as she picked her way around the awfulness that her father's house had become.

He had always been the best possible parent, and – until his recent stroke – a vibrant and independent man, who had packed his days reading biographies, learning Russian, and acting in local amateur dramatic productions, where he was in great demand because most of the other thespians were women. He had also made good use of his freedom pass and senior rail card, and had been in the habit of travelling to Cambridge for lunch with Annie on alternate Thursdays, and for long weekends several times a year.

Of course, there had been signs that he was ageing. How many years ago was it, Annie wondered, since she had started to take his arm when they crossed the road together? And when had she begun to notice how his neck was shrinking within the collar of the fleecy check shirts he always wore?

Still, she had always assumed that he had plenty of active years ahead. How abruptly things can change.

As a doctor, Annie had often witnessed the bewilderment in the eyes of adult offspring when their parents suddenly succumbed to serious illness. And when the phone call came to say that her father was in hospital, she had felt the very same expression of surprised outrage etched in her own features.

And there were more shocks in store.

On the day of his stroke, when Annie had driven to her father's house to pick up his pyjamas and other personal comforts, she had been faced with graphic evidence that – for many weeks – he had stopped looking after himself properly.

Annie had closed the door on the chaos that day. And though she had visited her father at his nursing home most weekends since then, she had never returned to her childhood home again till today.

She had planned that she might start the big clean-up. But, after five minutes of surveying the enormity of the task – mounds of papers and dirty plates and rubbish and clothes and books and CDs lying everywhere – she rapidly changed her mind.

Breathing deeply, she braced herself to go into the kitchen to make a black coffee. Her shoes squeaked and stuttered on the tacky floor. And she had to bleach a teacup before she could face drinking out of it.

She did fill a giant bin bag with produce from the fridge, but only because the seriously out-of-date pies and quiches were sporting a mould that Alexander Fleming would have killed for.

Afterwards, she toured the rest of the house, struggling with mind-battering emotions and memories, quite unable to settle to any one task.

Upstairs, in the room that had been hers, she burst into tears. She would have liked to have thrown herself on the bed too – like she used to do as a teenager when life seemed terminally unfair – but it was covered with box files, a year's supply of unopened *Reader's Digest*, and, very oddly, six velvet curtains in cellophane wrappers. So, she wiped her eyes, locked up, and drove to his nursing home.

The Willows was a large white building, overlooking the river, with well-tended gardens which most of the residents were too poorly to notice or use.

Annie rang the bell, sighing impatiently, while she waited for a member of staff to unlock the door.

Every time she visited, she hated this moment – and hated the fact that her father had to be here.

But he had to live somewhere. And, crucially, this home was in the catchment area of the medical practice that had looked after her family for decades.

Inside, her nostrils twitched in response to the assault of smells: furniture polish, disinfectant, simmering beef mince – and urine.

She was just about to summon up her cheerful face and go in search of the old stranger who nowadays masqueraded as her father, when the bossy, string-bean thin manager, whose smile was as false as her talon-like nails, waylaid her.

'Have you got a mo?' she asked.

String-bean was not at The Willows full-time, being some sort of *uber-führer* in charge of all the homes in the group. The fact that she was present, and demanding to see her, made Annie uneasy.

In her office, she graced Annie with a well-practised, sorrowful smile.

'I'm afraid,' she began in a syrupy voice, 'that Mr Buchanan has become something of a problem.'

'What d'you mean?'

'He's restless. And his doctor won't prescribe anything to tranquilise him, which makes life difficult for us. But you know what doctors are.'

'Yes, I do know,' Annie murmured, 'because I *am* one.'

String-bean did not bat an eyelid at the reproach. Instead, she detailed how Annie's gentle, honourable and sadly forgetful father had taken to wandering round the premises in the wee small hours, without any clothes on – and how the previous night, he had stumbled into the room of an elderly female resident, who had promptly become hysterical.

'I don't suppose this will go on,' said String-bean, 'but if it does, we may have to consider whether indeed this is the ideal placement for – um – Derek.'

45

'Duncan,' Annie corrected her. 'His name is Duncan. And,' she went on even though she knew she was being illogical, 'he's not just any old bloke. I don't suppose you've read the notes I prepared when he came in, but he was an accountant at Thames Television, here in Teddington, in the real glory days. And he was well-loved by stars like Tommy Cooper and Michael Aspel.'

'And your point is?'

Annie sighed, because of course there *was* no point except that she wanted everyone to know that her father had once commanded huge budgets, and been a strikingly attractive man, and not at all like the shambling figure he had become.

String-bean reassembled her concerned expression. 'I know this is hard for you.'

Too damn right, thought Annie as she entertained a brief fantasy of strangling the other woman by her sinewy neck. But it would be of no help if she lost her temper. Much as she loathed the horrible truth that her father needed to be in a home, she had been told by a local doctor that The Willows was the best of its kind in the area.

She took a deep breath. 'I'll talk to the GP,' she lied.

String-bean nodded, apparently mollified and Annie was able to escape. Quickly, she found a care-worker who let her out of the building so she could buy flowers for the poor woman who had been shocked by her father's inappropriate visit.

Naturally, when she returned and presented them, the elderly and demented lady had long forgotten her night-time trauma, and had no clue why some harassed visitor was thrusting a bouquet at her. And Annie knew that her father would have no memory of his nocturnal adventures either.

She found him, shrunken and blank-looking in the corner of the communal sitting room, attempting to eat his mince and mash. It was obviously a huge effort, because the stroke had weakened his right hand, so she started to spoon-feed him.

'I should be feeding maself,' he said suddenly. 'I'm a big boy now, Mother.'

'Dad, I'm Annie. I'm your daughter.'

'Ach, away wi' ye,' he said. His illness had robbed him of his toned-down accent, and reinstated the patois of his youth.

Huw Edwards was reading the one o'clock news on the television in the corner. No one was watching him.

As her father tired of the main course, one of the carers whisked his plate away and replaced it with pudding.

His eyes twinkled at her. 'Thank you, bonnie lassie,' he said.

The woman smiled at him. Thank heavens that, apart from Stringbean, all the staff seemed affable and pleasant.

'Trifle!' Annie heard herself announce the arrival of his dessert in a Joyce Grenfell voice.

'Jolly super,' responded her father. And then he laughed at himself. 'Jolly super,' he repeated. And laughed. This went on …

'Dad,' Annie interrupted. 'Are you all right here, in this nursing home?'

He looked puzzled.

'Do you have friends?'

'You can go now, Mum,' he mumbled. And he closed his eyes.

'Dad … I'm your daughter.'

He said nothing more. So she picked up her bag and kissed his forehead.

'I love you.'

Her breath caught in her throat. Had her father just spoken? Or had her brain conjured up those words because she badly wanted to hear them. She studied him for a long moment. He did not move.

'I'm going then, Dad. I'm going to meet the girls in Brighton. It's Lucy's twenty-first this weekend.'

There was just the sound of deep breathing as his head fell forwards into sleep.

'How was Grandad?' Alice had arrived first at the Italian restaurant in Brighton that Lucy had chosen for her 'birthday dinner'. She had

had her long, straight, dark hair cut brutally short, and Annie was busy trying not to convey her shock at her daughter's appearance.

'Uh, well … much the same.'

She did not want to put a damper on this family celebration by discussing her father's undignified and debilitating illness. Mind you, Alice looked far from celebratory in her worn jeans and over-sized rugby shirt. Was she trying to appear as unattractive as possible? And if so, why?

'He should have been here tonight,' Annie went on. 'You know how he loved occasions. But I don't think I'll ever be able to bring him out of that home now. He's too confused.'

'I'm sure you're right, Mum. I've thought about going to see him. But he wouldn't know who I am.'

'I bet he would.'

'Mum, trust me. He wouldn't. He didn't even know me and Lucy at Christmas – and that was before his stroke.'

'Of course he did.'

'He didn't. When I turned up, he looked at me as if he'd never seen me before, and then he said: "And who's this young lady?".'

'I don't remember that.'

'Because I never told you; I don't suppose he even knows *you* now.'

'He may,' Annie's eyes welled up with tears.

'Poor Mum,' Alice said. 'It must be seriously hard for you. I've no idea how I'd cope if you got old and sick like that.' She took her mother's hand and stroked it.

Annie smiled blearily. 'Well, no one imagines it'll happen to *their* parent. But I will get old, at least I hope I will. The alternative isn't so great!'

Alice laughed. 'You look really cool tonight, Mum. And so-ooo young.'

Annie hugged her. 'You always know what to say.'

'I mean it. That purple is great on you.'

Annie had intended to wear her all-purpose black dress. But having caught the shopping bug the other day, and in an attempt

48

to chase away her lingering unhappiness about her father, she had gone in search of a new outfit as soon as she had checked into her seafront hotel.

Discovering an L.K.Bennett boutique just round the corner had been exciting, but expensive. Probably Janey, with her flair, would have mixed and matched – buying a dress in one shop, a shrug in another, and footwear somewhere else entirely. But once a helpful assistant attached herself, and enthusiastically fetched and carried a wide variety of frocks, shoes, belts and scarves for Annie to try on, she was content to stay where she was and adopt the young woman's eager suggestions. She probably now resembled a dummy in their shop window, but she was pleased with the result nonetheless.

The waiter brought their ordered bottle of rosé. And suddenly, there was Lucy, dressed in the tiniest of clingy frocks, chestnut brown hair swinging like a celebrity in a commercial, weaving through the crowded bar area, and acknowledging various people she knew as she made her way towards her mother and sister.

'Great here, isn't it?' she cried, excitedly. And she launched herself at Annie for a kiss and then hugged Alice.

Annie poured wine, and they all clinked glasses. 'Happy birthday for tomorrow,' she said.

'Thanks, Mum.' Lucy turned to her sister. 'Are you supposed to look bald?'

'Nice to see you too, Lucy,' snapped Alice.

Oh God, Annie thought. Why can't my two marvellous daughters be together for five minutes without starting a row?

Lucy retorted, 'You look like a dyke.'

'How politically correct you are,' sneered Alice. She had developed an angry red flush on both cheeks which Annie knew was a dangerous sign.

'You don't have to be politically correct to your own sister,' snarled Lucy.

'Just because you want to look like a slag.'

'Oh God, Ally. You're a bitch. At least I, like, put effort into my appearance. It's, like, you're saying to the world: "I'm so bloody brilliant – the clever one – I really don't have to dress up." But actually, I'm sure it's because you just can't be arsed. Still, you know what? You need to, like, start bothering, because you'll never get a guy otherwise.'

'I wouldn't want the sort of man who's attracted to someone just because she looks available.'

They both grunted and proceeded to ignore each other while keeping up individual conversations with their mother.

Alice told Annie about a recent operation that had gone particularly well, while Lucy waxed lyrical about the lecturer, or should that be 'lecherer', wondered Annie, whose charms she had now succumbed to. It seemed his name was Rik – with no 'c', just a 'k'. Annie sighed. In contrast to Lucy, who clearly thought this spelling was 'cool', Annie immediately marked down this Lothario as an idiotic pseud.

As she had feared, Annie learned that Rik was married, and that – naturally – his wife had never understood him (in other words, she probably understood him brilliantly), and that he was supposed to be separated.

She considered delivering a cautionary, and maybe even disapproving, sermon, but this was hardly the occasion.

Meanwhile, Lucy was chattering on about how fantastic Rik was in bed.

'I can't believe what I'm hearing, Lucy,' Alice screeched. 'You seem to think you're entitled to have any man you want, but what you're doing is just as bad as what Dad did to Mum. Don't you remember how that ripped our family apart? How *could* you think this is OK?'

Lucy looked stunned and perilously close to tears at Alice's onslaught. Fortunately, at that moment their main courses arrived – which defused the mood somewhat. But once their immediate hunger had been at least partially satisfied, Alice spoke up again.

'I wasn't going to say this, Lucy, but I think that Mum's got a right to know that the reason you turned down her offer of a party tomorrow is because Dad and Suzie are throwing one for you, at the Grand Hotel. I'm not coming by the way! I think Mum should also know that you're going shopping with them both in the morning, and that they're going to buy you ridiculously expensive designer shoes.'

Annie's heart started hammering in her chest. How could her daughter be this disloyal? Lucy paled under her mother's scrutiny.

So, it was true. Suddenly, she remembered how Arabella had seemed confused when Lucy's birthday had been mentioned. 'Is Auntie Bella coming?' she asked.

'No,' Lucy replied. 'She seems to have changed her mind at the last minute.'

'Perhaps she thought that you and your father had been rather underhand about the whole thing.'

Lucy paused for a moment, then pounced. 'Look, Mum. I didn't ask for, like, you and Dad to split up and make everything so awful. I know it wasn't your fault he found Suzie, but you probably neglected each other. And whatever you think of her, she makes Dad happy. And he *is* my dad. Even if he, like, murdered someone and went to prison, I still wouldn't drop him from my life, so I'm definitely not going to stop seeing him just because he left you. People split up and get divorced all the time. It's not, like, a crime.'

'No, it's not,' Annie murmured, and with as much dignity as she could drag together she excused herself and headed for the Ladies, where she remained until she felt reasonably confident that she was not going to weep or argue.

'I'm really sorry,' said Lucy when her mother returned. 'I know I've hurt you, but the last few months haven't been easy for us either.'

Alice put an arm round her sister's shoulders. 'No,' she agreed.

Annie nodded. The girls were right; she had to acknowledge that, even if she was inwardly furious at having been outmanoeuvred by Edward.

'Let's have another bottle of wine,' she suggested. 'And pudding.'

Both girls smiled and hugged her.

Lucy stroked Annie's arm as she spoke. 'Look, Mum. The fact is that things could have been much worse. We could have been, like, little kids – but we weren't – and we *had* left Cambridge, more or less.'

'Yeah,' agreed Alice. 'We had a lot of stability when we were small. But it's weird, you know, coming home to see you, and there being no Dad.'

'And,' Lucy went on, 'it's pretty sad knowing that it might be years till we get you and him in the same room – like, acting normally. I sometimes wonder if you'll even both come to my wedding.'

'Lucy! You don't think Rik wants to marry you?'

'Mum!' laughed Lucy. 'Get real. I won't be getting married for ages. But ... look, what's happening tomorrow is like a good example of how things are now. I should have, like, told you that Dad wanted to be part of my birthday. But I was stressed out, and afraid to let you know.'

'Well, I know now.'

'Yes, you do,' said Alice amiably. 'Sorry I forced the issue there.'

The three women beamed at each other and a rosy glow seemed to settle on them all. Or maybe, thought Annie, it's a 'rosé' glow – as they had had rather a lot of it!

'Perhaps it's taken this spat and eruption of tension to move us all on to a more honest place,' she said, her voice quavering just a touch.

'Mum, you sound as if you're on *Jeremy Kyle*! Lighten up,' ordered Lucy.

'All right. Pour me another drink!'

Annie had a slight hangover when Saturday dawned. But despite it, she felt cheerful, and delighted to be by the sea.

She ate an enormous breakfast – justifying it as an antidote to all the wine imbibed the night before – and sat in the window of the hotel, drinking coffee and having a thorough read of the papers.

As she had booked in for another night, she had plenty of time to enjoy herself. Originally, she had considered pottering round The Lanes, but the thought of accidentally meeting Edward in a trio with her lovely daughter and Simpering Suzie was too horrendous to contemplate.

Thankful that she had had the foresight to pack walking shoes and casual clothes, she decided to get some exercise.

Before long, she was driving out of Brighton, on the coast road towards Eastbourne, humming along with the radio and enjoying the sunshine.

Some fifteen miles later, she drew up at the Seven Sisters Country Park where she left the car, and rambled across the cliffs in the direction of Birling Gap.

She strode out on the springy turf. The birds were singing, and the views of the white cliffs set against the glorious mix of blues in the sky and sea were magnificent. And as the wind lifted her hair, she felt as though the Channel breezes were pumping pleasure and fresh stimulus into her brain.

Thinking about the events of the previous evening, she realised that she must be much more resilient now than even just a few weeks ago. Obviously, she did not like being excluded from Lucy's twenty-first. But she could cope with it, which was just as well because now that both daughters had accepted their father's new life, she and Edward would have to compete for their company at every birthday, Christmas and New Year.

And, as Lucy had said, what on earth would happen when she got married? Were the Templetons going to be one of those split-families who were civilised and civil to each other at their children's nuptials? It was hard to imagine.

And would Alice ever get married? It was ages since she had had a boyfriend.

Suddenly, she noticed a tall man of about fifty striding up behind her. He bore a slight resemblance to her 'lost opportunity' from Waitrose, but was taller and more tanned. He was walking with the aid of two long sticks, and, much to Annie's surprise, he fell into step with her.

'Hello,' he said. 'Have you done this walk before?'

'Yes. But not since my children were small – and the younger one is twenty-one today!'

'I'm Bruce,' he announced.

'And I'm Annie – nice to meet you.'

Bruce was very talkative and before long he had outlined details of various walks on the South Downs Way, and around it. He was quite distinguished looking, in a kind of posh-soldierly way. And Annie could not help feeling a small sense of triumph that he had chosen to speak to her.

'Well,' he suddenly changed the subject, 'don't think me rude but I need to walk faster than this.'

Annie was crestfallen. She had been attempting to lengthen her stride in a bid to keep pace with him and was becoming quite breathless.

'Oh, please,' she gasped, 'Go ahead.'

He looked over his shoulder at her. 'I'm going to have lunch at the National Trust place at Birling Gap. Might see you there?'

Her spirits zoomed skywards again.

'Perhaps,' she answered, not wishing to appear too keen.

It was about an hour before Annie reached the top of the final climb and then made her way down the last slope towards the café, her legs trembling with the unaccustomed effort. Obviously, despite cycling to the surgery several times a week, she was not as fit as she had thought.

Bruce was sitting alone at a table. 'I've finished lunch,' he said. 'But can I get you a cup of tea?'

She was weak with hunger as it seemed ages since breakfast, but felt it would be egregious to ask for a sandwich.

'Lovely.' She sank down on to the bench opposite.

He returned a moment later with two mugs, then produced a laptop from his rucksack, and switched it on.

'You probably noticed my Nordic poles,' he said.

She smiled broadly in an attempt to disguise the fact she had no idea what he was talking about. He indicated the long sticks he had been walking with.

'Nordic poles,' he repeated. 'You'll find using them will help you to achieve greater overall stamina and speed.'

And then he turned the laptop round so that Annie could see the screen, and played her a DVD featuring extraordinarily hearty-looking Scandinavians striding around a sunlit forest with long sticks.

After thirty minutes, she was losing the will to live, so she excused herself and prepared to leave.

'So, what was your name again?' asked Bruce.

'I must have made a big impression,' she muttered.

'Sorry.' He reached for a business card from his pocket and pushed it at her. 'If you want to buy any walking equipment, you can get it via my website, and I'm also running a group for novice walkers on Sundays that might interest you.'

A sales pitch. How mortifying. Not a chat-up at all.

Annie bade him a hasty farewell and went to the counter, where she bought a cheese and pickle sandwich to eat on the bus back to where she had left her car.

Once she had finally reached her hotel and soaked her aching body in a hot bath, she began to see the funny side of the morning, and texted Janey:

Thought I was being chatted up today, but the guy only wanted to sell me something! Still, I'm in the mood for lust, and am staying in Brighton tonight, so you never know, I might yet get lucky. A x.

'Annie,' said Dr Jonathan, 'this is Gareth.'

Her partner was all smiles as he introduced the new locum.

Gareth Rees was tall, about forty, with a honed, fit-looking body, and dark eyes which looked as though he was permanently amused by life.

'Hello, Annie,' he said in a deep Welsh baritone.

Annie's heart did a little flip at the timbre of his voice, which was as gorgeous as the rest of him.

'Gareth's booked in for the psychosexual conference in York that you're going to,' said Jonathan. 'Bit of a nuisance, as I could have used him here, while you're away!'

Gareth smiled broadly. 'Sorry about that. But since we're both attending, Annie, can I drive you there? I don't want to be pushy, mind, and you may want to go by train and catch up with reading or something.'

Annie felt quite flushed at the very thought of sitting close to him for several hours.

'I'd love to come with you.'

'Good. And are you staying at the Royal York Hotel?'

'Yes.'

'Me too. That's convenient!'

Yes, very convenient, she thought. She may not have struck lucky in Brighton on Saturday night – though she had had a thoroughly agreeable time watching an Ira Levin play at the Theatre Royal and then having dinner, alone, in a bustling restaurant – but, maybe Gareth?

When she had been married to Edward, she had always avoided the socializing that goes on after hours at medical conferences. But she was single now. And maybe this delightful younger man might help kick-start her adventures.

She sailed through the Monday morning surgery. Then she went shopping again. This time, she bought two beautiful bras, which gave her significant uplift and cleavage, and matching French knickers. She also treated herself to a bottle of CK Euphoria perfume, which smelt younger, lighter and more exciting than the Madame Rochas which Edward had bought her every birthday.

That night she was too excited to sleep. She felt like a teenager instead of a fifty-five-year-old. It was ridiculous. Probably nothing would happen with Gareth – or indeed with anyone else. But even just thinking of the possibility made her blush in the darkness.

'Mum! Rik's taking me to Paris on Saturday for a long weekend!'

She should never have answered Lucy's call, as she still had another patient to see and Gareth was due to arrive in fifteen minutes to drive them both to the conference.

Annie started to mutter the usual motherly warnings about being careful about STDs and pregnancy, since Lecherous Lecturer doubtless had had numerous nubile students before her, but this was greeted by world-weary sighs from the other end. So she gave up and wished her daughter a happy trip instead.

Her last patient was a newly diagnosed diabetic. Fortunately, she was a sensible woman, who has already started making serious lifestyle changes to bring her weight down and manage the condition. If only all patients were so cooperative.

There was just time afterwards to check her emails.

One was from her ex sister-in-law.

Hi, Annie. Great to see you the other night. Lots has happened since then. I want to tell you everything in person. I haven't even told Edward. Speak soon. Much love, Bella

That was intriguing.

Janey had emailed too.

Am away with Miguel. He was desperate for a break, so we did one of those last-minute deals. We're in Sicily. Only checking emails occasionally. Happy man-hunting! J x

Little did Janey know that the hunt was already afoot. Peering out of her window on to the street, she could see that Gareth was just arriving in his red sports car.

The journey began well. Even the A14, most unusually, had no traffic jams on it.

They stopped for tea some way up the A1, and Annie noted what perfect manners Gareth had. He was quick to open her car door, for example. And in the café he was pleasant to the waitress, and attentive to an elderly – and not entirely sane – woman at the next table who mistakenly thought she knew him.

His fingernails were beautifully manicured too, Annie noticed, as he poured tea for them both.

How marvellous he was. For the first time, she could really understand Janey's exhilaration at having a younger lover.

Back in the car, her mobile beeped with a new text.

'It's one of my daughters. 'Do you mind if I look at it?'

He beamed. 'Be my guest, Annie.'

That voice again. It was like molten chocolate.

Hi, Mum. Think u r off to sex conference 2day. Am sure that only docs very interested in the subject go to such things. They probably c it as chance to get in2 someone else's knickers! LOL. Alice xx

Annie laughed. For such a young medic, her daughter had developed a fine line in cynical wisdom.

Gareth grinned at her amusement. So, she plucked up courage to read the text to him.

He laughed too. Then he selected a CD – a soundtrack of Sondheim's *Follies*.

She smiled at him and settled further down in her seat. What fun this journey was turning out to be.

'Talking of sex,' he said, suddenly.

Annie felt herself redden.

'I was so pleased to be able to drive you today because I was sure you were a friendly and understanding person, and I wanted to tell you something, in case it makes a difference.'

She could feel her smile fixed to her face. Was this conversation going the way she had hoped? Maybe not. But she did not want to upset Gareth by looking surprised or uneasy.

And then he told her that he was gay.

Of course he was. Stylish clothes. Impeccable manners. Immaculate nails. Stephen Sondheim. She must have been blind. Gareth went on to tell her how he had had a girlfriend since university – and how he had fought against his natural urges for years. Also, how – despite there being a well-known Welsh rugby player, and a referee, who had come out as homosexual – he had not felt brave enough to continue living back home in Wales while he experimented with what he believed was his true orientation.

His confession lasted from Lincolnshire to the outskirts of York. And while it went on, Annie continued to smile encouragingly even though her face was beginning to ache. But inside, she felt stupid that she had imagined he might be attracted to her. She also felt totally idiotic that she had spent so much money on lingerie.

'And so,' he was saying, 'would this be a problem with you in using me as a locum?'

'No!' Annie quickly dismissed her own ruminations. 'No, of course not, Gareth; nor would it be any kind of issue if we decided to offer you a partnership when our senior partner retires.'

'Are you sure that Jonathan would feel the same?'

'Absolutely!'

'Aw, thanks, Annie. You're champion. I feel fantastic having got that off my chest. I hope you'll let me buy you dinner once we've checked in and registered.'

She smiled. 'That would be nice.'

From then on, Annie more or less wrote off any possible liaisons in York, though she did reread Alice's text a couple of times.

She was, in fact, slightly appalled with herself that she was taking her daughter's words as encouragement rather than as a warning. The trouble was that since her titillating dream, she had had one pressing ambition, and that was to get naked with a new man. She had been celibate long enough.

So, after dinner with Gareth, when she bumped into Howard, a widowed GP she had known for years – having once dated him

59

for a fortnight before she had met Edward – she accepted his offer of a late night drink.

She watched as he waited to be served at the bar. His mannerisms were the same as those of the boy he had once been. Of course he was not in Gareth's league. Not only was he much older, but he had the air of someone who had lived well rather than wisely. Still, there was a kind of hazy resemblance to the lived-in face and sardonic charm that make Bill Nighy so attractive. And as time ticked by, Annie realised that he was actually very good company.

When they had finished their drinks, Annie wondered, just for a moment, if Howard might invite her to his room. But he simply stood up and kissed her hand.

'Thanks, Howard,' she said. 'I haven't laughed that much in ages.'

'Nor me,' he grinned.

Then he asked her to have dinner with him the following night.

The conference, which was titled 'Sexual Medicine in Primary Care', was good in parts.

Some of the presentations were pretty depressing – like the one which detailed how mid-life adults were getting sexually transmitted diseases in unprecedented numbers – but there was also excellent information about treating men's erectile difficulties, and plenty of explicit DVDs and frank workshop discussions.

In their practice, Annie handled everything to do with sex and relationships because of Jonathan's insistence that he was useless in that area, so it was important for her to learn as much as she could.

Her interest though was definitely sharpened by the prospect of seeing Howard that evening. There was something rather thrilling about focusing on sex all day when there was a distinct chance that it might occur later. So, by the time she had spent eight hours studying the subject, she was feeling increasingly inclined to 'do the practical' – if Howard steered their encounter that way.

Excited, and wearing her new L.K.Bennett dress, she arrived in the restaurant ready for romance – and also for a substantial meal, having been too busy to eat for most of the day. Howard, however, hardly ate a thing. He toyed with his salad and left most of his chicken and all his potatoes. He also refused dessert, which meant that Annie felt she had to do the same.

She asked if he was all right.

Howard took her hand, lifted it to his lips and said that he needed to restrict himself to a light meal if he was to get lucky later.

'Why's that?' she asked.

'Come on, Doctor,' he chuckled. 'What does it mean when a guy of my age, hoping to seduce a lady, goes easy on the old calories?'

'Are you diabetic?'

'No.'

'Worried about your waistline?'

'Of course, but that's not it.'

He leant across so that he could whisper in her ear, 'Vi-ag-ra.'

Then, speaking more loudly, he went on, 'Weren't you listening when the lecturer said it works much better if taken on a relatively empty stomach?'

Obviously, she had not been, but this new information sent her mind into a spin at the thought that she was going to have her first encounter with a chemically-induced erection – surely a 'seminal' moment in any woman's life!

Upstairs in Howard's bedroom, she suddenly felt embarrassed. For a start, she had not brought any toiletries so she ended up using his toothbrush; after all, she was certainly going to exchange bodily fluids so it seemed pointless to be nervous about oral bacteria.

She was also unsure whether or not to cleanse her face. The truth was that she had never gone to bed in full make-up since before her engagement to Edward, and she could not help worrying that her maquillage would make a mess of the hotel's pillows. But as Howard pulled her close and kissed her, she decided to just go with it, and stop worrying.

The little blue pill certainly produced impressive tumescence. But unfortunately, Howard was rather too taken with the results, and kept admiring his dimensions in the mirror – which was distinctly off-putting. At one point, he even asked her if she was pleased with his 'manhood'. She decided not to reply because it was obvious that he was delighted enough for both of them.

But then he confessed that after his wife's death he had felt so guilty about having sex again that he had been impotent for ages, before trying Viagra. This confession immediately propelled Annie into 'sympathetic doctor mode', which promptly killed any passion she might have mustered.

There was something of a hiatus too when he searched around for a condom. This was another unexpected part of the process because of course if you have been married – and faithful – to one man for decades, you have forgotten all about getting a rubber on at the appropriate moment. However, having heard about rising sexual infection rates earlier, she certainly would not have considered having sex without one.

Sadly, the sex was dire, despite the extraordinary build-up to it. It was very much the roll-on, roll-off variety with no concessions to what Annie might have wanted.

She would have liked to say: 'Were you away from medical school when they studied the clitoris?' But she resisted the impulse. Instead, she affected a polite gasp of pleasure when he reached his climax – just in case he was concerned about her satisfaction, which he probably was not.

Never mind, thought Annie, one good thing was that Howard had been in such a hurry that she had been able to keep on her uplifting bra, and had not had to worry about her breast-droop.

Another bonus, she decided, was that at last she had got her first post-divorce sexual encounter out of the way.

She chose not to spend the night with him, because as soon as their coupling had ended, he spread-eagled himself across the bed and started snoring.

The next day, there was another full round of lectures and workshops and she kept out of Howard's way. In fact, she only bumped into him at the late-afternoon tea break.

'Thanks for last night,' he murmured.

The pleasure was all yours, she thought.

'And nice to see you again, Annie. But – and I hope you won't be offended – I'm not going to promise to call. I think if I'm going to go looking for "Miss Right", I'd prefer to find someone younger.'

She was incensed. This was not how it was supposed to go. She was the one who had planned to say that she would not see *him* again. How insulting and annoying he was.

Fortunately, at that moment Gareth waved to her across the crowded room. Howard noticed and looked at Annie with a quizzical expression.

The honest thing would have been to say that Gareth was just the locum who was driving her back to Cambridge – and that in any event, he was gay. But pride had to come before honesty.

'No problem, Howard,' she said. 'As you can see, I like them younger too.'

Chapter Four

Carole looked excited. 'Annie – thank heavens you're here. You're going to be a radio star and you need to ring them!'

'What?' She stopped in front of the reception desk.

'It's to do with the conference you were at last week. There was some coverage in the papers. That new local radio station saw it, and rang asking for a doctor to come in to talk about sexual health. Jonathan suggested you.'

'But I can't!'

'Of course you can. Do you think *he* could? He'd be hopeless. But he should have told you.'

'Where is he?'

'Gone walking with that nephew of his – Oliver – for a few days. Dr Gareth's doing his surgery. Didn't Jonathan tell you that either?'

'Well he didn't phone, but I didn't check my emails,' Annie admitted guiltily. The truth was that having arrived home late from the conference on Saturday night, she had had a lazy day on Sunday and had opted not to look at the computer.

Gareth was in the staff room. His eyes twinkled when he saw her. 'Coffee?' he offered.

'Yes, but shall I make my own? I'm a bit fussy.'

'Aren't we all?'

Annie laughed. 'Probably not as bad as me! I only allow myself three cups per day, so I want them absolutely right. We used to have a coffee-making machine in here, but it broke. And we settled on this brand of organic instant.'

Stop it, Annie, she told herself. You sound boring and middle-aged.

'Sorry, Gareth. Yes, please. I'd love you to make some.' Despite her best intentions she could not resist adding, 'But do you mind warming the milk in the microwave, and making it quite strong?'

'Leave it to me.' His deep Welsh voice exuded confidence. And the coffee turned out to be excellent.

The morning was hectic, and it was well past what should have been lunchtime before she found a moment to call the radio station.

Ellen, the producer, sounded so enthusiastic on the phone that – against her better judgement – Annie agreed to do the interview.

'It will be just a one-off though won't it?' she queried. 'I might be hopeless.'

'You won't be!'

So that was that. She was to be a 'radio doctor' on Wednesday – her day off – which she had planned to spend in London seeing both her father and Janey. But, she supposed, she could go afterwards.

Carole was clearly thrilled that they now had a 'media doctor' in the fold. Perhaps, thought Annie, she and Jonathan reckoned it might boost the number of patients in the practice. As if we need any more – she rolled her eyes as she walked past the heaving waiting room with its crying children and wearily fed-up parents.

'I'm terribly nervous.'

It was Wednesday morning, and Annie was speaking on the phone to Alice at their customarily early hour.

'Mum, you'll be fine.'

'And I've had to clear everything out of my bedroom because I've got decorators coming today. And later I'm going to London.'

'You don't normally have a day off in the week.'

'I forgot to tell you. Jonathan decided we must be more available to our patients, so we're going to offer morning and afternoon surgeries on Saturdays, and do one late night as well.'

'Hoorah! A general practice crawling into the twenty-first century!'

Annie ignored her daughter's sarcastic tone. 'Yes,' she went on. 'So, we're working different shift patterns and we've brought in this new guy, Gareth, more or less full-time too.'

'What's he like?'

'Welsh. Good looking. Makes great coffee. Drives a red sports car. Gay.'

'What's *that* got to do with anything? Really, Mum.'

'What?'

'Well, do you describe a new doctor who's *not* gay as "heterosexual"?'

'Oh, you can be so touchy. I only mentioned it because …' Should she say that she had been interested in his body before she learned about his orientation? Probably not! '… because he drove me to York last week, and spent most of the journey discussing how he'd just come out, and asking if it would make any difference to his job prospects with us.'

'Why *should* it make any difference? How awful that he should think it might. God, you'd think we were in the Ice Age.'

'You're on a very short fuse this morning.'

'Sorry, Mum. Maybe it's a generational thing.'

'Oh, clearly my views are only good for the scrap heap.'

'Actually, I think you're quite enlightened for someone …'

'As old as me?'

'Something like that.'

There was a pause, then, to Annie's great relief, Alice giggled.

'Mum, sorry. I'm a bit stressed out. It's probably because of Dad's wedding today, though I'm trying not to think about it.'

Annie had been on her feet, attempting to put on her trousers with one hand while holding the phone with the other. She sat down, heavily, on the bed. 'Could you repeat what you just said?'

'Dad's … Oh my God! He hasn't let you know, has he? He only told me and Lucy on Friday. I asked if he was going to speak to you, and he said "Of course". But he obviously hasn't.'

'They're getting married – *today*? Are you or Lucy going?'

'Definitely not. Lucy's in France anyway. And I couldn't possibly get time off to go to Venice.'

'*Venice?*'

'Oh, bollocks! I shouldn't be the one telling you all this.'

Annie breathed out so hard she felt her fringe lifting off her forehead.

'Alice,' she responded, as calmly as she could, 'it's fine. He should have told me, but he's a coward. I don't want him back now anyway – even if I'm not sure I want her to have him. But it was clear they would marry. Still, Venice …'

'Mum, I'm sorry but I must go.'

'Of course. Me too. Look, don't worry. I know you don't like what your dad is doing, but you have your own life. So does Lucy. And so do I – after all, I'm about to go on the radio!'

The studio was in an alley near St John's College; it was staffed by bright and personable individuals, and a very pleasant boy brought her quite drinkable coffee.

Ellen, her persuasive producer, then talked her through what Ruth the presenter might ask. This is a sign of the times, she thought. Women in control; men relegated to a hospitality role. Could she tell Alice that, or would she somehow get it wrong and end up being lambasted for some political incorrectness she knew nothing about?

'And then we'll take calls …'

'You mean that I'll have to talk to real people, and give advice?'

'Yes. That's no different from being in your health centre is it?'

'Suppose not,' Annie answered weakly, her mind going into overdrive about whether her medical insurance would cover her for broadcasting. Her heart started to race and her mouth felt dry. But before she could back out, the boy who had been looking after her urged her into the studio, seated her in front of a giant microphone with a bright red spongy cover on it, and helped her put a pair of headphones on.

Annie gazed at Ruth, the presenter, but she was busy sliding buttons up and down a complex-looking electronic desk and seemed oblivious to her guest's arrival. On the other hand, Ellen, who had retreated to a booth next door, was smiling encouragingly at her through the soundproofed glass between them.

Suddenly, Ruth started speaking into her own microphone and Annie heard herself being described as a 'sex expert', but there was no time to correct the error because the presenter was already firing difficult questions at her.

'Was that it?' she heard herself say as she found herself back in the holding area.

The hospitality boy nodded. 'They loved you.'

She grew an inch with pride before telling herself that they probably said the same thing to every new broadcaster.

In the same way as she had been urgently pushed into the studio, she was now, just as speedily, ejected on to the street. Obviously, this was simply another busy morning for them, and they had not the slightest interest in her staying around and talking about her performance.

She stood still, as bikes and pedestrians rushed past her. Had she really been on the radio? It felt like a dream. And it had gone so quickly; though her watch told her that she had been on air for thirty minutes. Her legs felt wobbly. She had had her regulation three coffees already today, but this was an emergency, so she headed to a nearby Costa and bought a cappuccino and an almond croissant.

There was nowhere to sit because the café was full of very settled-looking people of all ages, who appeared to be running businesses by laptop from the premises, while spinning out occasional cups of coffee. She hovered with her tray until a woman grudgingly moved a bag from the seat next to her.

A text pinged in her phone.

You were great. Specially bit about fifty-somethings getting back into the dating game and being desperate for sex.

It was from Carole. Had she really said that? She had no memory of it. She quickly texted Janey.

Just done that radio thing. Flashed past. Can't remember what I said. Is that normal? See you for lunch at 1.15. A x

Her phone rang in response. 'Annie! Well done!'

'Janey – it was awful. Like a conveyor belt in there. They said it was good, but I expect they encourage everyone.'

'No they don't. Anyway, you were terrific.'

'Their signal doesn't extend to Pimlico, surely?'

'It's digital. I heard you on my PC. You were great. I'm doing an interview on Radio 5 Live myself before we meet, and haven't read up on the topic yet. It's all frantic now. Little money. No nice car to pick you up. Welcome to the wacky world of twenty-first century media!'

Her phone rang again. Ellen, the producer, sounding rushed, told her she had done brilliantly, and asked her to come in at the same time in a fortnight.

A text arrived. 'That'll be Hollywood I expect,' Annie muttered to herself. Really, the whole morning was very odd.

It told her she had a voicemail, which turned out to be Arabella asking if she could come and stay the night. She sounded very nervy and tearful. Annie tried to call her back, but the line was engaged, so she texted her instead:

Of course. Are you OK? You're not upset about Edward's wedding are you? I'm just off to catch train. Will be in London with Janey, and then my dad. Back about 8. Hope not too late for you. Will bring in M & S food. x

On the train, Annie took stock of the morning and of the day to come. This was not how she had envisaged her day off. Of course she did not begrudge Arabella a visit – especially if she was upset and needed a listening ear. And, as it turned out, she had not minded being on the radio, and might even in time come to enjoy it. But when she had originally planned the day, she had seen it as a luxury which she could spend in a leisurely way without deadlines. I'm fifty-five, she thought, should my life be so packed with incident?

She looked around the railway carriage. Two mid-life women were taking their small grandchildren to London. They were laughing and giving the youngsters a summary of what they would do.

Every five minutes, one of the little girls asked, 'Is this London?'

Apart from the grannies, everyone else on the train seemed to be absorbed in their own technological world. Across the aisle, a businessman was tapping furiously on his laptop. And next to her, a woman of about thirty was viewing an episode of *The Young Montalbano* on her tablet. Annie felt rather old-fashioned as she opened up her newspaper.

London was terrifically busy. Janey had said it was the Olympics effect and that it had been noticeably noisier and more crowded since the summer of 2012. Joe Allen, their favourite restaurant, was packed too.

Annie ordered what she always ate there – black bean soup and chicken Caesar salad – despite having exhorted herself to break out and experiment.

'But you like it,' reassured Janey. 'And it's not as if you have it every day. It's four months since we were here. You're hardly stuck in your ways, you old tart. What's bugging you?'

Annie explained about Edward. 'Mostly, I don't mind. I mean, he and she were heading that way for a while. Venice though …'

'Maybe he felt that your break-up had ruined the city for him and he wanted to replace that with a happier memory.'

'Hmmn.'

'Or maybe the seriously-awful Suzie wanted a bit of that plush Danieli treatment for herself. She *is* marrying "up", sweetie. And she doubtless relishes the idea of being a consultant's wife and going to classy hotels. What a cow!'

Annie grimaced, but then grinned. 'Well, good luck to her!'

The women clinked their glasses of sparkling water, and proceeded to chat about Janey's work, and Miguel's hopes of setting up his own studio. Was he looking to Janey to fund that Annie wondered?

'You look a bit frazzled,' Janey observed. 'Are you still thinking about Edward's wedding?'

'What? Oh, no.' Should she admit that she was uneasy about how exhausted and thin Janey looked?

'The girls then – are they worrying you more than usual?'

'Oh, I don't know.' But then, suddenly, she found herself reporting her morning phone call with Alice, and relating the details of Lucy's birthday dinner in Brighton. 'She's always so abrupt these days. Is it pressure of work, or could there be some sort of emotional crisis going on?'

'Perhaps she's gay?'

'What?' Annie shrieked. 'Alice! Gay? Absolutely not.'

'Well, you're her mother; you know best. But why was she so cross with you about Gareth? And why did she come to Lucy's party with her hair cropped so short and wearing a rugby shirt? Maybe she's trying to tell you something!'

'Well, I suppose there could be worse things.'

'There'd probably be no grandchildren.'

'There might not be anyway. What worries me most is that she's so serious and takes life and work so much to heart. I don't even know if she sees her friends.'

'I expect she's just overworking. She had a good social network at school as I recall. People don't change that much.'

Annie glanced at her friend who seemed to be pushing her vege-table tostada round the plate rather than eating. It was worrying;

rather more worrying than whatever was going on with Alice. Should she say something?

Unsure, she changed tack. 'Tell me more about Miguel.'

And Janey did, and as she spoke she looked younger and happier, and Annie let her worries slip away.

After lunch, she took a train from Waterloo to Teddington to see her father, who slept the whole time she was there. She sat watching over him, while the inevitable television in the corner showed an old episode of *Midsomer Murders*.

Every now and again, she leant over and kissed his cheek but he never stirred. Should she wake him? It would be so marvellous if he opened his eyes and was suddenly normal again. It felt as if that should be possible. After all, he looked the same.

'I want my *mummy!*'

A few chairs from Annie, sat a very old woman who had just woken in great distress. 'Where's my mummy?' she screamed. 'Where is she? Mummy! Mummy, I want to go home.'

Oh, Dad, thought Annie, I hope your dreams are lovely because your waking life these days must be one long, hideous nightmare.

Her journey back from Teddington into central London, and then from King's Cross to Cambridge, was beset with various signalling and other operational problems, so all the way home she worried that Arabella would arrive before her.

Fortunately, she did not. But, inside the front door, there was mayhem. She had forgotten about the decorators and their dust sheets and boxes of tools. Dropping her bag and coat, she ran upstairs. Her bedroom had no curtains at the windows and was a mess of paint pots and rearranged furniture and step-ladders.

'It'll be nice when it's finished,' she told herself firmly as she closed the door on the disorder. But where was she to sleep? And, more to the point, if Arabella was not heading back to Henley tonight – and it would be awfully late if she did – where should she put her?

Quickly, she swept up the dust sheets from the stairs and hall, so that the house looked more normal, and put the Marks & Spencer chicken pieces in the oven. She was just preparing a salad when the doorbell rang.

Arabella – looking fraught but beautiful as ever – stood on the doorstep, a stuffed holdall in one hand, and a bottle of champagne in the other.

'No one knows you're my ex sister-in-law, do they?' she demanded. 'Thank heavens I called myself Arabella Gordon, rather than Templeton, when I started my acting career. I've never been so pleased about anything and it's not as if you're in the public eye.'

'I've been on the radio this morning, I'll have you know!' Annie giggled, then hauled Arabella in and shut the door. 'What's going on?'

'The press are parked outside my home.'

'Why? What's happened?'

'Darling, I *will* tell you. But can I have a shower and a cup of tea, and then a glass of bubbly and calm down? And when I've recovered from driving like a lunatic round the most circuitous route you can imagine, I'll spill the beans.'

'Is it serious?'

'Yes.' Arabella's eyes were happy, though glinting with tears. 'But quite wonderful at the same time.'

'Well, so long as you're all right. Look, go up. Sorry about the mess. Can you use the spare room? I was going to sleep there tonight and it's chaos at the moment because I've dumped loads of stuff from my bedroom in it. But I'll tidy it while you're in the shower. I'll sleep in Lucy's room. She's not been home in ages. Anyway, she's in Paris.'

Annie rushed around, plumping up cushions in the sitting room, adjusting the lighting, and tidying away medical journals.

Upstairs in the spare room, she bundled piles of books and clothes into a couple of large bin bags and threw them into Lucy's room. Fortunately, there were clean sheets on the spare room's bed. She quickly found Arabella a towelling bathrobe and some matching slippers, and put a couple of newish paperbacks on the bedside table. It was hardly the Ritz, but it would do.

Downstairs, she transferred the almost-cooked chicken and its red-wine sauce from its foil container into an earthenware oven dish, and swiftly sprinkled dried herbs on top. Next, having finished the salad, she popped Arabella's champagne in the freezer for a quick cool down, and then put on the kettle. At the same time she kept wondering what on earth had happened in her sister-in-law's normally glamorous and organised life to warrant her escape to Cambridge. Why were the press outside her home? Of course Arabella was well-known, but not a 'celebrity'. Neither was her partner Jeremy. He was just a jobbing, if rather upper-class, actor.

Last week, Arabella had said that Jeremy wanted more sex than she did, but surely they could not have split up over that. And in any event, why had she been so concerned that no one must know of her connection to Annie?

Starting to make a pot of tea Annie suddenly realised that she would sooner have a proper drink – so she uncorked the champagne, found two proper crystal flutes and poured a generous amount into one of them.

'Can I have one of those as well?' Arabella had quietly joined her in the kitchen. She was dressed in the robe and slippers Annie had provided, and her wet hair was swept up in a large bath towel. She looked pink and excited but somewhat older than usual. She was of course fifty-seven, though the public were not supposed to know that.

The kitchen was warm and smelt of herby chicken and they decided to stay in there to eat.

'I might just have a quick shower and come down in a dressing gown too,' said Annie.

'Yes, go. I'll toss the salad for you and sneak a top-up of bubbly while you're gone!'

When she returned, Annie asked, 'Are you sure about eating in here? It's bad enough I'm slobbing around in nightclothes and serving you a ready-meal – I feel I should make an effort to turn tonight into more of an occasion. The dining room is …'

'Absolutely not.' Arabella deployed her projected voice, which had – for decades – effortlessly reached the back row of theatres throughout the land.

So they stayed where they were and ate and laughed and downed the bottle of champagne. And, once Arabella had insisted that she would rather talk about herself later, Annie brought her up to date with her crazy day, and also about her recent trip to York and how she had mistaken Gareth's friendliness for ardour – and also how she had broken her celibate habit, though not memorably.

When there was a lull, they turned their attention to Edward's wedding.

'He's having a mid-life crisis, and she's a bitch on the make – but hey, let's hope they're happy,' said Arabella.

'Couldn't have put it better myself,' Annie muttered wryly.

After eating, they moved into the sitting room. Arabella threw herself on to a sofa, put her feet up and surrounded herself with cushions.

'Red or white?' Annie came in from the kitchen waving a bottle of Chardonnay in one hand and a Merlot in the other.

Arabella pointed at the Merlot. Then she reached in her pocket and drew out her phone. 'Can I just check this text?'

Annie nodded and disappeared to uncork the wine.

'I think,' she reflected, as she returned with two generous glasses of wine, and handed one to Arabella, 'that I may suffer for this in the morning, but what the hell!' Then she giggled and sat down in her favourite large armchair opposite Arabella's sofa. She felt slightly tipsy, but despite the mystery still surrounding her sister-in-law, her unease about Janey, and the news of Edward's remarriage, she was enjoying herself.

'OK,' Arabella took a deep, dramatic breath. 'Here's the thing …'

At that moment, the phone in the hall rang.

Annie waved an arm in its direction. 'Ignore it. I'm off-duty till tomorrow morning. The answer-phone will …'

Suddenly, she heard Lucy's voice.

'Mum, please pick up. Why aren't you answering texts? I've got to talk to you. Oh God ... Please don't be at the theatre or anything.'

Annie put down her glass, shrugged at Arabella and ran out to the hall.

'Lucy. Sorry.'

'Mum, I need to come home. I'm on my way.'

'Aren't you in Paris?'

'No, Rik dumped me. I've got as far as St Pancras. Can you come and get me?'

'No, I can't possibly.' Despite Lucy's anguished tone, Annie wanted to giggle. 'Sweetheart, I am sorry, and of course you must come home but I've got Arabella here and we've just had supper and lots to drink.'

'Oh I can't bear it!'

'Lucy, calm down.'

Arabella was at her elbow. 'Ask her not to tell anyone that I'm here,' she hissed.

'What?' asked Annie. 'Not you, Lucy. Hang on, Arabella's saying something.'

'Not a word about me being here,' Arabella implored her. '*Please* ask her not to tell anyone. *Anyone* at all.' Then she walked back into the sitting room.

'Did you hear that?' Annie asked her daughter.

'Not properly.'

'Arabella is asking you not to tell anyone that she's here. It's important.'

'All right. Who would I tell, anyway? What the fuck is up?'

'Lucy, please. Actually I don't know. There's some sort of crisis. She's about to tell me, but she'll be staying here tonight.'

'Oh no! Sorry to be horrible. I just need to come home and chill in my own bedroom.'

Annie winced.

'OK, love, can you get a train?'

'That's why I'm phoning, Mum, I was so upset I, like, left the hotel in Paris in a hurry. I had my Eurostar ticket in my pocket but I forgot my purse. Luckily for me, I met this really cool French guy at the station in Paris and he, like, bought me coffee and sandwiches and talked to some official about getting me on the train even though I wasn't booked on that one. He was meeting some friends later, so he sat with me till the Eurostar left, and he was, like, really helpful. But I can't get to Cambridge, and my battery's going. Oh God!'

'Could you go and stay with Alice?'

'No!' Annie held the receiver at arm's length while her younger daughter explained loudly why seeing her sister would not suit her.

'All right. Find a cab that will take a credit card and I'll settle up when you get here.'

Suddenly Lucy's voice brightened. 'That's cool, Mum. Thanks. Love you. See you later.'

Annie put her head round the sitting room door. Arabella was sending a text but she quickly put her phone down.

'I reckon,' said Annie, picking up her wine glass and stretching out in her chair again, 'we've got about an hour till my heartbroken daughter arrives in a taxi that's going to cost a fortune. And in that time, I'm going to have to move all my stuff out of her room and into Alice's before she gets here or there'll be hell to pay. She doesn't believe mothers should cross the threshold of their daughter's space. It's going to be a long enough night listening to the blow-by-blow account of her rejection by the plonkerino lecherer, without having to endure one of her monologues on boundaries.'

Arabella nodded. 'I didn't mean to interfere on the phone. I was just nervous about being found. But it probably doesn't matter now – despite my exit in disguise earlier and then driving round two supermarket car parks before hitting the open road.'

'Why? This is getting more and more mysterious.'

'Well, according to a text I've just had, the press are publishing the story anyway, so it'll be common knowledge by the morning.'

'But what will?'

'You know I said I wasn't getting on so well with Jeremy?'

Annie nodded.

'To be honest, I didn't tell you everything. You see, I've been seeing someone else, secretly, and it's wonderful and we've fallen massively in love. And he's perfect – and adores me.'

'But that's marvellous!'

'In most ways, yes …'

'And in other ways?'

'Well, he's been married to someone else for forty-two years.'

'Ah, not so good.'

'No. And the very, very bad thing is that … he's Jeremy's father.'

'What!'

'I know!'

'Oh, my God!'

'It *is* bad.'

'But he's …'

'Exactly … he's the Home Secretary.'

Chapter Five

Annie punched her pillow in the hope of making it more comfortable. Lucy, in the adjoining twin bed, had fallen asleep – mid-sentence – well over an hour ago.

The temperature in Biarritz was much higher than it had been at home and there was barely any breeze from the open window.

Worse than that, the bed clothes were dreadful. Brushed nylon! They reminded her of horrible 'digs' back in her junior doctor days. And, just to pile on the agony, the bottom sheet was too small for the mattress, so it was wrinkling beneath her.

She cast her mind back to the last vacation – not counting the Venetian fiasco – she had spent with Edward. It had been in Nice. How blithely she had taken for granted the perfect service, the elegant bathroom and the silky bed linen. This place, chosen by Lucy, was more like a student hostel than a hotel, and was about as removed from that delightful 'French Style' as it was possible to be.

The idea for a trip to Biarritz had evolved out of the long night in Cambridge when Arabella had bared her secrets, and the rejected Lucy had turned up eager to recount the saga of her ruined relationship.

Apparently, she and the lecherous lecturer had spent a couple of days in Paris visiting museums and talking about Art History – as well as having very athletic sex. Presumably, Annie had speculated, he had been able to claim the trip, and her daughter's charms, as a tax-deductible expense.

Unfortunately, their Parisian carousing had been interrupted – while they were in the act as it were – by Rik's mobile.

'He really snapped at me, Mum, and yelled that I must keep silent. And guess what? It was his *mistress* on the phone. And of course, he's got a wife too.'

Arabella and Annie had gasped in unison.

'I suddenly realised,' Lucy had continued, 'that I was mad to be involved with him. He said that he's, like, had this mistress for ten years. I felt so-ooo bad – especially as I was like helping him cheat on her *and* his wife. It had been fun till then. But I was shocked. So, I was just about to dump him – when he got in first. I've been like … blind,' she had sobbed. 'But I will miss the sex, which was fantastic.'

The two older women had tried to look casual and worldly-wise, despite being stunned by Lucy's candour. As Arabella had said later, 'It's strange to have that kind of conversation with someone you remember reading to at bedtime.'

'I know!' Annie had agreed. 'While Lucy was speaking, I got a sudden image of her as a curly-haired toddler sitting on her potty. But now she's an expert on the difference between a clitoral and G-spot orgasm!'

The following day, Lucy had continued to be tearful, so Annie had suggested that once the summer term ended they should take a few days' break.

Those 'few days' had sounded fun at the time. Right now, in her airless hotel room, they seemed like a life-sentence.

If she were at home, she could get up, and heat some milk, and potter around and read before returning to her comfortable bed with its high thread-count Egyptian cotton sheets.

Lucy made a little snuffly noise and turned over. She was probably enjoying happy dreams of Jean-Pierre, the gorgeous boy who had picked them up at Biarritz airport.

It turned out that this young man was the 'cool guy' who had come to Lucy's rescue on her way home from Paris. During their encounter at Gare du Nord they had managed to exchange a great deal of information. He had told Lucy that he was studying fashion design, and that he lived on the Left Bank with his mother, who had been a super-model, but now had some high-powered job in haute couture. He had also mentioned that he was planning to spend much of the summer on his father's boat near Biarritz.

Having been introduced to Jean-Pierre earlier, Annie was not at all surprised that – when given free rein to choose a holiday destination – Lucy had picked this one so that she could see her 'hero' again. The lad was tall, well-mannered, beautiful, and black.

'I hope he fancies me,' Lucy had confided to her mother once Jean-Pierre had left and they were eating dinner. 'But whatever happens, I'm gonna love being in Biarritz. There are, like, surfers everywhere – and they're *hot!*'

Morning came eventually. There were spectacular views from their bedroom of the sea and beach, which Annie had not been able to see in the dusk the previous night, and the breakfast was very jolly. Best of all, the sun was shining brightly, and she was looking forward to spending time with her lovely daughter.

'It's great, isn't it, Mum?' Lucy had been texting, but looked up from her phone and beamed. 'Aren't you glad we came?'

Annie smiled back, feeding off her daughter's delight. 'Very glad.'

They planned a walk round the town, and then a relaxing morning on the nearby beach.

'Let's go then,' Lucy jumped up and headed for the front door.

'Sweetheart, I need to pick up my hat and go to the loo and so on. Can you give me five minutes?'

Upstairs, she brushed her teeth and renewed her lipstick. Then she debated whether her legs were a touch too old or too pale for the white cotton shorts she was wearing, but decided to risk them anyway.

Lucy was outside the front of the hotel, as arranged, but so was Jean-Pierre. Most politely, he offered to escort them both round town, but as Annie glanced at this young man's fixed-gaze on Lucy, and then at her daughter's dancing eyes, she quickly changed her plans.

'You two go. I'll do my own thing.'

'But, Mum, I'm supposed to be having time with you.'

'I know, love. But when I was upstairs I had a call from the surgery and I need to talk to someone about something ...' She had always been a terrible liar, but Jean-Pierre and Lucy were so wrapped up in each other that they did not appear to notice.

'Well, if you're sure,' Lucy said – and the two of them disappeared rapidly.

Annie walked a hundred yards down the street till she came to the wall that encircled the horseshoe-shaped Port Vieux beach. She leaned against it as she reached for her mobile phone, keeping up the pretence that she had something important to do. And, because nothing else occurred to her, she did ring the surgery, only to be reprimanded by Carole, who said she should be enjoying her holiday and not giving any thought to the practice.

For a moment, she felt nervous and alone. What was she going to do with herself, especially if Lucy spent all her time with Jean-Pierre?

She gazed around her. The beach looked inviting. The weather was hot. There were no clouds in the sky.

You *can* do this, she urged herself. There had been holidays with Edward where she had longed to have time alone. Now she had it.

She would start by seeking out some good coffee.

A pretty café, decked out in pastel shades that reminded her of Edinburgh rock, attracted her. And as she sat outside in a mint-green chair, with the sun on her face, sipping her first *grande crème* of the holiday, she realised that she was going to be fine. Ten minutes later, she decided that she would be even finer if she could buy a British newspaper.

She finished her coffee, paid her bill, and tried the nearest *tabac*. They only sold local papers but told her about the *Maison de la Presse*, which was a short walk away.

Soon, she was passing the *grande plage*. Lucy had been quite right about the hordes of young people in the resort. Somehow, Annie had imagined that Biarritz would be quaintly old-world and traditional, like a Gallic Broadstairs. Instead, it was bustling with fit and spirited surfers and their admirers.

With a sense of triumph, she secured the last *Daily Telegraph* in the shop. She rarely read a paper thoroughly at home, but today she had time to enjoy it.

As she edged nearer to the front of the queue to pay, she could not help noticing the man in front of her. He was around her age, tall and athletic-looking, with casually uncombed pepper-and-salt hair, and wearing smart sailing clothes with expensive-looking leather deck shoes. He had two children in tow – a girl of about seven, and a boy of pre-school age. He was chatting to the girl in American-accented English, but then, when he addressed the smaller child, he switched to what sounded like perfect French.

Just then, the boy became bored and started jumping around; he bumped into Annie, dropping the colouring book and crayons that he was waiting to buy.

She bent down to help him retrieve them.

The man knelt down simultaneously, looking straight into Annie's eyes before helping her up as she handed over the child's purchases. 'I am so sorry,' he apologised.

'How did you know not to speak to me in French?' she asked.

'*Madame*,' he answered, 'you have what they call around here *l'air anglo-saxon*!'

'That doesn't sound good.'

'On the contrary.' His eyes twinkled in a very attractive way. 'It is much admired and copied in these parts.'

He put out his hand. 'Greg Harmanan,' he announced.

'Annie Templeton.' She shook his hand, which felt dry and muscly compared with her own.

At that moment, Greg's family reached the head of the queue and he paid for their items, chatting at the same time with easy charm to the assistant who obviously knew him. He grinned at Annie as he gathered up the children and left.

Annie felt quite flushed and flustered. It was probably the heat of the shop. She paid for her paper and made for the exit, only to find that Greg was waiting for her.

'I feel the least we can do is to buy you some good coffee,' he offered. 'Young Oscar packs quite a punch when he runs into people. I know, I have the bruises to prove it.'

The café opposite was large and light and airy, with huge gleaming mirrors.

The waitress appeared to be somewhat overwhelmed by the number of customers, but when she saw Greg, she smoothed down her long white apron, tucked a stray strand of hair back into her chignon and advanced towards him for a kiss on both cheeks, which left her looking rather pink.

Before long, she was back with a large pot of coffee and an even larger jug of hot milk as well as a plate of tiny almond biscuits. The children, with a little help from Greg, quickly made their own milky drinks with just a hint of coffee. The little girl, who, it seemed, was called Nancy, supervised her brother.

Greg poured coffee for Annie and added milk till she was satisfied with the colour.

'You know *exactly* what you want,' he teased. She felt herself blush slightly.

'Sorry,' she laughed. 'At my surgery, everyone leaves me to make my own because I'm too particular!'

He studied her with his head on one side. 'Your surgery? You're a doctor?'

She nodded and proceeded to take a sip of her delicious beverage.

Her heart began to race. Probably the coffee was stronger than she was used to. And she had drunk a *grande crème* just half an hour ago.

He turned from her for a moment to attend to Oscar, who wanted advice on which crayon to use for the picture he was drawing. Annie watched as Greg spoke seriously and attentively to his son. She could see that the child idolised his father.

Nancy interrupted and suggested that she and Oscar should go and play outside. There was a patch of beach right in their eyeline.

'Stay where I can see you, honey,' Greg said firmly.

The very cute Oscar weighed up his options. Annie could tell that he was torn between his drawing and the promise of fun with his sister. Not for the first time, she wondered what it would have been like to have had a son. Certainly, Edward had wanted one, very badly.

'You can finish this later,' Greg counselled his child, in English – and the little boy ran out of the café after his sister.

'So, you have bilingual children?'

Greg smiled. 'I'm American, as you doubtless realized. I have three children, who all have different mothers. I was thirty-one when I had my first son, who's grown up now. Then Nancy came along when I was married to my second wife and splitting my time between France and the States. Then I – this was not my finest hour – I was having difficulties with my wife and I – uh – got the nanny pregnant. She's French – which I guess is why I talk to Oscar mostly in French. I never married her, but even though we no longer have any kind of attachment, she lives with us. Nancy is based with her mom in Boston during school terms, but comes to me for vacations.'

'Sounds very, um, civilised,' remarked Annie, unsure if she was saying the right thing.

'It is now. But there's been a hell of a lot of blood on the carpet in the past. Still – important that you know.'

'Why?'

Greg reached across the table and stroked her arm.

'Just because.'

Really, thought Annie, he was too smooth for his own good. But he was very good looking. And awfully nice. She felt slightly breathless.

85

'Look, Greg, thanks for the coffee. I must go. My daughter's with me. She'll wonder where I am.'

'Of course.' He stood up, and gave a little bow. Then he smiled at her in that sparkly way he had.

'I don't suppose you'll want to come,' he went on. 'But – uh – there's a very historic tea room in town. And you British love tea, as we all know. If you could bear to spend an hour or so there with me tomorrow afternoon, it'd be awesome. I won't have the kids with me.'

'That's nice of you,' Annie responded. Her head was telling her to refuse him, politely, which she fully intended to do.

'It's called the Miremont.' He quickly sketched some simple directions on a paper napkin. 'It's easy to find, and has wonderful patisserie. But you may be busy.'

'Yes. So, I don't think …' Then she looked at him again and took a deep breath. 'Actually, I'd love to come.'

His eyes and mouth engaged in a huge expansive smile. 'I look forward to it. Shall we say three?'

She swallowed. What was she doing? She should state, right now, that she had meant to say 'no'.

He was still smiling at her.

'Fine.' Then she made for the exit, half-stumbling into a chair in her hurry to leave.

Well, she berated herself as she strode away, you made a right hash of that. Why did you accept when you have no intention of going? Why did you have to be so clumsy? You looked a complete idiot.

She walked and walked, not sure where she was going. This man, though most attractive, was obviously trouble. It would be crazy to see him again.

She found she was climbing a steep hill, but she did not slow her brisk pace. It helped to just keep moving. And it did not matter where she went because round every corner there was another breathtaking view of the coastline, or another interesting house to look at.

After a further half mile or so, she found a shady seat under some pine trees, and as she sat down, she took out her mobile and called her own landline in Cambridge.

'Darling!' cried Arabella. 'I was about to text you. I've got a telly job! Some new medical drama set in the '50s. The actress who was going to do it had a big bust-up with the director and left. He's a nightmare by the way, so I'm not surprised. I think my name came up because I was in people's minds after all the media coverage of me going off with my boyfriend's father! I'm playing the matron. Remember those? A wise and kindly lady! God – it doesn't seem long ago that I used to get booked to play the "crumpet". Now, I'm the dried-up old prune munificently sharing her views on everything that life has thrown at her.'

'Anything less like a dried-up prune would be hard to imagine.'

'You always say the right things. Anyway, it's work – and much as I've loved hiding away in your house, I need to face the music and get on with life.'

'Well the press stuff has calmed down hasn't it? How's the Home Secretary coping?'

'The Prime Minister is standing by him. That's what he was most worried about, I think.'

'What about the wife – what's her name – Jeremy's mother?'

'The saintly Mildred. Well, she hates me and has told everyone that I not only broke Jeremy's heart, but prised Martin away from an idyll-ically happy marriage – though of course she and most of their friends know that he had several affairs through the years. But Martin's giving her the house, which she's very pleased about. And Jeremy has been staying with her, and I think she always preferred him to her husband.'

'Gosh. Lots going on then. Are you all right?'

'Brilliant. I'm massively in love and being spoilt rotten. You should see the presents that arrive every day. Flowers, Jo Malone candles, chocolates … Of course, I won't be eating them, as I don't want to be a *fat* matron, so I'll leave them for you!'

Annie laughed.

'So,' Arabella continued, 'I'm off later. I'll lock up and post the keys back through the front door when I go. We're filming in Bristol for at least six weeks. Now, how's your holiday?'

'Well, Lucy is very taken with the young gorgeous guy who rescued her in Paris and is staying somewhere near here with his family – so I don't think I'll see much of her. The hotel is ghastly. Biarritz is great.'

'Is there's something you're not telling me?'

'Well, I don't want to bother you.'

'Don't tell me you've met someone?'

'Kind of.' And suddenly the words were pouring out of her about how appealing Greg was, but how he had a terrible track record and had probably taken endless other women to this particular tea shop. 'So I meant to say, "no thank you" when he invited me. But instead I agreed. What shall I do?'

'You obviously *want* to go. And you could do with some charming company. Think of him as "just for Biarritz" rather than for life. And he can hardly rape you mid-afternoon in a tea shop!'

As Annie walked slowly back to the hotel she replayed Arabella's words in her head. He could be a distraction in Biarritz, and forgotten thereafter.

By the evening, when she finally met up with Lucy at dinner, she had become glad, and even slightly excited, that she had accepted the invitation.

Lucy was thrilled to hear that her mother had been propositioned over coffee, but she was even more delighted with her own day and keen to detail what she had done with Jean-Pierre, and how she loved Biarritz, and had met so many 'cool' people.

Much to Annie's surprise, she slept well. But next morning she awoke feeling very nervous – and her anxiety intensified through the morning, particularly after Lucy disappeared to go surfing with Jean-Pierre.

She sat on the beach and tried to read, but could not concentrate. Why did this man have to have such an effect on her? After all, they were only meeting for tea.

After lunch, she focused on her appearance. Lucy had told her she must wear a dress. So she put on one of the two she had with her, before changing it for the other one. Then she opted for the first one again. This might have gone on indefinitely, had she not run out of time.

Just before leaving for her 'rendezvous', she tried to call Janey for some advice, but got no answer. So she phoned Diana, but failed to reach her either. And Arabella was probably rehearsing.

Who would have thought that life would be so complex at this point in all our lives, Annie mused. I'm sure that when we were in our twenties and thirties we assumed that by now we would be sauntering around in a settled, mature and tranquil way. Little did we know!

Greg waved and stood up when she entered the tea room, which was even more beautiful than he had described. One end of it faced on to the street but the other overlooked the sea, which – this afternoon – was piercingly blue. The smell of creamy confections was heady and delicious, and the salon's belle époque decor delightful. As she reached him, she saw that he had combed his hair, and that he was wearing a navy linen suit, albeit in a louche and casual way.

He was unlike anyone she had been connected with before, and her pulse raced at the possibilities that she knew were being offered to her.

'Stunning place,' she murmured, looking around, trying hard to avoid his brown eyes which she knew were searching for hers.

He came round to her side of the little table and helped her to be seated. An electric shock ran through her body as their hands touched.

He offered her a menu.

'You choose,' she suggested. 'I'm sure you know what's good.'

'I think I probably do at that!' He smiled broadly, exposing his immaculate American teeth.

Pink mousse-like cakes arrived; they were shaped in little mounds and each was topped with a miniature strawberry.

Oh heavens. How very French. They look like breasts.

'They do, don't they?' He laughed.

She looked puzzled. Surely she had not spoken her thoughts aloud? He was grinning at her. She grinned back. And suddenly everything was easy. Tea, cake, handsome man. More tea, plus endless chatter as they recounted their life-stories.

He told her that he worked in the aeronautical industry, in Toulouse, but that he also spent a couple of months each year lecturing at Harvard.

'It's a terrific life, Annie. One foot in each of two very different worlds. A boat in St Jean de Luz. Great weather. I'm a lucky guy.'

The second teapot ran dry.

'Shall I order another?' he volunteered.

She heard herself say, 'I imagine you've got other plans.'

'Am I that obvious?' he asked. 'Could be! That has been suggested before!'

Ouch, she thought. He was not even going to pretend that he was unused to picking up women, let alone that she was different or special. But she knew that it was no longer a question of whether she was going to have sex with Greg, but when. Maybe for her own sense of decency, she should delay.

'What are you up to tomorrow?' she asked.

He did a little writing motion above his head to indicate to the waitress that he wanted his bill. It came quickly. Just as speedily he put down two 20 euro notes and, taking Annie's arm, led her back on to the street.

They stood close together, facing each other.

'I'm too old to play games, Annie. I *do* have plans in mind for this afternoon, as you suggested. You see, tomorrow I have to be in Toulouse for a conference. I'm staying overnight at my apartment there because we have American clients coming in for a meeting first thing Thursday. Then I need to come back and host Nancy's birthday party that afternoon. So, if not now, I can't see you till Friday. I will be free then, all day. But the weekend is difficult.'

'And I go home on Saturday.'

She looked at him. Had she ever felt like this before? Lustfully and urgently wanting someone because he was just so sexy and it felt so right? Her breasts felt as though they were bursting out of her dress in a bid to be caressed. But there was limited time. They had this afternoon, then really only one more day. How was she going to feel if she chastely bade him 'goodbye' now? Relieved, or regretful?

She stood on tiptoe and kissed his cheek. 'Did your plans for today involve me?'

'I'll say!'

'OK.' Her voice came out as a whisper. 'Let's try them. Where, um, shall we go?'

'I've got a hotel room. Let me say quickly that I don't have it just in case I get lucky! I book it for the entire summer – it's a kinda office as well as a bedroom, because I often need to work and it's way away from the noise of the kids. Will you come?'

She nodded. How on earth was she going to tell Diana or Arabella or Janey? She was not wanton. Never had been. This was so unlike her. But she had an overpowering urge to sample what was on offer.

Unlike her encounter with Howard in York, sex with Greg far exceeded not only her hopes but all previous experiences.

She found that she had no fear. No angst about her breasts looking droopy. No anxiety that she had never got round to having a bikini-wax. No concern that she would have to make a fuss about him using a condom, because he was well-prepared and as keen to be safe as she was. Everything fitted together incredibly well, and the sense of huge pleasure and satisfaction was overwhelming. She smiled at him as, breathless, they drew apart.

'What are you thinking?' he drawled.

'Something about only just realising what I've been missing.'

He propped himself up on one elbow. 'Me too.'

'Oh, come on, Greg. You're a very experienced man and lover.'

91

He grinned. 'But this is special. And so are you.'

Sometime later, he encouraged her to sit down on top of him, facing away from him. Then he slid himself into her and pulled her shoulders down so that her whole unclothed body was lying on top of his body and they were both looking up at the ceiling.

Warm, refreshing breezes from the open window drifted over her nakedness. She felt weightless, excited and liberated.

'It's called the "Free as air" position,' he explained. 'Do you like it?'

'Mmmn,' she answered, because she very definitely did. With no effort at all, her pleasure peaked again. She slid off him, then slept.

He woke her with a glass of champagne. She sat up in bed, not bothering to cover herself with a sheet, and sipped her drink appreciatively.

'It's what summer afternoons are for. Making leisurely and glorious love and then drinking a bottle of something special before doing it all again.'

'You're insatiable,' she laughed.

He took the glass from her and kissed her very deeply and thoroughly.

'Not normally,' he contradicted her. 'But I am with you! I feel years younger than I did yesterday morning, before we met. You have a swell effect on me. And that's a real appropriate word, believe me! Can we do it again?'

'There's nothing I'd like more,' she answered politely. Then she laughed, and so did he.

Later, as she lay on her back, his tousled head between her thighs, the voile curtains at the windows billowing in the marine air, she felt very unlike her normal self. But she did not feel like anyone else either – simply a sort of extension of herself that she had never known was there. It was a strange but joyous feeling.

The next day, she felt sore, but it was a happy soreness – almost a badge of honour. It was similar to the sense of accomplishment she had felt years ago, when she had played long tennis matches, and ached everywhere afterwards, but in a good way.

Lucy stayed with her for the morning and they pottered around the town, but it was obvious her thoughts were elsewhere. Whether it was as obvious to her daughter that Annie's thoughts were also in an entirely different place, she was unsure.

In truth, after a Mediterranean lunch of fresh seafood and French bread and salad and one glass each of a dry and delicious white wine, Annie was not sorry when Lucy went off to meet Jean-Pierre.

She lay on the beach, under a parasol, and read her Kindle, and – from time to time – drifted off to sleep.

Later she texted Janey.

U always want me 2 be more adventurous, so u'll be pleased 2 know I was seduced yesterday by v sexy American. He knows his stuff! V sore today. But I want more! Not like me at all! Sadly, man is busy 2day and 2morrow. We have Friday, but I come home Saturday. How u? A x

Janey did not reply, which was strange. She was normally so quick to text or pick up the phone.

Annie shrugged away her disappointment. Then she went back to her reading. She finished Nora Ephron's *I Feel Bad About My Neck;* she had always loved the late-author's writing, but this was one title she had never read before. She surveyed the Kindle's other contents and selected the latest John le Carré – but before long, she fell asleep again.

Later that night, replete with sun, a good dinner and a shared bottle of wine with Lucy, she was ready for bed.

Now I have finally taken leave, she reflected, I seem to have realised just how tired I am.

She remembered Jonathan's concern for her when he had gently reminded her how often people get over a crisis, only then to feel exhausted or ill. It had been kind of him to suggest she might want some sort of sabbatical. Maybe if she took one, she could come back to Biarritz later in the summer. There was considerable attraction in that idea.

Lucy finally vacated the bathroom, and as she did so, her phone pinged, and she grabbed it.

'Hmmm. Jean-Pierre's texted to say we can't meet up tomorrow. There's a family party, and he says his dad needs help in organising it. You don't think he's tired of me do you?'

Annie smiled at her daughter's worried face. 'I doubt it, my sweet. I'm sure he thinks you're adorable.'

Lucy's eyes lit up and the uncertainty left her expression. 'Are you seeing *your* man again?'

'Possibly on Friday. He's away on business.'

'OK then. Why don't we do something special tomorrow?'

'I could hire a car and we could go up over the mountains into Spain?'

'Really? Mum, that'd be amazing. Is that, like, a long way away?'

Annie laughed. 'Geography's never been your strong point!'

'I know. But we're not near the Costa del Sol are we?'

Annie laughed again. 'No, we're not. Spain's a big place!'

She headed into the bathroom smiling to herself. From inside the paper-thin door she could hear Lucy's phone.

Then her daughter's voice: 'I miss you already.'

There was a quite a long silence.

'That'd be awesome. I need to clear it with my mother but are you sure? OK, speak in the morning ... Me too.'

'Mum?'

Annie opened the bathroom door and continued cleaning her make-up from her face. 'Was that your lovely young man?'

'Of course! How many guys do you think I've got on the go? He's got a plan – but I don't know how you'll feel about it. Would you mind if I didn't come back with you on Saturday?'

'Why?'

'Jean-Pierre says that the rest of his family are going to be away next week. His kid brother's going off somewhere, and his dad is

94

taking his sister to Switzerland. So he's asking me to stay with him on the boat. You should see it, Mum, it's fab. It's, like, long and all polished wood and really, really old. Most of the other boats around it are kind of, like, white and plastic but this is beautiful. And, well, we haven't had sex yet – completely – because, after Rik, I thought that I should take my time. But I can't wait really, and if we had the boat to ourselves ...'

Oh my baby, thought Annie.

'Don't be sad, Mum, it'll be great.'

'I'm not sad, sweetheart. Well, maybe sometimes I'm a bit wistful because you've grown up so very much. But really, I just love you and want to keep you safe.'

'Mum! I *am* safe. Jean-Pierre's a great boy and his family are obviously loaded. So?'

'Lucy, of course you can stay. You will use contra ...'

'Mum. Please! I don't want to get pregnant any more than you want me to. Now, if we're going all the way to Spain tomorrow, we need to get some rest.'

'We had a trip to Spain yesterday,' Annie told Greg. 'We went up through the Pass of Roncesvalles and had a walk and visited the church and had a meal. I don't think my daughter had a clue which bit of the country we were in! But it was lovely.'

They were sitting over lunch on the terrace of Greg's hotel, eating in a very leisurely fashion but mutually aware of the frisson of anticipation between them.

He is just for Biarritz, Annie kept reminding herself, remembering Arabella's words. Still, perhaps she could come back.

'Do you stay here for another month or so?' she asked as Greg emptied the bottle of Chablis they were drinking into their two glasses.

'Yup. It sure is handy having that boat.'

'Oh, so your boat is quite big is it? Do you all stay on it?'

'Sure ... all mod cons. But we've got a bit of a hiatus next week. Oscar's mom is taking him to Provence to see her mother, and because it was Nancy's birthday yesterday I'm taking her on a little trip too, but we'll be back in a week. I'm sorry you're going home. Will you have any more vacation this summer? Could I tempt you back?'

Annie blushed and smiled. 'You never know.'

In his room, he swept her into a huge hug and then locked his lips on to hers. Suddenly, they were tearing at each other's clothes.

So this really does happen, she thought happily. Not just in films.

It was the last conscious cognition she had for a while, as intense pleasure took over. Making love with Greg was like nothing she had known before. She was noisy. Abandoned. Unashamed of her drive for each climax – and wickedly grateful every time she got there.

But there was tenderness too. As they lay together, temporarily spent, he stroked her arm and later she found herself tracing his lips with her forefinger.

It was almost dark when they finally rolled apart.

He rang for room service.

'Will your daughter be worried? Do you need to call her?'

Annie struggled to come back to the present. 'Um, I think it's fine. She's met a boy here. She … it's very sweet. I think she'll barely give me a thought!'

'If she's as lovely as her mother, then that is one lucky guy!'

They ate smoked salmon and bread together, and drank a glass of champagne.

'At home, this amount of booze in one day would give me a headache!'

'We've paced ourselves,' he laughed. 'And had plenty of exercise! I just wish you weren't going home tomorrow, and that I didn't have to take Nancy to Lucerne.'

'You're taking your daughter to *Switzerland*?'

'Yup. To tell you the truth, I'd like her to go to school there. It'll take a lot to persuade her mom though.'

'Greg, tell me about your grown-up son – you haven't said much about him. What's he like?'

'He's a great kid. We didn't meet much when he was young because his mom was very bitter about the divorce for a while. She was a top model. From Martinique originally, but she made the big time in Paris.'

'So is your son ... um ...?'

'Black? Sure is – and he's a pretty hot guy, let me tell you.'

'I can imagine that he's lovely with you and the super-model as parents. What's his name?'

'Jean-Pierre.'

Annie took Greg's hands in her own. 'Great name. And I bet you've been a terrific father – to all these kids.'

He looked puzzled. 'Is anything wrong?'

She shook her head. 'No, no. I just feel quite emotional about families. And yours is – well – it's a complicated one. Blended, as we say nowadays.'

'There *is* something wrong, Annie. What is it?'

She leapt out of bed and started pulling on her clothes. 'I think that after all, I do feel a bit guilty about my daughter. I'd better go.'

'Can I see you off tomorrow?'

'Greg,' she said seriously. 'I don't want you to. Let's just leave things here, in this room. It's been amazing. But I don't want to do a grand goodbye. Do you mind?'

He shook his head. 'But you will think about coming back?'

'I promise I shall think about it a great deal,' she answered quietly.

The next morning, Annie took a lengthy walk around Biarritz. She could hardly believe how much she had hated this town just a few days previously. Now, it would always be part of her.

The sun was shining. People were happy. The views were wonderful. It was hard to tear herself away.

Back at the hotel, as she pushed the last of her toiletries into her suitcase, there was an awkward moment when Lucy announced that she was coming to the airport. It was the last thing she wanted.

'It's a waste of your time, pet,' she said, firmly. 'I'm just going to get a taxi and check in. Have fun with Jean-Pierre instead.'

Lucy threw her arms round her mother's neck. 'Thanks for bringing me here, Mum. I'll never forget it.'

Annie smiled. 'Neither will I.' She could see a taxi drawing up on the street below. 'Must go. Here ...' she produced a bundle of euros that she had drawn out from a nearby ATM. 'I don't want you to be short of money.'

'Mum! That's a *lot*!'

Annie kissed her daughter, swept up her luggage and ran downstairs and out to the waiting cab. Inside the vehicle, she forced herself to look back and wave, then she settled into her seat and opened a newspaper to make sure that the driver did not speak to her, or notice that she had started to weep.

Greg had been a holiday diversion, she reminded herself. That was all. He would be a poor bet as a lifelong project. But he had sparked off something very powerful in her body and mind, and it was going to be tough to relinquish it.

Just before the taxi drew up at the terminal building, she pulled out a small mirror from her bag and checked that her distress had not damaged her make-up.

There was a mass of people disembarking from taxis and other cars. The driver fetched her a luggage trolley and put her suitcase on to it. She tipped him and turned to go into the terminal.

'Annie!'

Tears welled up in her eyes. He should not have come. But she was so very pleased that he had.

She found herself wrapped in his long arms. His lips searched for hers. Willingly, she allowed herself to be kissed deeply and passionately.

Eventually, he drew back and looked at her.

'I just don't get why you left so suddenly last night. We have something special going on here. I know I have a lousy romantic history but ...'

98

'Shall we get a cup of coffee, Greg?'

He nodded, and within moments he had steered her and her trolley into the terminal building, seated her in a little café and swiftly – while others were prevaricating and dithering – got himself served with two cappuccinos.

She beamed at him. 'You're a man of action!'

'Thank you, ma'am … I've been thinking. I know the summer is hectic and I have all these kids staying. But Nancy will go back to the States in a month, and Jean-Pierre will return to Paris. I can come to England for a weekend. You can come here. Or Paris. We could make this work. People have long-distance relationships these days.'

'Greg, I wasn't going to tell you this, but since you've turned up this morning I will. Remember I said that my daughter had met a young guy here?'

'Sure.'

'His name is Jean-Pierre.'

'That's a coincidence. Oh, wait a minute … wait a *minute* …'

'I only realised last night myself. He's a very fine boy, by the way. A credit to you.'

'Your daughter and my son are … making out.'

'To tell you the truth I never quite know what that means. But I think they are about to celebrate their lust by staying in bed on your boat for a whole week!'

'Well, heck. But does that make a difference?'

Annie took his hand and held it tightly. 'It *does*,' she said. 'After all, we might end up as grandparents to the same children!' She giggled then, and – after a moment – so did he.

'Oh God, will we tell them?'

'No, we will not,' she insisted. 'Don't you remember what it felt like when you realised what your mum and dad must have done to produce you?'

'Do you always have to be this goddam sensible?'

Annie smiled. 'I have to go and check in. But I'm glad you came to see me off. This is a better "goodbye". So, thanks for doing that.'

She stood up and kissed him, and then left without turning back.

The check-in queue was mercifully short, and in less than ten minutes, she had lodged her suitcase and was wandering towards the departures gate.

'De da, de da da da,

De da da, da da da ...'

Someone was humming the big song from *Casablanca*.

Greg caught her hand just as she was about to head into the Security section.

'Don't go,' he pleaded. 'Give us a chance.'

'Greg, this has been a holiday romance. That's all. You know it. I know it. I've loved it – I'm sure you realise that. But ...'

'I guess we'll always have Biarritz,' he murmured with an attempt at a Humphrey Bogart accent.

She smiled up at him. 'I have to go or I'll cry again – and I definitely won't do it as elegantly as Ingrid Bergman.'

Forcing herself, she took a big step away from him, and then another and another. She looked back. He was still there, as she had known he would be.

Blowing him a kiss, she turned away for the last time and walked purposefully into an area where he could not follow.

Chapter Six

Getting rid of her verbose patient – who lingered, hand on door-knob, insisting that 'there's just one more thing, Doctor' – was not just a nightmare, but a necessity.

With seconds to spare, Annie reached the sanctuary of the staff lavatory. It was her fourth visit in the past hour.

She knew what the trouble was, though she had not had it for decades. How many women had she treated with cystitis she wondered? She would have even more sympathy with patients who had it in the future. It was awful; the price to be paid – presumably – for unexpected and energetic sex.

Carole was in the staff room when she emerged, somewhat shakily, from the cubicle.

'Are you OK? You look a bit …'

'Cystitis,' Annie mouthed at her.

'Ooh. Painful!'

Annie shrugged. 'It's not terminal. How many more patients are there this morning? I want to pop out and buy some bicarb.'

Carole put down her coffee and made for the door. 'I'll go and get some. There are two more appointments. Can you manage them?'

Annie nodded. She hoped she could.

As soon as the last patient had gone, Carole slipped back into the consulting room with her purchase, and Annie quickly made up a solution of water and bicarbonate of soda and drank it down. It was horrible. But she knew that it would soothe her bladder.

After half an hour of trying to distract herself with paperwork and emails, she spooned more bicarbonate of soda into a glass, mixed it with water, and forced herself to drink it.

Carole popped her head round the door. 'Any better?'

'Improving,' Annie murmured.

'You should go home.'

'I can't. It's the practice meeting this afternoon, and then Jonathan and I are booked to go to a postgraduate lecture about eye diseases at Addenbrooke's this evening.'

Carole shrugged her shoulders and disappeared again, only to reappear minutes later with a hot water bottle.

'Put this on your tummy.'

'Where did you find that?'

'I keep it in the staff room cupboard. Regard it as a gift from a sympathetic sufferer.'

'Thanks. I really owe you,' gasped Annie. 'I … Oh, I have to …'

'Don't speak,' smiled Carole. 'Just go!'

A couple of glasses of bicarbonate solution later – and after a quick nap on her examination couch – Annie recovered sufficiently to attend the weekly staff meeting.

Jonathan was full of ideas, as was Gareth, who was a lively contributor and beginning to make his mark on the practice.

Annie was quiet, but she hoped that no one would notice. At least her pain had subsided, and she managed to sit through the meeting without having to excuse herself during it.

'Well, that was good, wasn't it?' Jonathan was all smiles.

'Yes,' she agreed. 'Gareth is a good addition.'

Jonathan nodded and departed, leaving Annie alone in the staff room. She glanced at her watch. There was half an hour before she need cycle to the postgraduate meeting. The sofa she was sitting on was much more comfortable than the furniture in her consulting room, so she swung her legs up and stretched out. Really, she should use this spare time to catch up on medical journals. Instead, she rummaged in her large handbag for her mobile.

There was a text from Janey:

I want to hear about your trip.

Annie could see that the text had arrived during her morning surgery. She quickly rang Janey, but got her voicemail, so she texted instead.

Sorry. Only just seen your text. Been one of those days. Ring you later. Hope all ok. A xx.

Jonathan came into the staff room wearing a slightly worried expression. She forced herself to sit up and smile, but he said nothing and disappeared again.

In a moment, she would summon the energy to put on some make-up. She really was much better. Thank heavens for the old remedy that she had read about – thirty years ago now – in a self-help book. The author deserved a medal.

She felt herself drifting off to sleep. Trying to resist, she reminded herself that she should be leaving soon.

'Annie …'

She struggled to sit up and shake off the lethargy that was claiming her.

'Annie,' Jonathan repeated. 'You're not well. Don't bother to come to the meeting.'

'I'm about to get ready. I'll see you there.'

'You're not going on your bike.'

'Of course. Some fresh air will wake me up.'

'Do me a favour and come in my car. I want to talk to you anyway.'

Annie looked at Jonathan's earnest face. In truth, she did not relish a bike ride this afternoon.

She nodded. 'OK,' she agreed, then swept up her bag and headed for the Ladies. She still had some discomfort, but that awful sense of urgency had eased.

Unusually, the traffic was quite light and they were at Addenbrooke's in no time. Jonathan had not talked about anything in particular during the short trip. In fact he had hardly said a word. Then again, neither had she.

He dropped her at the main entrance and drove off to find a parking space.

A gaggle of GPs was gathered at the table where coffee and tea was laid out for them. Annie knew that either beverage would be likely to spark off more bladder irritation, so she reached for a bottle of water instead.

The meeting began with a clinical quiz. The eye specialists had brought along several patients, and invited the GPs to examine them, and write down a diagnosis.

One man had woken up recently to find himself suddenly and totally blind. That certainly puts things in perspective, thought Annie.

Jonathan, it turned out, was brilliant on eyes. He got maximum marks. She had one diagnosis wrong.

'No disgrace in that,' he reassured her with a smile. 'You're more of a "below the waist" medic!'

She laughed as they found seats in preparation for the lecture.

'That's better,' he murmured. 'You're starting to look more like you.'

He had a very comforting presence, Annie mused, as she tried to concentrate on the ophthalmologist who was outlining the crucial symptoms in various eye diseases.

When the specialist's lecture finished, she clapped extra loudly in a bid to compensate for her attention lapses.

'Just one more talk,' Jonathan murmured.

The last speaker's PowerPoint presentation was clear and easy to follow. He also finished on time, which was a real bonus.

It was a shame that her bike was still at the surgery, but she could easily pick up a taxi at the front of the hospital and be home and in a bath in twenty minutes.

'You haven't got transport now,' Jonathan interrupted her thoughts. 'How about we grab a bite to eat? As I said earlier, I really need to talk to you. But I didn't ... well, you know, I felt ... you'd got enough on your plate keeping awake for the presentation. Well done by the way. I'm sure you've been feeling lousy. Do you want to tell me what's wrong? You're normally so hale and hearty.'

'It's nothing serious. I'm just a bit uncomfortable.'

'Gynae?'

'No. UTI.'

What should she do? Really, she just wanted to go home. She and Jonathan had never eaten together before – well, not outside medical parties at hospitals or their own practice – but she could see he was keen to talk. So maybe she should go. Also, she realised suddenly, having not eaten since breakfast time, she was hungry.

'All right.' His rather terse words interrupted her deliberations. 'Let's just get you home.'

Oh, she thought. He thinks I am not interested in his plans.

'Jonathan, sorry, I'm a bit slow on the uptake today. I'd love it if we had supper. And I really want to hear what it is you need to talk to me about.'

His expression brightened immediately, and he stood back to let her leave the room in front of him.

'Wait inside the main door,' he said. 'I bet the temperature's much lower than it was in south-west France. What's happened to our summer? I'll get the car.' And he raced off.

He drove to the pub in her own village, which served Thai food. She had only eaten there once before – with Edward – when it had opened.

Since her visit, there had been an outbreak of elephant ornaments in the dining area. But the rest of the pub still looked like a typical village hostelry with its brass fittings and polished bar.

'Is this all right?' Jonathan asked. 'I just thought it would be near, and you could get to bed afterwards.'

'It's lovely. I should eat here more, now that Edward's no longer around. He wasn't keen on the food; more of a carvery sort of man.'

Jonathan offered the wine list to Annie. She shook her head, and he suggested jasmine tea.

'Perfect,' she said. 'But wouldn't you like a glass of wine? Don't let me inhibit you.'

'I don't drink at all if I'm driving.'

How very different he was from Edward.

He went to the counter and ordered and paid for a mixture of several different hot dishes and rice which he tucked into enthusiastically when they arrived. Annie smiled at his evident enjoyment as she ate somewhat smaller portions herself.

'Have you been to Thailand?' he asked suddenly.

'No. I've never been further east than India; one reason for that was that Edward never got round to taking all his leave entitlement, so the idea of long-haul holidays rarely came up. Anyway, there's still so much of Europe I want to see.'

'Me too! I'd like to do more walking in the Alps, for example. Then there are areas of Scotland and Ireland I don't know at all.'

'You must do a lot of walking.'

'Yes – often with my nephew Oliver. It's one of the things we can do together. Do you?'

'I'd like to do more. I used to walk with my dad. He's a Scot and quite rugged ... well, he used to be. But Edward wasn't interested.'

'What was your husband like when you were ill?'

Annie appeared surprised by the question.

'Sorry, was that a bit personal?' Jonathan looked flustered.

'Not at all. I ... I don't think I ever let him know when I was poorly.'

'You *are* very self-reliant and capable.'

'Me?'

Jonathan grinned. 'Yes! You like to be in control, and you like making other people better and not making a fuss yourself. All of which makes you a very good partner at the practice!'

'Gosh, that's … well, maybe, if it *is* true, that's just as well. Edward wasn't good with illness. Well, I suppose he'd have been fine at dealing with fractures if the kids had ever had any … mind you, one year when we went skiing, I had a bad fall. You might have thought with his specialty that he'd have been interested in that, but he just turned back briefly, to ask if I could move my legs and my arms, then carried on down the hill. Fortunately, the ski instructor got me to my feet and helped me.'

'Not over-blessed with sympathy then?'

'I suppose he had other qualities – but he's using them up on someone else now.'

Watching Jonathan, she knew that he would not have left her lying shocked and hurt in the snow.

'You're a nice man,' she said suddenly. 'I'm sure you had plenty of other things to do tonight, but bringing me here was kind of you. I probably wouldn't have bothered to eat if it had been left to me.'

He seemed to blush slightly but it was hard to tell in the subdued lighting. He was obviously not good at accepting compliments, which was rather endearing.

Jonathan quickly changed the subject and outlined his latest plans for extending their surgery hours. Then he moved on to his news – which was that their older, and distinctly eccentric, partner had decided to return to work. He looked distressed, and Annie was equally upset. Dr Margaret was not an asset in the NHS as it had become, and it was hard to see how she would fit in with their new plans. Also, might her return mean that – even with the extra hours – there would no longer be enough work for Gareth? He was a good doctor, and would doubtless soon be in demand with other health centres in Cambridge, but it would be a pity not to be able to use him as much, since he was infinitely more effective than Margaret would ever be.

'That's a real drag ...' Annie began.

'It is. And there are implications for Gareth.'

'I was thinking that myself.'

Jonathan looked at her thoughtfully. 'You know, Annie,' he ran his forefinger around the rim of his glass of water, and then cleared his throat. 'I still maintain that you could do with some time off. And with both Margaret and Gareth around, perhaps ... only if you want to of course ... this would be a good time to have it. The fact that you've come back from less than a week off somewhat, um ... unwell and tired ... I mean ... Does this suggest you perhaps ought to catch up on rest?'

Did she want more time? She had thought so on holiday, but that had been when she had thought she might return to Biarritz. She did feel exhausted. But there again, she had not been well today. And maybe her mood was on the low side after having such excitement in France, and it being so brief – a brief encounter.

'Annie.' Jonathan's voice broke in on her rumination. 'You're out on your feet. Let me drive you home.'

'I only live a hundred yards away, which you'd know if you'd ever accepted any of my party invitations!'

'I'm not good at parties,' he admitted. 'Right, let's *walk* you home!' He opened the pub door and shepherded her through it.

She smiled at him. In their thirteen years as colleagues, this was the longest period they had ever spent on their own, outside of a medical situation, and she was amazed at how pleasant it was.

As they turned into her drive, Annie shrieked in surprise. Her friend Diana was knocking at the front door. 'Aren't you in Scotland?' Annie asked as she rushed forward to hug her.

'Just home for a day,' explained Diana. 'I had to tidy up a few loose ends, but I popped round because I've got lots to tell you.'

'Um,' Annie stood back and gestured at her colleague. 'Diana, this is Jonathan, my partner at the practice. Why don't you both come in and have a cup of tea?'

'Well, I ...' Diana looked from Jonathan to Annie.

'I'm going,' Jonathan said quickly. 'Annie hasn't been well. We've just been to a medical meeting and had something to eat. I'm relieved to deliver her into a friend's hands. Good to meet you.' He did a swift about-turn and disappeared from the drive.

Inside the front door, Diana looked apologetic. 'I didn't mean to frighten him away.'

'He's shy,' Annie explained as she walked into the kitchen and put the kettle on. 'Don't mind him. We were only talking business.'

'You're not seeing each other then?'

'Jonathan? No! We just work together.'

'What did he mean about you being ill?'

'Oh, it was nothing.' Annie put some cups and saucers on a tray and found some stem-ginger biscuits. 'I had cystitis today. It's almost over now; nothing serious.'

Just at that moment, the kettle boiled and Annie busied herself with making tea. Then the two women wandered through to the sitting room and sat down in armchairs overlooking the rear garden.

Annie appraised her friend. She was looking very well, and more relaxed than usual, dressed casually as she was in navy chinos and a pink shirt. Her steely-grey hair had been allowed to grow longer too. Funny how most women's response to romantic trauma is to try a new style, Annie thought.

They talked about the Scottish Borders and Diana's brother and his home. Annie could tell that her friend was downplaying its grandeur, but it was obviously a proper, baronial-style castle surrounded by acres of land that ran down to the River Tweed.

'What do you do with your time there?' Annie asked.

'I run a lot. I've joined the tennis club. And I've read masses of books. There's a library at my brother's … and I've also done a great deal of thinking, including about my job. And I've realised that I don't want to do physiotherapy any more. Not sure why. Maybe it's because of Rupert, or because I'm sixty next year. Anyway, my partner is taking over the practice. So I came down to sign the relevant legal papers and pick up some summer clothes while I was at it – that's in the hope that it will eventually get warmer!'

Annie stared at her friend while she spoke so matter-of-factly about discarding a major part of her life. She felt concerned that Diana's plan to give up her job might be just the start of a series of changes. What if she left Cambridge altogether? That would be a huge blow.

Diana was her only close companion in the village. And with the girls gone to London and Sussex, and Edward off the radar, so much had already altered …

'What are you thinking about?' Diana asked. 'Or are you just tired?'

'Bit of both, I suppose. Our lives are so different now compared with a couple of years ago.'

'I know. What do you think are the biggest things – about being single – after decades of marriage?'

'Hard to say; they change, don't they, as time moves on? For ages, I kept our bedroom just as it was – probably because I thought Edward might come back. But then, once I realised I didn't *want* him to return, I felt I needed to alter it. So, I've had it painted a lovely Mediterranean burnt-orange colour. Edward would have hated it!'

'Sounds heavenly. I'd love to have a look before I go if I may. Anything else?'

'Well, when you're single, if you clean the kitchen, it *stays* clean!'

'Was Edward messy? I can't imagine it.'

'Not really. But living alone is very different from having someone else around. Everything is where you left it … I expect Rupert has noticed some changes in *your* house. For a start he may realise now just how much you used to do for him!'

Diana raised her eyes heavenward, but said nothing.

'Do you think the two of you will ever get back together?'

'I haven't decided,' Diana answered, quietly. 'But, it doesn't feel likely, though sometimes I do miss him. We used to do so much together, well, socially at least. Thing is though, I've had a few, well, "dates", I suppose you'd call them … with a friend of my brother. He's a judge. We've had dinner in Edinburgh and been to Scottish Opera. No hanky-panky or anything. Just a chaste kiss at the end of the evening, but it makes you aware that there are other men.'

Annie smiled. 'I know.'

'Oh, do tell me what happened in Biarritz.'

So, Annie did. But first she told her friend about Lucy's heartbreak, and how in a weak moment she had promised to take her daughter away. She also described Arabella's recent upheaval, which – having been ensconced in the ancestral castle – Diana had managed to miss. Then, taking a deep breath, she launched into an account of her liaison with Greg. She felt rather anxious that Diana would be appalled, but in fact her friend was eager for details.

'And you're really not going to see him again – because of Lucy?' Diana asked.

Annie shrugged her shoulders. 'It would never have worked. And, the funny thing is, although it was just last week, it already seems like a dream. But, it was just great to feel hugely sexual and to find out that it all worked.'

'I must say, I'd like that too.' Diana looked pensive, then she jumped up. 'Can I look at your bedroom before I go?'

'Of course. I'll pop into the downstairs loo while you do.'

'Oh, I forgot about your problem.'

'So did I – which must mean I'm better! After you go, I must try and speak to my friend Janey. I can never seem to track her down at the moment.'

'Too busy with her young lover, I imagine,' chortled Diana, as she took the stairs two at a time.

Janey did not answer her landline, or her mobile. So, Annie left messages on both. She also emailed her, with a brief description of her passion-filled days in Biarritz, and their painful legacy today. Finally, she tried a text:

111

Have you found another best friend? We haven't spoken for ages. You can't be in bed with Miguel all the time! Sorry not to get back to you this morning. Was rushing to the loo every five minutes. Cystitis! Better now. Hope you're OK. Not like you to maintain 'radio silence'. Lots of love, A x

It was eleven days later – despite numerous attempts by Annie to reach her best friend – before the two women finally spoke.

During that time, Annie had fully recovered from her bladder problems, lost count of the number of surgeries she had done, and been a radio 'expert' again.

She had also had various texts from Lucy, who was clearly in some sort of sunshiny sexual heaven, and heard from Diana who was delighted to be back in Scotland.

It was Friday, late evening, and Annie was watching Wimbledon on her television. To some extent it was a bitter-sweet experience, because she and Edward had gone to the tournament every year, and despite the fact that she no longer had any wish to be with him, there were moments when she missed events or occasions that reminded her of their long life together.

Federer had just won a set, and his opponent had gone off for a 'comfort-break'. The cameras roamed around the stands picking out celebrities and other spectators of interest. These were mostly young and beautiful, but there was also an old gentleman in his panama who was obviously asleep.

Annie sauntered out to the kitchen for a glass of Chablis. The summer had finally come back and – for the first time this year – the evening was long and hot and full of fragrant promise.

She gazed out of the window at her garden. On such a night as this, she thought, it would be lovely to sit outside and enjoy a light supper and drink good wine.

She and Edward had bought all the necessary garden furniture for al fresco dining, but they had never used it except at their annual barbecue – an occasion Annie had hated because Edward got drunk and burned the food, every year without exception.

Back in the sitting room, she noticed that Federer's opponent had called for the trainer, so play had still not resumed and there were more shots of the crowd.

'Ewwww! Oh God.'

There, on Centre Court, sat her ex-husband and Simpering Suzie, who was kissing his ear. Worse than that, he did not look at all embarrassed.

At that moment, the phone rang.

'Sorry I've been so elusive …'

'Janey! If you're at home, turn on BBC1 now. Oh, don't bother, they've gone.'

'What? Who?'

'Wimbledon. You know how Edward and I always used to go, and how he was always very proper about it and we had to dress up and everything. Well, there was a shot of him in the crowd just now, canoodling with you-know-who and he … well he looked relaxed, and not at all formal, and as if he was having fun.'

'Well, darling,' Janey remarked blithely, 'that's what he left home for, wasn't it?'

There was silence for a moment, and then Annie heard the unmistakeable sound of her best friend sobbing.

'Janey, what is it?'

'I just sounded like a real bitch and …' She was crying too much to continue.

'No you didn't. You're right about Edward. It hurts, but it's true.'

'Sorry,' Janey sniffed and then blew her nose. 'I don't know what's wrong with me. Maybe I'm a bit down. What did his fancy woman look like, by the way?'

'Summery and – now I come to think of it – rather plumper than I remember.'

Janey attempted a light-hearted laugh. 'There you are then, there *is* a God.'

Annie giggled. Then, suddenly serious, she asked, 'Are you really feeling down? Please tell me. After all, you were my "go-to" agony aunt through my trauma. So it'd be awful if you couldn't ... you know ... open up to me. And although you'll probably deny it, I feel you've been avoiding me.'

'OK, I have. I'm been trying to make sense of how I feel. It might be my age. I feel uncomfortable and kind of full in my tummy all the time. And I wee more. And I've got a sort of back-ache. Of course that's probably muscular. But do all these things happen in mid-life? You never talk about the menopause.'

'I've been lucky. It must have begun in the Edward days, but it never bothered me and I don't even remember how long it is since I had my last period. Believe me, for a doctor, that is a terrible and inefficient admission!'

'Did you lose your libido?'

'There was so little sex on offer I didn't notice!'

'Was your appetite poor?'

'Only for about a week when Edward first left. But, coming back to sex for a moment, is everything OK with you and Miguel?'

'Yeah – it's just that I can't be bothered. I suppose I feel permanently pre-menstrual. And bloated. And actually, sex has hurt me a bit lately. Maybe I'm just getting older. Right, I've had my moan now. What's *really* wrong is that I don't have enough work. And what I *do* have I'm bored with, or it doesn't bring in enough dosh.'

'Why don't you come up here for the weekend?'

'I wish I could. But I've got two articles to write, so I must do them, even though they're for an editor who looks about twelve and hasn't a bloody clue.'

Annie was content to let Janey have a rant. And towards the end of the phone call her friend sounded more cheerful. But this did little to dispel Annie's unease about her.

Of course there had been tears and heartache over Janey's various – and usually unsuitable and unhealthy – romances. But such setbacks had never altered her essentially optimistic attitude. And she had always loved her job and never tired of it before.

The Federer match was over and the Wimbledon transmission was ending. It was cooler now, but still a beautiful evening. Annie wandered out into the garden and watered the pots of geraniums standing on the terrace outside her sitting room. She loved the earthy smell of the plants.

Her maternal grandfather had been a keen gardener who had had a greenhouse full of geraniums. Annie had never grown them until after Edward had left. But now they seemed to connect her to all that had been good in her childhood. It was funny how a link to early life now seemed so much more relevant than it used to be when she was bringing up her own girls.

She would have some supper now. Watch TV. There was a ballet on Sky Arts that she would enjoy.

In the kitchen, she prepared a salad and opened a pack of smoked mackerel.

'I'm getting so lazy,' she chided herself as she poured out a fresh glass of Chablis.

She was just sitting down in the sitting room to her meal on a tray when the phone rang. It was Arabella, full of joy and happiness. Being in love with Martin was clearly like a life-giving injection for her.

'How's your medical drama going?'

Arabella groaned. 'We film every single day, including weekends. We have to. The scripts are so poor that they don't work, and we have to rewrite them on the hoof.'

Despite her disgust at the series, Arabella laughed and joked and barely drew breath for a good ten minutes. This was how Janey used to be, thought Annie sadly. What has happened? Maybe she's fallen out of love, but is that all?'

'So,' Arabella was saying. 'Are you seeing the handsome American again?'

'I'd forgotten you didn't know the end of that story. It turned out he was the father of Lucy's boyfriend!'

Arabella roared with laughter, while Annie recounted how exciting the lovemaking had been, but how she had worked out the family connection and finished with him.

'Never mind. You're back in the saddle, as it were! What else is happening?'

'I just saw Edward on TV while I was watching Wimbledon.' Annie went on to describe the episode with Suzie, and also mentioned that she thought her replacement had put on weight.

Arabella giggled and did a little bitching of her own about her brother's new wife. Everything amused her these days. And it was infectious. As Annie put down the receiver at the end of the call she could feel herself smiling broadly.

She finished her supper and switched on the ballet. Dance was one of the hobbies she had reconnected with after the end of her marriage. Before Edward, she and Janey used to queue up for cheap seats at the Royal Opera House. Then they would always have pasta and a bottle of red wine at a Spaghetti House nearby.

Annie's heart started pounding.

'Oh, my God,' she whispered as a chilling realisation took hold of her. 'Not Janey.'

She must think. Think what to do. Think what to say. But not sound alarming. And that was going to be very difficult, if not impossible, now that she knew – almost beyond doubt – exactly what was wrong with her friend.

Chapter Seven

By eight o'clock the following morning, Annie was halfway down the M11. Being Saturday, there was no commuter traffic, and she was making swift progress on her journey to London.

She had had no difficulty in leaving home early, because her 'eureka' moment of the evening before had robbed her of sleep.

All her usual wind-down routines – hot milk, an even hotter bath, and drops of lavender oil on the pillow – had failed to relax her.

Eventually, sometime after two she had dozed for a while, but her slumber had been laced with terrifying dreams, so once daylight had dawned she had abandoned her bed.

During the long hours of worry, she had decided that she must talk to Janey as soon as possible, but in person, rather than on the phone.

Her friend had said that she was going to write two articles over the weekend, so she should be at home. But what time might she be up and at her desk?

In the old days, Annie had known Janey's routine almost as well as her own. Customarily, her friend would rise early and work hard throughout an extended morning, then take a nap before continuing to write, and then going out to eat or drink, or both.

How much had her schedule altered to accommodate Miguel? Did he sleep late? It seemed likely, as he taught in the evenings and probably ate dinner afterwards. Could she, or should she, speak frankly in front of him? And if not, where could she and Janey have this vital conversation?

She adjusted her position slightly, then raised and dropped her shoulders a couple of times in an attempt to ease the tension in her neck and back. The car seats were normally comfortable, but today everything hurt.

She loved this little Fiat – having traded in her Picasso People Carrier a few months ago. She should have done it before; it had been years since she had been required to ferry her girls to school or to discos. But for a while, she had needed a vehicle with sufficient space to convey them back and forth to university. Even that had stopped now. Alice had her own car. And Lucy always seemed to have a devoted boyfriend who wanted to transport her – and her considerable baggage – to and from Sussex.

Realising that she was no longer the first-choice chauffeur had been a slightly painful discovery. It had been one of those landmark stages – such as the day when your child stops wanting a hug at the school gates, or refuses to hold hands when crossing a road. Mixed feelings, she mused, are an integral part of motherhood.

The old car had also played a part in her marriage as it had been her role to drive Edward back from any function or dinner party they had attended together, so that he could drink as much as he wanted, which was usually a lot. She could not imagine him poured into this petite and pretty vehicle with its cream paintwork, white steering wheel and scarlet fascia and upholstery. Doubtless he would consider it cramped and frivolous. But it suited her.

She cast her mind back to the day when she had eased Diana into the passenger seat, and then learned of her marital crisis. Though barely two months had elapsed, it was obvious that the situation between Diana and Rupert had become less dramatic and that, in time, some sort of new normality would emerge. So, it probably followed that, eventually, Janey's crisis would gain a new perspective – though she wished she could feel optimistic about its outcome.

For the hundredth time, she ran over all the symptoms that her friend had mentioned in the past weeks: bloating, weight loss, little appetite, feeling full almost as soon as she had started eating, urinating more frequently, backache, pain during sex …

How could she have been so slow to link all these 'danger signs' together? Or to recognise what they might mean?

'Not your finest moment, Doctor,' she snapped at herself.

She would like to discuss the probable diagnosis with another medic. But who? She considered Alice, but this was hardly her field. In any event, she must not mention Janey's name until and unless her friend was prepared to go public with her condition. And Alice was so shrewd, she might well guess who her mother was talking about.

Perhaps Jonathan? He would be helpful. She filed the idea away and turned her attention to the route into central London. She rarely drove in the capital these days, and everyone seemed to drive faster here than they did in Cambridge.

It was almost nine when she reached Pimlico. Janey's second-floor flat was in an elegant Regency building on the corner of a quiet square. It would cost a fortune to buy now, but Janey had purchased it during the recession of the early 1990s when its owners had been desperate to sell.

Back then, Janey had been the health editor on a breakfast television programme, as well as an agony aunt in both a women's magazine and a popular Sunday newspaper. On top of that, she had just published a book on relationships that sold so well it made the Top 10 Paperbacks list in *The Guardian*.

'Thank God the readers don't know that my own love life is a bloody shambles,' she had joked to Annie, on more than one occasion.

Janey had had no viable partner during this hectic period. Just one of the married variety, who had turned up when he could get away from either his wife, or the editor's chair of a national broadsheet.

Though her love life had continued to be messy, her career had blossomed until the credit crunch of 2008.

'I'm older now. Less fashionable. It's going to really hurt,' she had told Annie when she had rung with the news that she had lost two of her regular jobs in one week.

But she had survived, and – as she always did – kept laughing.

Annie parked in the square round the corner from Janey's flat, locked her car, took a deep breath and walked to the front door. She paused before ringing the doorbell.

'Hello, yes?' Her friend's voice, slightly croaky, came over the intercom system.

Annie announced herself.

Just as if she had been expecting her, Janey said, 'I think it's coffee time. I'll be down in a moment.'

Annie suddenly felt queasy. Bewildered too. She had expected to be buzzed into the building and to have to explain what she was doing there.

Five minutes went by. She paced up and down until Janey appeared, all in a rush. She hugged Annie without quite looking her in the eye, then, taking her arm, marched her round the corner to a French patisserie and coffee shop.

'You must have left at the crack of dawn. How about we murder a couple of *pains au chocolat*?'

Annie nodded.

'They do a marvellous *grande crème* here as well.'

Annie smiled at Janey's enthusiasm. 'Sounds good.'

Janey ordered from the counter while Annie picked a table as far from the other customers as possible. She watched her friend, who appeared to be in no hurry to join her. Janey seemed even thinner than when they had last met for lunch. Her hair looked greyish – as if she hadn't bothered with the strawberry blonde rinse for a while – and had been scraped back into a giant butterfly clip. She was wearing old jeans and a purple sweatshirt – the colour of which would normally have suited her, but now merely emphasised how pale she had become.

Eventually, Janey brought over the pastries, and the girl from behind the counter carried the coffees.

As she sat down, Janey half-looked at Annie.

'You're awfully smart today. Nice sundress. That turquoise suits you. And your hair is great. I like it longer. You must have washed and blow-dried it this morning.'

'I've been up a long time.'

'Ah.' Janey stirred her coffee with apparent concentration.

'So, are you surprised to see me?' Annie ventured, and immediately felt exasperated with herself. What did that mean? For sixty miles, she had carefully rehearsed what she needed to say.

Janey licked her spoon and set it on the saucer. 'Not entirely.'

'Do you want to know *why* I'm here?'

Janey reached for Annie's hand and held it very tightly for a moment before letting go. 'I *know* why you're here. You've come to congratulate me for finally getting down to a size six!'

'What?'

'That's my attempt – probably my last one for a while – to be funny. I had hoped that you wouldn't come to the same conclusion as me. I deliberately avoided talking to you for a while – once I started googling the symptoms … because I wasn't ready, I suppose, to accept or deal with everything. Then yesterday evening, I knew I'd given you various clues and I decided – because you didn't immediately hint at a diagnosis – that maybe I was just doing that "worried well" thing. After all, health journalists are notoriously neurotic about themselves. But you're here. So, now it seems that, like me, you think there's a high chance I've got ovarian cancer.' Janey's eyes filled with tears.

Annie grabbed both of her friend's hands and held on to them, blinking furiously to stop herself from crying too.

'I suppose …' Annie fought to keep her voice steady. '… I should have realised that with your sort of knowledge …'

'The worst thing,' Janey sighed as she pulled her hands out of Annie's grasp, 'is that I recall writing about it maybe twenty years ago. I remember some of the exact words too: "Sadly, by the time a patient is aware enough of her symptoms to visit a doctor, it's often too late." So, I know that my chances are pretty dire.'

121

'Janey, listen. I won't give you false reassurance. But things have moved on. I mean, at Addenbrooke's, their stats are quite encouraging. It's obviously a centre of excellence, but there are equally expert hospitals in London. What we need to do is try to keep calm and get a blood test done, and see where we go from there.'

Janey took a gulp of coffee. Then she said, 'I suppose you mean a CA 125 test?'

'You *have* done your homework,' Annie murmured. 'You haven't by any chance booked an appointment with your GP as well have you?'

'I know I should have done ...' Janey suddenly looked lost and slightly shrunken.

'Don't worry. Do they open on Saturday? I could come with you. Explain it's an emergency. Mind you, there's no way they'd get that blood result back today.'

'Should I try to get a private appointment with a specialist? What would that cost?'

'I'll tell you what we could do,' Annie decided. 'There's a laboratory in Wimpole Street. I could request a blood test for you – and we could go this morning.'

Janey shifted in her seat. She picked up the uneaten *pain au chocolat* and broke it in two, then replaced both halves on her plate. 'I don't want to be a nightmare, and I know I need this done urgently, but I want to finish the articles I'm working on. God knows I need the money.'

Annie sighed inwardly. Janey was afraid, which was understandable. But she was focusing on matters that ultimately were irrelevant compared with the much bigger issue of keeping herself alive.

Annie changed tack. 'My medical bag's in the car. Would you let me take your blood? Then I can drive it over to the laboratory.'

Janey looked stunned. 'I can't believe this is happening,' she mumbled. 'Not to me. And yet ... Well, why *not* to me? OK. Yes, please can you take blood from me – and can we do it in your car?'

Annie tried hard to keep her face expressionless. Janey was obviously struggling with doom-laden thoughts, but the car was not suitable.

'We need to do it in your flat,' she stated firmly. 'It'll be simpler and more hygienic.'

Janey slumped back in her chair and stared into the distance. Annie watched her for a moment before swinging into action. She walked round behind her friend's seat and encouraged her to stand. Then she slipped her right arm around Janey's waist. 'C'mon. You've got work to do.'

As she helped Janey to her feet, Annie noticed that the pretty French waitress had come over, all smiles, to clear the table. She watched as the girl hesitated and took in the barely drunk coffee and uneaten pastries before gazing at the two of them and then retreating. We must look as traumatised as we feel, Annie surmised, as she gently pushed Janey towards the door.

When they reached Annie's car, Janey leant against it while Annie opened the boot and pulled out her medical bag.

'Right – let's go. 'Have you got your keys?'

'Oh God, I hope so. I don't want to wake Miguel.' Janey patted her pockets and started to sob again as she rummaged in her capacious shoulder bag.

'Let me look,' Annie suggested. 'Here they are! It's OK.'

Their progress up to the flat was slow. If only, Annie kept thinking … if only I'd realised sooner.

Janey opened her front door, and tiptoed in. She was obviously worried about waking her boyfriend. But this was an emergency. If he loved her, surely he would want to know that she might have something seriously wrong with her.

Annie looked around her as she walked from the small hallway into the spacious double-aspect sitting room. Janey's home had always been immaculate, but now a large sports bag – with sweaty exercise clothes spilling out of it – had been dropped casually on the floor just inside the door, bundles of DVDs lay on the sofa, and some technological gadget, with a mass of cables coming out of it, was taking up most of the surface of the glass coffee table.

'He's young,' Janey whispered conspiratorially in answer to Annie's silent criticism.

Not that young, thought Annie. Young, compared with us, it's true. But thirty-eight isn't nineteen.

She had only met Miguel once. At the time, he had struck her as attractive and charming. But she had never been in Janey's apartment since he had moved in, and what she saw all around her, hardened her heart against him. No wonder Janey had wanted the blood test done in the car.

She noticed that Miguel had made his presence felt in the bathroom too. Wet towels lay in a heap near, rather than in, the laundry basket.

In a slightly embarrassed way, Janey swept them up before sitting down on the edge of the bath.

In preparation for taking the blood, Annie swabbed Janey's arm. Then when she had the specimen, she completed the procedure by applying a plaster over the pinprick hole.

'OK. Shall I leave you to your work and go to the lab?' she asked.

'Do you mind? Thanks for sorting it. I know I should come but I want to get writing, and do normal things.'

Annie leaned over and kissed her cheek. 'Janey, we both think you may have this … illness to face. But you may not. Even if the CA 125 is high, it might indicate something else.'

Janey looked unconvinced.

Outside, Annie sat in her car and mentally replayed the morning's events. The conversation she had dreaded had proved much easier than she had anticipated, but there were other worries now – most of which majored on Miguel.

She drove off, only getting lost once on her way – which was something of a record for her in London. Luckily, she found a parking space right outside the laboratory, and once inside, she was relieved to find that the receptionist was helpful. Scanning the form that

Annie had presented with the blood, the woman noted the URGENT request at the top of it, and said quietly, 'We're not too busy this morning, Doctor; we'll have the result for you in four hours.'

Back on the street, Annie was at a loss. What now, she wondered? She was in the West End, with spare time to shop, or visit a gallery but with no inclination to do either.

She opted to drive to the nearby car park in Cavendish Square and then go to her medical club.

Her stomach was churning. She had not felt like eating breakfast before she left and certainly had not done justice to the brunch with Janey, so she made her way to the members' café and ordered a cappuccino and croissant.

Her coffee was good and she passed some time skimming through a couple of newspapers that were lying around. Afterwards, she deliberated over whether or not she could ring Jonathan. The trouble was that he would be in the middle of the Saturday morning surgery, which was proving popular with their patients. Also, it might be better to wait till she had a diagnosis before discussing it with him. It was so difficult to know what to do.

Unsettled, and uncertain, she left the café and the club and walked the short distance to John Lewis so that she could buy Janey a present.

An hour or so later, with purchases in hand – none of which seemed quite what she had wanted – she walked back to the club with the intention of going to the library where she knew she would be able to find journals and text books on ovarian cancer.

As she approached the lift to take her there, an extremely large man exited from it. He stared at her, glanced away, and then looked again.

'You're Anne Buchanan!' he announced loudly.

The fact that he called her by her maiden name and used 'Anne' rather than 'Annie' meant that he had known her sometime before her marriage.

She smiled and offered her hand – and as he grasped it, she perceived that there *was* something familiar about him. It was just that the rather sweet chubby face she remembered was now surrounded by a much larger, jowly one. He had been a student with her in medical school.

'Do they still call you "Jumbo"?' she asked, as his nickname sprang to mind.

'I'm afraid so,' he laughed.

'Did you become a GP?' She played for time.

'No, I went into ENT, in Edinburgh – same as Colin. I still see a lot of him.'

Colin had been her boyfriend throughout her training.

'What are you doing in London?' she asked.

'There was a conference here yesterday. I'm taking my wife to the theatre this afternoon before we fly home. What about you?'

'Well, I live and work in Cambridge these days, but right now, I'm hanging around to get a blood test result for a CA 125. My best friend may have ovarian cancer.'

'Oh God. That's rotten luck,' Jumbo sympathised. 'You should talk to Professor Prue Spears.'

'Prue Spears? I've read papers by her.'

'I'm not surprised. I know she's published a lot of literature on female cancers. She's at the Royal Marsden now. Funnily enough, she was in here earlier. Apparently, she has a private clinic in Harley Street on Saturdays. You should pop round and see her. Number 10, she said.'

'I can't do that. I don't know her.'

'Yes, you do. She was one of the few English medical students at Edinburgh – like you.'

'Actually, I'm not wholly English. My dad's a Scot.'

'I never knew that. Anyway, Prue was the year above us. Prudence Smythson. You must remember … Totally brilliant.'

At that moment, Jumbo's wife emerged from the lift pushing two cases. He introduced her as Caroline.

'Must go,' he said cheerily, as – waddling slightly – he set off for reception. 'Look us up if you're ever in Edinburgh,' he called over his shoulder as he disappeared round the corner.

126

With only 'Jumbo' to go on, that could be difficult, thought Annie, but meeting him had been extremely useful; she had had no idea that she had actually known the eminent Prue Spears all those years ago. Could she really go and seek her advice?

A visit to the library to read up on women's cancers certainly did not improve her mood, but at least it occupied her time till she could return to the lab.

As she walked up Wimpole Street, Annie's steps grew slower and her heart heavier. It would be wonderful to get good news but she did not expect it.

The result of the test was every bit as bad as she had feared. Clutching the ripped open envelope she quickly left the building and stood outside, breathing deeply. Absent-mindedly, she stepped off the kerb. A taxi hooted at her. She jumped back.

'Pull yourself together, Annie,' she berated herself.

In a daze, she negotiated the short distance to Harley Street and quickly found the right house.

The smiling and smart receptionist was polite but guarded as Annie asked if Professor Spears was in the building.

'I believe so. Have you got an appointment?'

'No. Sorry. I'm a doctor. We knew each other at medical school. I … I just heard she was here today. I'd love to catch up with her for ten minutes if she has a break. I'm Dr Templeton, but she'll know me as Buchanan.'

'Leave it with me.' The woman, whose name badge indicated that she was called Jill, gestured to the room opposite her desk. 'Take a seat in the waiting room. I'll try to intercept her between patients.'

Annie helped herself to extra-cold bubbling water from a machine in the corner, and then looked for somewhere to sit among the cosmopolitan mass of individuals who were dotted around the room waiting their turn. She chose a sofa next to an engaging little Asian boy and his mother. The child immediately showed her his Fisher Price Chatter Telephone. She smiled. Her girls had had an earlier version of the same toy when they had been small. She played with him, pretending to ring up a friend. He laughed in that completely uninhibited way young children have. Annie laughed too, but suddenly found that her eyes were blurred with tears.

Fortunately, Jill appeared in the doorway at that moment and called out, 'Ravi Patel?' And the child and his mother trotted off for their appointment.

Annie blew her nose and reached for a copy of *Good Housekeeping*, which she failed to open.

Looking out of the window at passers-by in Harley Street, she was aware that today was likely to be routinely uneventful for most of them. Janey, on the other hand, was going to have to deal with the unpalatable certainly that her life was about to change for ever. How many of the individuals in the waiting room were also going to get a life-threatening diagnosis, she wondered. Fortunately many of them looked quite well.

A text pinged into her phone. It was from Arabella who was clearly fizzing with joy and energy. She had decided to sell her Henley house. Everything was going brilliantly – even though the television drama was driving her mad! Annie grinned, and then switched her phone off as an elderly and very lame gentleman shuffled into the waiting room.

Making his way over to her sofa, he squeezed in beside her, huffing and puffing with the effort. One of his walking sticks fell and banged her on the ankle. She ought to be nice, but she really wanted to push him away, or at least extricate herself and go and sit on the other side of the room where there were a couple of empty chairs. Would that be very rude? She stayed where she was and attempted to visualise Lake Geneva, which was a tried and trusted calm-inducing technique of hers.

Suddenly, a woman of a certain age, with beautifully-cut silvery grey hair and dressed in a white shirt and black trousers – much like Annie's own 'uniform' at the surgery – appeared in the doorway, gazing around with an enquiring expression. Annie stood up and walked towards her. Prue Spears smiled. 'Goodness me! Anne Buchanan. How many years has it been?'

They shook hands. Prue led the way downstairs to a kitchen in the basement and offered Annie some tea.

'I've got a break of fifteen minutes and I'm gasping,' she explained before selecting two mugs from a cupboard, dropping a teabag into each of them and adding boiling water. As she spooned out the teabags into a rubbish bin, she spoke again.

'We could sit in here. But we may be disturbed. Would you prefer the consulting room?'

Annie nodded.

Inside the room, Prue took one of the armchairs in front of the desk and offered Annie the other one.

'So, Anne …'

'Do call me "Annie". That's how I'm known now.'

'Funny how we're much less formal as we age!'

'Yes. You were very much "Prudence" as I remember.'

Prue winced. 'Don't remind me. We were so serious. Mind you, I think women *had* to be back then. There were so many chauvinistic professors who assumed that we'd never be any use as medics because we'd be off having babies every five minutes. So, what's up?'

'Is it obvious that I want to pick your brains?'

'Pretty much,' Prue replied.

'To tell you the truth, I'd never connected Professor Prue Spears with the very brilliant Prudence Smythson! But I bumped into someone this morning who knew us both. Trouble is, all I can remember is that his nickname was "Jumbo"!'

'Yes, I met him earlier too. I had to ask what his real name was. It's Trevor Davidson.'

'Oh! That only rings the faintest of bells. Still, he did me a huge favour in telling me you were here. It's about my friend …'

Prue Spears reached for a pad and took notes, listening carefully – without interrupting – while Annie recounted all she knew and had discerned about Janey.

'So, you've had her CA 125 done this morning?'

Annie nodded and produced the envelope. 'You'll know far more than me what this means.'

Prue quickly read the information. 'Could I see her? Where is she?'

'Pimlico. It would be marvellous if you could. But I'll pay.'

'You will *not* pay,' Prue retorted, in a voice that made it plain there was to be no argument.

'OK. Well, what about the usual consultants' currency?'

Prue looked puzzled.

Annie grinned. 'Whenever my ex-husband saw a fellow doctor, a case of Prosecco used to appear.'

'You may have found my weak spot!' laughed Prue.

She was an attractive woman – much more so than her younger self – even if she was plumper than Annie remembered. And though she was grey-haired, it was obvious that she had the character and confidence to carry it off. She would be well able to afford the best colourist in London, so she must have chosen to let nature take its course.

'How soon could you see her?' Annie prompted.

'In the morning. Say 9.30?'

'You're working on Sunday! Don't you ever sleep?'

Prue laughed again. 'I'm not usually here as much as this. But we're off to our Suffolk hideaway in about ten days, so I'm getting ahead. I'll examine Janey, and do an ultrasound, and we'll take it from there. Let's just swap mobile numbers.'

Once they had both tinkered with their phones, Annie went to shake hands with her, but Prue opened her arms and gave her a huge hug. 'You take care of yourself,' she counselled as she pulled back. 'We're talking about your very best friend. And what happens to her is going to have a big impact on you too.'

In the street outside she rang Janey, who did not pick up her phone, so Annie texted a message, telling her about the consultation the following morning, and promising to ring later.

There was little she could do now; not if Janey was working, and less than keen to see her, so she collected her car and drove out to Teddington.

Her father seemed brighter than on her recent visits, so she sat with him in his room, and played Scottish songs on his CD player. There was a glint in his eye today which made him seem almost his normal self. And every now and again he would join in with the words.

'My love she's but a lassie yet,' he warbled, taking Annie's hand and kissing it.

She stayed longer than she had planned because both she and he were having such a good time. He probably had no real sense of who she was. And he had no idea either of where he was, or of what he had had for lunch, but the words of Robert Burns – seared into his brain at school – tumbled out of him with barely an error.

After he grew too tired to sing, he fell asleep, so Annie found a carer and asked to be let out of the building.

She decided to leave her car where it was and to walk for a while. Wandering away from the river and into the main street, she realised she was exhausted. Was she going to drive back to Cambridge now? And then motor back in the morning so she could accompany Janey to Harley Street?

She rang her friend again, this time on her landline, but got her answerphone.

'Just to let you know,' Annie said, 'that I'm in Teddington at the moment. Do you want to meet up later or anything? Or I could just meet you in Harley Street in the morning? I think I'll be in London overnight … somewhere.'

She wasn't sure how much more she should say, so she terminated the call.

It was pretty certain that Janey would not offer her a bed for the night, as she would have done pre-Miguel. But perhaps they could still spend some time together.

She had only walked a few steps when Janey called back.

'I'm taking Miguel out for dinner tonight to explain what's going on. He's a very special guy, Annie.' She sounded quite brittle and challenging.

Annie did her best to colour her own voice with a degree of warmth which she did not feel. 'I know. He's made you very happy. Of course you must spend time with him. It's going to be hard on him too.'

But would it be? Annie wondered as she walked rather aimlessly along the high street that had changed so much since her childhood. She noticed that a tea shop which her mother had loved had become a Mexican grill. There would be no proper teapots in there … no cake …

Maybe Alice would put her up?

Her daughter's mobile went straight to voicemail. She left a message saying she was in town. Two minutes later, she received a brief text.

Mum. Sorry to have missed you. Not at home. Working. See you soon. Love Ally.

Perhaps then, the club might have a room? She tapped out their number, and was relieved to be told that they had.

During her drive back into central London, she kept passing pubs and cafés where people were sitting outside and enjoying the early evening sunshine while they ate and drank. Paused at traffic lights, she could hear excited chat and hoots of laughter from the al fresco customers at an obviously popular hostelry, which was bedecked with a mass of colourful hanging baskets. She felt a stab of envy for anyone who was enjoying a carefree summer Saturday.

After garaging the car, and registering for her room, she paid a visit to John Lewis to buy cleansing wipes and a toothbrush, as well as a shirt and some navy cropped trousers; the sundress which Janey had admired earlier was far too grubby and creased to wear another day.

Then she went to the food hall and bought a bottle of Sauvignon Blanc, a bunch of grapes, a box of strawberries and a chicken sandwich.

It was just past eight. If she had had someone to do it with, she would have been delighted to freshen up with a shower and then go out for dinner. But it appeared that everyone in her life was busy, or somewhere different from where they normally were.

In her room, she laid out her picnic and took her first sip of wine. She switched on the television and found the BBC rolling news.

A text arrived from Lucy in Biarritz, which made her smile.

Everything gr8 here, JP wonderful. His dad is cool too. He is paying us to do some office work for him. Amazing! Wish you could come back before I leave. Was thinking his dad could be just your type! LOL xx

As Annie ate her impromptu meal and drank rather too much of the wine, she allowed her mind to rerun her brief, lustful episode with Greg. Though it was recent, it seemed like a century ago.

She was in bed by ten o'clock, exhausted by all of the day's happenings and her early start.

How, she pondered, as she stretched down beneath the sheets, do people my age – with careers, children, parents going gaga and their friends falling ill, or in or out of love – ever have the spare capacity to sort out a new romance? Even if she had a man at the moment, when would she see him?

It was her last thought of the day.

Next morning, she arrived in Harley Street in plenty of time.

Sitting in the waiting room, she checked her watch every thirty seconds.

Janey did not appear till 9.29. Her voice was slightly shrill as she over-explained why she was almost late. 'I got the 24 bus up to Trafalgar Square. It's such a beautiful morning and everything looked so wonderful. You know, if you stand with your back to the National Gallery, and look to the left of Nelson's Column, you can see all the Union Jacks fluttering on government buildings down Whitehall. And in the distance you can even see the one on top of Victoria Tower at the far end of the Houses of Parliament. London's just the best city. I've never tired of it … not since I moved from Hertfordshire, just before I met you.'

It was typical of Janey to want to pack in a few last good experiences before facing up to potentially bad ones.

'You'll like Prue.' Annie changed the subject. 'Let her do the worrying for you now. She's the expert. Shall I come in with you?'

Janey bit her lip, appearing to consider the suggestion, but then shook her head.

'Have you got pen and paper?' asked Annie. 'You might want to make notes. Sometimes it's hard to remember everything.'

'Don't worry, you old tart.'

Annie tried to smile at her friend's attempt to sound like her normal self, despite the drama unfolding in her life.

The receptionist came into the room and called Janey's name. Annie settled down for a long wait and opened the Sunday paper she had brought. Unable to focus on it, she stared out of the window on to Harley Street.

Restlessly, she texted Lucy and Alice and Arabella and Diana – about nothing in particular, but it helped to keep her occupied.

Some thirty minutes later, she looked up to see Janey in the doorway. It was obvious that she had been crying. 'Come outside,' she mouthed at Annie.

Annie jumped up, grabbed her bag and phone and newspaper and followed her friend on to the street.

Janey said nothing for a moment, then with her eyes firmly fixed on the pavement, she began to speak.

'OK, here's the thing … I'm really pleased that Prue is going to look after me. First thing to say is that she says I can be treated on the NHS, so that's a worry off my mind, because of course these days I no longer have any health insurance. She's done an ultrasound.

134

Apparently it doesn't look good. She needs to make some arrangements and wants to do more tests. I'm going to be waiting around for ages. So, I think the best thing would be for you to go.'

'Go! Go where?'

'Go home. I can email you later when I'm more together.'

Annie gazed at her friend, who continued to study her feet.

'Is there nothing at all I can do?' she pressed, gently.

Janey looked at her, then said, 'You got me here. And I'm very grateful.'

Annie did not understand; could not begin to understand, but it seemed pointless to argue. She pulled Janey close, hugged her and then let her go.

'I'll be off then. Email me when you're ready.'

Janey nodded and went back inside the building.

Annie stood motionless until a couple coming up the street, talking and laughing, accidentally bumped into her. Was it worth staying for a while in case Janey changed her mind? Perhaps later she might want to talk about what was to happen to her?

She wandered down the road and into Cavendish Square where she sat down on an empty seat and breathed deeply. After a while, she gathered herself together, collected her car and set out for Cambridgeshire.

Ninety minutes later, she was motoring down the main street of Little Trumpford, which was looking at its most delightful in the sunshine. She meandered through her house and out into the garden, where she sat for a minute or two before deciding that she needed to be busy. By early evening, she had – somewhat robotically – completed what she regarded as an impressive list of cleaning jobs, inside the house and out.

All the time, she had been on 'full alert' for a phone call, a text, or an email. But there had been no communication.

Being July, it was not actually the longest day of the year, but it certainly felt like it.

Chapter Eight

She was early. The crematorium was not yet a quarter full, and she could see no one she knew. Such mourners as had already arrived were dressed in black; she was wearing navy. Obviously, this was not to be a trendy 'celebration of life' with a 'colourful dress code'. Maybe that could only happen when the deceased had enjoyed a long and productive existence and was done with the business of living. This was altogether different, being both sudden and shocking.

Her mind drifted back six days to Prue's phone call which had come just before her Monday morning surgery. Initially, Annie had panicked, fearing that the other woman had rung about Janey.

'No,' Prue had explained. 'Jumbo! He had a massive heart attack as he was getting off the plane in Edinburgh.'

'But we both saw him, and he was fine,' Annie had protested, knowing that she was making no sense, yet feeling somehow unable to be logical.

'I know. One minute he was fighting fit and the next he was dead.'

'I must go to the funeral,' Annie had said, thinking aloud. 'It's only right, since one of the last things he did was try to help with Janey.'

'Well, it's next Saturday, late afternoon, in Edinburgh. *Will* you go? It would help me feel better about not getting there myself. I'm operating that day.'

After the phone call, everything about Monday morning had gone wrong. For a start, she had been worried sick about Janey, who had not been in touch since they had parted company in Harley Street the morning before.

Then Mad Margaret, the senior partner, had arrived unannounced to do a surgery, and for some obscure reason had elected to do it in Annie's room. It had seemed easier not to argue – particularly since the older doctor had been looking even wilder than usual, with her un-brushed hair, and cardigan dotted with egg stains.

So Annie had decamped into a small office where there were no medical forms or rubber gloves or any of the paraphernalia that every doctor needs for consultations, and the whole session had been thoroughly discombobulating.

Thankfully, at the end of the morning, Janey had rung, but she had sounded so strained and tired that Annie had been filled with foreboding that her friend's life was already ebbing away.

What she had learned from the conversation was that Janey was going to have surgery within days, and that it would involve the removal of her womb as well as her ovaries. And that chemotherapy would follow.

With the annoyance of accommodating Mad Margaret still fresh in her mind, Annie had suddenly decided to adopt Jonathan's suggestion that she should take time off. And, thinking that Janey would be pleased, she had suggested basing herself in London while her friend was in hospital, so that she could visit regularly.

'Gosh, that's lovely of you,' Janey had mumbled, sounding – briefly – as if she was delighted. But she had continued, 'Not sure I'll want anyone to see me though. I mean, a girl's got *some* pride. I'm going to look repulsive and lose my hair. So, I'd rather you didn't.'

And now it was Saturday; the day that Janey was having her surgery. But she was four hundred miles away, in Edinburgh, at Jumbo's funeral.

The crematorium was filling up. New arrivals were having to squeeze into rows already populated with friends of the deceased. There was a rustle beside her, and a tap on her shoulder.

'Abs!'

Annie jumped at the voice and at the use of her old nickname, which she had almost forgotten. Looking up, she saw a figure in a pin-striped suit. As she registered his laughing brown eyes, beneath curly hair which no longer colour-matched them, her heart gladdened and she jumped up to hug her former boyfriend.

'Oh, Colin. This is so sad.'

'I know.' He sat down beside her. 'Are you here alone?'

She nodded, just as the sound of bagpipes wheezed into action and a kilted figure appeared in the doorway behind them, ahead of an extremely large hardwood coffin topped with lilies and heather.

The procession advanced to the old Scots tune of 'Rowan Tree'. It was her father's favourite melody.

Later, at the post-funeral refreshments, which Colin insisted on calling the 'the purvey', she observed, 'So, that's the first death of anyone in our year. Bit of a landmark.'

'Mmmn,' Colin agreed. 'Wake-up call.'

'Yes. Makes you think, about stuff you still want to do.'

'And state of health,' he added. 'I'm overweight. My cholesterol's too high. Ditto my blood pressure. Oh, there's Caroline, the grieving widow. She looks in shock.'

'I'm not surprised. I met her in London for the first time a week ago today. She was happily organising Jumbo, and they were going to the theatre. She looks like a ghost now. I must go and say something to her, though what, I'm not sure.'

'I need a drink first, I'll be over there.' Colin indicated a quiet corner right at the end of the buffet table where no one had as yet attacked the plates of sandwiches.

Annie spoke to Caroline who seemed to have no memory of who she was. And since it seemed cruel to remind her that they

138

had met for the first time only hours before Jumbo had fatally collapsed, she kept her condolences brief.

'Heavens above! It's Buchanan!' cried a voice, in a broad Glaswegian accent that neither time nor success had diluted.

It belonged to Gordon – a man she had known well in medical school. He waved, then stuffed a ham sandwich into his mouth with one hand and held out a glass in the other for more red wine. The wine-pourer was Alastair, another former classmate. They were clearly drowning their sorrows at considerable speed and eager to open the memory bank of their student days.

In the middle of a story about someone vomiting in the anatomy rooms, Annie caught Colin's eye and he beckoned the three of them over.

'Gordon! And Alastair – is it true that you're still doing ortho-paedics in that doss-hole that passes for a hospital in the Midlands? I hope you've got a decent private practice to make up for all that squalor!'

Alastair bridled. 'There've been loads of improvements since the enquiry,' he muttered. But Colin was busy fetching a cup of tea for Annie and failed to react.

Alastair refilled his glass of wine and waited till Colin sat down again.

'You're seriously fat, old man,' he jeered, poking Colin in his rotund tummy.

'Thanks for that.' Colin winced. 'At least I don't look wizened and wrinkly like you and all those disgustingly healthy, thin people.'

'No chance! You're a dead ringer for Mrs Doubtfire!'

'How's the boring Ear Nose and Throat world?' Gordon challenged Colin, determined not to be outdone in the joshing depart-ment. 'One damn grommet after another?'

'Can't be as bad as doing general practice in Glasgow. God, I'd hate that – a waiting room full of folk comparing the colour of their phlegm.'

Why do men do this to each other? Annie wondered. Edward had been just the same.

'You're not saying much, Abs,' Colin observed, when there was a lull in the volley of insults.

'Abs! God. Yes – that's what we called you,' Alastair broke in. 'I'd forgotten. Why was that? Were we dissecting someone's six-pack at the time?' The three men guffawed.

Annie laughed. 'You three haven't changed at all. I think it was something to do with that, plus of course A B were my initials.'

'So, you're no longer a Buchanan.' Gordon deduced.

'No. I married a guy called Edward Templeton.'

'Templeton! He's a great surgeon. Pretty dull lecturer though,' announced Alastair, before realising he had been less than diplomatic. 'Sorry, Abs.'

Annie grinned. 'Don't worry. He left me for a younger woman last year. We're divorced.'

Gordon chuckled. 'You should have married Colin. You were made for each other – practically joined at the hip in medical school.'

Colin jumped up to find another bottle of wine. 'She wouldn't have me.'

Annie smilingly allowed the conversation to flow over her head. Every now and again, and surreptitiously, she glanced at her watch. Janey's operation should be over now. But, not being next of kin or family, she really had no right to ring up the hospital to try to find out what had transpired in the operating theatre.

'Pretty dry old do, this,' Alastair was complaining, as he upended the nearest bottle of red into his glass and cast his eye around the room for another.

'Well, I suppose it's all been rather hurried and difficult,' Annie pointed out, as she made an effort to return to what was happening all around her. 'It's not like he died after a long illness, where the family would have had time to plan.'

'Quite right.' Alastair nodded. 'Stand corrected. Got a train to catch anyway.'

'Me too,' Gordon joined in. 'I think most people are on the move. No one seems to have the appetite to turn it into a decent wake.'

Colin leant over and whispered in Annie's ear. 'The two of them are obviously off to get hammered. I don't particularly want to join them, do you?'

Annie shook her head.

'Dinner then?'

It was only seven o'clock but felt much later. 'Nice idea,' she agreed.

They walked for a while, slipping into a dimly-remembered sense of familiarity. Then Colin hailed a passing taxi, which they took to Haymarket.

'I can't remember if this place existed when we were students,' he said, pushing open the door of an Indian restaurant. 'But it's been here for decades. Lucky we're early. It'll be mobbed later.'

Colin ordered the mixed vegetable Thali for them both, and a couple of Indian beers.

They had rarely met since Annie had moved back to London, and when they had, they had not been alone. Each of them could recall a couple of weddings which they had both attended in the late '80s, but these had taken place after she and Edward had married, so he had been there too.

'I don't suppose,' she reflected, 'that we've had a real conversation together since we were an item. We always got on well though didn't we?'

'We were *very* good friends, Abs.' His voice was gentle and warm.

She took his hand across the poppadum dish, knowing that his memories were mirroring her own. 'I suppose we did a lot of growing up together *and* got each other through the exams.'

'True. Particularly the anatomy. Dear Lord, I hated that. I just wanted to treat real people, and those two years cutting up dead ones almost finished me. If you hadn't been around, I'd have chucked it.'

'I never knew that.'

'A chap has to have *some* secrets!'

She released his hand, contriving to pat it gently as she let go.

He was wearing a very large wristwatch and she noticed that it was half past eight. Janey should be back on the ward by now.

The next part of the Thali arrived and Colin fell on it as if he had not eaten for days. He signalled to the waiter that he would like extra chutney and more naan.

'I'll start the diet tomorrow,' he chuckled.

'Really?'

'Of course not. I never do. I ought to exercise more. That's a better way to get rid of the blubber for me. I used to have a mate who ran serious distances and I would train with him, but he got married and went to Bristol, because his wife was a professor and had small children and couldn't move to Edinburgh. Sign of the times, isn't it – women being the more successful partner? New romances being forged with people who've already got families. Very complicated!'

'Too complicated for you? Did you never consider settling down?'

'Not seriously. Mind you, some got away while I was thinking about it. And I would have married you.'

'We were too young,' she said quickly.

'Yes. In actual fact I rather like my life as it is. My home is how I want it. I do stuff with male mates – go to the rugby and so on. I've got a selection of female friends who don't mind coming to the odd concert at the Usher Hall, though, I often go alone. I have plenty of time to myself, and mostly I like it that way. I bet loads of guys would love to be me! We're not all cut out to be devoted and faithful – or good fathers.'

'Do you mind that you never had children?' she asked.

'Not at all, if I'm honest. I suppose I should pretend. Might sound better! But with you it seems pointless. You'd see right through me. You probably feel very differently though. It's girls you have, isn't it? Tell me about them.'

So she did – while Colin energetically consumed the remains of their meal and another couple of Cobra beers. And when she had finished, she took a deep breath, and told him all about Janey's operation, and also about her friend's resolute independence and refusal of company or help.

Inevitably, she shed a few tears but Colin continued listening and simply handed her a paper napkin to wipe her eyes.

'That's really rough,' he murmured. 'For your friend, of course, but also for you and I can see why you feel side-lined.'

'It's crazy to mind about not being wanted or needed. But Janey had such a role in getting me over Edward, that it's hard to accept she wants to manage this crisis without me.'

He nodded. 'Shall we have coffee at my place? You could ring Janey's hospital from there. It's only ten minutes' walk.'

Colin's home, an imposing, detached, stone-built house near Murrayfield rugby ground, seemed slightly familiar.

'Was this where your father was the local GP?'

'Well remembered.' He smiled, and ushered her through to a lived-in, sprawling kitchen which overlooked the Pentland Hills.

'It's getting dark now,' he continued, 'but this view is the main reason I couldn't let the house go when my mother died. I'm not very sentimental about families, but this is a happy place and for as long as I'm in Edinburgh, I'll be here.'

'Will you ever leave?'

'Funnily enough I think I might. Recently, I've been restless. Like most of us docs, I'm pissed off with the bureaucracy of the NHS and I don't fancy doing private work full-time. So sometimes I think it'd be good to do something different. How long are you in Edinburgh, by the way, and where are you laying your weary head tonight?'

'I'm at the Old Waverley. That's a bit of a nostalgia trip, as it's where my dad used to stay when he came up during my student days. I'm taking the train home tomorrow afternoon.'

'Could we have lunch before you go?'

'Actually, I've got a friend joining me.'

Colin looked disappointed.

'I don't suppose,' Annie added swiftly, 'that she'd mind if you tagged along. Why don't you come?'

He grinned. 'Don't want to cramp your style if you're going to do a lot of girly gossiping.'

143

'Diana's not that kind of woman. She's a physio. Feisty. Posh. No nonsense – but a very good friend.'

Colin jiggled with an espresso machine that looked as if it rarely saw any use.

'What sort of coffee can I get you?'

'Does it do decaf?'

'Mmmn. It probably could if I knew how. I've got *instant* decaf.'

'That'll do fine.'

'Thank God. The last girlfriend left this as a parting gift. I've never quite worked out how to use it. By the way, do you want to call the hospital about your friend?' He nodded towards a phone in a bracket on the wall.

'I don't suppose they'll tell me much.'

'Say you're her doctor.'

'Ooh, I don't think I'd better. But, I'll call anyway. Thanks.'

While she was waiting to be put through to the ward, Colin quickly made two mugs of coffee and added milk and then waved an opened box of chocolate biscuits in front of her, which she declined with a smile. He took two and wandered off to his sitting room.

'Staff Nurse speaking.'

'Good evening. I'm ringing about Janey Durrant.'

'Are you family, or next of kin?'

'No. Actually, she has no family. But I'm her best friend.'

'Well, she's not back on the ward yet. I don't think I can give you any further information. Sorry.'

'Does that mean she's still in the recovery suite? She's not in ICU is she?'

There was a pause. Annie got the impression that the nurse was checking up with a superior on what to say.

'Sorry.' The Staff Nurse sounded genuinely sympathetic. 'All I can tell you is that we expect Ms Durrant back on the ward later.'

'Well, that's probably a good sign, isn't it? Is there … can you tell me anything else?'

'Not tonight. Perhaps you could call tomorrow.'

Annie replaced the receiver and went in search of Colin, who was lying on a large sofa, having removed his jacket and tie and shoes. He stood up as she arrived.

'So, what's the latest?'

'Not back on the ward yet. What do you think that means?'

'Well, you know how things are – emergency with a previous patient perhaps? Or maybe your friend's surgery was extensive. There are a dozen possibilities.'

Annie nodded, suddenly feeling shaky and slightly odd.

'Come on, now,' Colin was at her side. 'You look pale, Abs. Sit down. Here's your coffee. I'll get you a brandy.'

'I don't drink spirits.'

He gave her a quick hug. 'Don't argue, pet,' he said as he strode over to a well-stocked drinks trolley in the corner.

'I'm sorry,' she whispered.

He pressed a heavy crystal glass containing a generous measure into her hands. 'Drink that, and you'll perk up no end!'

She sipped at it. And, rather to her surprise, felt better for it.

'You say that Prue operated. Why don't you ring *her*?'

'Well, I don't want to put her in an embarrassing situation. I know that I kind of referred Janey to her, but I'm not her GP and I don't really have the right to information.'

'I could ring. She probably remembers me, and she might be able to say something.'

Annie shook her head. 'No, I can't ask you to do that. I'll text her. I'll tell her Jumbo's funeral went well and just add something about hoping Janey's op was OK.'

Colin disappeared for a moment and then returned with Annie's handbag which she had left in the kitchen.

'Go on then,' he urged. 'You'll feel better when you've done it.'

Annie sipped more brandy, then rummaged in her bag for her phone.

'Oh! My daughter Alice has texted. Still, that can wait.'

145

Annie punched out her message to Prue and then put her phone away.

'Let's have a trip down memory lane!' Colin was standing by a hi-fi deck with a record turntable on the top of it. He rifled through a stack of vinyl discs as he spoke.

Annie's phoned pinged. She grabbed at it.

'It's from Prue. She says: *Poor Jumbo. Still can't believe what happened to him. As for Janey, try not to worry. She was late getting into theatre, as op before her did not go well. Janey poorly but OK. Everything going according to plan. Love, Prue.* What do you think that all means?'

Colin shrugged. 'It sounds as if Janey's doing as well as can be expected. I mean, you and I both know they'll have a better idea when the lab reports come back and when they see how the chemo goes. It'll be a long haul.'

Annie looked across at her former boyfriend. 'Thanks. I'm so glad I'm with you.'

Colin came and sat on the sofa with her and hugged her, and then kissed her on the lips. They both felt her resistance.

'No spark is there?' He grimaced. 'That was always the problem, as I remember.'

'Sorry.'

'Don't be. We were more like brother and sister.'

Annie smiled. 'I'm afraid so. But it's lovely being in touch again.'

'Well, let's *keep* in touch,' he said. And with that he bounded over to the record player and put on a Fats Waller LP.

He returned to the sofa and once he had sat down, she snuggled up to him and tucked her feet under his legs, just like she had done years ago when they were a couple.

She stayed with Colin, listening to jazz and chatting about old times till she became sleepy, at which point he phoned for a taxi.

'One for the road, before you go? I'm going to have a nightcap.'

She grinned at him. 'I don't have your capacity!'

'Not many calories in brandy are there?' he joked, as he helped himself to a large one.

Suddenly, she remembered Jumbo – and felt a pang of anxiety about Colin. She hoped that he might start thinking about losing weight and getting fitter, sooner rather than later.

He walked her to the front door and hugged her. As the cooling night air hit her, she realised that she was really rather 'squiffy', as her father might have said.

The taxi pulled up and Colin helped her into it.

'Great evening, Abs,' he said, and he stood waving till the taxi was out of sight.

Back in her room in the Old Waverley Hotel, she stood for a moment looking out at the Scott memorial and thinking about her father. He had loved Edinburgh, though not enough to return to live and work here. His career as the chief accountant at Thames Television had spanned decades and was the great stimulus of his life. And even when he retired, he had been more drawn to the friends and colleagues who mattered to him down south than family or friends in Scotland.

Annie left the window open while she prepared for bed, enjoying the sounds of a Saturday night in Princes Street.

She was about to charge up her phone when she remembered that Alice had texted her earlier.

Hi, Mum. Got a few days off and wonder if it would help if I started clearing up Grandad's house. I know it's got to be done and you hate being there. I could stay over there for a few days and sort. Let me know. Alice xx

Annie read the text and then reread it. It was typical of Alice to be kind but this was right out of the blue. She could not even remember discussing her feelings about her father's house.

Still, there was no doubt that the huge task of cleaning up and clearing out his home was one she had been putting it off. She had vaguely thought it might be a chore to tackle when she had some extended leave. But now that Janey had insisted she did not want her around, would she still take time off? And if she did, what would she do with it?

Poor Janey. She would have been pumped full of analgesics and sedatives, so she should not be in pain. But when she woke up, would she be frightened? Resigned? Relieved?

She picked up her phone again and texted Janey with one short sentence: *Thinking of you.*

Then she considered ringing Alice, but as it was well past midnight, she texted instead: *Kind idea. Am in Edinburgh at a funeral. Will call tomorrow. Love, Mum xx*

And finally, she texted Diana: *Really looking forward to seeing you tomorrow. Hope you don't mind, have invited an old boyfriend to join us for lunch. He was at the funeral. Have told him 12.30 so you and I can still meet at 12 and have a catch-up. Do say if not OK. Love, Annie*

She turned off the light and slid down under the light bedcovers.

For the first time in ages, she felt a real ache; an ache for someone to curl around as she slept. She grabbed a pillow and held it to her breasts in an attempt to comfort herself.

It was now some fifteen months since she had spent a whole night with a man. She supposed that she and Edward must have lain together, close and companionably entwined, at some point. It was hard to remember. Of course, during their early years, their sleep had often been disturbed. As a junior doctor, Edward had frequently been called in to the Royal National Orthopaedic hospital. And, as a young GP, she had had to cover house calls overnight – back in the days when all practices did their own nocturnal visits.

As for the later years of the marriage, Annie had learned to stay very much on her side of the bed, because Edward had not been keen to cuddle, except when he had wanted swift sexual relief.

So why did she ache now?

Was it because the first of their classmates had died, which had made her realise how life was whizzing by? Or because of Janey lying in her hospital bed – minus various organs – weak and ill? Or because of the closeness she had enjoyed with Colin?

It was a pity that she had no desire for him. In all probability he was not very attracted to her either, but she knew he would have tested that out if she had given him the chance.

She felt herself drifting into sleep, and in that half-dreamlike state she found that she was visualising Jonathan, which was very strange, but oddly soothing.

Annie and Diana sat sipping coffee in a French restaurant in the Grassmarket.

Annie had walked from her hotel and was slightly damp, as it was a showery morning and she had neglected to bring an umbrella.

The friends brought each other up to date with what had happened in their lives since they had last met. And Diana pointedly said how much she had enjoyed meeting Jonathan during her very brief visit to Cambridge.

'He struck me as a really nice man. Lovely smile.'

'Sounds like he made quite an impression,' Annie teased.

'Well, I wouldn't push him out of bed,' laughed Diana.

'You've changed! I thought that life in the Borders would bring out some sort of Presbyterian side in you, but I was way off the mark.'

'Let's get some wine,' Diana suggested, and she mouthed an instruction to a passing waiter. 'I just think that Jonathan would be perfect for you. You looked good together.'

'Oh, no. He's very shy, and definitely not interested. Also, we work together. How messy would it be if … you know … it all went wrong?'

'So you do have *some* feelings for him?'

Annie felt herself blush. 'No, I don't. But, I have found myself thinking about him occasionally. I suppose, till recently, I've never been conscious of him in any way other than as a colleague. But we did have a rather sweet time together in the local pub that day you met him and he's always very kind.'

Suddenly, Annie saw Colin in the doorway. She waved and he rushed in.

'Oh! It's you!' Diana and Colin said in unison.

Annie looked puzzled. 'You know each other?'

'No,' they chorused, then laughed.

Diana gestured to Colin that he should sit down and join them. He beamed at her and offered his hand.

'Colin Galbraith!'

'Diana Audley!'

'Good to meet you properly,' Colin said. Then he swivelled in his chair to face Annie. 'Diana and I don't know each other at all – but, funnily enough, I've been thinking of plucking up my courage to speak to her. We keep turning up at the same lunchtime music concerts at Edinburgh University.'

'Yes,' Diana's eyes were sparkling. 'I'd begun to wonder if you were stalking me. And now that you're here, I'm certain of it!' She giggled, suddenly looking much younger than her fifty-nine years.

She poured a generous amount of red wine into Colin's glass and he signalled for a jug of water and dispensed it into their three tumblers.

'What's good here?' Annie asked as she scanned the menu.

'You've got to have the coq au vin,' Colin insisted. 'It's their speciality.'

'Absolutely,' agreed Diana.

The three of them ordered, then Annie sat back and watched while the other two chatted as if they had known each other for ages.

She heard the sound of a text arriving in her phone.

'Sorry, do you mind if I check this?' she interrupted, but Colin and Diana were too deep in conversation to notice.

She was hoping to hear from Janey, but the message was from Alice. *Are you free to talk now?*

She is really keen to do this house clearance, thought Annie. It was strange. Why would anyone want to spend their precious days off doing something so unappealing?

Just as she was considering calling Alice, her phone rang and she excused herself, and went outside to talk.

'You probably saved my life.' The voice was drowsy and faint.

'Janey! Are you OK?'

'Well, you know, not ready for a salsa session exactly ...' She tried to laugh. 'Ooh, that hurt.'

'Take it easy.' Annie smiled, feeling a huge emotional burden rolling off her shoulders.

'I don't think there's much option. But I *am* happy. Part of me wondered if I'd ever wake up – or that, if I did, I'd be told that everything was hopeless. But it seems it's not. I've got a chance. A good chance ...'

'Are you having any visitors?'

'No.'

'Not even Miguel?'

'*Specially* not Miguel. I look horrendous. In fact, I've told him he's got to move out for a while when I'm out of hospital and having chemo.'

'Wouldn't it help to have someone around?'

'Not my style, Annie.'

'Well, you're your own boss. By the way, I said to the nurse last night that you'd got no family. Was that right?'

Janey had always been secretive about her past.

'It *is* right,' she murmured. 'After my mum died – shortly before you and I met – there was no one else. No siblings, no father. So I turned up in London and reinvented myself, and never looked back!'

'Are you OK though? Don't you feel lonely?'

'No. Now, let's talk about you.'

'I'm having lunch in Edinburgh. But you sound tired so I'll tell you the rest another day.'

'Thanks, Annie.'

'What for?'

'Pretty much everything!'

Annie sat down for a moment at an empty outside table. The sun was out now, glinting on the damp cobblestones of the Grassmarket. It was very cheering and it boosted the gladness that had exploded in her heart on hearing from her closest friend.

A group of Lycra-clad, whippet-thin men cycled past. Couples walked by, hand in hand. In the pub on the corner, there was a large number of noisy and sweaty runners downing pints. A family of tourists sauntered towards her – debating, in French, which café they should favour for lunch. Annie smiled at how seriously they were taking the decision, as she rose to her feet and returned to the restaurant.

Inside, the smell of garlicky, proper homemade cooking wrapped itself around her. She reached her own table just as two waiters delivered mini copper saucepans packed with chicken pieces in a rich and aromatic sauce.

'This is going to be delicious,' she announced confidently as she sat down.

Diana smiled at her. 'I'm so glad you're here; this is one of my favourite places to eat in this city. I presume from your demeanour that that was a good phone call?'

Annie nodded into Diana's laughing eyes. 'It was! Janey called, and she sounds OK.'

Diana leant over and kissed her on the cheek and Colin poured out wine for them all so that they could toast Janey. A look of promise and very definite attraction passed between Colin and Diana, she noticed, as they all clinked glasses before devouring their delicious lunch.

Well, who'd have thought it? Annie mused as she settled back into her train seat some hours later. Her two friends had delivered her to Waverley Station, and had waved her off together as if they were a long-established couple.

It had been amazing to see them so excited and animated in each other's company. Would they go their separate ways now – Diana back to the Borders and Colin to his solitary existence, in the well-heeled

152

area of Murrayfield? Somehow she doubted it. Maybe they would go for a walk. Up to the castle perhaps? Take tea in a hotel? Talk some more. Go for dinner? And what then?

She drifted off to sleep – relaxed in her relief about Janey and slightly pink from two lunchtime glasses of wine. When she woke, the couple opposite her were preparing to leave the train at Durham so she decided that, with fewer people around her, she could probably call Alice.

'Oh, Mum. Thank heavens.'

'Are you OK, darling?'

'Of course.'

'You sound anxious.'

'Just trying to get you to agree about Grandad's house, Mum, that's all.' Alice sounded tense and irritable.

'It's so kind of you.'

'It's the least I can do. I haven't helped in any way since he got ill. I'm sure clearing out his place will be horrible – but it'd be much worse for you because you grew up there.'

'Well, thank you.'

'Is that nosey neighbour still next door?'

'No, she moved. It's a young couple now. The woman is called Damali, and she's nearly always in because they have a baby. She's got a key. I'll text and ask her to give it to you.'

'Great. Can you do it now? I want to start this evening.'

Annie wondered whether to ask what the rush was, but decided against it.

'Where are you, by the way?' Alice continued.

'I'm on a train back from Edinburgh. I came up yesterday morning for a funeral, no one you know. In fact I hardly knew him myself but we were medical students together.'

'You weren't too upset were you, Mum?'

'No, but he was the first of our year to die. It's sad.'

'Yeah, I can imagine.'

'So, you're all right?'

'Of course, Mum. Talk soon!' And with that, Alice terminated the call.

Annie quickly texted her father's neighbour about the house key, and then sat back to examine her thoughts.

What on earth was this Alice business all about? Had she rowed with her flatmates? It seemed unlikely. She had lived with the same three girls since medical school. Did she therefore want time and space somewhere else? Had she just fully realised that her grandfather was never going to return home? Did she feel guilty about him? Was she going through some sort of crisis? Annie remembered again her lunch with Janey, when her friend had suggested that Alice might be gay.

Not for the first time, Annie wished that her split from Edward had been less hostile. He had never been over-burdened with insight into how their girls' minds worked. But he was their father. Still, this matter was probably too vague to discuss with him even if they could have a relatively civilised conversation. So far, they had failed to manage that, and ringing from a train would not be an ideal start.

It was late when she arrived home, and she was so tired that she had to force herself to remove her make-up and floss her teeth.

Sleep came quickly. And so – far too soon – did the following morning. She had slept better than she had since first learning of Janey's diagnosis, and she would have liked to have slumbered on.

Fortunately, when she reached the surgery, she learned that Mad Margaret had rung in to say that the last week had proved so stressful she was staying at home until further notice. With a sigh of relief, Annie settled herself into her own room, and buzzed in her first patient.

During the staff meeting later, she found herself gazing at Jonathan. For the first time she noticed that he had beautiful and expressive hands.

It had been strange talking to Diana about him. Could he possibly have any interest in her? It seemed unlikely. In any event, as she had said to Diana, changing their relationship from that of colleagues to a romantic couple would be so fraught with danger. It was – as her girls might say – probably 'better not to go there'.

After the meeting, there were endless forms to be filled out and emails to be attended to. As she often did these days, Annie pondered on how much the job had changed – and how, with all the bureaucracy, it was harder to prioritise what she had come into the profession to do, which was 'good doctoring'.

Through her consulting room's open door, she could hear Gareth and Jonathan talking and laughing together.

The young Welshman was a much more relaxed individual than Jonathan. Annie felt pleased that her partner had another male medic around the place. Gareth was obviously having a good effect on him.

She wandered through to reception and as she arrived, a loud guffaw sounded from the direction of the staff room.

Carole jerked her head towards the laughter. 'Those two get on so well, I'm beginning to think that Jonathan might be gay too!'

Annie grinned. 'Oh no, I don't think so. He's been married.'

'That doesn't mean anything nowadays.'

'Mmmn, well, OK, but I'm pretty sure he …' She shrugged her shoulders and left the sentence unfinished as she walked along the corridor towards her colleagues.

In the doorway, she paused and stood watching them. They were engrossed in conversation and did not see her for a moment. Once they realised she was there, Gareth tapped Jonathan's arm and they sprang apart. There was a slightly embarrassed giggle.

Feeling a mite uncomfortable herself, Annie walked over to the kettle, which had recently boiled, and made a cup of coffee.

The men continued to converse, but so softly that she could not hear them properly till Gareth raised his voice above a whisper.

'Jonathan – just go and ask her.'

Annie turned towards them with an enquiring look on her face. 'Ask me what?'

Jonathan blushed and looked down at his shoes. He continued to study them for several seconds.

'It can't be that difficult,' she murmured.

'Well,' he said at last, 'I was wondering if you could give me some tips about making my house a bit more comfortable and user-friendly.'

Whatever she had expected, this was not it. 'I'm not exactly Laurence Llewelyn-Bowen you know!'

'You must be much more expert than me.'

Gareth breathed out sharply and loudly. 'You're impossible, Jonathan,' he snapped.

Was the younger doctor cross or just pretending? It was hard to tell.

'Say what you really want,' he prompted.

Jonathan reddened again. 'Well, Annie, the truth is I'm going to have a housemate.'

She noticed that a look of exasperation crossed Gareth's face and that he shook his head.

'Oh, that's nice,' she responded vaguely. 'Is it anyone I know?'

Jonathan nodded, and turned towards Gareth, who rolled his eyes and sighed but then grinned broadly, and said, 'Yes, Annie, it's me. I'm moving in with Jonathan. God knows if it will work out – but we're going to give it a go.'

Chapter Nine

'I didn't think you'd be at work today.'

Janey's voice on the phone sounded slightly more robust than it had last time they had spoken.

'I'm off tomorrow, being Sunday, but other than that I'm working six days a week for a while – mostly because Gareth's been moving into Jonathan's house, so he's taken leave. Haven't a clue what's going on, but it definitely involves loads of decorating and new curtains!'

'Must be true love.'

'You think?'

Annie remained undecided whether Jonathan was simply offering lodgings to the younger doctor, or something more personal. Carole was convinced that they were lovers. Janey, who had never met either man, was tending to the practice manager's view.

'Of course, I only know what you've told me,' Janey added. 'But all that upheaval sounds more like a relationship than a business arrangement. You don't mind, do you?'

'Mind?' Annie answered quickly. 'Why would I? So long as they're happy.'

'I wondered whether you had any secret designs on Jonathan yourself?'

'Certainly not!' Annie was grateful she had never confided to Janey that she had felt some stirrings of interest in her colleague. It was bad enough that she had hinted as much to Diana. 'Shall we speak tomorrow?'

'Great.'

'I'll call early. I know you're up at the crack of dawn. Hospitals never let patients have a lie-in! I suppose you wouldn't like a chat in person instead?'

'Absolutely not. I look hideous. I look forward to you phoning, though.'

Annie grinned. 'OK, I'll ring about eight, and after that, I'm driving to Henley to help Arabella, who's moving house. But I'm going via Teddington so I can see Dad – and I hope to pop in on Alice too.'

Unfortunately, the next morning, she learned by text that Alice had to work throughout the weekend. But after seeing her father, who slept throughout her visit, Annie could not resist driving round to his house.

It had been transformed. Two beds – the one she had slept in as a child and the double in the spare room – were made up with new, colourful linen. The fridge was well-stocked. And the chaos that had been her father's sitting room had morphed into a spacious living space, smelling of furniture polish and the roses, which were in a vase on the windowsill.

Looking out of the window, Annie could see that the wheelie bin was overflowing and a dozen black bin bags were stacked beside it.

Her heart swelled with gratitude at what Alice had achieved. She quickly rang her daughter's number; inevitably it went to voicemail.

'Alice, it's Mum. I can't believe how much you've done. It's wonderful. I can't thank you enough. I owe you the biggest hug and well, something else nice … maybe money for a holiday? After all, I took Lucy away, so you should have a treat too. Love you.'

As she left the house, she saw that Damali, the young woman who lived next door, was playing with her baby in the neighbouring garden.

'Wonderful day,' Damali greeted her. 'How is your poor father?'

Annie was gratified at the question – from someone who barely knew him and was young enough to be his grandchild.

'Not bad, thank you, but he's unlikely ever to come home again.'

Damali nodded, respectfully. Then her face brightened. 'Your daughter and her partner are obviously enjoying the house. I hear them laughing all the time. And ...' she gestured to the pile of bin bags, '... they've been very busy.'

Annie stopped on the path. 'Yes, I can see.' Then she waved to the baby, and made for her car.

Once she had started the engine and driven away, she said the word aloud: 'Partner.' Then she repeated it: 'Partner.' Alice had a *partner*.

Remembering how Janey had questioned Alice's sexual orientation, Annie wished that she had established whether the 'partner' was male or female. It would have been awkward though as she would have had to betray how little she knew about her daughter's love life. Why did Alice have to be so secretive? If it had been Lucy, she would have heard the partner's entire life-history by now.

Annie switched on the radio and started to sing along to it as she motored out of Teddington. It was wonderful to know that Alice was happy. That she had someone in her life. That she wasn't just devoted to her career, and destined to end up lonely and old, in a flat just a stone's throw from whichever hospital she was working in.

She was still thinking about Alice when she turned into the driveway of Arabella's house in Henley where another major clean-up was in operation.

The front door was ajar and as she walked towards it, her sister-in-law bounded down the stairs to meet her. She was wearing jeans and an outsize man's shirt, but somehow contrived to look glamorous. Naturally, she was wearing full make-up; and her hair, though casually gathered up in a clip behind her head, was prettily tumbling round her face. She looked eager, happy and fulfilled.

'I bet you're ready for coffee.' Arabella grabbed Annie's arm and led her into a kitchen littered with half-filled packing cases and numerous piles of rubbish.

'You look so great,' Annie murmured as Arabella pushed down the plunger on her cafetière. 'I doubt if you've ever looked happier!'

'Really?'

'Yes, really.' Annie grinned as her ex sister-in-law rushed around, defrosting a couple of croissants and stacking up a pile of newspapers that had fallen over.

Arabella came to a sudden halt, and gazed around. 'My God, the recycling collectors are going to have a fit! There's twenty years' backlog of junk in this house, and it's all got to go. Hopefully, they'll take a lot of it. I'm sorting the rest into completely unusable rubbish, which will have to go to the dump, charity shop donations and stuff Jeremy has yet to collect.'

The microwave bleeped, and she ran over to extract the croissants.

Annie giggled. 'You're like a new butterfly – just out of its chrysalis – flitting around, excitedly exploring life!'

'D'you know,' Arabella paused and put both hands firmly on her hips in a dramatic gesture, 'I couldn't have put that better myself.' Then she laughed again, bubbling over with delight at how her life was panning out.

Annie sipped her excellent coffee and nibbled at the croissant, which was buttery and delicious. 'Mmmn, lovely. Thanks. Have you got any work plans?'

'I have. Do you remember the very first play you saw me in?'

'Very well! It was in Southwold, which I fell in love with, and it was soon after Edward and I met. Something by Agatha Christie?'

'Impressive memory! Yes, it was at the summer repertory theatre. And, for the first time since then, I'm going back!'

'Isn't that a somewhat low-key job for you?'

'The awful TV hospital drama is finally finished. I don't have anything else lined up. And the people who run Southwold got in touch when the news broke about Martin and me, so I just thought it would be fun to go and do a couple of productions. Like you, I love the town. Wonderful air there – very energising. Anyway, Martin's in the throes of finalising the details of his divorce, and soon he'll be busy in his Norfolk constituency – for most of the parliamentary recess – placating irate party-workers, who think he's behaved badly.'

'Sounds grim.'

'He says it'll involve loads of boring pub lunches and chicken dinners. So, we're going to be apart for a while, but soon we'll be together full-time – and in the meantime, I might as well enjoy a last bit of single life. You should take time off and come to Southwold too!'

Annie glanced up, mug in hand. 'I might do that.' Then, brushing croissant crumbs off her top, she stood up. 'OK, what can I do?'

'Could you bear to tackle the garage? I've been putting it off.'

Annie was quietly delighted to find that Arabella's garage was in an even worse state than her own – which had become so cluttered in recent months that her car had to be left in the driveway.

It was odd how helping a friend seemed much less of a chore than having a blitz on her own chaos. And while she worked, she was able to think … Who would have thought that Arabella would find love, verve and energy with an older man, having ended the romance with her toy boy? It somehow seemed the wrong way round.

Arabella interrupted her thoughts. 'I'm just packing my cookery books,' she called from the kitchen, 'and wondering if I still need all seventy-two copies of the *Cordon Bleu* magazine that I bought as a teenager!'

Annie laughed. 'Sounds like you've cherished them for so long you should keep them.'

'Mmmn, but if Martin is keeping everything that *he's* treasured over the years too, we're going to need a palace to put it all in!'

'I know you're not living together yet, but does being with him feel different compared with someone younger?'

'Definitely! Especially the sex! But I've got to a stage in life where it seems to suit me. Jeremy was very goal-oriented – had to have at least five orgasms a week or he thought his balls would explode! Martin's past all that. I know we're still a novelty for each other, but he'll spend ages just kissing me. Of course I think he really loves me, whereas Jeremy probably took up with me originally because he was in awe of me, and therefore rather pleased with himself that he could pull this sophisticated and – at that time – more successful actor. Naturally, that wore thin after a while. One can't be impressive permanently!'

'Oh, I'm sure *you* are!'

'Darling, you say the sweetest things! I think I must always have had a bit of a thing for Martin. It's odd actually because sometimes in bed he runs out of energy, but I really don't mind. We cuddle up and go to sleep, or have a cup of coffee and some fruit cake, then try again. Life's just normal with him.'

'If you don't mind my saying so, it's not exactly normal to be "doing" the Home Secretary!'

'Not for you perhaps, but it is for me!'

Annie grinned to herself.

'He may give up at the next election,' Arabella went on. 'We thought we might buy an old camper van and potter round Europe.'

That sounded very companionable and heart-warming. And Annie felt a sliver of envy for Arabella's new relationship and her plans, even if they seemed somewhat unlikely or impractical.

'Aren't you both more "five-star" sort of people?'

'Who knows?' answered Arabella with a giggle in her throat. 'I think what the last few months have taught me is that everything's possible. And anyway … oh … your phone's going.'

Annie rose to her feet and edged herself out of the garage. She reached her handbag just as the ringing stopped.

The number came up as that of her father's neighbour.

She called back quickly. 'Damali, you rang me. Is there a problem?'

'No – it's just that I forgot to tell you something. It's about that lady, Marianne Walshe, your father's friend. She came round a few days ago. Apparently, she's been in Canada for six months – since before your father's stroke actually – because her daughter had a premature baby and she went there to help. She told me she'd only just heard about your dad. She wants to see him.'

'Heavens! That's quite a shock. I'm ashamed to say that I know nothing about her. Were they, I mean, was she like a girlfriend?'

'Oh yes.'

'I wonder why Dad never said. Maybe I should ring her.'

'That might be best. I'll text you her number.'

'Thanks, Damali. Uh, just before you go, do you know when Alice is coming back?'

'Haven't a clue. But *his* car has just turned up. Do you want to talk to him?'

'Oh my goodness, no. Definitely not. But *his* car you said … like Alice's *partner's* car?'

'Yeah?' The girl sounded puzzled.

'Terrific. Thank you. Goodbye.'

Arabella looked up from the cupboard she was clearing and slowly raised an eyebrow. It was an expressive and enquiring gesture – and probably something she had perfected for a television role.

Annie smiled at her. 'It seems that Alice, finally, has a boyfriend, which is excellent news. I'd been worried that she was lonely, and Janey had a theory that she might be gay. But according to my dad's neighbour, she has a bloke. Also, interestingly, it seems to be the case that my dad has – or had – a lady friend. Perhaps they met at the amateur dramatics.'

'Very likely,' Arabella agreed. 'Men are like gold dust in am-dram. I should think he had his pick!'

It was almost midnight by the time Annie arrived home.

Letting herself into her empty house, she noticed that there was a message on her answerphone in the hall.

Hoping it might be Alice, she played it.

'Annie!' It was Diana's voice. 'I can't thank you enough for introducing me to Colin. I just wanted to check you're happy that he and I … well, it's a bit late to check now, in fact. We, um, did the deed earlier today. And it was brilliant. I won't say more. I hope your daughters aren't home for the weekend and listening to this! But thanks. I feel so great. Thanks.'

Annie ambled through to her kitchen to make a decaffeinated coffee, and sighed. It was not that she wanted Colin for herself. She was delighted for Diana, but she missed her. And now, it seemed most unlikely that she would return to Cambridge any time soon.

Two years ago, she reflected, her life had seemed settled and certain. Not very exciting perhaps, but everyone was where she expected them to be. If she had been asked what the future held for her and all her friends and family, she would have predicted, confidently, that nothing much would alter. What had happened to them all?

And what, for example, would she learn at work tomorrow? Would it become clearer whether Gareth and Jonathan were romantically attached? And did it matter? Jonathan was such a good man. She seemed to have realised that rather late in the day.

As for her father and Alice …

Her phone vibrated with a message from Janey.

Texting under the covers as can't sleep. But don't text back if you get this or I'll be in trouble! Miguel is being awkward about moving out when I leave hospital. Obviously, he didn't take me seriously when I originally told him. But I need my space. Am I being hateful? And if so, surely I can be hateful when I'm this ill? Speak soon. J x

Annie grinned. She was greatly cheered to be contacted by Janey and delighted that Janey did not want her lover around while she recovered – because that definitely made her feel better about being kept at arm's length herself.

Having harboured less than charitable thoughts about Miguel since she had seen the havoc he had wrought in Janey's flat, she now allowed herself the rather mean theory that his reluctance to move out might be more than a little about having to pay rent somewhere else.

'Ooh, you are a bitch,' she sniggered as she climbed the stairs to bed.

Jonathan was sprawled on one of the sofas, drinking a cup of tea when she entered into the staff room before the nightmare that was Monday Morning Surgery. He was all smiles.

'Gareth is such a taskmaster,' he announced as he watched her making her first coffee of the day. 'I've been at it all weekend!'

'Sorry?' Had he meant what she thought he had said?

'Been painting the house.'

'Ah.' She nodded. 'How's it going? You and him?'

'Well, early days,' admitted Jonathan. 'But good, I would say. Will I see you at lunchtime? I'll get the sandwiches. I could even bring you in a coffee if I can be sure to get it just how you like it, which of course is a real challenge!' And off he went to do his surgery, whistling as he walked down the corridor.

Jonathan seemed much easier in her company this morning. Was it simply that making a new friend in Gareth had made him feel more confident – which in turn had led to him becoming more socially adept? Or was it, as Carole and Janey both suspected, that he was gay and in good spirits about being in a relationship with the Welsh doctor?

If he was gay, did he assume that they all knew? And was that the reason that he now seemed more relaxed and warm with her?

Her head was buzzing with questions to which she had no answers.

The next evening, she learned that she was going to have to find answers to a whole multitude of relationship issues, for the radio show the following day.

'Not the usual old stuff, though,' cautioned Ellen the producer, who had come to the health centre after Annie's evening surgery. 'I want to look at people who were heterosexual but are now flirting with bisexuality. Also, late relationships. People in their fifties.'

'Oh, *that* late!' Annie roared with laughter.

Ellen blushed. 'You know what I mean.'

'Anything else?'

'Um – mid-life people finding out that their parents are having affairs – that kind of thing.'

'Yes, that is quite an eye-opener,' murmured Annie.

'So, maybe focus on relationship situations which might once have seemed unusual, but which are becoming common.'

'Fine, but shouldn't you have a psychotherapist or counsellor for all of this? None of it is really medical.'

'No, the listeners know you. And they know you talk common sense. And you can always bung in your safe sex messages!'

Annie sat back in her chair, and peered at Ellen. She had come to enjoy working with this intelligent and positive young woman.

'What are you looking at?'

'I'm not sure,' Annie answered. 'You just look a bit different. I mean you're always bright and enthusiastic – but today, it's more so.'

Ellen sat upright. 'Does it show?'

'What?'

'My secret?'

'You're not pregnant?'

'God no, that wouldn't be cause for celebration. I've got a new job. It's top secret – but I've been dying to tell someone. You won't breathe a word will you?'

Annie smiled slowly. 'Think of it like patient confidentiality.'

'Great. I'm going to work on TV – for a company who are doing a new show for Channel 4!'

166

'That's fantastic.'

'I *know*. Trouble is, it might mean this is the last programme for you. Once I leave Cambridge, there'll be a new producer, and changes.'

'That's OK,' Annie responded, though part of her felt strangely disappointed.

The following morning when her radio slot was over, she felt even more disconsolate. It had gone well, and she had come to enjoy broadcasting. It was more rewarding than she would have imagined.

Back at the surgery, a waiting room full of patients occupied her attention and she pushed her feelings about the programme to the back of her mind. But she decided to discuss it with Jonathan later. Perhaps they could approach another local radio station to see if they wanted a medical slot?

At lunchtime, Jonathan had arrived in the staff room before her, and she could not help noticing how attractive he looked in a blue shirt that brought out the colour of his eyes.

It was her turn to go and buy the sandwiches, and she watched Jonathan as he perused the local deli's rather battered take-away menu which they kept on a shelf behind the communal kettle.

Suddenly, Carole appeared in the doorway. 'Jonathan! Dr Gareth has fallen off a ladder at your house. He's hurt his back. He's possibly been unconscious – according to your cleaning lady.'

'Christ!'

Annie observed her colleague struggling to process the information. Normally unflappable, he paled, then threw the menu down and raced out of the room. Annie heard his car start up and an uncharacteristic screech of tyres as he drove off.

Carole looked bewildered. 'He was very upset.'

'Well, if anyone's unconscious it's a cause for concern. *I'm* concerned,' Annie declared. 'Have they called an ambulance?'

'Oh I don't think so,' Carole answered. 'The cleaner, who sounds as if she comes from Eastern Europe somewhere, wasn't easy to understand, but she did say that he was sitting up and drinking tea.'

'Well, you didn't tell Jonathan that,' Annie barked. 'He's gone off in a terrible state. Suppose he has an accident?'

Carole backed out of the room at Annie's tone, raising her hands in front of her in a defensive gesture.

'Bloody hell!' Annie bellowed to the empty room. The last thing she needed was for her practice manager to go moody on her.

She had no appetite now – not for eating alone when she had been looking forward to having time with Jonathan – so she picked up her bag and set off for the front entrance. Wondering if she should apologise to Carole, she hesitated in the reception area. The other woman was nowhere to be seen. So she told one of the receptionists that she was going out for an hour, but that she wanted to be contacted if there was news of Gareth.

She walked swiftly, with her head down; this, after all, would not be a propitious moment to be recognised by a patient who might want to discuss some malady or other.

Crossing the river at a brisk pace, she made for The Backs and strode along as fast as she could. It was windy and much less sunny than of late. She hoped the summer was not about to abandon them.

As she reached the entrance to the gardens of Clare College, her phone rang.

'Mum, have you got a second?'

'Hi, Alice. Yes – I've gone out for a walk.'

'That doesn't normally happen, does it?'

'Oh, you know, sometimes fresh air calls.' Annie was aware that she was dissembling, but was not keen to explain what was going on in her mind, mostly because she could not identify what it was herself.

'Yes, I know the feeling. I'd love to get out today, preferably back to Teddington. But I'm in Theatre till really late. Do you want to know why I called?'

Annie felt her shoulders relax, and she smiled. 'That would be good. By the way, I meant what I said about giving you money for a holiday. You could get away either alone or with a friend. You must be due some time off.'

Tell me about your boyfriend, she thought. Please tell me …

'Not possible right now. Mum, listen, I know Damali, the next door neighbour in Teddington, gave you that woman's number – Grandad's friend, Marianne – have you rung her?'

'No.'

'Well, I think you should. She came round to Grandad's house – and I was in this time – and it's obvious that she's been part of his life for years. I told her where he is by the way. Hope that's all right. And she wants to meet you.'

'Oh – I don't feel I can deal with her right now.'

'Mum! This isn't like you. What's wrong?'

'Grandad never told me anything about her. Why didn't he tell me? I'm sick of people not telling me things. She can't have been very important. Anyway, he won't know who she is now, he doesn't know what day it is.'

'Mum, you've said yourself that he may understand more than we appreciate. She's really nice. I think Grandad would want you to be kind to her.'

'Oh, do you?' Annie knew that she sounded overwrought and was embarrassed by it. Trying to calm herself, she sat down on a nearby bench.

Alice tried again. 'Maybe at some level in his brain he'd enjoy having her around. Just because someone's demented doesn't mean to say that all their feelings and desires have been eradicated.'

'Alice – slow down. This is all too much.'

'Look, Mum, he's still Grandad. Current research suggests that people can do better if they're treated as if they still have some basic characteristics and faculties.'

'I didn't know you were such an expert in dementia!'

'You're in a very strange mood today.'

169

'I'm sorry.' Annie was close to tears.

'I think it's *you* who needs a holiday, Mum.' Alice's voice sounded concerned. 'Apart from Biarritz, you haven't been away since you were with Dad. And you've got a lot on your plate.'

You don't know the half of it, Annie brooded. There was Gareth's accident. And Jonathan. Suppose he crashed his car? Her heart felt heavy at the very idea of any harm coming to him. And Janey was certainly not out of the woods, and might not make it. And Diana was away.

'Sorry, Alice. I'm sure you're right. About everything. I'll ring the lady – at some point.'

'Well, that's the thing, Mum,' Alice responded quickly. 'She's got a sister, who lives in Huntingdon and she's going there today, and she'd like to meet you while she's in Cambridgeshire.'

'Does she drive then? Surely she's a bit old for that?'

'Mum …' Alice sounded as if she was reasoning with a distraught child. 'She's a lot younger than Grandad. She looks about – I dunno – less than seventy. So, you will ring her, won't you?'

It was easier to agree, though as yet Annie was not sure that she wanted, or could cope with, this further complication.

'So,' she changed the subject. 'Tell me what's happening in your life – apart from tidying up the Teddington house and orthopaedics?'

'God, is that the time? Must go. Love you, Mum.'

Back at the surgery, Annie sought out Carole.

'I didn't mean to be rude,' she apologised.

Carole shrugged her shoulders. 'I know. I think it's me. My own life is so boring that I'm getting a bit of a thrill from the new romance between Jonathan and Gareth. Cheers me up.'

'You really think they're in a relationship?'

'A hundred per cent! Gareth's OK by the way. Jonathan phoned. Apparently he hadn't had any breakfast, because he felt queasy after having too much to drink last night, and then he'd been rushing around and I think he felt faint and kind of slid off the ladder. He's bruised but fine.'

'Thank God. And, Jonathan is all right?'

Carole looked puzzled. 'Yeah.' Then her expression lightened. 'It's nice they've got each other, isn't it?'

Annie's 'mmmn' sounded less delighted than it should have been. So she quickly asked, 'How are things in your house?'

'My husband's still keen on moving to Australia. Feels a bit drastic – so I've said he should go alone and see if he likes it, and then if it's great, like he hopes, I'll come with the kids.'

'But do you want to go?' Annie was horrified that what had seemed like a vague notion was becoming a real prospect; one that would deprive the practice of the best manager they had ever had.

'I don't know what I want,' Carole sighed. 'I just want something different!'

Annie nodded sympathetically.

'Talking of different,' Carole sighed again. 'She who must be obeyed phoned and is planning to come back to work again in a fortnight.'

'Mad Margaret?'

'Yup.'

'Oh God.' Annie's head dropped right back and she stared up at the ceiling before exhaling loudly.

'And so say all of us,' Carole mumbled as she turned back to her computer.

In her consulting room, Annie took a long look at herself in the mirror. *Did* she need a holiday? The face staring out at her was that of a tired mid-life woman. However, she thought, in the NHS who *isn't* exhausted? She renewed her lipstick and mascara and blusher. Was that better? Not much. If their senior partner came back, life would become even more stressful. Perhaps she should take that break.

Looking at her watch, she remembered her promise to ring Marianne Walshe.

Marianne picked up the phone after just one ring. She had a pleasant, educated voice, and was quite assertive.

'I know this is a lot to ask – particularly as I understand you never knew anything about me – but today, or rather this evening, would be best for me. I'm setting off soon. My sister's expecting me tonight, but I could come to you on the way.'

It *is* a lot to ask, Annie thought. Still, she might as well get it over with. She did not have to like the woman. She just had to be sure that her father would want to have contact with her.

She heard herself agreeing, and saying that she would be home by seven and then giving her address. She was about to issue directions but Marianne interrupted her.

'Don't worry, I'm not a bad map reader – and I've got satnav.'

'Oh,' said Annie weakly. 'Well, I'll have the kettle on.'

With that, she put the phone down, took a couple of deep breaths and buzzed in her first patient of the afternoon.

When she arrived home, Marianne was standing beside her car in the driveway. Determined not to let her irritation show – despite having anticipated the luxury of five minutes to herself before the visitor showed up – she leapt out of her Fiat, and shook the older woman's hand vigorously.

As Alice had said, her father's 'friend' was much younger than him. She was slim, with Celtic colouring and slightly freckled skin. Though her hair was greying, there were still auburn lights in it. And she had a warm but nervous smile.

'This must be awkward for you,' Marianne murmured. 'I'm sorry.'

Annie's heart was racing. She felt almost rooted to the spot. This woman and her father … It was hard to get her head around the various possibilities. What had she expected? Maybe someone who slightly resembled her own mother? But Marianne was totally different in build, in colouring, in manner …

'Sorry,' she managed. 'Let's get in. Sorry.'

Inside the house, she led the way into her sitting room.

'How lovely. L-shaped. Unusual – and a wonderful view of your terrace, and all those gorgeous geraniums.'

172

Annie licked her dry lips and then smiled. 'Yes, that's what I like about it too. And my father, he likes, liked this room. When he was staying, he would sit here reading the papers.'

'Duncan does love his newspapers,' Marianne agreed.

'Tea, or a drink?' Annie asked.

'Could I have tea, but also the teeniest glass of red wine too? I mustn't have any more as I've still got fifteen miles to go to my sister's. But, to be honest, a small amount of alcohol would be welcome.'

'I know what you mean,' Annie replied. 'Oh, there's a downstairs cloakroom – first door on the left in the hall.'

'Thanks,' Marianne said. 'I will just avail myself of that.'

Annie mulled over her first impressions of Marianne as she walked into the kitchen to fill the kettle. 'Avail' was just the sort of word her father would have used. She was unsure what she had expected from, or of, this woman, but it was easy to see that she was an interesting and intelligent person.

She poured out a small glass of Rioja for Marianne and a rather larger glass of Chablis for herself, then took them through to the sitting room before returning to the kitchen to finish making the tea. She laid a tray and started to carry it along the hall, almost colliding with Marianne as she emerged from the cloakroom. They both apologised and stepped sideways to allow the other to pass, but somehow contrived, at the same time, to bump into each other.

'Sorry, clumsy of me,' Marianne murmured.

Annie took a long look at her. 'Not at all. This is a strange situation, and it's probably worse for you than for me. I've only known about you for a few days, whereas you've probably been aware of my existence for a while and may well have imagined this meeting.'

Annie guided her guest into the sitting room and sat on the sofa, putting the tray on the coffee table in front of her. Marianne selected the armchair opposite.

'Dr Templeton …'

'Please call me Annie.'

'OK. Thank you. Annie. I *have* known about you for a long time; for a *very* long time, at least twenty-five years.'

Annie gasped.

'In fact,' Marianne continued, 'I've seen you before. My home's in Pinner, not far from where you and your ex-husband moved to when your children were tiny. I'm afraid I used to wander past your place, and I saw you ... once or twice. I couldn't resist finding out what Duncan's beloved daughter was like.'

Annie shook her head in disbelief.

'Shall I be entirely honest?' Marianne ventured. 'You're obviously going to be shocked, but perhaps it's best.'

Annie poured tea for them both and handed a cup to Marianne. She noticed that her own hand was trembling, just a little, as she offered sugar and a plate of biscuits, both of which were declined.

'Go for it,' she answered firmly.

And Marianne did. She made no attempt to hide the fact that she and Annie's father had met almost three decades ago when they had both worked for Thames Television, and that they had embarked on an illicit relationship shortly thereafter. She was junior to him in the Accounts Department, but had rapidly progressed through the company and held various senior managerial roles. Marianne had remained there till 2006, though of course Duncan had long retired by then. They had both been married when they met. She remained married, to a vicar whom she would never leave but did not love – at least not in the way she loved Duncan.

'I know,' reflected Annie at one point, 'that my parents weren't happy together. My mother wasn't an easy person. They were not tactile, but I never guessed that my father had someone else, especially so long before Mum died.'

'I'm not proud of that, Annie. But I used to console myself that not only was I not the first of your father's girlfriends, but that if I hadn't succumbed to his charms, he'd have found someone else. We felt as good as married in many ways. We were the whole world to each other. I hate the word "needs" – but people have them. Your father has always been a very loving, virile man. I fell completely under his spell even though there's a gap of seventeen years between us. In contrast, my husband and I are pleasant companions, nothing more. Our daughter is my only child. I had her not long before I met Duncan. Once he and I were together I felt I couldn't have more babies. It wouldn't have been right.'

Annie nodded, trying to come to terms with a whole new side to the father she thought she had known so well.

'Once my mother died,' she said, 'I mean that's … fifteen years ago, why didn't you and Dad get together?'

'Well, I wanted to – but I didn't think it was fair on my husband, or daughter. Duncan understood. And that's why, I think, he never told you about me. I used to wonder what would happen if one of us got ill or died – and of course I was out of the country when your dad fell ill. I knew something must have happened because, though we wouldn't have had much contact while I was in Canada, he would normally have texted me at least twice a week. So when no texts came, I knew there was a problem, but I didn't know what to do. And after I came back, I was still uncertain. So, I did nothing – till last week. Suddenly, I couldn't bear not knowing any more, and that's when I spoke to the neighbour.'

'Have you seen Dad yet? I know Alice told you where he was.'

'She did. But I haven't. I felt I needed your blessing first.'

'He's vastly changed,' Annie mumbled, almost to herself. 'A couple of his friends went to see him when he was in hospital. But they dropped away. I'm the only person who's visited him for months.'

'And you may want it to stay like that. Just you, and your dad. You're very close.'

Annie tried to keep her voice steady. 'But you and Dad are very close too. I never knew. But I know now. So do go soon.'

Marianne sprang to her feet. 'I'd better leave – because I want to cry and I don't want to do that in front of you,' she said briskly.

'I understand exactly what you mean,' Annie agreed as she walked out of the sitting room and towards the front door.

The two women stood together in the hall. Annie was aware of a desire to be alone, but – at the same time – of a strange reluctance to let Marianne go. Just a few hours ago, she would never have believed what comfort she would derive from meeting another individual who loved the father she adored.

'It's been good to talk about him.' Annie's voice was a whisper.

Marianne nodded. 'I just want to see him and hold him.'

Annie felt a tear run down her cheek. And then another. 'I want you to do that too. It's important. My mother didn't put her arms round him, *ever*, as far as I remember. I'm sure you've brought him comfort and closeness that he wouldn't have had otherwise. Mum wasn't a bad woman, but she wasn't warm, even with me. My dad gave me lots of cuddles though. Lots and lots.'

'You must miss that.' Marianne smiled, mistily. Then she took Annie in her arms, hugged her, and left.

Chapter Ten

As Annie turned off the A12 on to the smaller road which would lead to the coast, the radio began playing the old Mungo Jerry hit, 'In the Summertime'. Smiling broadly, she began tapping out its pulsating rhythm on the steering wheel as she drove.

Before long, she was passing the Southwold town sign with its model seagull on top. From there, she could see the tower of St Edmund's, the mediaeval parish church – which was an excellent landmark, because Arabella had said that her rented cottage was in the square in front of it.

Her former sister-in-law had been acting in the summer repertory theatre for the past three weeks. Annie had hoped to join her sooner, but the practice had been busy, and it was only now – the last Tuesday in August – that she had finally managed to get away. Unfortunately, Arabella would leave this Sunday, but Annie planned to stay on.

At her journey's end, she parked the car, threw open its door, then closed her eyes for a moment. The scent of old-fashioned roses mixed with fresh clean salty air tickled at her nostrils, and as she took a deep breath, the tension that lived in her shoulders seemed to roll away.

'Are you coming in? I've put the kettle on!' Arabella pulled her out of the car and hugged her, before helping to extract Annie's two holdalls from the boot.

The exterior of Arabella's temporary home was traditional-pink, with an arch of vibrantly-coloured summer blooms round the front door. It looked like the cover photo of a Suffolk guide book. But inside, where Annie might have expected to see an inglenook fireplace, beams, chintzy curtains and copper coal scuttles, she found a minimalist interior with pale grey walls, light-coloured furniture, natural wood floors and silver blinds.

Arabella smiled as she observed Annie's reaction.

'The woman who owns it is an artist; it was her late mother's home. Apparently, it was ultra-traditional with thirty-year-old carpets and brasses and everything. The old dear died recently, and it sounds like she was barely cold before the daughter renovated it – sounds like she hated Mum, and Mum's taste, in equal measure!'

'Extraordinary,' Annie murmured. 'Is the owner really happy for me to rent this when you go?'

'Absolutely! She's desperate for the money.'

Annie gazed around her. She could already visualise herself sitting and reading in the small garden she had spied out of the rear window. And she could cook if she wanted to … perhaps go to the harbour and buy fresh fish.

'Now,' Arabella's voice interrupted her thoughts, 'what I mustn't forget, is that I've got to go to work! I'm only free this afternoon because the rest of them are rehearsing next week's play, which of course I'm not in. I need to eat before the performance. We could have something here, but there's a lovely pub near the lighthouse which does delicious food.'

Annie smiled at the whirlwind that was Arabella. 'Whatever suits you.'

'Pub then. Crab salads OK? I'll ring and order in case they're busy when we get there. We can have a cuppa here first. Do you need a shower? Want to change?'

'All of that. Tea first, if there's time?'

'There's time. By the way, the actors usually go for a drink at the end of the evening, will you come?'

'Sounds good.' Annie stood looking out of the front window on to the public green and at the splendid church which dominated it. 'It's wonderful here.'

'I know.' Arabella pressed a mug of tea into her hands. 'I'll shower while you have that. Later, I must tell you about my lovely Martin. I'm going to see him tomorrow, in Norwich. I'm so excited. You can come with me if you like.'

Annie grinned as the retreating figure of her ex sister-in-law sprinted niftily up the spiral staircase that connected the two floors.

She sat at the scrubbed kitchen table on a pale blue wooden chair with a plump yellow cushion, and stared out of the window. The rear garden was a mass of decking, surrounded by gravel, with a few potted shrubs and roses dotted here and there. There were mirrors, and a tiny water feature, and it was surrounded by a bright blue-painted brick wall, which made the area entirely private.

'Beautiful,' she whispered.

She could hear Arabella splashing around upstairs; then there was another sound, from the depths of her bag, indicating that she had a text. It was from Carole.

Envy you getting away. Dr Margaret's been at her most annoying today. Her surgery seriously overran, and Gareth had to see three of her patients. Then she decided to change her skirt in the staff room when he was having a cup of tea. Not a pretty sight! He complained. She got furious and said she'd been working here since before he was born. We're going to have to do something about her. Hopefully, will be sorted by time you come back. Happy holidays!

Arabella called from upstairs, 'I'm out of the shower. So, having seen it, are you really happy to stay on here? I haven't pushed you into it or anything?'

'I'm so delighted, I can't tell you. I'm not sure how long I'll stay exactly, so will the owner do me a sort of weekly agreement?'

'Yeah, don't worry. She hasn't got any more bookings this year.'

Excited, Annie swept up one of her holdalls and headed up the spiral staircase. Presumably, there had once been conventional stairs, but this arrangement created much more space.

Arabella had run up the steps, but she was more cautious. She would be braver in time. And she had time now; time for everything.

'It's a very happy place to be,' she answered, when one of the company asked what she thought of Southwold.

The actors were sitting together in The Swan hotel bar. Arabella, the undisputed star of the Alan Ayckbourn play they had just performed, was in the centre of them. Annie sat at the edge of the group.

A woman behind the bar shouted, 'Last orders!'

Annie jumped up. 'OK, everyone!' She raised her voice to gain their attention. 'What do you want to drink?'

'You can't buy a round for us all …' Arabella began.

'No,' another actor added, but less convincingly.

Annie stood her ground. 'I'm on holiday. I've been very well entertained by all of you. It's the least I can do.'

'I'll give you a hand,' offered the man beside her.

She turned towards him. 'Shall I just buy wine all round?'

'Might be easiest,' he agreed. As he stood up, she saw that he was not much taller than her, and carrying slightly too much weight, but that he had a winning smile and deep dimples. Annie thanked him and led the way to the bar

She bought four bottles of Chilean Chardonnay and her helper gathered up a dozen clean glasses, then proceeded to pour wine for everyone. Giving one to Annie, he winked as he touched his glass to hers.

'Thanks, kind lady. I don't know where you sprang from, but this is uncommonly decent of you. I'm Henry.'

'I know,' she answered. 'I saw you in the play. I'm Annie. I'm staying with Arabella, who's my friend and ex sister-in-law. Cheers!'

Now that she looked at him closely, she realised he was not as young as the majority of the company, being, most likely, about thirty-five.

'Are you in the business too?' he asked.

'Heavens, no. I'm a doctor.'

'Really? My father's a medic.'

'You weren't tempted to follow in his footsteps?'

Henry choked on his wine. 'Never! I went into the City. Did quite well initially, but then I was at Lehman Brothers when that collapsed. I regrouped and had a couple of good jobs after that, but I think the fact that it no longer felt secure made me realise it was time to do something else. Also, in a way, I didn't really approve of how I was making a living!'

'It's quite a leap from international finance to rep in Southwold!'

'I know. But acting was always my dream.' He glanced somewhat furtively towards the others who were chatting with Arabella, and lowered his voice. 'I'd always done amateur dramatics. I keep that quiet here, because thespians tend to be disparaging about it. But it must have done me some good because when I left the City, I managed to scrape into the Central School of Speech and Drama. I've spent the last three years training as an actor. And now I *am* one. This is my first job!'

'You were very good tonight,' Annie congratulated him quickly.

He beamed. 'That's kind, but it's a small role. Next week is my big challenge. I'm playing Gabriel Oak in *Far From the Madding Crowd*.'

'That takes me back; I was force-fed the book at school and didn't like it at all. I haven't seen the recent film, but I loved the old one. Course, I didn't see it when it came out, because I was only eight! But I've seen it twice since, and lusted after Alan Bates!'

'Well, he played *my* part. But I'm hoping most of the audience won't remember him. Not only was he awfully good, but – very unlike me – he had all those tousled, sexy curls!'

Annie studied Henry's head. His brown hair, which was swept back, was rather thin. She took a sip of wine, unsure what to say.

Fortunately, at that moment, a wiry, rather anguished-looking boy who had been sitting at their table pushed past her, cigarette packet in hand, heading for the exit. Clearly, Arabella's attraction was not as great as his need for nicotine.

'So,' Henry went on, 'I've talked to the director today about shaving my head.'

'That's dedication!'

'Not really. There's a bit of a worry that I might look like a gangster. But I'm game to give it a go. Being bald certainly hasn't done Patrick Stewart any harm!'

They both laughed, just as Annie noticed – out of the corner of her eye – that Arabella was on her feet.

'Sorry, Henry,' she murmured. 'I think we're about to leave, but it's been very nice talking to you. I'm staying on after Arabella goes, so I'll definitely come and see your performance next week.'

Henry jumped up and kissed her on both cheeks. 'I'll hold you to that,' he responded cheerily, then he slid into the seat that Arabella had vacated, and topped up his wine glass.

'They adore you, don't they, all those young actors?'

It was the following morning. Annie was driving to Norwich and Arabella was map reading.

'Maybe,' Arabella replied. 'But of course they also hope that I might put in a word for them if I get another telly, or a West End role. I always used to attach *myself* to the best-known thesp in any group I worked in! It's what you do. You were getting on awfully well with Henry.'

'He's rather different from the others.'

'Yes. It's obvious he made shedloads of money in the City, so that puts him in a different league. Also, he's shy – especially with women – in that public school way he has. And he's older, even though he's just out of drama school. I think it's taken him a while to integrate with the company.'

'How will he cope with that big role next week?'

'I think he'll be good enough.'

'Talk about damning with faint praise!'

Arabella giggled. 'Well, he may seize his chance and reveal hidden talents. Oooh ...' Arabella swiftly turned the road atlas upside down. 'Turn left here, I think. Sorry, I'm hopeless.'

Annie laughed. She much preferred driving to navigating, so on balance this was the better arrangement, even if they were lost.

As she slowed down and tried to read the city road signs, her phone suddenly vibrated in her pocket, but she ignored it.

'Oh, I see where we are,' Arabella announced in her bold and carrying voice. 'It's on the next corner. Are you sure you don't want to have lunch with us?'

Annie drew into the kerb and stopped on a double yellow line.

'You haven't seen Martin for four weeks. The last thing you want is me there. Anyway, I expect he'll have got a room!'

Arabella hooted with laughter. 'Of course he won't.'

Annie grinned. 'We'll see.'

Arabella hugged her. 'What will you do on your own? I've no idea where you're going to park, or ...'

'Just go,' insisted Annie. 'I'll pick you up at four. It'll all be fine.'

Arabella leapt out of the car, blew her a kiss and disappeared into the Maid's Head Hotel as Annie slipped into first gear and drove away.

She parked near the river and then walked back uphill towards the city, using the cathedral spire as her guide.

Soon, she found what she was looking for in the shape of a delightful tea room on the old cobbled street called Elm Hill, and before long, she was settled in the quiet interior, drinking a cappuccino, and eating an egg sandwich made with crusty tomato-bread. She glanced at a newspaper someone had left, but then pulled her phone from her pocket and checked who had been calling her.

Half-disappointed that there were no messages from the health centre, she realised that she had obviously not yet relinquished work-mode, if she hoped that they were unable to manage without her. Her two missed calls were from Marianne and Lucy. Neither had left a message.

Probably Marianne had been to see Annie's father again, which she now did several times a week.

Annie had grown increasingly grateful to her. Now that her parent had another visitor, and a regular one at that, she felt relatively guilt-free about taking a break from him as well as from work.

What she had not anticipated – and what had become a real comfort – was how much she enjoyed talking to Marianne about her father. They shared stories about him, which brought the real man back into focus for her in a very heartening way.

She took another bite of her sandwich as her attention turned to Arabella. Could she and Martin sit openly together, eating lunch, in one of the city's main hotels? Of course his Norfolk constituency did not include Norwich itself, but a Home Secretary – particularly one who has recently left his wife for a well-known actress – has a pretty high profile.

She was thrilled for Arabella that she was so happy; just as she had been for Janey when she had first found Miguel. But thinking about the 'Spanish dreamboat' now cast a temporary shadow on her mood. Everything had seemed so idyllic for them in the early days. But he did not appear to be 'the rock' her friend needed at the moment. Mind you, he probably felt bewildered at Janey's demand that he stay away while she had chemotherapy.

By contrast, Arabella's romance seemed much more promising. She had emerged from her toy boy era, and was now calmly content with someone older. Surely this would work out well?

What *had* worked out well – and Annie was incredibly grateful for it – was her own relationship with her ex sister-in-law, which had become closer since her divorce from Edward. In fact, she had spent far more time alone with Arabella in the past few months than she ever had before. And she liked it.

Arabella's friendship had become as vital and valuable to her as that of Diana or Janey. Of course, when you no longer live with a man, she thought, you have much more time for your friends.

During her marriage, these few days in Southwold with Arabella would have been out of the question. Edward had had firm views about her being home to cook dinner at night. On the rare occasions when work had precluded her from feeding him, he had moaned about having to make do with a bowl of cornflakes. It was absurd. He was an able man who could easily have worked out how to make toast, or heat up something in the microwave. How had she put up with it? Why had she never rebelled?

If I ever live with anyone again, she mused, I would want to keep some independence … we would not, after all, be bringing up a family … there must be a different etiquette … I might want to have a night in town with Janey … assuming things go well health-wise … or to see Arabella in a play, but not necessarily have to catch the last train back.

Suddenly, she thought of Jonathan. He was an independent spirit. He certainly liked to go off walking on his own. How would Gareth react to *that*?

After lunch, she wandered outside, where she found a bench under a tree, and settled herself down to make some calls. First, she tried Janey. There was no answer. She was probably out having chemotherapy. There was no reply either when she phoned Lucy. Marianne, on the other hand, picked up immediately.

'Annie! How lovely of you to phone back. I just wanted to say I hope you have a good break. Don't worry about your father. He seems … well, you know … some days more alert than others.'

'It's wonderful that you see him so often, Marianne,' Annie said. 'When you first visited him, it must have been a terrible shock. I wouldn't have blamed you if you'd never gone again.'

'Annie!' There was the tiniest hint of reproach in Marianne's voice. 'I love him. Always have. Always will. I want to be there for him.'

Annie felt her eyes moisten. 'Thanks. Speak soon.'

She pocketed her phone and resolutely set off to make the most of her time. She had never been to Norwich before and wanted to cram in as much as possible.

The ancient cathedral beckoned. Inside, an organist was practising something by Bach. It sounded wonderful in that huge space and she noticed that, as she moved around, her footsteps were walking in time to the music.

As she gazed up at the majestic ceiling, a man standing nearby suddenly – and loudly – addressed his female partner.

'The cathedral was finished in 1145, my dear. That's *centuries* before the construction of Machu Picchu, which is – after all – nothing but a bunch of old terraces and rocks! Why you would like to go there, I simply can't imagine. Not when we have all this in England.'

Annie noticed that the woman turned her head away from her spouse; she said nothing but her shoulders sagged.

That tells a story, thought Annie. Of course the cathedral was breathtaking, but she could imagine a scenario where this woman had dutifully put the man's career first, brought up his children, dreamt of one day seeing the world …

She remembered her emotion in Venice on the night that Edward had announced he was leaving her. She had taken refuge for a while in a beautiful Venetian church, telling herself that she would never recover from the pain. How wrong she had been. Her only regret now was that she had not left *him*, before he abandoned her in favour of Simpering Suzie.

She felt a powerful urge to walk up to the sad woman, who was staring into space, and to take her by the arm, lead her out of the cathedral and say: 'Run like hell and never look back.'

She failed to summon sufficient courage, and her lack of it plagued her for the rest of the day.

Outside, rain threatened. She had intended seeing the castle, but instead she pottered around some shops in a quiet pedestrianized street where she bought homemade soap for Arabella, and a book about East Anglia for herself.

The time sped by and she suddenly realised that she must retrieve her Fiat if she was to meet Arabella at four o'clock.

She had just reached the car park when Lucy texted:

Pls call me.

'I tried to get back to you earlier,' Annie said once she had reached her daughter. 'By the way, is this costing me a fortune?'

'No! I'm not in France! Didn't I tell you I was coming back to England?'

'No.'

'Oh!'

'So are you back in Brighton?'

'No, Mum. I'm here – at home. Where are *you*? You didn't come back last night and there's no milk in the fridge.'

'Sweetie, that's because I'm on holiday.'

'Oh … Well, I need to do some work before term begins and I thought I'd do it here.'

'Well, darling, that's fine. But I'm not going to be around.'

'Where are you, then?'

'I'm in Southwold with Auntie Bella.'

'But how long for?'

'Dunno, actually I'm going to rent the house where she's been staying. It's pink and traditional on the outside and really modern inside. It's in the little square in front of the church. It's lovely. You could come and stay if you like.'

'Sounds cool. But I've got lots to catch up with here.'

'Let me know, sweetheart. I need to go because I've got to pick up your aunt. She's on stage later.'

'OK. Love you.'

Arabella was flushed and glowing as she jumped into the car.

While she negotiated the one-way system, Annie said nothing but simply concentrated on finding the right lane. She had already got lost more than once today, and the traffic was beginning to build up.

'Good!' She suddenly saw a signpost to Beccles. 'That's what we want, isn't it? Thank goodness. So, OK, was I right, or was I right?'

'Right about what?' Arabella feigned ignorance.

187

'Did he get a room? I *know* he did. You *look* as if he did.'

Arabella giggled. 'What it is to be so clever! OK, yes he did. And he was marvellous. And I miss him already.'

Annie reached across and patted Arabella's arm. 'You'll soon be together.'

'I know. He's just got to spend another few days in the constituency house. I'd love to go and join him there when I finish on Saturday, but he doesn't think that's wise yet. Still, the good news is that he's rented a flat in Dolphin Square, which of course is very convenient for the House of Commons, and we're going to live there till we decide where and what we should buy.'

'That's round the corner from Janey. When are you moving in?'

'Not exactly sure. First – in fact as soon as Martin leaves Norfolk – we're off to the south of France, and I absolutely cannot wait!'

The next few days passed in a gentle, unstructured way – reading, talking, laughing, walking, shopping and having coffee in the delightful tea room by the children's boating lake.

All too soon, it was Saturday.

Annie walked round to the theatre with Arabella, intending to see the play again, but it was sold out.

'You can come and perch in our crowded dressing room,' Arabella suggested. 'Or sit in the graveyard; that's our "green room", you know! Might be a bit damp tonight, though.'

Anne shook her head. 'I'd only get in the way. I'll see you at The Swan later.'

Though it was drizzling slightly, she enthusiastically set off to walk to the harbour and back. Then she returned to the cottage and made herself a cottage cheese salad, which she ate to the accompaniment of a Prom concert on the radio.

She arrived at The Swan before Arabella, and bought them both a glass of rosé. The actors turned up in noisy, expansive mood, and there was a lot of hugging of the company members who were leaving. The thin, troubled-looking boy who kept going outside to smoke was one of them.

'He's not been a great asset,' Arabella whispered to Annie. 'Takes himself far too seriously.'

'Ooh, you're a harsh woman.' Annie grinned at her friend.

'It's a harsh business,' Arabella replied brusquely.

At that moment, Henry arrived, and announced that he was 'in the chair' and proceeded to buy several bottles of champagne. After dispensing drinks to all the cast, he squeezed into a seat beside Annie.

She was about to ask Henry and Arabella how the performance had gone, but she suddenly realised that her sister-in-law had mysteriously melted away and was talking to an elderly man in the corner.

'I was wondering …' Henry ventured. 'Please say if I'm seriously out of order here … whether … assuming Arabella is leaving early tomorrow … you might like to come out for lunch? I'll be going over my lines in the morning, but I can't stick at that for too long. I'm going to get nervous if I spend the day alone, so you would be doing me a huge favour.'

Annie looked puzzled. Why on earth would this much younger man want to spend time with her?

'Of course, you may have plans,' he pressed her.

'Uh, no. No I don't. I think the owner of the cottage talked about popping round with the rental agreement, but she didn't say when. Are you sure? What about the others?'

'I *am* sure. I see enough of them as it is. I thought we could drive to Oulton Broad. It might be fun.'

Annie smiled at him. 'It *would* be fun.'

'Terrific!' He reached for a champagne bottle and topped up both their glasses.

'But why,' Annie asked Arabella as they strolled back to the cottage, 'do you think he wants to take me to lunch? Is he lonely?'

'He fancies you.'

'He can't possibly.'

'Well, he does. He asked me earlier what time I was leaving tomorrow. That's why I went over and talked to the boring but

189

sweet old chap who comes to all the productions. I needed to give poor Henry a chance to chat you up.'

'He's young enough to be my son.'

'So?'

'Well, suppose he wants to … you know … I don't think I could.'

'Well, you may not. But there again, you may. And if you do, it might do you a power of good!'

Had it, she wondered as he rolled off her? Had it done her a 'power of good'?

'Sorry,' he moaned into the pillows. 'Far, far too soon. I was too anxious. How embarrassing. I'm hopeless at this sort of thing.'

Annie leant over and kissed him lightly on the lips before saying, 'First times with new people can be very awkward.'

He turned to look at her. 'I don't often get a second chance.'

She smiled at him. 'Well, I've got lots of time to spend in any way that I want, and I think we should have another go later.'

'Oh, I don't know. That may be all I can manage.'

'I really don't think so,' Annie disagreed as she gave him an encouraging and intimate caress, before leaving the bed and heading downstairs.

Arabella had said that when she and Martin had any problems in bed, they adjourned for a pot of tea and a slab of fruit cake. By great good luck Annie could provide both.

She had not foreseen that they might have sex.

Henry had turned up at noon, as planned, soon after Arabella had left. What failed to go to plan was the weather.

After the light showers of the past few days, a full-blown storm had swept in, just in time to ruin everyone's Sunday. It brought with it the sort of serious rain that bounces off streets and finds its way inside the collar of even the sturdiest waterproof.

They had driven through it to Oulton Broad and watched hordes of disconsolate trippers mooching around in inadequate clothing.

'Thank heavens I booked,' Henry had said as he parked in a nearby pub car park. 'I imagine that loads of these people will be hoping to get into somewhere for a hot lunch.'

They had wiped the steamy window with a napkin so that they could see the rainy view.

'It must be gorgeous on a sunny day,' Annie had said, brightly.

He had sighed. 'This isn't what I planned.'

Fortunately, the grilled Dover soles they had ordered were huge, moist and delicious. Neither of them wanted alcohol after their drinking session of the night before, so they drank sparkling water and then coffee.

By the end of the meal, far from the weather improving, it had worsened, and a dense, wet fog hung in the air.

'I don't think this is going to be fun, after all,' Henry had moaned as he stared out of the window.

'Actually,' Annie had tried to inject an optimistic tone into her voice, 'I really like walking by water in the rain, but I think this is a bit much, even for me!'

'Thank heavens for that,' he had said.

And so, they had driven back through the narrow, winding lanes to Southwold, sitting on the front of their seats in order to get a better view out of the windscreen.

Then, just as they had reached the outskirts of the resort, the downpour suddenly stopped, and by the time they had pulled up outside Annie's holiday home, the sun was shining, and there was a rainbow over the town.

They had dried off the table and chairs that stood on the decking outside the back door and Annie had opened a bottle of Chablis. Before long, the day had taken a completely different turn.

Quite how it had resulted in them heading for her bedroom, she was unclear. There had been a kiss. And cuddle. Then more kissing, and touching …

The kettle boiled, bringing her back to the present.

I expect I should feel ashamed of myself, she thought as she cut two generous slices of fruit cake and put them on a plate on the tray.

Still, what was the point in delaying an action, once it had become a question of 'when' rather than 'if'?

Returning to the bedroom, she could see that Henry had smoothed the bed down and opened the window.

'Are you sure you're not fed up with me?' he asked, nervously.

'Not at all,' she answered. 'It's very kind of you to take pity on an old lady who hasn't seen much action between the sheets for a while.'

He laughed, then took the tray from her, put it down on the bedside table and tickled her till she fell giggling back on to the bed.

'Stop it, Henry,' she chided. 'Tea and cake first.'

'You're terrifying,' he said, only half in jest.

'Well you'd better do what you're told then!'

And he did. They ate, they drank, and then, in a gentle and soothing way, she touched and stroked him and showed him how to reciprocate in ways that would arouse and pleasure her.

He did have rather nice equipment, she realised. Of course she had had the most sensational time with Greg back in the early summer, and it did not seem at all likely that she was going to replicate the highs of that particular relationship. But Henry did look fresher – and his intimate parts much less in need of ironing.

This time round, he lasted much longer. Long enough for her to really enjoy what they did, particularly since he was a quick learner about how to use his fingers at critical moments.

It felt good, she thought as she slid away from him, avoiding the rather large damp patch, and covered herself with the sheet they had thrown off a moment previously. Not fantastic, but very nice.

Dreamily, she sank into that kind of after-sex reverie which provides the ultimate sense of relaxation. There were voices under the window … possibly people walking to Evensong. She heard a car pull away, and another arrive. There was a slamming of doors and a cheery: 'Bye and thank you so much.'

Then, suddenly wide awake and horrified, she realised who the voice belonged to. Swiftly, she swung herself out of bed and, hiding herself with the curtains, peered down through the open window at the female figure who was now knocking at the door.

'Oh my God!'

'Annie, what is it? Don't be upset.' Henry struggled to sit up and shake off his post-coital torpor. 'We're not doing anything wrong. You're single. I'm single. We don't have to answer the door. And even if we do, you're a very modern woman ...'

'Mmmn, well this is a bit *too* modern,' she gasped as she rummaged in a drawer for a sweatshirt and a pair of shorts. 'Please go into the bathroom. Take your clothes. Put them on. Pretend you've been rehearsing your lines. And don't come down for a minute or two. I'm sorry to panic – but it looks like my daughter's arrived.'

Chapter Eleven

The knocking grew more persistent as she crept down the spiral staircase, pressing the tea tray to her chest.

From inside the front door, she yelled, 'Just coming. Sorry. I've double locked it.' Thank heavens she had. 'Got to find keys …' That was a lie as they were in the door.

She ran out to the little back garden, quickly laid out the used crockery on the table, and arranged the chairs to look as though she had been sitting there.

Then she sprinted to the front door and unlocked it, trying hard to assemble her expression into one of delighted surprise at the sight of her daughter.

'Lucy!' she shrieked, gathering her younger child into a huge hug. 'Where did you spring from?'

'It was so sudden, Mum,' Lucy answered, as Annie released her from their embrace and led the way into the house. 'And you'd described the place so well on the phone, it was easy to find.'

'Tell me everything.'

Her daughter had changed during her stay in France. Her tumbling, chestnut curls had been tamed into smooth blow-dried waves, her shorts were beautifully tailored, her ruched top was an unusual mustard-colour and perfectly showed off her graceful curves. Also, she was wearing elegant suede ankle boots which emphasised the trimness of her ankles. I know I'm biased, thought Annie, but she is stunning.

'Mum, you're not listening.'

'Sorry, love, I was just enjoying looking at you.'

'Oh! Cool. Well, you know Mr Dawson the dentist, who used to live in the village? His son, who I knew at school, was, like, visiting friends in Little Trumpford, and we bumped into each other. He said he was driving to Woodbridge, because his parents have retired there. And I said you were in Southwold, and that I might be going to see you, and he said he would bring me because it was, like, almost on his way. I think he possibly fancies me, so all the way here I've been talking about Jean-Pierre to put him off!' She giggled.

Annie could not help but laugh – then she hugged her irrepressible daughter again.

'I'm sorry if you'd knocked before,' she said. 'I was dozing in the garden. Come and see it, it's so sweet. Oh, and don't get a shock but there's an actor upstairs learning his lines in the bathroom. He's … um … a friend of Auntie Bella's … in the same company. I think his lodgings were noisy. Arabella had let him work round here some days and I thought it was unfair not to let him continue. He's got a big part in this week's play.'

As she spoke, she realised – not for the first time – that she was a hopeless liar. She was over-explaining, and would doubtless not quite remember later what she had said. Fortunately, her daughter appeared to be too intent on surveying the open-plan room, and the pretty garden, to register much of what her mother was saying. And it occurred to Annie that not only did Lucy have a most unsuspicious nature, but that she would not imagine – for one second – that this actor could have designs on her parent.

'Tea? Or wine?'

Lucy leaned over and planted a loud kiss on her mother's cheek. 'Is there cake?'

Annie nodded.

'Tea and cake then, please – that's what I missed most in France. Jean-Pierre says "hello" by the way. I had such a good time in Biarritz with his dad and family. The dad's great – but a bit of a player. He's had at least three different girlfriends over the summer!'

'Gosh!' Annie headed for the kitchen area, hoping that she was not blushing at the sound of Greg's name or reputation.

Lucy followed her, chatting away. 'And then I loved my time in Paris. Jean-Pierre's mum is sensationally beautiful – black like him and gorgeous, and her fashion designs are, like, amazing. You must meet her.'

'This is serious then, you and Jean-Pierre?' Annie queried as she cut generous slices of fruit cake and boiled the kettle.

'Totally,' answered Lucy. 'I miss him so much. But I have to finish my degree, he understands that. We're going to have some weekends together. And I've invited him home for Christmas. I hope that's OK?'

'Hello!' Henry's voice announced his arrival at the foot of the stairs.

Lucy turned to look at him. 'Hi! I'm Lucy!'

'Henry,' he announced, as he walked over to her before shaking hands very formally.

'Mum says you're here to study your lines. Where's your script? I could read your cues. I used to do it for my auntie when she came to stay.'

Henry looked stricken. 'Oh no, I couldn't possibly. I uh … well … I have a bit of a headache actually … been at it too long … probably going to go off now and just do that … thing …'

'What thing?' Lucy looked puzzled.

'Uh … got to go and see someone … actually … in the pub … but very good to meet you …'

'Tea before you go?' Annie suggested, trying to suppress a smile at his embarrassment.

'Oh! Very kind … but probably not,' he answered. 'I … to tell you the truth, I … need a drink … well, I don't *need* it, but …'

Annie grinned. 'Off you go then. Good luck tomorrow!'

'Is he a bit weird?' Lucy asked as he slammed the front door.

'I don't think so,' Annie replied as she carried the tray out to the garden. 'You just had a devastating effect on him. He's awfully shy.'

'I made a complete arse of myself,' Henry maintained. His self-criticism sounded slightly comical – coming as it did in such posh, rounded vowels.

Annie kissed his furrowed brow. 'It's a week ago. Forget it.'

They were in bed together for the first time since the day that Lucy had arrived.

She and her daughter had packed a lot into seven days; they had explored Southwold, walked on the pier and eaten far too many afternoon teas in cafés, visited the lighthouse, shopped for fish at the harbour, bought jewellery in the famous Amber Shop, and generally had a wonderful time. However, she had not been surprised when Lucy had announced that one week was enough, and that she had sorted herself a lift to London with a couple she had met in the bar at The Swan.

'I'll text Alice and see if I can stay the night with her,' Lucy had said as she hurriedly packed her rucksack in preparation for her imminent departure.

'Do you mean that you haven't fixed who you're staying with in London tonight?' Annie never ceased to be amazed at how this confident child of hers saw no reason to make arrangements in advance – relying instead on her mobile, once she was on the move. 'Alice might have other plans. Have you been in touch at all?'

'Just, you know, like a couple of texts here and there.'

Annie had chewed on her lip wondering whether she should drop a hint that Alice had a boyfriend.

'Anyway,' Lucy went on. 'No worries. There are, like, plenty of other people I can stay with. Chill, Mum, it'll be OK. I'm going back to Brighton tomorrow. Got work to do before term starts. I'll call you later.'

Within five minutes of her departure, Annie had texted Henry to tell him that the coast was clear.

She smiled as he reached across the bed and put his arm around her. Snuggling into his shoulder, she murmured, 'I'm getting used to your bald head; I think it's rather sexy.'

He hauled himself into a more upright sitting position and stared at his image in the dressing table mirror. 'Mmmn, not sure,' he said. 'One thing though, my head's a better colour than it was when I shaved it on Monday. I wasn't prepared for how pale it would look! Thank God we've had lots of sun this week.' Then he grabbed Annie and kissed her again.

His enthusiasm for her was pleasing, but boisterous. 'Steady on,' she protested.

'Sorry, but I've been lusting after you constantly. Your daughter was sweet, but I've been praying she would leave! Now that she has, I want to spend every minute in bed with you that I can. There's only one more week of rehearsals, then the daytimes will be free and …'

'I might need a rest sometimes,' she giggled.

'Not you,' he responded as he disappeared under the bedclothes.

'Ooh Henry,' she gasped.

How lucky it was that Lucy had not interrupted them the previous Sunday until after they had made love for the second time. Had her daughter turned up after the initial, rather unsuccessful attempt, Henry would have been nursing his embarrassment all week and they might never have made it back into the bedroom.

What he was doing for her now was really quite … delightful and surprisingly gratifying. His confidence was clearly growing.

Eight days later, from the darkness of her seat near the front of the stalls, Annie was watching Henry with a mixture of pride and gladness. It was the first night of the last play of the season – Noel Coward's *Private Lives* – and her lover was playing Victor. He was funny, and had captured that uptight and morally-superior character perfectly.

Henry's agent was in the audience tonight, and Annie hoped that the lady – who was renowned for plain speaking – would be kind to him afterwards.

She was certainly loud, Annie registered later, when the honoured-guest, who was tall, with crimson-coloured hair that hung in a dead straight, asymmetric style around a long face, turned up on Henry's arm at The Swan. Annie watched as the agent swiftly downed a large gin and tonic and proceeded to order another in a voice that resonated with drama: 'Sweetie, I've had *such* a day; one drink simply isn't going to *touch* the sides.'

Smiling to herself, Annie turned to talk to the two youngest women in the company, who worked very long hours for little money as Assistant Stage Managers and small-part players. One of them, Trish, was having boyfriend trouble and was bent on extracting advice from anyone who would listen.

Meanwhile, Henry was pouring alcohol down his agent's throat and listening to her utterings with rapt, sycophantic attention. He did not introduce her to Annie or to the rest of the group, though a couple of male actors lingered nearby, obviously longing to be admitted to the agent's presence.

One of them finally managed to beguile his way into the charmed circle by laughing loudly at the agent's stories and offering to buy her a drink. Not long afterwards, Henry backed away and set off for the Gents, catching Annie's eye as he did so and gesturing with his head that she should follow.

In the quiet corridor he pinned her against the wall and showered her with kisses.

She laughed and fended him off. 'How's it going?'

'Good. She liked me as Victor and she's putting me up for another Noel Coward play that's going out on tour.'

'How exciting!'

'I know. But it would start almost immediately, which is terrific, in a way. But I don't know where it leaves us. I'd been thinking that if you're staying on here, I might stick around too.'

'Oh!' Annie was taken aback. She had always assumed that Henry would leave at the end of the week, and she had begun to prepare for being on her own. She had come for rest, recuperation, and solitude; but since her arrival, someone else – in the shape of Arabella or Lucy or Henry – had been with her almost constantly. 'Well,' she said, 'let's see what happens. Good luck! I'm going now.'

'I'll come over later.'

'Henry.' She put her hand on his arm. 'Let's leave it for tonight. Your agent's probably going to want to drink for hours yet. And, don't forget, she's got your career in her hands at this stage. There's always tomorrow.' She kissed him quickly then returned to the bar before leaving, to offer a sympathetic farewell to Trish the lovesick girl.

She was not sorry to have time to herself even though her activities with Henry had become increasingly satisfying. Much to her own surprise, she had revelled in her role as the older woman teaching her younger lover everything she knew. Previously, she had never seen herself as any kind of expert; certainly, she had never been in a relationship before where she had dictated the sexual menu. It had been stimulating.

The first name that came into her head on waking the next day was not, however, Henry's – because her heart was beating rapidly after a saucy dream about Patrick Pace. She had missed seeing her fantasy-man, there being no television in the cottage.

Smiling at the memory as she breakfasted outside in the sunshine, she tried to ignore the autumnal chill that tinged the air.

Her phone rang.

'Can you talk, or is Lover Boy there?' asked Janey.

'His agent came to the play last night. I left them drinking and came home alone.'

'Oh – not so good.'

'Actually, it was fine. And I had a rather lascivious dream about someone on TV who shall remain nameless.'

'Not Patrick Pace again. You're stuck in a rut!'

Annie giggled. 'Well, it's a very nice rut. Have you recovered enough to start thinking about getting up close and personal again with Miguel, or is he still being kept at bay?'

'I've been horrid to him, haven't I? Still, the boy will live.'

It was heartening to hear Janey sounding so much more like her normal self.

'How's he coping?'

'He's been dossing on some friend's sofa, and I've been quite impressed by how he's dealt with things. To be honest – and this was probably because I was worried and tired before the op – he'd started to get on my nerves. But he's rung every day and I'm going to see him soon. My hair's very wispy with the chemo, but I feel better, so I bought a blonde wig off the internet, which really rather suits me!'

'Can I come and see that?'

Annie held her breath in the pause.

'Maybe ... I have missed you, you old tart.'

Annie laughed.

'By the way,' Janey continued, 'I had my follow-up appointment with Prue. All pretty good. She's going to Suffolk this weekend – I think you know she's got a holiday home – and I get the impression it's not far from you. I suggested she look you up. Hope that's OK.'

Prue rang shortly afterwards, just as Annie had sat down again in the garden, having fetched a sweater and a second cup of coffee.

By common yet unspoken consent, the two women avoided any discussion of Janey in their phone conversation. Annie was fully aware that by now Prue would have some idea – though not an exact one – of her friend's prognosis. But she could not seek details, any more than Prue could share them.

'I hadn't realised,' said Prue, 'that you'd taken yourself off to Southwold. We've got a place near Aldeburgh. I'm coming up early on Friday. I don't suppose you're free for lunch? My husband won't arrive till later, so it would be just us.'

Annie enjoyed chatting to the other doctor. There was something gratifying and grounding about being in touch with someone who had known her before she married, or became a mother, or a GP.

'I love talking to you,' Prue said, suddenly.

Annie replied warmly, 'I love it too. I wonder now why we weren't better friends in Edinburgh?'

'I was awfully serious. You seemed much more popular – particularly with men. I think I was shy of you.'

'There was only ever Colin,' Annie said. 'I wasn't one of the "cool" girls, as my daughters would say. But I wish we'd known each other better. Trouble was, I felt seriously intimidated by your brilliance.'

Prue hooted with laughter. 'What rot! Anyway, must go – I'll text our address.'

In bed with Henry later, she found herself talking about Janey and Prue. He listened politely, but his mind was obviously on the lovemaking that they both knew would follow.

She rolled over and looked into his eyes. He responded by grabbing both of her breasts. It was a gesture that might have felt exciting later in the proceedings, but was slightly rough at this stage.

'Henry,' she reproved him. 'Treat me gently, will you?'

'Sorry. I'm just really keen to do it, as I couldn't be here last night. I thought my bloody agent would never go to bed. She must have been seriously hung-over this morning. God knows I was. Still, she texted me earlier to say I've got an audition for that Noel Coward tour on Thursday – first thing – in London. So I'm driving down tomorrow night after the show. I don't suppose you'd like to come with me?'

She shook her head. 'Will you be back in time for the play that night?'

'Yes, but I won't see you tomorrow now. That makes *two* nights without sex this week!'

'It's shocking being you,' she laughed and gave him a playful kiss.

Later, lying in his arms, she murmured, 'After we've parted, some lovely and lucky younger woman is going to have a great time in bed with you.'

'Don't say that, Annie. I want us to stay together.' His face was earnest.

'Henry,' she chided him, gently. 'No, you don't. We've been good for each other. It's been lovely, and – if I say so myself – you may have learned a few things.'

'Oh, masses,' he agreed enthusiastically. 'And I've got loads more confidence. After Sadie, my girlfriend, left me, I thought I'd never manage to do it again – and whenever I tried it out, it went wrong, like the first time with you.'

'You poor boy! I had no idea you'd had your heart broken.'

'Not sure about my heart, but I was certainly crushed. We lived together for a year, but I found out that she used to pick up guys in clubs. Pretty rough types as it turned out.'

A troubling thought lodged in Annie's mind, but she parked it at the back of her brain to think about later.

'Well, I'm sure you're over her now.'

'Yes,' he agreed. 'And that's thanks to you. Please don't end it.'

'The thing is, Henry, you're not in love with me.'

'I know that …'

Annie smiled at how quickly, and unflatteringly, he admitted to his lack of deep feeling.

'I thought it might grow though,' he added quickly.

She patted his arm affectionately. 'I'm not in love with you either. But I like you. You're a fine fellow!'

They both laughed.

'Also,' she continued, 'I don't think either of us would be comfortable with going public about our relationship. I certainly didn't want to own up to Lucy about you. And you never considered introducing me to your agent as your girlfriend.'

He ran one hand over his shaved head before speaking. 'Actually,' he said, 'my parents are coming to the last night on Saturday. I had been wondering what to say or do about you.'

'I should say and do nothing,' she advised. 'I'll probably be at the last performance, but I won't get in your way.'

'That'll be *another* night we can't be together. And if I get the Noel Coward part, the rehearsals start almost immediately.'

'Things are just winding down, Henry,' she murmured. 'I'll always remember you – and my summer in Southwold – but this was never going to be long-term.'

He looked sad for a moment, but then nodded. 'What about Friday?' he asked.

'A final flurry of passion, do you mean?'

'That's what I'm hoping.'

'You're on,' she said. 'Now, sleep.'

'I just want to sleep for a week, Mum. Can I come and stay?'

It was Friday, and Annie had been on the point of driving to Prue's house for lunch when Alice phoned.

'Of course, sweetheart. I'd love to see you. You've been quite elusive.'

'Sorry. Shall I turn up about five?'

Henry would be upset, she thought, as she locked the front door and stepped into her car. She had promised to spend tonight with him. But he would have to understand that older lovers have complicated lives, and that adult children comprised part of those complexities.

Prue's house was larger than the cottage Annie was renting in Southwold, but it had the same delightful 'holiday-feel' about it. You could tell that it was massively loved, and also that its owners prioritised relaxation over fresh decor or tidiness.

'Do you think it qualifies as "shabby chic"?' Prue queried as she watched Annie forming her first impressions.

Annie grinned.

'I bought this the year Alan and I married,' Prue reminisced. 'In the early days with him, I used to escape here whenever his adolescent sons came for the weekend. I was a hopeless step-parent at the beginning … terrified of children … I hadn't even lived with anyone before I met Alan – and I was over forty then. So this was my sanctuary. Everyone was very patient with me. Now the boys use it with their partners. And we all get on well.'

'It must be hard learning how to be a step-parent. No one grows up expecting to be one. How did you meet Alan?'

'A colleague knew him. She dragged me along to a lecture he was giving all about moving populations and climate change. There were drinks afterwards and we got chatting and we haven't stopped since! I never thought I'd marry. And I certainly didn't plan on shacking up with a brilliant but unambitious anthropologist who's hopelessly impractical, but nonetheless, fascinating and rather wonderful.'

'He sounds great.'

'Yes, he is, even though he's terribly eccentric. I used to mind that if we went to posh dinners I'd be in my "finery" and he'd be dressed in corduroy trousers that looked like he'd slept in them. But I gave up trying to change him, and it no longer bothers me. More than that, I've come to realise that I'd be far more selfish and intolerant if I didn't have him. I'm sure I'm more mentally stable as part of a couple than I would be alone. We need someone to care for and to be compassionate about. I'd be so bossy if I was single. Some of my students probably think I'm bossy enough as it is!' She jumped up. 'I hope you're ready to eat. I'm supposed to be on a diet to bring my cholesterol down, so I've gone for healthy-ish stuff.'

Prue disappeared into the kitchen and returned with a smoked salmon mousse and a huge bowl of salad.

'How did you do all this when you only left London this morning?'

'I didn't. Waitrose did.' Prue laughed. 'Why slave over something you'll do inadequately when you can buy it, beautifully done, and ready to eat?'

Annie raised her glass in salute. 'I couldn't agree more.'

The lunch was very convivial, even though Annie refused any alcohol, because of all the Suffolk lanes she would have to negotiate back to Southwold.

She could sense a genuine and growing friendship with Prue; one that she was aware was of equal value to them both.

Initially, they talked about their medical school days, but gradually they discovered that they had evolved into very similar mid-life women with a number of shared interests. They both liked to walk and cycle and preferred European holidays to long-haul ones. Also, Prue loved the theatre and – it turned out – had seen Arabella in several plays.

'It's so good we met each other again,' Prue reflected as she gathered up their empty plates and replaced them with pudding dishes and big bowls of Greek yoghurt and fruit salad.

Annie nodded. Then she looked pensive for a moment before saying, 'Do you find that this is a much more turbulent time in life than you would ever have imagined when we were younger?'

'Absolutely – that's one reason why meeting up with you again couldn't have happened at a better time. I don't mean it to sound as if I've latched on to you simply to boost my tally of good mates! But my very best friend – and someone I thought would always be round the corner – recently dumped her husband and upped sticks to run a yoga retreat in a village in Greece. We Skype and so on, but it's not the same. Another woman I used to like, retired early and has become so seriously boring that I can't bear her company.'

Annie grinned. 'I haven't had that happen exactly. But Arabella is awfully busy with her passion for the Home Secretary! Then my local friend, Diana, is no longer local because her husband and she had their differences and she went off to stay in Scotland. I saw her when I went up for Jumbo's funeral and introduced her to Colin Galbraith, and they've been inseparable ever since! Lovely for them of course, but I miss her.'

'I'm sure. And of course Janey is somewhat out of the picture.'

'We should do something together,' Annie said quickly. 'Do you like ballet?'

'I love it. As it happens, I've got tickets for *The Winter's Tale* at Covent Garden soon. If you'd come with me, Alan would be thrilled. He pretends to enjoy it to please me, but he loathes it really.'

'My former husband hated it too. Years ago, I used to go with Janey.'

Prue looked her straight in the eye. 'And I hope you will again,' she said firmly.

'Me too.' Annie sighed. 'I haven't seen her at all, not since that day at your consulting room. She's been very private about her illness, and didn't want any visitors. She obviously hated the idea of being weak, and of losing her hair.'

Prue looked thoughtful. 'I've had other patients react like that. But it would be a shame to waste time.'

Annie studied the dark purple juice of her fruit salad. Was Prue giving her a clue about Janey's recovery, or possible lack of it?

'I miss her a lot.' Annie's voice cracked. 'Of course we speak most days, but, well, I haven't wanted to bother her with any of my worries and usually I ask her advice all the time.'

'She may well miss that aspect of your friendship herself.'

'Do you think so?'

Prue nodded.

All the way back to Southwold, Annie pondered on what Prue had said. Maybe during Janey's illness she had unwittingly treated her so differently that she had made her friend uneasy. Had she sounded too solicitous? Overly sympathetic? It had been hard not to let her anxiety and concern show, but perhaps Janey just wanted to restore their usual banter and for Annie to ask for – and receive – the advice that Janey was so good at providing.

Back in Southwold, she stopped at a bakery to buy some treats for her daughter's visit, and was only just back at the cottage, and unloading her shopping, when Alice arrived.

She stood on the doorstep – pale, thin, and tired-looking in a crumpled black T-shirt and faded jeans that had probably fitted her once but which were now far too big and held up with an old black belt. There was a pause, then Annie held out her arms and her daughter launched herself into them.

If only, thought Annie, as they drew apart, I could sit her on my knee like I used to do when something went wrong with her school day.

'Can I use your bathroom, Mum?' Alice looked distracted.

'Upstairs, love. And the single room up there is yours.'

As Annie made tea in the kitchen area and filled a plate with the cupcakes and chocolate brownies she had bought, she suddenly remembered the panic of Lucy's arrival, less than three weeks previously. She could laugh about it now, especially since that visit had turned out so happily. If only this one would.

While Alice remained upstairs and she was waiting for the kettle to boil, she checked her phone.

Henry had texted in response to her message which had said they could no longer meet that night. It was obvious he was disappointed, but he was also excited because he had heard that he had got the part on the Noel Coward tour. He suggested she bring Alice to The Swan later.

As Annie filled the teapot, her daughter crept up behind her and hugged her, but said nothing. And she remained silent as she sipped at her tea and nibbled at the lemon icing on top of a cupcake.

Eventually, Annie risked a comment. 'You don't look as if life is treating you very well, darling.'

Immediately, she felt anxious that she had said the wrong thing and that her attempt to get her daughter to open up about her problems sounded contrived and awkward. After a moment or two, she picked up the teapot and walked over to Alice to top up her mug.

The younger woman forced a smile, which did not reach her eyes. Then she muttered, 'Do you think that some people always find life more difficult than others?'

Annie held her breath for a moment, desperate to find the right words. She played for time by returning to the sofa and sitting down and then asking a question of her own. 'By "some people", do you mean Lucy?'

Alice put her head on one side and appeared to be carefully considering the question. Then she spoke, 'Perhaps I do. But I was thinking of Dad too. One of the things I need to tell you is that he … they … are having a baby.'

'What!' It had never occurred to Annie that Edward would start a new family.

'It's true. In January. They waited till they were sure things were going OK before telling Lucy and me. It's a boy.'

Annie felt as though someone had punched her hard in the stomach. Edward had always wanted a son. How ironic it was that her replacement – whom so many of her friends had ridiculed – was able to provide him with the one thing she had failed to deliver.

'Also, I've given up orthopaedics.'

'What!' Annie cried again. 'Why? You've always wanted to do it.'

'It's bloody hard work, and I've come to the conclusion that I'm not physically tough enough. Also, I've finally faced up to the fact that – at one level – I think I went into it to get closer to Dad. He's never been proud of us, has he? He loves Lucy and me, in his own way, but I don't think he rates us, somehow. You wouldn't believe how excited he is that he's going to have a son. I find it … insulting.' Alice burst into tears and her face screwed up into a mixture of pain and rage – just like it used to do when she was a child and something unjust happened.

Annie felt as though her heart would explode with grief for her daughter. 'You're such a little thing,' she murmured, 'even if you are twenty-five. Would you like to sit on my lap?'

Alice sniffed and dabbed at her eyes with a scrap of tissue. 'No. But I would like a hug,' she whispered as she moved across the room and sank into the sofa beside her mother. Annie cuddled her, then kissed the top of her head. Her hair had grown over the past six months. It was still short, but it was pretty now, rather than severe.

'What are you going to do, workwise?' Annie asked, after Alice's weeping appeared to have stopped.

'Well, I've taken a temporary job as a research assistant at UCL. It's routine, so I don't have to worry about it after I've left work for the day.'

'And where are you living?' Annie asked. 'Still at Grandad's?'

Alice's body suddenly shook with renewed sobbing. 'No,' she managed, eventually. 'I've gone back to my own flat.'

Annie's pulse was beating loudly in her neck. Should she let slip that she knew Alice had a boyfriend?

'Are your flatmates helpful?' she ventured, knowing that she was being too timid and too opaque.

'Yes. Thing is, Mum, I was seeing a guy for a while, but it didn't really work out.'

Annie breathed out sharply, before kissing her daughter's forehead, and hugging her even more tightly.

'Thanks,' Alice whispered.

What now, Annie wondered. What can I say?

Alice struggled to free herself and sit up. 'Can we talk again later? I haven't been sleeping and I'm so tired. I feel I could rest now.'

'Of course, pet. Go on up, I'll come and tuck you in.'

Alice got to her feet, wearily, and attempted to smile. 'That's very nice,' she murmured. 'You used to say that when I was little.'

'Where's your daughter then?' Henry demanded when she walked into the bar later. It was obvious, from the empty bottles on the table that he had been treating himself – and some other members of the cast – in the wake of his good news.

Trish, the young woman who had appeared so heartbroken about her love-life just the other night, was sitting beside him looking quite proprietorial.

'We're celebrating my new job,' he announced, as he found a clean glass and poured out some wine for Annie.

She raised her glass in his direction before sipping from it.

'Congratulations!'

'Thanks. Of course I realise that whoever was to have played the part must have dropped out, because everyone else has been cast for a while.'

Annie smiled at him fondly. 'Arabella got her most recent TV series because another actress walked out of the production. It happens all the time.'

He nodded. Then he gave her an aggrieved look. 'So, your daughter didn't want to come for a drink then?'

He was slightly drunk. And maybe he did not believe that she had cancelled their rendezvous because of Alice.

'She's asleep,' Annie said firmly. 'She's been working crazy hours and she's exhausted. I think, probably, I'd better get back to her. I expect I'll bring her to meet you all tomorrow.'

She stood up, reached over and kissed Henry on the cheek and smiled broadly at the cheered-up young woman by his side.

On her walk back to the cottage Annie contemplated the possibility that Trish might end up in Henry's bed at the end of the evening. She felt much like the Marschallin at the conclusion of *Der Rosenkavalier* when she gives her blessing to her boy-lover's new romance. Smiling to herself, she unlocked the front door.

Upstairs, she crept into Alice's room. Her daughter did not stir. She looked about fourteen lying there in an old, oversized rugby shirt. Was that the one she had worn to Lucy's birthday dinner?

She softly kissed Alice's cheek, then tiptoed out of the room, shutting the door behind her. Downstairs, she made a mug of hot chocolate. Then, remembering her lunchtime conversation with Prue – she texted Janey.

Don't suppose you're still up, are you? A x

Her phone rang in response.

'Wasn't this the night you were supposed to be doing your final performance with Lover Boy?'

'Alice is here,' Annie murmured. 'I'm whispering because she's asleep upstairs. Mind you, she's dead to the world.'

'What's going on?'

'I haven't got to the bottom of it yet. But one thing that's really distressed her is that Edward's going to be a father again.'

'God Almighty! Isn't Floozy Suzie rather long in the tooth for motherhood?'

Annie sighed. 'I'd assumed so.'

'Are you all right about it?'

'Actually, it is upsetting – not on the scale of what's happened to you. But, apparently, they're having a boy. And of course he always wanted a son. I think I'd be more upset were it not for Alice taking it so badly. She's devastated. I could do with your advice, perhaps we could talk if Alice goes out tomorrow?'

'Of course. Love to help. Tomorrow would be great. I'm going to have to go in a minute anyway. Miguel is in the bath but he won't be much longer.'

'Oh! Things *have* moved on since we spoke.'

'Mmmn, well …'

'Is everything OK?'

'Yes and no.' Janey lowered her voice. 'Having been on my own for weeks, I rather resent all his stuff being around. I'm trying not to be hateful, but we had a bit of a row. He said he'll never feel this is his home and suggested I sell up, and we move out of town. But you know me. I came to the big city when I was twenty, and never considered leaving. I mean, can you see me somewhere like South Croydon?

Annie had to admit that she could not.

'I'd better go. I shouldn't complain. Not everyone has a really cool, devoted and hot Spanish boyfriend!'

It was hard for Annie to settle after their conversation; her brain seemed to be buzzing with thousands of thoughts about family and friends.

She was anxious about Janey's health and her relationship and her future. Had Prue been hinting that the long-term prospects were poor?

Then there was Henry. She had said 'goodbye' to him. It was a landmark moment and she would miss him. It had been strange but enjoyable to have a man in her bed again and to have someone to make breakfast for.

And there was her daughter to worry about; poor little, serious-faced Alice. Why did she want to change medical specialties when she had been doing so well? Why was she so upset about Edward having a son? And what had happened with the boyfriend who had been staying with her in Teddington?

'They laugh all the time,' her father's neighbour had said. How had it gone so badly wrong, so soon?

Her hot chocolate was cold, so she made another and carried it up to her bedroom.

Propped up against her pillows, she forced herself to read the paper which she had never got round to opening.

She must have dozed off. The paper had slid off the bed and was lying in a heap on the floor. She was still holding her – now empty – mug. Fortunately, she did not appear to have spilled hot chocolate on the white duvet cover. She switched off the light. Damn, she thought. I forgot to take my make-up off.

It was nine-thirty when she woke.

She took a shower and wiped off the remains of yesterday's mascara before creeping down the stairs quietly, so as not to wake Alice.

Outside, there had been a change of wind-direction, so she was sheltered in the little garden. It was sunny, and warmer than it had been for days.

She felt a surge of joy that perhaps the summer might not yet be over, and also that Alice would be able to see Southwold at its best. They could sit at the charming café by the boating lake, and maybe go to one of the town's excellent pubs for lunch.

A bowl of muesli and two cups of coffee later, Annie felt much revived. She found her phone and checked the latest BBC news headlines on it. Pleased that there was nothing too dramatic or awful listed there, she turned her attention back to her child. It was 10.45. Surely Alice was not going to sleep all day?

She laid her phone down on the garden table and walked inside, then tiptoed up the stairs. Hovering outside her daughter's room, she listened intently for any sound of activity. There was none, so she opened the door, just a crack.

The bed was empty.

Annie stood in the doorway, fighting an unaccountable and unreasonable wave of panic.

She must have got up before I awoke, Annie reasoned. She probably decided not to disturb me, saw it was a lovely day and went out for some fresh air. That was the obvious explanation.

She walked back into her own bedroom, and looked out of the window, trying to think calmly.

She recalled that Alice's car had been parked right behind hers yesterday, so where was it?

Turning away, she suddenly saw a sheet of paper on the floor that looked as if it had been torn out of a notepad. It must have been put under her door while she slept.

Dear Mum,

I love you so much. Thanks for being so kind. And thanks for always being there. But I've got things to sort out in my head and I think I need to do it alone. I thought I'd feel better if I got out of London, but I don't. So it's best I go back and face things.

Don't be disappointed in me. I am doing my best – though it's not a very GOOD best at the moment.

Loads of love, Ally. xx

Annie sat down on the bed. She read and reread the note. Of course Alice would be all right in the end, but she wanted to magic a happy life for her right now, this minute. The pain of not being able to do so was excruciating.

Suddenly, she heard her phone ring. Thank God, she thought, as she ran down the stairs and out into the garden to find it. It would be Alice. She could talk to her, find out more, maybe persuade her to come back if she had not driven too far.

'Annie!' cried Janey. 'Guess what? After you and I spoke last night, I had a terrible row with Miguel. But then the weirdest thing happened. He went down on one knee and asked me to marry him. I was stunned because no one else has ever proposed to me. I should have said "no" of course, but before I knew what I was doing, I'd said "yes". So, I seem to be engaged!'

Chapter Twelve

There was an end-of-season atmosphere in the small town.

On Saturday evening, The Southwold Summer Theatre company had brought down their final curtain of the year. Annie, feeling far too anxious about Alice, had not gone to the performance, but had looked in on the after-show party.

Initially, Henry had not noticed her, engrossed as he had been with his parents and Trish. But Annie had walked past his group and caught his eye. He had smiled broadly, his dimples much in evidence, but he had not stood up, or encouraged her to join him and his companions.

Then, yesterday, her plan had been to take a long walk and have a Sunday lunch at The Crown. But the bad weather had thwarted her, and she had retired, wet, cold and windswept to the cottage, where she had eaten scrambled eggs on toast instead of the roast beef she had looked forward to. She had also lit the wood-burning stove for the first time, before settling down on the sofa with the papers.

Later, she had dipped into her well-stocked Kindle and sipped a glass or two of Rioja while playing music on her iPod. Annoyingly, when listening to Elkie Brooks singing 'Lilac Wine', she had found herself, quite inappropriately, thinking about Jonathan.

In the evening, she had rung Janey and Arabella and Diana, and texted Alice – several times – but had had no response. It had been a relaxing day, she supposed, but she was not sorry it was over.

And now it was Monday and still stormy, though the wind had dropped slightly.

After breakfast, she ventured out on to the almost empty streets. She bought a fisherman's sweater for herself and an engagement card for Janey, before turning into one of her favourite tea shops.

The windows were steamed up, and there was a smell of damp rubber and plastic as the heat of the interior dried out the customers' macs and kagouls.

Compared with a month ago, the clientele was older and less affluent. It was comprised almost entirely of determinedly cheerful women, munching on teacakes, and chuckling as they constantly reminded each other: 'you have to laugh about the weather!'

Annie glanced at her phone. Alice still had not been in touch since her swift departure more than forty-eight hours ago. Should she text again? Would her daughter welcome the message as a sign that Mum was rooting for her and willing everything to be OK? Or would it be regarded as unhelpfully intrusive? Her thumbs twitched to make contact but her head ruled against it.

'She's a lovely doctor,' the elderly woman at the next table was saying to her companion. 'Very kind. Always puts herself out for you.'

Annie jumped up, stuffed her phone into an inner pocket, struggled into her waterproofs, swept up her shopping, then paid and departed.

The rain had eased slightly, so she made her way along the High Street and then strode towards Gun Hill, where she stood, gazing at the grey, churning sea. Till now, she mused, I've loved staying here. But ... what now?

Turning her collar up against the swirling wind, she plodded down the hill, deliberating as she went.

Partly, she liked the idea of meandering round the resort as the weather deteriorated; she could read, walk, go to tea shops, join the public library, treat herself – from time to time – to a mouth-watering Omelette Arnold Bennett at The Swan.

However, the truth was – and sometimes she wished this were different – she was not over fond of her own company. I suppose, she acknowledged, that I think I want time to myself, but mostly I prefer to be with other people.

Recalling the two women discussing their GPs in the tea room, she felt a rush of nostalgia for her life in Cambridge. I'm a doctor, she thought. I should be doctoring.

What had Carole decided about Australia? Was their senior partner still causing havoc? How was Gareth?

She did not want to think about Jonathan. It was annoying how, in quiet moments, his name or face cropped up in her thoughts or dreams. It was pathetic of her; particularly since her interest in him had only really developed after she had learned that he was gay, and therefore unavailable.

She had always intended to visit London before returning to the health centre, so maybe she should do that. Janey was almost certainly ready to see her again, and she could catch up with her father and Arabella too. Additionally, there was the not insignificant matter of getting herself tested at a genito-urinary medicine clinic.

All in all, there seemed to be nothing to keep her in Suffolk; no real reason why she should not ring her landlord, pack up and return to her own home.

Her house in Little Trumpford felt enormous compared with the Southwold cottage. She wandered around it, stroking furniture surfaces, plumping up cushions, and remembering wisps of conversations that had taken place in different rooms over the years.

Among the post, which had been stacked up by the neighbour who had kept an eye on the property, were several picture postcards from Colin, detailing the progress of his romance with Diana. She laughed out loud. He had got it bad!

It was good to be home. Did she really want to go to London? She was less certain now. It was almost four o'clock. The late afternoon

218

surgery would soon start. Might this be a good time to drop in and see how things were?

Carole spotted her as she pushed open the front door: 'Oh, thank goodness! Let me hug you to see if you're real.'

Annie chuckled and submitted to the unaccustomed contact with her practice manager.

'Did you miss me then?'

Carole released her grip on her Annie's arms and looked at her gravely. 'More than you will ever know. Come and have a cup of tea.'

Jonathan was in the staff room. She felt herself blushing at the sight of him and turned away quickly in the hope that neither he nor Carole had noticed.

Fortunately, Jonathan chose that moment to drop a number of files he had been carrying. They clattered, untidily, to the floor and he busied himself with regathering them. Meanwhile, Carole was filling the kettle.

I think I got away with that, Annie thought. But she was rattled at her reaction to her colleague.

'Great to see you, Annie,' Jonathan commented, without looking at her. 'Must dash …' He exited in the direction of his consulting room.

Carole raised her eyebrows, before muttering, 'What's wrong with that man?'

Annie sat on one of the sagging sofas. 'Is everything all right with him and Gareth?'

'I think so,' Carole answered as she washed a couple of mugs for their tea. 'But they're both being driven mad by Dr Margaret.'

'I'd assumed that would be resolved by now.'

Carole sighed. 'It's been a right saga. She fell out with the local pharmacist because he's young and wants computer print-out prescriptions and she insists on handwriting them, as you know, and uses Latin phrases which he doesn't understand. Then it turns out that the Clinical Commissioning Group didn't know she was back working and she shouldn't have been, because she hasn't had a recent appraisal. Also, some patient she saw earlier in the summer has made a formal complaint about her. It's a nightmare. *And* she treats Jonathan and Gareth like idiots.'

'What a mess. And what's happening about you and your husband?'

'He's flying to Australia next week, without me obviously, to check it out.'

'Are you OK with that?'

'Fine.'

Annie was just wondering whether Carole was putting a brave face on her situation, or was genuinely happy at the prospect of a marital sabbatical, when one of the receptionists appeared in the doorway and beckoned to the practice manager.

Most untypically, Carole swore under her breath. Then she said, more loudly: 'Can't *anybody* cope with *anything* while I have a cuppa?'

Annie threw her a sympathetic glance. 'Go! I'll make the tea. Hopefully you'll be back shortly and we can carry on catching-up.'

The teabags had changed. Someone had bought 'own brand' ones from the nearest supermarket, instead of Yorkshire Gold. Don't say anything, she cautioned herself. You are far too pernickety. But she felt unsettled. What other changes had happened in her absence?

She swizzled the teabags around in the boiling water, and added milk. Then she carried her own mug over to the sofa and reached for a copy of the *BMJ* as she sat down.

Before long, Carole reappeared.

'I made your …' Annie began.

Carole nodded and sat down opposite her. 'When were you thinking of coming back to work?'

Annie was surprised at the straight and sudden nature of the question. Of course, Carole had schedules to draw up. It was not an unreasonable query.

'Sorry to ask, but Jonathan's in a strange mood today. He says that he and Gareth need to deal with Margaret, and that if you're around it'll complicate things because she'll try to get you on her side.'

'Well,' Annie answered, after a pause. 'He could be right, but there's nothing going on that I don't know about, is there?'

Carole looked confused. 'Not as far as *I* know.'

'It's unusual for Jonathan to be so ...'

'Is "rude" the word you're searching for?' Carole sounded exasperated.

'No! Jonathan is the sweetest ... I mean he's politeness itself.'

'Not today, he's not,' Carole grumbled.

'I shouldn't have come in unexpectedly.'

'That's ridiculous. It can't be anything to do with you. Shall we say that you'll start again a fortnight today? Hopefully Margaret will have gone. Life can return to normal.'

'Seems fine,' Annie agreed. But she didn't feel fine. There was something oddly strained about the health centre today, and she was relieved that she had more time away from it.

Four afternoons later, approaching Janey's apartment for the first time since her operation, she felt strangely nervous.

What would her best friend look like? Would Miguel be there?

She took a deep breath and rang the bell for Flat Three.

'Come up, you old tart.' Janey's voice on the intercom was reassuringly normal.

There was a buzzing noise and Annie leant on the large front door till it yielded.

Upstairs, Miguel was waiting for her. 'Annie!' He kissed her hand, then each of her cheeks. 'You are looking so, so wonderful.'

She smiled at him. He was as gorgeous as she remembered. 'Congratulations on your engagement,' she said. 'I hope you'll be very happy.'

He nodded, then wrapping a muscly arm around her waist, he propelled her into the sitting room where Janey was lying on a sofa, working at her laptop. She waved for Annie to sit down beside her.

'Sorry, just let me finish this paragraph.'

Annie watched as Janey swiftly tapped away at her keyboard, noticing at once that her left-hand ring finger was adorned with a platinum band set with several small blue stones.

As she continued to observe her friend, Annie was heartened to see that she looked quite well, if pale. However, her wig came as something of a shock, because it was very blonde. Of course in Annie's mind's eye, Janey was forever auburn, even if time and hair dye had altered that original colour. Was she still as thin? It was hard to tell as Janey was dressed up warmly in black leather trousers and a huge sweater. But she certainly seemed confident and happy, despite the trauma she had been through.

'There!' Janey shut the laptop and jumped up to hug Annie. 'Oh God, I have missed you,' she murmured softly into her friend's neck.

'Well, whose fault is that?' laughed Annie.

'Touché!'

Miguel reappeared, offering to make coffee.

Janey padded over to him in her sock-clad feet. 'You're too good to me, lover,' she purred. Then she turned to Annie. 'And he does make the most divine coffee, but …' she slightly pouted at her man, with her head coquettishly on one side, 'do you mind if Annie and I go out? It's a lovely afternoon.'

He pulled Janey towards him in a move that looked like something he normally executed on the dance floor, then he gazed at her in a lingering and liquid-eyed sort of way before releasing her with a small bow and backing out of the room.

'He is *such* a sweetheart,' Janey declared briskly as she walked into the hall, stepped into a pair of outdoor shoes, and grabbed a duffle coat. 'Shall we get coffee round the corner a bit later? I fancy sitting outside in a patch of sunlight while it lasts. Will you be warm enough?'

The extensive gardens in the middle of St George's Square were sheltered from the autumnal breeze, but before long the sun dipped, and with it the temperature. So the two women abandoned their seats and began to walk around the perimeter, chatting as they went.

Annie told Janey all about her father, and how good it was to see him regularly while she was staying in his house. And how when she had gone in to see him two days ago, Marianne had been sitting with him, stroking his hand while he slept.

'I really didn't want to disturb them,' she said. 'It was so sweet.'

'How lovely,' Janey murmured as she drew her coat more tightly round her before taking Annie's arm.

'God knows if he has any concept of who she is, and why she's suddenly appeared in his life again, but I'm sure she's good for him. He definitely looks more "with it" than he did before I went to Southwold.'

'Isn't it good that your dad found true happiness – even if you never knew about it! We should focus on *your* happiness now. Could Henry be the one, and are you going to carry on seeing him?'

'Absolutely not, but – since you've mentioned him – I want to tell you something.'

And she launched, with some embarrassment, into a confession about having had to go to a GUM clinic.

'Everyone has unwise sex at some point,' Janey sympathised.

'Yes – but I'm fifty-five and talk about this kind of mistake to patients all the time. I just assumed that because Henry was nervous and apparently inexperienced he was unlikely to have an STI. As it turns out, I was right. He didn't have one. But he *might* have.'

'So, that's OK.'

'Not really. I'm mortified that I temporarily forgot that people like Henry can have former partners, who may have had risky sex.'

'Well, you're in the clear. That's the main thing – probably time now for you to get on the internet dating wagon. It'll do you …'

Annie felt a pull on her arm as Janey stumbled and seemed – suddenly – to be breathing very heavily.

'D'you know,' Annie said quickly. 'I could really do with a hot drink. Have we done enough exercise for one day?'

Her friend nodded, and they headed out of the gardens and along the road that would take them to the French patisserie.

In the warm café, and with most of a mug of hot chocolate inside her, Janey began to look better. It was early days yet, there would be ups and downs.

'Did you want to ask my opinion about Alice?' Janey's voice interrupted Annie's thoughts.

'I'd like to.'

'Go on then.'

So she did – at some length. She described how unusually tense and difficult Alice had seemed for months. How the neighbour at Teddington had mentioned a boyfriend – and what had transpired when Alice had spent those few hours in Southwold.

'So, when she went up to bed, having arrived to stay in your cottage, did she seem OK?'

'Well, she was sad, and very tired. But I thought that having begun to talk to me, we'd continue the conversation next morning.'

'I expect,' Janey surmised, 'she woke after the first decent rest she'd had for a while. You were asleep, obviously. And she suddenly felt alone and miserable and that getting away hadn't been the answer and she needed to go back. I've been there myself. It's a horrid feeling.'

'But why has she cut herself off from me? I want to help her.'

Janey leant across the table and patted Annie's hand. 'Of course you do, Mrs Fix-It! You love improving things for us all. That's why you're a good doctor. But sometimes people have to do things their own way.'

Annie nodded, aware that Janey was not simply talking about Alice.

Janey went on, 'Alice probably feels mortified that this guy seemed the right one, but has dumped her. I mean, she's not like her sister. She doesn't flit from one male to another, or fall in love easily.'

'She had a sweet boyfriend in the sixth form. And I think there was something with the brother of one of her flatmates for a while – but nothing has affected her like this.'

'He could be married.' Janey suggested.

Annie smiled confidently. 'Oh no. That's one thing I'm sure of. Alice has very strong moral beliefs. Remember how she was when Lucy was seeing Ric the lecherer? She was deeply offended that her sister would sleep with a married man.'

Later, driving back to Teddington, Annie replayed their long conversation in her mind. It had felt so good to unburden herself.

She had never fully realised before Janey was ill exactly how the dynamic of their friendship worked. It had taken a major event to help her to see that although she was responsible for sorting the medical problems of thousands of people, when it came to her own life, she always looked to Janey for advice and support. It was lucky that her friend rejoiced in that role.

As Annie got out of the car at her father's house and unlocked the front door, she remembered Janey slipping in that mention of internet dating. And therefore she was not surprised, when she checked her emails on her father's old and very slow computer, to find that her friend had not only registered Annie on to a couple of websites, but had started arranging her matches.

Online dating was the last thing she wanted to think about, but she was so delighted to have her friend back in organising mode that she supposed she would go along with it.

Before leaving to meet the first of her dates, she glanced again at Janey's instructions.

Avoid lunch or dinner. Coffee/tea/drink all fine. You might want to beat a hasty retreat! Don't talk about job too much. You'll be too intimidating! Focus on mutual interests.

Annie smiled as she noted her friend's recommendations. Now, all she had to do was to drive to nearby Twickenham – and there, meet Roger.

She pushed open the door of the all-day bar and saw him immediately. As he had promised, he was sitting near the mock fire in the middle of the room. He had highly-polished shoes, a blazer and a cravat. A cravat! Dear God, can you still buy those she wondered?

His eyes lit up when he saw her. He jumped up and lurched forwards, apparently eager to plant a kiss on her cheek. Quickly, she held out a hand to be shaken.

'I think,' he said. 'Not that I'm used to this kind thing, but the form is that, on a first meeting, each participant gets his or her own refreshment.'

'Fine by me,' she smiled.

As she waited for the noisy coffee machine to steam her milk to a high enough temperature, Annie viewed Roger in a mirror above the bar. He was about sixty. Dapper. A little tubby. Not overly tall. Perfectly respectable-looking, but her heart was not in this outing, and she wondered how soon she might decently leave without seeming rude.

'Ah, not a drinker, then,' he said with discernible disappointment as she returned, carrying her cappuccino.

'Bit early for me,' she murmured.

He raised his eyebrows. 'Ah well, once you retire, there's no reason not to drink whenever you want to. And the excellent thing here is that mid-afternoon, you get a deal – steak and kidney pie and a pint. Had my grub earlier. Very fine!'

She stirred her coffee, stifling an urge to giggle.

'And they do two-for-one meals on Monday, which is really top value. You couldn't get a better meal anywhere. And, if I say so myself, I travel a lot, so I know what I'm talking about.' He paused to take a deep gulp of his ale.

'Last month, for example, I took a young lady to the continent for a long weekend. I managed to get a cut-price deal on the overnight ferry crossing. And if you make sure you're one of the first on board, you can get good reclining seats so you don't need

226

a cabin. Of course, with the ferries taking care of two nights, you're only shelling out for one night's accommodation – and I found a pretty decent B and B …'

'And are you still seeing that "young lady"?' Annie asked innocently.

He removed his beer glass from his lips. 'No! She rang me after we returned to say she'd gone back to her husband. I was bloody annoyed because I had rather pushed the boat out on her account.'

'That would be the ferry boat, would it?' Annie muttered, gazing at her rapidly disappearing coffee. 'Yes, I suppose some women can be awfully ungrateful.'

'You can say that again,' he remarked before he launched into a story about another 'young lady' who had let him down.

Surreptitiously, she glanced at her watch. Janey had said she might ring to see if she was coping.

Fortunately, a couple of minutes later, her friend obliged.

'So sorry,' she explained to Roger, 'I have to get this …' Then ignoring Janey's whispered question about how things were going, she spoke loudly into the phone: 'Darling … Oh no! No, of course. I'll come right away!'

'Trouble?' Roger's brown eyes – which had, up until now, twinkled with a benign expression – gazed somewhat angrily at her.

'I'm afraid so. My daughter's having a crisis at the moment. And I have to go. That's what Mums are for.' She stood up. 'I would thank you for the coffee, but since I bought my own I won't bother. Goodbye.'

He harrumphed. 'Well, I *must* say … Maybe another time?'

She was halfway to the door. 'Probably not,' she cried over her shoulder.

'Why are they all called "Roger"?' Annie asked when she phoned her friend later. 'Is it a code, meaning that they want sex?'

'I'm not sure you're taking this in the right spirit,' Janey giggled. 'To be honest, I don't know the answer to your question. But there are a lot of "Rogers" so I thought I'd just pick three of them and then there's no danger you'll forget their names or call them by the wrong one. Trust me, they hate that. I once went through a whole lunch calling some guy "Brian" when his name was Graham.'

'Aren't you glad you've got Miguel and you don't have to do this any more?'

'Yes, and no,' answered her friend, rather enigmatically.

'OK, tell me about Roger Two.'

'He looks quite hot, but his picture is probably years out of date. He's supposed to be fifty, and in the music business. You're to meet him at Charing Cross mainline station tomorrow, 3.30, at the end of Platform 6.'

She was there far too early and, not wanting to look over-eager – which she was not – or sad – which she hoped she was not – she went for a wander round Boots. Eventually, she bought an electric toothbrush and toothpaste, mostly because she was standing in the dental area when the security man walked past her for the sixth time, eyeing her suspiciously.

The Boots plastic carrier would not fit into the small handbag she had chosen, and she felt it detracted somewhat from the image she was trying to create.

She walked slowly towards the end of Platform 6 and waited. Fortunately, Roger appeared almost immediately. He had less hair – and what there was of it was greyer – than in the picture Janey had emailed her, but his smile was genuine and welcoming. He was casually dressed in a jumper, jeans and trainers and a weathered biker jacket.

'I thought we might walk up to Covent Garden,' he suggested. He looked at her shoes. 'Are you up for a ten-minute stroll?'

'Sure,' she agreed.

'Let me take that.' He wrested the carrier bag from her before she could protest and they set off.

He was recently divorced, he told her. And he had two adult children, one of whom was a nurse. 'So that's a coincidence,' he said.

'Sorry?'

'She's a nurse, you're a nurse.'

Annie knew she looked bewildered.

'Don't tell me you lied on your profile and that you're really some awful admin person?'

She blushed. Janey must have changed her occupation, thinking that 'doctor' was too intimidating.

'No. I just forgot that I put it down. I … you know … um … some men have … a thing about nurses' uniforms …' Oh God, she thought, what on earth possessed me to say that?

Fortunately, he laughed and put his arm around her. She felt this was a bit soon in the proceedings but it was not an unpleasant sensation. He was interesting and easy on the eye, and his smell was attractive.

They chatted amiably as they walked up St Martin's Lane and into Long Acre.

'My office is over there,' he said, waving in a northerly direction. 'And my flat's just the other side of the Opera House.'

'And what is it you do, exactly?' she asked.

'I'll tell you everything over a pot of tea,' he answered. They stopped outside Marks & Spencer. 'Oh, I just want to pop in here … Croissants and fruit for breakfast, do you think? You're probably not a bacon and egg sort of girl.'

'Breakfast!' She looked at him, horrified. 'I thought I was meeting you for afternoon tea.'

'Well you are,' he smiled. 'But there's not much point wasting time at our age, love.'

'What!' She wished she could think of something witty or cutting to say, but nothing came to mind.

'We're mid-life people of the world. I mean, you obviously thought sex would be on the cards otherwise you wouldn't have bought a toothbrush …'

'Oh my God,' she shrieked. 'This is just awful. I am so, so out of my depth here.' She grabbed her carrier bag. 'I have to go.'

'Your loss, sweetheart,' he dismissed her with a shrug.

Too furious to stand and argue, she raced across the road, almost colliding with a bicycle-rickshaw. She felt stupid and naïve, which made her even angrier. She was furious with him, with internet dating, and with her own handling of the incident. However, five minutes of power-striding later, she began to see the comical side of the situation. And by the time she happened upon the Maggi Hambling statue of Oscar Wilde in Adelaide Street she was giggling.

Sitting on the bench that formed part of the sculpture, she texted Janey: *Frog rather than prince. Will ring later.*

Roger Three was late. Very late. Not that she minded. It was a pleasant if breezy afternoon, and the drive to the tea shop near Kew Gardens – where he had suggested meeting – had not taken long.

She sipped her cup of tea and then, because she had not had lunch, she ordered a home-made flapjack and demolished it swiftly.

There was still no sign of Roger. She finished reading her copy of *The Guardian* and ordered another pot of tea. Eventually, she rang the mobile number he had given her.

He sounded breathless as he explained that his car had broken down and that he had lost her mobile number.

'Not very organised, I know,' he apologised.

'Don't worry. It's a nerve-racking business!'

'Thanks for being understanding,' he said. 'Could we meet tomorrow?'

This was ridiculous, she thought as she ordered her second pot of tea the following day.

'You live round here?' asked the teenage waitress in the tea shop.

'No, I'm supposed to be meeting someone.'

'Oh … it's just I remember you from yesterday.'

Annie finished her paper and wondered whether to eat something.

'Can I get you anything else?' the girl asked when she brought the fresh tea.

'I don't know. Oh, let's go mad. I'll have a fruit scone.'

The waitress returned almost immediately with a warm scone and a small pot of home-made jam.

'Lovely!' Annie smiled.

'Look, I'm not being funny or anything ...' The girl's voice was conspiratorial. 'But are you waiting for a man called Roger?'

Annie paused in her act of opening the small jar of jam. 'Yes. Why? Do you know him?'

'Never seen him,' answered the young woman. 'But you're not the first person he's stood up. I think the last lady said he had a phobia.'

'A phobia! What sort of phobia?'

'Something like where he can't leave the house?'

Annie laughed. 'Oh God. Agoraphobia.'

'Yeah, that's it. Is it serious?'

Annie smiled ruefully. 'Well, it obviously is for him.'

She finished her tea and paid. 'I don't think I'll give him a third chance, so I probably won't be here again,' she said to the waitress.

'Don't blame you. Men, eh!'

Annie smiled and left. It occurred to her that the best use of the rest of the afternoon would be to go and see her father.

The care-worker at The Willows opened the front door to her with a tired smile. 'His lady-friend has just gone,' she said. 'He's in the television room.'

Her father was sitting up straight and wearing a smart tweed jacket and a new tie. Marianne had obviously taken over his wardrobe since coming back into his life, and it had been a good move. Probably, at some level, her father felt more like himself because he was *dressed* more like himself.

He smiled at her. 'Hello, lassie,' then he winked.

'Hi, Dad.'

He looked puzzled.

'I'm your daughter Annie, remember?'

He nodded furiously, though whether to emphasise that he did really know her, or to mask the fact that he didn't, was unclear.

They watched *Pointless* on TV together. Some part of his brain seemed to enjoy it. But as soon as it was over, he began to nod off.

'I'll see you again soon, Dad,' she murmured.

He forced himself to reopen his eyes. 'Will you come again tomorrow, Mary?'

Was that his name for Marianne?

She paused for a moment, then smiled and gave him a quick kiss on the cheek. 'Definitely,' she promised.

This was not how I thought the evening would go, she thought as she finished her email to Roger, giving him links to a support group for agoraphobics and also some material from the Royal College of Psychiatrists about cognitive behaviour therapy. She tried not to be patronising, but she did want him to understand that he could get treatment, free, and probably without waiting too long, if only he would tell someone about his condition.

'Shall we avoid Rogers from now on?' Janey asked when she phoned later. 'None of them seems to be up to much!'

'Actually, I've decided that this cyber-dating lark isn't for me.'

'That's crazy, you old tart. You've hardly got going yet. You mustn't be put off so easily.'

'The trouble is, and I know it's sad, but I really need to tell you … I have feelings for Jonathan, my colleague.'

'The *gay* one?'

'Well, yes.'

'Annie, be realistic. That's never going to happen. And you don't want to live out your old age alone do you?'

Annie considered the question. 'Not entirely sure at the moment … Do you think Roger Three will be upset that I've found out about his problem and emailed about it?'

'Not if he's sensible. Probably he'll ring you as soon as we're off the phone and ask you to come over to his place.'

'Well, I won't be going,' laughed Annie. 'I'll speak to you tomorrow.'

Her phone rang immediately. It made her jump. Janey must have sixth sense.

'Hello,' she answered, cautiously.

A woman's voice cried: 'Annie!'

So it wasn't Roger Three after all.

'It's Ellen.'

She must know an 'Ellen' but could not place her.

'From the Cambridge radio station.'

'Ellen! Sorry. I was miles away. How's your new job?'

'It's fantastic. It's a topical live late-evening show. We have a different presenter every week. Different guests. Loads of work. Terrifying, but I love it. Have you seen it?'

'Sorry no … I've been away in Suffolk living in a cottage without a television.'

'Never mind. But look, Annie, a paper's just been published in the *European Journal of Sexual Medicine* all about rates of sexually transmitted diseases, and the fact that, in the UK, the biggest percentage increase is in the over-fifties. Right up your street, I thought. So can you come on tomorrow evening and talk about it? You should have plenty of time to get to us after your afternoon surgery. Jon Snow's probably going to be this week's presenter. He's so nice.'

'I'm in London, well, Teddington. On holiday. But I couldn't possibly do it. I'm sorry. Local radio's one thing …'

'It's exactly the same.'

'How can it be? This is *television*.'

'But you look great and you know the subject.'

She could feel herself being swayed by this flattering and likeable young woman. Maybe I could do it, she thought. I might be hopeless at internet dating but perhaps I could do this. It would be awful to be one of those older people who never tries anything new.

'Well …'

'Good,' said Ellen. 'You'll really be helping me. I'll email you details of the studio. It's in Great Portland Street. Come about 9.45 so I can talk you through it. We go on air at half past ten.'

This was crazy. She really should decline, but somehow she heard herself agree. As she ended the call, she thought of Janey, and quickly called her. The evening would be much less frightening if she could persuade her friend to come with her.

'Oh, marvellous!' Janey was delighted. 'You'll be great and I'd love to come. I'll put the wig in rollers. I've probably hidden away for too long. This'll do us both good!'

'Annie!' Ellen appeared round the green room door and rushed in to hug her. 'So glad you're here.'

'Thanks,' she said, then drawing Janey forward, she began to introduce her friend but Ellen interrupted her.

'Oh my God. You're Janey Durrant. I used to love you on breakfast TV when I was growing up. And then when you wrote that sex column in *More* magazine, I was such a fan. You taught me everything!'

Janey beamed. 'Really? That's nice to know.'

Ellen giggled. 'God, it's so hectic here. Lots to do … Annie, you'll be fine. All you've got to do is quickly read these notes.' She thrust a folder into Annie's hands. 'Back later,' she said as she sprinted towards the door.

Annie and Janey looked at each other.

'What *am* I doing here?' Annie said in a stage whisper. '*You're* the broadcaster. I must have been mad!'

'I'm not a broadcaster nowadays – only odd bits and pieces for companies with no money to spend. You'll be great. Just read the brief, while I toddle along the corridor and find a loo.'

Annie opened the sheaf of papers and found, much to her surprise, that she was not going to be the only interviewee for the item. To a degree, she was relieved as she felt it removed a certain pressure, but it was clear there would be something of a debate because the other guest was a reactionary doctor, whose stance was that everyone not in a heterosexual marriage should simply abstain from sexual contact. He had dominated question-times in various conferences she had been to over the years, and she had formed a fervent dislike of him.

234

She felt her heart thumping. Where was Janey? She would have liked to run her thoughts past her friend. How feisty should she be?

The sound was off on the monitor at the far end of the green room, but she could see the opening titles of the programme and as they mixed through to the presenter's desk, she spied Patrick Pace.

'Oh my God,' she moaned aloud, just as Ellen reappeared. 'Ellen! I can't possibly do this. You said that Jon Snow was presenting and I ...'

'Exciting isn't it? I couldn't believe it when Pace agreed to do it. Of course you can work with him. You'll be fine!'

How could she explain her decades of devotion to this particular broadcaster, or that she felt weak at the knees at the thought of meeting him in real life? Not that television was anything like real life, she thought as Ellen led her down a corridor and through a tremendously heavy door into the studio. She found herself standing behind the set, though she could see what was happening on a nearby monitor. It was dark where she was, and there were cables everywhere. Suddenly, a scruffy man emerged out of the shadows and put a radio microphone on her, clipping it to her lapel, and taping its wire to the inside of her jacket and then slotting it into a little radio pack that was housed in a pocket of a black belt which he asked her to tie round her waist.

'Don't worry,' the soundman whispered. 'No one will see it. You'll be sitting down.'

The other doctor hovered nearby. His face looked both arrogant and scornful as he observed her for a moment before extending a bony hand to be shaken. She noticed that he smirked as he turned away.

The previous item had just ended and they were quickly into a film insert about sexual behaviour.

'Right!' Someone in baggy jeans and headphones appeared and ushered her and the other guest on to the set before indicating that they should sit one each side of Patrick Pace, who was busy scribbling something on a pad in front of him and talking to an unseen person about a politician who was to appear later.

He was utterly magnificent. God-like. And she could see how super-fit he was beneath his beautiful jacket. He smiled in her direction and then turned to the other guest and nodded curtly. Had they met before, she wondered?

Then a voice said, 'Coming to studio in five seconds ...'

'So,' Patrick began, 'to talk about these apparently shocking figures I'm joined by Dr Hugo Wickham from the Hoover Bradley Family Institute and Dr Annie Templeton, who is a GP from Cambridge and a sexual medicine specialist.'

Specialist! Oh my God, she thought. That sounds far too grand for what I do. Should I ...?

But the interview had begun and Dr Wickham had launched into his tirade, condemning lax modern morals, criticising ageing baby-boomers who, to his mind, had always followed their selfish inclinations rather than the rules of society which had served this country well in previous generations. Did he mention gay marriage as well? She got lost in his argument. He ranted on and on. It would be her turn soon. She would need to give advice but from a modern and liberal perspective.

Suppose though, she said something stupid? Or lost her train of thought? What if her hero found her wanting in some way, had to repeat a question, or grew impatient – as she knew he could?

'Dr Templeton,' he turned to her, not smiling, but with a twinkle in his eye. 'Let's hear from you.'

She paused, nervously. Then seeing Wickham's self-satisfied, smug expression, she took a breath and she was off.

Did she really say the word 'dinosaur'? She thought she must have done. Patrick Pace looked quite gleeful.

'Surely,' she said, 'as we all have the prospect of living longer than former generations, no one would expect us to remain in unhappy marriages indefinitely, or to be celibate after we've been widowed or divorced. But of course it's important to be careful. You may think that you've taken up with someone suitable. But no one comes packaged with a label on the forehead telling you whether he or she has a sexual infection. And being older is – as the figures show – no protection against an STI. It's easy you know, to fall for – say – a shy widower, who was married to his first wife for thirty-five years, and to assume there's no risk to you. But supposing that widower's wife used to have a lover, and suppose that lover was someone who played around? I'm not saying this invariably happens, but it can. So, we need to wise-up and not assume that a new encounter is infection-free. Whether or not Dr Wickham thinks people in mid-life should be "putting it about" – I think his phrase was – the fact is that they *are* sexually active and they mostly want to remain so for as long as possible. But they need to practise safer sex strategies – which basically come down to having an absolute rule that you don't bed someone new without using a condom. And no one, man or woman, should feel embarrassed about carrying one …'

'Welcome back!' Carole looked up from the reception desk. 'And congratulations on your TV appearance. You were fantastic. You should get your own series!'

Annie smiled but shook her head. 'Oh no. Once is enough, but it was quite fun – in a terrifying sort of way – and I've had so many emails from people who hate the other doctor, that I haven't answered them all yet!'

Carole laughed. 'The kettle's boiled. We've bought in plenty of your favourite brands of tea and coffee! And our big news is that – as of last Friday – Dr Margaret has officially retired. We have it in writing.'

'Thank heavens! I must tell Jonathan that he was right to keep me out of the way.'

'Oh, didn't you know? He's taken leave this week. Gone to Florence, I think. It's just you and Gareth.'

Had her expression given anything away, she wondered as she made her way to the staff room? She had been urging herself to act normally around Jonathan. But perhaps it was a good thing that she had time to work her way back into a normal routine without him distracting her. She made coffee and was about to sit down with it when Carole appeared.

'There's a doctor to see you. She's got a baby with her – probably about ten months old. She's moving here and wants to go on your list. Shall I ask her to come back at lunchtime?'

'She's not poorly is she? Or the baby?'

'She said not. She just wanted to meet you.'

'Well,' Annie glanced at her watch. 'No time like the present.' She took a quick gulp of her coffee then put the mug in the sink, before following Carole back to reception.

A tall, elegant Asian woman stood there, jiggling her baby on her hip. She had glorious black hair cut into a long shiny swinging bob with a fringe, and she was dressed in an expensive-looking navy trouser suit and crisp white shirt.

Annie smiled broadly at her visitor. 'Hello! Gosh, what a lovely little boy you have.' She took his tiny hand for moment and gently stroked it. Then she turned back to his mother: 'What's his name?'

'Bahir Anthony,' she answered, fixing Annie with a penetrating gaze. 'And I'm Dr Jaspal Kaur.'

'Good to meet you. Come into the surgery and have a quick chat,' Annie invited her, leading the way.

Inside, she indicated a chair.

'I prefer to stand.' The younger doctor's tone was assertive, maybe even hostile.

'OK. So, are you a GP yourself?'

'No, I'm a diabetic specialist.'

'And you're coming to work in Cambridge?'

'I'm not actually. I … I wasn't entirely truthful with your practice manager. I don't want to go on your list. I just wanted to meet you.'

Annie looked puzzled.

'I saw you on a Channel 4 programme.'

Annie beamed at her.

Dr Jaspal did not smile back. 'I realised at once who you were. You're very like *her*.'

Annie was thoroughly disconcerted by the other woman's tone. 'I'm sorry, but I don't know what you're talking about. And I don't think I can pursue this now. There's a waiting room filling up with patients …'

'My married name is Jackson,' the other doctor announced. '*Now* do you understand?'

Annie shook her head vigorously. 'No, I don't.'

'Well let me spell it out for you,' Dr Kaur snapped – at which point her previously docile son began wailing loudly.

Annie raised her voice. 'Please do.'

'Your daughter is in a relationship with my husband, and …'

Annie felt a wave of relief. There was obviously a mistake.

'No,' she interrupted. 'That can't be right. Lucy's in love with a French boy.'

'Who the hell is Lucy?' The visitor shouted over her child's deafening cries. 'I don't know any Lucy. *She's* not having an affair with Tony. It's *Alice* I'm talking about. Alice Templeton.'

Chapter Thirteen

Her morning surgery had passed in a blur; she hoped she had not missed anything vital. She had then worked through lunch, dealing with countless emails, and prescriptions, and with the sort of pointless form filling that drove all doctors to distraction.

Now, sitting over a quick cup of coffee in the staff room, she finally revisited – sentence by sentence – the horror of Dr Jaspal Kaur's earlier visit, and decided to text Janey. That done, she sighed and stood up, ready for her afternoon surgery.

Gareth, who was sitting nearby looked across at her. 'What's wrong, Annie?' His voice was gentle.

She smiled at him. 'No wonder the patients think you're "ever such a nice doctor"!'

He grinned.

'There's a crisis with one of my daughters.'

Gareth put down the journal he had been reading and came over to put his arms around her. To her surprise, she relaxed in them, enjoying the close contact.

'That's better,' he whispered as he released her. 'Pity that Jonathan's not here to comfort you.'

'Yes – he's a very kind man,' she murmured.

'Maybe this isn't the time, Annie, but you know the day he was trying to say something to you in here – the day he told you that I was going to move in with him?'

'Yes,' she turned away and busied herself with some papers.

'You were aware of what he was trying to tell you, weren't you? About his feelings?'

'Oh yes,' she responded, as she moved towards the door.

'And how did you feel about that?'

'Really,' she answered, 'it's nothing to do with me.'

She left then, oblivious to the puzzled expression on Gareth's face. Why on earth, she wondered, did he want to know what she thought of their gay relationship? It made no sense.

Fortunately, most of the late afternoon surgery was routine – comprising, as it did, people with coughs, colds, muscular aches and 'odd feelings'. But her last patient required more time and thought.

Barbara Lawson had consulted Annie for years. She was someone who had always put other people first, having been a teacher, a local councillor, and founder of a women's refuge. Annie admired and liked her, and regarded her as a tireless force for good. However today, disturbingly, she looked fatigued and older than her seventy years.

'I booked your final appointment for the day. I know it'll take a while. I hope you're not in a rush,' she began.

Of course not,' Annie replied. Barbara Lawson was not a hysteric or a hypochondriac. If she thought that her consultation merited a longer than average slot, then she was undoubtedly right. 'Would you like some tea? I was thinking of having a cup.'

'That would be welcome.'

Annie could see tears in Barbara's eyes as she left her for a moment to ask one of the receptionists if she would bring the drinks.

It took half an hour or so to determine that this selfless and stoical woman almost certainly had a secondary carcinoma – having had breast cancer two decades previously.

'I was warned this might happen,' Mrs Lawson explained. 'But of course you always hope it won't. I've had aches in my ribs – and a lump in my armpit – for about five weeks. But you were away, and I decided I'd sooner wait to see you.'

'That may not have been the wisest option.' Annie rebuked her gently.

'I know. But I ran it past a friend who's a Macmillan Nurse. She was very honest.'

The two women discussed referrals and treatment options, most of which this well-informed patient calmly but firmly refused.

'I'll have a scan,' she agreed. 'Just to see the extent of the problem, but probably I'm not going to agree to radio or chemotherapy. I doubt if my prospects are good, and I'd sooner enjoy what time I have left without lots of pointless intervention.'

'It might not be pointless, though. There've been huge advances since you had your mastectomy.'

Barbara remained polite but implacable. 'I don't have children or a partner. My only close relative is my sister, and she lives in Australia. Luckily, I have masses of friends – in fact the best bunch of brilliant women that you could wish to meet – who'll be there for me. But I don't want to prolong their agony or mine.'

It was a very sober Annie who drove home.

The sound of an incoming text made her jump. She was near Waitrose so she pulled in to the supermarket car park hoping that the message might have come from Alice.

It was from Janey: *Just read your message. Home now. Call me.*

So she did, and immediately launched into an account of Dr Kaur's visit that morning.

'Of course you're upset,' soothed Janey. 'But Alice isn't a criminal. She's just having an affair. People do. God knows I've had enough. You've never been judgemental with me.'

'You're right.' Annie knew when she was losing an argument with Janey, and had no energy to pursue this one. The truth was that she was appalled by her daughter's behaviour, but she did not want to confide that fact, even to her best friend. How could Alice have used her grandfather's house – under the guise of cleaning it up – to pursue her sordid liaison? It was so duplicitous; so unlike her, with her high moral standards. And how could she have had allowed herself to become so close to her boss when she knew that his wife was so newly a mother? I love Alice so much, she thought. But I really don't like, or understand, her at the moment.

'Are you listening to me?' Janey's voice broke into her thoughts.

'Sorry. I'm not making sense today. I'm just going to do a routine shop now – get the freezer stocked up and so on – and then have a quiet evening at home watching something bland on the box.'

Her mind was not on the shopping. Before long, her trolley contained far more free-range chicken breasts, fruit, vegetables and soya yoghurts than she could possibly consume before their sell-by dates.

'Get a grip,' she whispered to herself as she walked to the checkout, having decided not to put anything back on the shelves, but simply to get out of the supermarket quickly.

'Dear lady!' declaimed an upper-class male voice.

She looked up. Rupert – Diana's husband – was in front of her in the queue. He looked older, thinner and less smart than when she had seen him last. There was a button missing from his shirt, which was gaping open under his Guards tie.

He peered into her laden trolley. 'Looks like you're planning a feast!'

She smiled weakly, noting that his basket contained only one tin of potatoes, a packet of frozen spinach and a pork chop.

'How are you, Rupert?'

'So-so. I imagine Diana told you she's away and that we are having certain marital difficulties?'

He has absolutely no idea that I know everything, she realized; how he likes being a kitchen slave and being beaten, and has a dominatrix in Wales.

'We should get together one evening,' he was saying. 'You're on your own too. We could be company for each …'

'Uh, nice idea, Rupert. I've got a lot on though.'

He nodded. 'Understood.'

She immediately felt remorseful at her brusqueness. 'Still,' she said quickly. 'We have to eat and um, company is always good to have. Can I just get through this week and I could cook dinner one night?'

He brightened immediately. 'Excellent suggestion.'

Fortunately, at that point he reached the head of the queue. After he had paid, he looked back and asked if she could manage all her purchases herself.

She smiled. 'Yes, don't worry. I'll put a note through your door about dinner.'

He gave her a little military salute and walked away. As she watched him she resolved to contact Diana and tell her how down-at-heel Rupert was looking, so she texted as soon as she reached her car. Then she headed home, grateful that she could have a gentle evening to herself to try to process the developments of this extraordinary day.

'What time do you call this?'

Lucy stood in the hall, wearing an apron and holding a wooden spatula. She rushed forward to help Annie with her shopping bags, and carried them into the kitchen.

'Come in the sitting room and have a drink, Mum,' she said, in a firm but encouraging voice. 'I don't want you interfering with the dinner. Just chill – and I'll, like, pull the last bits together, now you're here.'

'Lucy, where did you spring from? And, why?'

'Tell you everything in a moment.'

'OK.'

This was just one more unusual happening in an already bizarre day, she decided. Sinking into her favourite sofa, she smiled broadly at her younger daughter. 'I haven't a clue what's going on, but it's marvellous to see you.'

Lucy placed a glass of red wine in her mother's hands and sprinted back to the kitchen.

Annie recalled that the last time Lucy had cooked anything in this house it had been a fried egg on top of beans on toast. Maybe she had extended her repertoire since then. The interesting point though was why she was here. Was it because of Alice? The girls had never been close. Would Lucy have a clue about – or be remotely interested in – her sister's love-life? On the other hand, it must be too much of a coincidence that she had turned up on the very day that Dr Jaspal had dropped her bombshell.

'Come through, Mum,' Lucy called. Annie picked up her glass and followed the voice.

'My goodness. Proper dinner – in the dining room.'

'Yes, I thought we'd do it elegantly!'

Annie looked in some wonder at her grown-up daughter who seemed so confident and stylish. She then took in the beautifully-presented spread on the table. Where had Lucy learned such skills?

As if in answer to her mother's question, Lucy explained, 'I've been in Paris this weekend with Jean-Pierre and his mum, Simone. And she sent me home with all of this food in a cold bag. I'm pretty sure she thinks I eat rubbish when I'm away from them! So I thought I'd share it with you.'

'Sweetheart,' Annie exclaimed, as she sat down, 'that is so, so great. And it all looks delicious.'

'Well, I hope it will be. Bon appétit!'

The food tasted even better than it looked. The main dish consisted of tiny, rare slices of roast beef tossed in a delightful dressing with pieces of mango and pumpkin. There was coconut rice too. And various green leaves, and chopped green beans, and some tiny sautéed potatoes.

'It seems like you've got a bit of a finishing-school situation going on in Paris,' Annie laughed, for the first time that day.

Lucy laughed too. 'I know, Mum. I'm so lucky. Simone used to work for her father. He was a chef, and came from Martinique to Paris when she was small, and worked his way up in classy hotels and then later had his own restaurant. I've, like, learned so much from her – about fashion too of course. And it's all thanks to you. I know I'd already met Jean-Pierre in Paris after I left "old arsehole" there and had to get home. But if you hadn't, like, taken me to Biarritz we probably wouldn't have got together.'

Annie had almost forgotten about the lecherous lecturer, Rik – with no 'c' in his name.

'Oh, Rik, yes … do you have to go to any of his classes this year?'

'No. I chose another course-option so I don't see him. I can't think now how I ever, like, got into that. But then we all make mistakes!'

Annie scrutinised her daughter's expression. Was she talking about Alice?

Lucy smiled at her. 'Let's finish this, then have dessert. Later, we can go through to the sitting room and talk.'

It was a very strange feeling to realise how wise Lucy had become. She had always been flighty and slightly edgy and unconventional. But now, here she was adopting a feeding and caring role, and acting with a calm maturity that Annie had never witnessed before. It was comforting if – paradoxically – disconcerting.

When the pudding came, it was a warm apple, almond and caramel tart with a light, crumbly topping, served with a bowl of crème fraiche.

'More wine?' Lucy was at her elbow.

Annie nodded, then she glanced at the label. 'My goodness, this must have cost you a fortune.'

Lucy giggled. 'No way! I called in on Dad after I got to Cambridge, and he gave it to me.'

'Well don't tell him you squandered it on me!'

'Actually, Mum,' Lucy sounded rather serious. 'He *suggested* I share it with you tonight. He thought you'd like it.'

'That was kind.'

'You two don't have to be enemies forever.'

'I know. But I'm not sure I'm quite ready to stop being an enemy. How is he anyway?'

'Really happy with Suzie. Totally thrilled he's going to be a dad again. Funny, I don't remember him being very interested in us

246

when we were kids – *still* not that interested, is he? I had to tell him about Ally, by the way.'

So this visit *was* about Alice. Lucy was dealing with 'the parents' so that Alice did not have to. Trying to sound calm and unemotional she asked about Edward's reaction.

'He didn't seem to think it had much to do with him.'

'Mmmn. Nothing new there, then!' Annie grimaced. 'So – you're here about Alice?'

'Yup. Let's move to the sitting room, shall we?'

Once settled, Annie asked Lucy what she knew about Alice and her clandestine lover.

'Mum, I can tell you're really upset and cross. Ally *said* you'd be furious. That you'd, like, think she'd totally lost her understanding of right and wrong.'

Annie reminded Lucy of her twenty-first birthday dinner when Alice had been so upset about the lecherous lecturer and about Lucy's lack of concern at the hurt it might do to his wife.

'*That* was Alice,' Annie's voice was emphatic. 'The Alice I know. Also, she's hardly had any boyfriends. So why now? And why does she have to pick someone who's not free?'

'You don't always choose who you fall in love with.'

'Lucy, I appreciate that you want to believe that this thing is bigger than both of them.' She sighed deeply and came to a halt.

'You think they'll get over each other?'

'Of course!' It's a matter of choice. We're not animals. We have highly-developed brains!'

'Ally was so right about you, Mum.'

'I don't know if that's good or bad,' Annie retorted.

'Look, Mum, she's not seeing him any more and I don't think *I'd* be that strong. Not if I felt like she does. And he, like, really loves her. By the way, I don't know what she sees in him. He's older – about thirty-five or something – and pale and very ordinary and, like, not cool at all. Just interested in the job and gadgets – like Dad, come to think of it. Ally said that the wife was coming to see you.'

'She did. This morning. They have the sweetest baby boy – a child who needs both parents. And how Alice could do this to a … well … an Asian woman … it somehow makes it worse.'

'What!' Lucy looked angry. '*Why* is that worse? That's discrimination, Mum. That's as bad as saying you wouldn't want Alice to marry a non-white doctor.'

'Don't be ridiculous. It's the very *opposite* of that.'

'No, it's not, Mum. You're almost saying that the wife is disadvantaged. Well, she's not. She's a clever, professional woman from the Midlands – and she comes from a rich Sikh family, who are, like, very westernised. You seem to think she's some sort of earth-mother from a remote village in India. That's totally wrong, Mum. You have to wise up.'

Annie was stunned. She had become used to Alice questioning her views from time to time. But now it was Lucy too. Growing up, she had been embarrassed by her father describing some neighbours as 'brown people'. Now, horribly, she was embarrassing her own children.

'Where *is* Alice?' she asked, suddenly tearful.

Lucy rushed over and hugged her. 'Mum, don't be upset. You're a good person, and a great mother.'

'Well, that's nice to know,' she murmured, as Lucy released her and sank down on the carpet beside her mother's chair. 'But please tell me where she is.'

'OK. I took her with me to Paris, last Friday. Simone is looking after her.'

'Why? *I'm* her mother.'

'Mum, she, like, doesn't want to see you right now. She's really upset. *Really*. I mean, it's not like me and her have ever been close, but I feel for her now. I've only known about everything for a few days. She texted me. And then came down to Brighton to talk. She looked, like, totally awful. She's gone a bit mad, I think.'

For the first time Annie's heart lurched with pity for her older daughter and tears coursed down her cheeks.

'You need to sleep, Mum. I'll come up in a moment with a hot water bottle. Get to bed.'

Annie nodded obediently, before walking out of the dining room and setting off up the stairs. Turning at the top she saw Lucy watching her. In as reassuring a voice as she could manufacture, she said, 'I don't want you to have to feel responsible for me – much as I'm glad that you're here.'

'Don't worry, Mum.' Lucy was grinning broadly. 'It's only temporary! I'm not up for pushing you around in a wheelchair and cutting up your food just yet! I'm going tomorrow and you'll have to cope on your own – though I bet Janey and Auntie Bella and Diana will give you advice. Just remember though, they're not exactly an advert for clean living, are they?'

Upstairs, Annie was about to put her phone on charge when a vivid vision of Alice – tearful, distressed and lost – filled her mind. So she sent a text:

Are you all right? We will talk when you want. Mum x

As Janey had said, Alice was not a criminal. She had always been the most decent of people – which made what was going on all the more incomprehensible. With a little shake of the head, Annie attempted to banish the muddle that was swirling around in her brain. Then, fearful that she could not escape her thoughts except by chemical intervention, she broke one of her almost-absolute rules and took a sleeping pill.

He should have thought of that before. X

Struggling to wake up from the 'knock out' she had delivered to her system the night before, Annie gazed at the text but could not force her brain to make sense of it.

Then she noticed the sender. It was Diana. So this message was about Rupert and a response to Annie's text of the previous evening. Obviously, her friend was not going to be diverted from her current course of pleasure just because her husband was finding life difficult.

Another text appeared: *Sorry, pressed SEND before I meant to. Just to say am in Corsica with Colin. Loving it. And him. All going wonderfully. And it's sunny! Will never be able to thank you enough for introducing us. How are you?*

How *was* she? Probably better than yesterday. And it seemed pointless bothering Diana with her anguish about Alice. So she texted: *Fine. So pleased you're both happy. xx*

Much to her surprise, Lucy was awake already. She could hear her in the shower at the end of the landing. Annie ran her own bath and jumped in – reminding herself of her long-held belief that there was little in life that could not be improved with a soak in hot water.

She had just emerged from the tub and was wrapping herself in a large, warm towel when Lucy appeared in the doorway, bearing a cup and saucer.

'Tea?'

Annie chuckled. 'No one else has ever looked after me as well as this,' she said as she reached out a damp arm to accept the drink.

'What about your mother? I don't really remember Granny ...'

'Well, she died when you were six. No, she wasn't a very motherly type. My dad was the one who put plasters on my knee and helped with homework. But there again ...'

Lucy had been about to leave her mother's bathroom, but she turned back. 'What?'

'Do you know about Marianne? Did Alice mention her?'

'No, who's she?'

Annie quickly told her about her father and his long-term love – and about how Marianne now visited him almost daily.

'I can't believe it,' Lucy cried. '*Grandad!*'

'I found it hard to believe too, to begin with. But they had – and probably still have – a very real love for each other.'

'Not so different from Alice and Tony then.' Lucy pointed out.

Annie reflected for a moment. 'At least Marianne and Grandad didn't break up any marriages. Still, I do wonder now whether my mother *knew* that he had someone else. She wasn't very affectionate at the best of times. But maybe life was difficult for her – more difficult than I suspected.'

Lucy looked at her watch. 'Are you going in by bike or car?'

'I haven't looked out yet to see what the weather's doing. Why? Would you like me to drop you at the station?'

Lucy grinned. 'I was hoping you could.'

Annie laughed. 'It's the least I can do. Thanks for being so helpful.'

'It's nothing, Mum. And when you next see Grandad, give him a huge hug from me.'

'And that's a hug from Lucy,' she said to her father the following Sunday.

'Ah, that's nice, lassie,' he answered.

She looked at him intently. Had he understood? Did he know who Lucy was? Who *she* was?

He carried on talking, 'Lovely lassie. I love a lassie …'

'That's a song, Dad.'

'It is, right enough. By Hans Christian Andersen.'

She laughed. 'No, Dad, it's …'

'It is so,' he contradicted her, his lip trembling like an aggrieved toddler.

'Perhaps it is,' she said, as she patted his arm. 'Come on, are we going to have a little potter round the garden?'

He looked out of the window. It was a grey day.

'I want a wee jam sandwich,' he announced.

'OK, it'll be teatime soon. We'll have a walk another time.'

She sat with him for a while till, inevitably, he fell asleep.

Ideally, she would like to leave now – but it seemed heartless when she had not yet been here half an hour. She sighed. It was all so pointless. Thinking suddenly about Barbara Lawson, her patient with terminal cancer whose time was surely running out

251

though she had so much yet to offer, Annie felt a sense of infuria-tion and frustration at the universe and its inexplicabilities.

It was not as if she wanted her father to die. But in his normal, previous life, he would never have regarded this as a viable exist-ence. Really, she told herself, as a doctor she should be used to the unfair lottery that determines who will breathe another day, and who will not.

Marianne put her head round the door. When Annie failed to see her, she knocked, gently. 'Annie, you don't look like someone who's just had several weeks off work.'

Annie turned. 'Marianne! I'm glad you're here. I was just having a philosophical moment that was leading me down a deeply depressing path. I'd better go, back to Cambridge.'

Marianne hesitated in the doorway, and in so doing, uninten-tionally – or perhaps not – blocked Annie's route to the exit.

'Why don't we have a cup of tea first?' she suggested.

'Good idea. Will they get us one here do you think?'

'They will. But I wouldn't recommend it, unless you like some-thing that tastes as though someone's swept it off the factory floor! Let's go back to your dad's place. I'll come and see Duncan later.'

They drove, in their own cars, the short distance to the house. Annie arrived first and put the kettle on. Then, because she had stayed the night before, she quickly ran upstairs to gather up her overnight case. She looked somewhat longingly at the bed. Maybe, instead of rushing off now, she should sleep here tonight. She could set her alarm for five o'clock, and drive back in time for morning surgery.

Suddenly, she realised that Marianne was on the front doorstep and that the bell no longer worked.

'You should have a key,' Annie apologised as she led the other woman through to the kitchen.

'Would you be happy to let me have one?'

'Of course. I imagine you used to spend a lot of time in this house with my dad after my mother died.'

Marianne nodded with a faraway look in her eye.

'You should definitely have a key. After all, if you'd ever chosen to leave your husband, you'd have lived here. It's only because you're a decent and honourable person that that never happened. Not like some people.'

Suddenly, the floodgates opened and Annie divulged everything she knew about Alice and her lover. Once started, she could not stop. Marianne took over the making of the tea while Annie leaned on the sink and poured her heart out.

'And she brought him here,' Annie cried angrily. 'She was most insistent that she wanted to sort out this place for me – and she did. But what I know now is that she needed this house so that they had somewhere – where no one would know them – they could sleep together.'

Marianne put her arm around Annie's waist and encouraged her to sit down at the kitchen table. She put a mug of tea before her.

'Am I the right person to advise you about your daughter, Annie?' Marianne asked with a half-smile on her concerned face. 'I'm someone who had an affair with your father while your mother was alive and I carried it on afterwards; and I've deceived my husband, who is a wonderful person, for almost three decades.'

'But you didn't take Dad away from me. And you didn't split up your home or remove your daughter from her father. It's the baby and the young mother that I can't get my head around.'

'I know.' Marianne reached over the table and took her hand. 'But there may be details about the situation that you don't know about. You need to speak to Alice.'

'She won't talk to me.'

'Well, she will in time. She's probably appalled with herself.'

Annie nodded grimly. 'I'm sure that's true. And apparently she isn't seeing him any more. So that's to her credit. Marianne, I don't want to pry, but, after all, you'd have been my step-mum if things had turned out differently …'

Marianne smiled. 'That would have been so nice. Go on, ask anything you like.'

'It's about my mother. I wondered if she knew about you and Dad.'

Marianne stood up and fetched the teapot and refreshed both their mugs. Annie helped herself to milk.

'I don't know. Theirs was a strange marriage, wasn't it? They got together, apparently, when he was on an accountancy course in London. He hadn't long left Scotland and he hardly knew anyone. They met at a party. They both got drunk and fell into bed together that night, and you were the result!'

'I never knew that.'

'Well, I've no reason to doubt Duncan's story. Your mother had left her home – in the West Country, I think – with high aspirations. I understand she'd been very strictly brought up and had been desperate to get away. She was training to be a dentist. But the pregnancy put paid to that. Duncan had to marry her. I think they both resented the other for the rest of her life. He, because he didn't love her, and she because she never became a dentist, or had the life she'd planned.'

'How awful. Why did they stay together? Torturing each other?'

'People just did.'

'But was that a good idea? Surely there's more to life?'

'We all do what we think is right, I suppose.'

Annie had a vision of Dr Kaur's baby bouncing in his mother's arms, and then of her sad and teary daughter as she had last seen her in the Southwold cottage. 'It's hard to know just what *is* right though, isn't it?'

The first person she bumped into at the surgery the following morning was Jonathan. He looked tanned, and his curly hair had grown since she had last seen him. She had been preparing herself for their meeting during the whole of her early drive from Teddington. Act naturally, she said to herself, but despite her best efforts she could not persuade her heart to beat slower. It was most perverse of her, she knew, to be attracted to him now – now that he was happy and in a gay relationship. Had he always been gay? He had never, so far as she knew, had a male partner before. On the other hand, she had not heard of any female ones either – though of course he had once been married.

He looked at her somewhat warily but then smiled. 'Can I bring you in a sandwich at lunchtime – before the meeting?'

'Yes please,' she answered quickly. 'That would be lovely.'

But would it, she wondered? Only if she could act sensibly.

It was a week since Barbara Lawson had been in about her lump and her pain. She was the first patient this morning. Annie was not looking forward to confirming what – probably – this very sensible woman already knew, which was that the prognosis was poor. Typically, once the consultation started, and Annie had explained the result of her scan, Barbara made no fuss.

Annie told Jonathan about it at lunchtime, over their ciabatta sandwiches, and they talked about how hard it was to deal with terminal illness in people who were still active contributors to life.

'It's quite irrational,' she admitted, 'and please don't think I'm going crazy or anything. But yesterday, I found myself wishing that my father would die instead of Barbara. I'd never have told Edward that. He'd have winced and berated me for engaging in airy-fairy, unscientific nonsense.'

'Well, *I* know exactly what you mean. But, I suppose you have to choose who you confide that kind of stuff to. I … I remember wishing much the same about a horrid grumpy woman who kept presenting with symptom after symptom, insisting she'd got a terminal illness. She hadn't of course. But at the same time, I had a much younger patient who *was* dying, of leukaemia. She was wonderful, even though she was having to come to terms with the certainty that she wouldn't live to see her kids grow up. You can't help but feel life is unjust.'

She looked across the staff room at him, slumped in the shabby sofa, and she smiled. As he smiled back, her heart skipped a beat.

'Annie,' he murmured. 'Gareth told me you're aware of my position and that yours is somewhat different …'

She had been thinking about Barbara and was not sure she had understood. Her position. What did that mean?

'I won't,' he was saying, 'mention this again, but it won't stop us working together, will it? It doesn't make things awkward for you?'

She had no idea what he was talking about but he obviously needed reassurance. Poor Jonathan. 'Um, I ... I love working with you, Jonathan. Is that OK?'

He beamed at her. 'It's ... good,' he answered.

'So, everything's all right?'

He nodded, just as Gareth burst in, full of energy and ready for the staff meeting.

'Doesn't he look great?' Gareth pointed at Jonathan. 'Must have been sunny in Florence ... that nephew is a lucky guy.'

Annie decided to leave the men talking while she went to check her personal emails and texts before their meeting began.

Yet again, there was nothing from Alice so Annie sent another short but friendly text.

Janey had emailed her. *Just started another round of chemo. Thinking that when I get my next week off it, I'd like to get away. Any ideas?*

Annie quickly called her friend. 'My partner, Jonathan, has just come back from Florence, and had wonderful weather.'

'Mmmn. Thing is – since I met Miguel I've taken him away to the sun several times, but I can't help feeling he ought to get used to the fact that it's not warm in the UK in the winter, and learn to put up with it. But I'm desperate to have a break away because he keeps trying to drag me out house-hunting in the suburbs. I'm resisting of course because there's *no* way that's happening! So, to come back to the holiday idea, I was wondering about the cottage you had in Southwold.'

'Terrific idea! I'll email you the details. Would Miguel like it?'

'Well,' Janey answered, quite sharply, 'I bloody well hope so ... How are things with Alice?'

256

I am just so lucky with friends, Annie thought later, having also spoken about Alice to Arabella. The fact that she had nothing to report about her daughter did not seem to deter Janey or her ex sister-in-law from constantly offering advice and emotional comfort.

Of course, neither of them could fully appreciate what Annie perceived as the enormity of the situation. To them, people fell in love – not always wisely – and it either worked out or it did not. Annie knew that she was having a peculiar, and probably unreasonable, reaction to Alice's affair, but she seemed unable to alter it.

Some days later – in one of their quiet moments at the surgery – she decided to discuss the situation with Jonathan. In return, he confided in her about his frustration with his nephew, Oliver. Annie had not realised before that his young relative had no living parents.

'My sister and her husband died in a road accident when he was a baby,' Jonathan explained. 'His paternal grandparents brought him up, but since they died, I'm virtually the only family he has. I'm nothing like a parent, of course, but one has to try.'

He went on to elaborate about the Florence trip.

'I took him away with me to help him get some perspective on his current relationship. The truth is, his girlfriend's a poisonous bitch.'

Annie was completely taken aback. She had never heard her colleague express such a negative comment about anyone.

'He's just too naïve,' Jonathan continued. 'She reins him in when she hasn't got anyone else, then dumps him when someone more interesting comes on the scene. I want to shake him and make him realise that there must be better options out there.'

Annie nodded disconsolately. 'That's the sort of thing I'd tell Alice, if only she'd get in touch.'

More days passed. Routinely, each morning, Annie reached for her phone before getting out of bed, to text her daughter. When no answer came, she threw herself into her working day, then tried – without conspicuous success – to ban all thoughts of Alice from her mind.

It was November now. She had not seen her daughter since late September, and it was weeks since Lucy had taken her sister to Paris. Where was she now? It was agony not knowing her location, or state of mind.

Then, one evening when she stooped to pick up the post from her doormat, she found a handwritten letter.

She carried it through to the kitchen. The white C5 envelope of the sort that business mail often arrived in, looked like a personal note, and though it was not in Alice's handwriting, she had a strong sense that it concerned her daughter. She tore it open.

Dear Dr Templeton,

I am very sorry for the trouble I am causing you and Alice and the rest of your family. I know that Jaspal came to see you. That must have been a shock for you.

I would very much welcome the chance to meet you. I don't know if I can explain our situation, but I want to try. I am hoping Alice is in touch with you, but she was so anxious about your reaction to our love for each other that I worry she may not have been.

It is a desperate situation for everyone. Please help if you can.

Kind regards,

Tony

Annie poured herself a glass of wine. She should eat something but had no appetite. Instead, she texted Alice to tell her that she had heard from Tony. Hoping that this message would spur her daughter into replying, she watched her mobile for what seemed like ages. There was no message, so she texted Lucy.

Tony has written to me. He wants to meet. Don't see the point.
But I badly want to see Alice. Where is she? Do you know? Love,
Mum.

Lucy called back immediately, sounding worried. 'I've no idea,
Mum. I s'pose she's back in London. She left Paris after a week;
Jean-Pierre's mum was very upset about it but couldn't stop her.
As far as I know, she's not in contact with anyone. I don't under-
stand because, you know me, I, like, well, I couldn't *not* talk to
people.'

For the first time, it occurred to Annie that Alice could be so
seriously disturbed that she might kill herself. She must do something. Would seeing Tony help? He had put his mobile number
at the foot of the letter. She had absolutely no wish to be in contact
with this man, but she texted him all the same.

Tony, I'm afraid that I don't want to see you. Sorry if that sounds
rude. But I am so worried about Alice. Do you know if she is with
friends or in touch with any of them? Can you tell me where she
is? I'd been assuming she was in France but now know she isn't.
Annie Templeton.

Tony texted back immediately.

Know nothing. But she has told me she is safe and getting on with
her life. Have to believe that or would lose my mind.

Annie paced around the kitchen. Up till now, she had not actually
tried to phone Alice. But perhaps she should try.

Inevitably, her daughter's phone went to voicemail. 'Darling,'
Annie said, 'it's Mum. I know you're really suffering. I am so, so
sorry. To be honest, I was cross and upset after Dr Kaur came to
see me, but now I'm just worried sick about you. Please don't do
anything silly. Can we meet? If not, please just text and let me

259

know how you are. I know you're trying to do the right thing by not seeing Tony. As I said in my text earlier, he wants to meet me. Maybe I should agree. I love you, Alice, so much.'

Was there anything else she could do? She did not think so but she hated feeling so impotent. It was rather late to ring Janey – anyway, she and Miguel were in Southwold and it would be unfair to disturb them. Diana had returned from Corsica but she knew nothing about the Alice situation. As for Arabella, she was probably already wrapped round Martin, and having a romantic night.

More than anything, she realised, she would really like to talk to Jonathan again, but she was loath to interrupt his down-time with Gareth, even though she knew he would listen and support her.

Suddenly hungry, she decided to make a slice of cheese on toast. She had just taken a bite out of it and switched on the television to catch the end of *Newsnight* when her landline rang.

The girls rarely used that phone, generally preferring mobiles. It was almost eleven. Perhaps it was a wrong number. She let it go to the answerphone.

'Anne.' The male voice was one she knew well, but had not heard since they had agreed to have no contact other than through lawyers, and that had been more than a year ago.

'Sorry to call at this hour but I thought we should talk about Alice …'

Annie jumped up and grabbed the receiver. 'Edward,' she said. Then she stopped, unsure of how to go on.

'How are you?' he asked, rather formally.

'Fine. Good … apart from worrying about our daughter. You?'

'Excellent. You heard I'd married again and am going to have a son?'

'Yes, the girls told me. Congratulations.'

'Thanks.'

Not wanting to prolong the small talk, she asked, 'So, have you heard from Alice?'

'No, but I've been thinking ...'

'I'm so worried for her, Edward. She's totally unlike Lucy. I don't think she's ever fallen for anyone before and this is massive.'

'I agree,' he responded quietly.

'And tonight, I suddenly thought that, well, that she might kill herself.'

'Anne. Please. Alice does *not* have a hysterical personality.'

'Do you mean that I do?'

'No!' He was obviously struggling to be patient and civil. 'I didn't mean that. You're a warm and good person. Not hysterical. Not usually.'

'OK, what do we do? She can't have this man. The wife has a baby!'

'Anne, look at it from the chap's point of view. Perhaps he married, as many of us do, because all his friends were, and he thought it was time he settled down and had children.'

'Is that what happened to us?'

'Pretty much.'

'So you didn't love me then?'

'Of course I loved you.' He sounded exasperated. 'I probably even believed I was *in* love with you. But I know now, because I feel totally different about Suzie, that ... well, that there are various kinds of love. Maybe having married his wife, Tony then fell for Alice and perhaps this is the real thing for them.'

'But surely they have to get over it?'

'I'm not sure. I've checked up, and apparently Tony is a very good surgeon – and should get a consultant's job before long. He's a decent sort. Not a serial adulterer. But I gather he's had time off work for stress. The powers-that-be won't put up with that kind of thing for long. If it goes on it'll damage his career prospects.'

'Is that all you care about? His job? Because he's in orthopaedics, and that's something you understand?'

'No, but his training and expertise shouldn't be wasted.'

'What about *her* career?'

'Well, I heard she'd jacked in the orthopaedics. She should never have chosen it in the first place.'

Annie kept her voice as calm and reasonable as she could. 'Did it ever occur to you that she did it to get closer to you?'

'What? I didn't know that.'

'You didn't know lots of things,' Annie's voice was weary. 'She's been trying to please you and get your attention since she left my womb. And I know for certain that one of the things that's upset her most recently is how cock-a-hoop you are that you're having a son. She told me she found it "insulting".'

Edward went quiet. Then he announced, 'Right! I'm going to phone her. Now!'

'But I've texted her every day for weeks without success. Perhaps she's thrown her phone away, or let the battery run down.'

'I doubt that. Alice is a sensible person. People don't alter their basic characteristics, even if they're so in love they can't see straight.'

'But why should she respond to you when she hasn't replied to me?'

'Because I'm not going to be sympathetic and diffident and appeasing, like you undoubtedly have been. I'm going to demand that she thinks of you and me and Lucy, and stops behaving like a broken-hearted heroine in a tawdry novel, and bloody well gets in touch.'

'Well, *that* should work.' Annie did not bother to disguise the contempt and sarcasm in her voice.

He ignored her. 'What I'm also going to do is to give her my blessing.'

'For what?'

'I'm going to tell her that if she really loves him and he loves her, I think they should be together – and marry, if they want to. I'd never have done such a thing before I met Suzie.'

'That really changed everything for you, didn't it?' Annie's tone was full of wonder.

'It did,' he replied.

There was a warmth and pride in his voice that was hard to reconcile with her memories of the man to whom she had once been wed.

'As you say, probably I haven't been the best father to the girls, but knowing what I know now, I want them to experience true love. And if this is Alice's main chance, I want her to grab it.'

Chapter Fourteen

Waiting for Prue to emerge from the Ladies, Annie rummaged in her bag for her mobile phone and switched it on. As it bubbled into life, she scrolled through her texts, searching for the one from Alice, which had arrived the night that Edward had phoned her.

Immediately after that conversation, and true to his word, her ex-husband had left a message on their daughter's voicemail. Clearly, his unvarnished words had spurred her into action.

Annie's relief at hearing from Alice had been overwhelming. Perversely, she had been almost equally relieved that Edward had not managed to persuade their child to actually talk to him. It would have been infuriating had he scored even greater success with his first intervention.

She reread the text – for at least the hundredth time:

Sorry. Didn't mean to be selfish or worry you both. Just so unsure what to do. Am in Bristol. PLEASE don't come here. Staying with old friend. Doing locum shifts in A & E. Am not suicidal. Just very, very sad. Wish I could wake up to find I have no feelings for Tony. But I don't think this will ever happen. Love, Ally

Looking up, she noticed that the crowds leaving the Opera House were thinning out, and that Prue was standing on the slope below the box office, looking around for her.

'Sorry,' Annie apologised. 'I'm pathetically rereading Alice's text. It's a bit like my security blanket!'

Prue squeezed her arm fondly.

'Thanks,' said Annie. 'And for bringing me here tonight. It's great that you're a ballet-nut too!'

'I know!' agreed Prue as the two women walked towards the Bow Street exit. 'What a pity we didn't know each other better in Edinburgh. Mind you, I don't remember dance being much on offer at the time.'

'No. Anyway, you never did anything but study!'

'I was a terrible swot. If I could wind back the clock, and give my younger self some advice, I'd definitely tell her to get out more.'

Annie laughed. 'Still, your single-mindedness took you a long way!'

'Perhaps.' Prue looked pensive. 'But I'm pleased to have learned some sense, and to lead a more balanced life these days. A night like this is priceless, isn't it? Thank heavens that one of Jumbo's last acts in life was to bring us together.'

'We should have toasted him over dinner. Do you want to get a drink now, before we go our separate ways?'

'To be honest,' Prue glanced at her watch, 'I don't. I have to be up at six.'

'Me too.'

'Have you got to get back to do a surgery?'

'No, it's my day off. But I'm meeting Tony – Alice's lover – at seven, before he starts work!'

'How do you feel about that?'

'Nervous. But I expect he's feeling worse.'

Annie stayed overnight at her medical club, and the following morning it was just a short walk to the café where she and Tony had elected to meet.

Hovering outside, she peered through the windows. A lot of tired-looking people were sitting hunched over large cups of coffee, fiddling with their phones or tablets.

The only customer not thus engrossed was a thin, pale, fair-haired man, who was staring into space out of eyes circled by deep, panda-like shadows.

She headed towards him. He jumped up to welcome her, somehow managing at the same time to spill most of his hot drink on to the table. In a flurry of apologies and amid much mopping up, he insisted on going to the counter to buy coffee for them both.

'Anything to eat?' he asked, eager to please.

She shook her head. How anxious he was – and how young; despite his pallor and obvious stress, he was boyish for thirty-five. It was hard to imagine him commanding authority in the brutal, demanding world of orthopaedics.

'Thanks for coming,' he started, as soon as he returned with cappuccinos for them both. 'I'm sure you hate me, and hate what I've done to Alice.'

'She's a grown-up, Tony. It must have been *her* idea to inveigle me into letting her use my father's house, under the pretext of cleaning it up.'

'She did clean it up, though. Really efficiently,' he protested.

'I'm sure you helped.'

'Well …'

'You both did a great job. But what I'm upset about is that I was used.'

Tony sighed. 'I'm sure that's my fault. We had to find somewhere … anonymous. Jaspal was away visiting her parents with my son and obviously it would have been unthinkable for Alice to come to our house. I know you think we shouldn't have given in to the feelings we have for each other. But they were overwhelming.'

His eyes filled with tears as he went on to describe how he had felt his pulse quicken the first day that Alice had joined the Department – and how he had fought against his emotions. He described her as beautiful, petite, angelic, diligent, super-bright … Annie wondered when he was going to complete his list of compliments, but he seemed to have an inexhaustible supply of them.

Eventually, she intervened. 'I think I've got the picture, Tony.'

'I don't want you to think that I'm praising Alice to try to make you like me.'

Annie had come to this meeting ready to do battle, and also to state unequivocally that what the pair of them had done to Jaspal and their baby was wrong. However, she found herself saying, 'I don't dislike you, Tony. I don't know you, but I'm sure that normally you're a good and nice man. And I don't think for one moment that you're trying to humour me by praising my daughter. I believe you really love her. But that's not the point.'

'It's the *whole* point,' he exploded. Then he blew his nose noisily, and attempted to compose himself. 'She is my very soul. I need her to complete me. Life without her is torture.'

'You're far too poetic to be an orthopaedic surgeon. Are you sure you're in the right specialty?'

'I'm sure,' he replied firmly.

'Sorry,' she muttered. 'I was being flippant.'

He looked confused.

'Don't forget,' Annie continued, 'I was married to an orthopod for decades and he wasn't known for his poetic side. Well, not till he left *me*! I suppose one of my concerns is that – despite your endless stream of compliments about Alice – you probably felt just as strongly for Jaspal not so long ago.'

'I can see how you would think that, but I didn't.' Tony nervously swept his rather floppy hair out of his eyes with his right hand, then sat forward in his chair. 'That's what I want to tell you. That's what's important and it's why I believe – hope – that one day Alice and I can be together.'

'Are you living with Jaspal and your little boy at the moment?'

He nodded.

'How's that going?'

He gazed at the table. 'Really awful,' he muttered.

'I don't suppose you're trying very hard to make it work.'

She saw him grimace. 'I suppose I deserve that,' he murmured, refusing still to meet Annie's eye. 'But I *have* tried, actually. I've tried to be at home more for my son, and to provide the security for him that any father should give his child. I've even tried to have sex with Jaspal, but we've both agreed that it's not working, and I am therefore sleeping – or rather *not* sleeping – in the spare room.'

'It sounds pretty hopeless,' Annie conceded.

He lifted his head and gazed at her. 'I don't expect sympathy. More coffee?'

She stood up. 'I'm going to get them. And I'm buying you something to eat. You look as if you're going to pass out.'

As she queued for their drinks she realised that it was impossible to be angry with this young man. What had happened to him and Alice was obviously huge for them both. But that did not make it right.

'Eat that,' she ordered as she returned and placed a fruit salad and a large croissant and jam in front of him. 'I'm just thinking of the Health Service, you understand. They need good surgeons, and the way you're going, you're likely to be off work for months with an ulcer or severe anxiety, or both.'

He gazed at her as she retook her seat. His hair was in his eyes again, but – squinting through it – he was obviously trying to assess what her mood was. She could see him daring to hope that she was being kind to him. Against her better judgement, she smiled.

Visibly encouraged, he embarked on the story of how he had come to be married to Jaspal.

During their student days they had lived in the same shared student house. There had been four boys and two girls. Three were originally from the Indian sub-continent, one was Canadian, one Ghanaian – and the sixth was Tony.

'We were a diverse group. Jaspal's parents were rich, and so were the family of the other girl. The rest of us came from relatively humble homes. I had no religious faith, neither did a couple of the others, but Jaspal kept up the appearance of adhering to Sikhism, and one guy was a devout Moslem and the Canadian chap was a Catholic. But we all got on well.'

Tony went on to describe how Jaspal's father – despite being of a liberal persuasion – had hoped that she might marry a Sikh.

'She would disappear at weekends to meet men who had been approved by her parents. She used to call it "Husband Shopping"! She wasn't averse to the idea. I think she believed it was a good way to find the right partner.'

As it had turned out, Jaspal had been much too independent for the taste of many of her suitors. And out of the potential partners who had been prepared to 'put up with' her career and ambition, there was none she was partial to.

Her father had not given up hope of a match, but he had not pressed her either. And as time wore on, and she qualified and – like all junior doctors – spent a couple of years working so many hours that any social life was out of the question, the subject of an arranged marriage was quietly dropped.

She had not seemed concerned about settling down, being a ferociously ambitious woman, intent on working hard and enjoying her interesting group of friends.

'Apart from our racial differences, we were really alike,' Tony said. 'I'd had few girlfriends. I was very focused on my career. Hopeless at sport, except cricket. I was definitely the product of a minor public school, and a late starter sexually. She was modest and had been quite strictly brought up. We used to joke that if we got to forty and neither of us had found anyone, we might set up home together.'

'But neither of you is forty yet.'

'True,' he agreed. 'What no one could have foreseen was that Jaspal would wake up on her thirty-fourth birthday and feel broody.

So we sort of brought forward our plans and tried sharing a bed occasionally.'

'And how did things go?'

'We used to say we were just practising – to see if a marriage between us might work. The sex wasn't great, but of course she had no experience at all, and I had *practically* none, so I just thought it would get better. Of course, as you know, she's a beautiful woman – frankly, right out of my league – but the odd thing was that she wasn't aware of that. We used condoms to start with, but then she went on the Pill. She only took it for a short time. She said it didn't suit her, but I think she just wanted a baby – and that's the reason she stopped it.'

'Do you mean you were tricked into marrying her?'

'No! We were good friends and we'd always planned that we might end up together – though I'd have preferred not to have had a child so early in the scheme of things. But I wasn't unduly upset when she became pregnant. I suppose I thought that no one else might ever want me. And her family were remarkably good about everything. We had a big wedding … very colourful … I was carried along with it. Also, her parents insisted on buying us a terrific house in Islington. Then Bahir was born and I was very taken with fatherhood. To be honest, I thought I was happy. Everything might have been fine – but Alice turned up in February this year, and by April, I was completely besotted.'

He paused and took a large gulp of coffee before continuing.

'I'm sure Alice tried to suppress her feelings just as I did. There was a time when she seemed determined to make herself as unattractive as possible. She had her hair cut so short she was almost bald and she wore baggy clothes.'

'I remember,' Annie murmured, as a vision of her older daughter at Lucy's twenty-first birthday came to mind.

Tony's own memories made his eyes moisten again. 'It didn't work though,' he whispered. 'She was still lovely.'

'I'm assuming that Jaspal doesn't want you to leave her?'

'No. And Alice is hell-bent on forgetting me. She says we'll never be happy because we're upsetting so many people. Since she visited you in Suffolk, I've only seen her once. That's why I wanted to meet you. I'm hoping you'll tell her you understand, and that you're not cross with her. It might not make a difference immediately – especially while Jaspal is set on keeping the marriage going – but it might in the end. And I will wait. For as long as it takes.'

Annie emerged from her deep muscle massage. She felt strangely lightheaded as she rejoined Arabella, who was stretched out in an isolated area of the spa at The Corinthia, sipping green tea with honey.

'This is the most marvellous treat. Thank you.'

'Think nothing of it.' Arabella looked amused at Annie's dreamily vague appearance. 'I'd been to this hotel to various events and launches, and one day I had some spare time and decided to take a look at their spa. And I was hooked! Don't you just love it? I've been dying to get you here.'

'It's wonderful,' Annie whispered, as she took in the black marbled walls and the floor lighting. 'It feels so luxurious. I normally never come to places like this. I worry that I'll find them intimidating, and won't know what to do!'

Arabella hooted with laughter, then swiftly clasped her hand over her mouth.

'It's awfully quiet, isn't it?' she mouthed. 'Bit like being in a cathedral.'

Annie smiled and nodded as, by unspoken consent, they stretched out for a while until Arabella suggested they had facials.

'No, you go,' Annie urged her. 'I won't bother; I'm really tired. Usually, I've seen fifteen patients by this point in the morning, and today all I've done is meet Tony. But I'm exhausted.'

'Well, family affairs are always more draining than work!' Arabella remarked airily as she set off for the treatment room.

271

Later, they ordered coffee, before swimming in the pool and then ending their visit with ten minutes in the steam room.

Upstairs, as they lunched in one of the hotel's restaurants, the tranquil atmosphere they had enjoyed all morning seemed to cling to them like an invisible mist, and they were less chatty than usual.

'I think,' Arabella ventured after a long period of silence, 'that Martin comes here for lunch sometimes. It's so near the House.'

'I'm not surprised. The food's marvellous, isn't it?'

Arabella nodded enthusiastically as she savoured a mouthful of scallops in walnut sauce.

Annie took a sip of mineral water. 'Is everything still going well?'

'Better than that.' Arabella smiled at her. 'It's wonderful. His divorce will be through in January, and then we'll get married. *Very* quietly.'

Annie raised her eyebrows, as she looked at her friend. 'Oh, yeah?'

'You can mock,' laughed Arabella. 'But that's what we want. *You* must come of course. On the subject of weddings, do tell me more about meeting Alice's boyfriend.'

'Talk about the moral maze! I now don't know what to think. But I'm going to text Alice and tell her that I like Tony and that I'm not cross with her. Other than that, I suppose I just have to let them sort it, if they can.'

Feeling very lazy, she took a bus from Whitehall to Oxford Street. She had no real deadlines for the rest of the day, apart from meeting Janey for tea at the medical club.

Once there, she installed herself in the café and read the papers before flicking through her texts, just in case Alice had contacted her. There was a new message, but it was from Tony, thanking her for meeting him earlier. She certainly could not fault his manners.

'So, what was he like?' Janey burst in and threw herself down in the seat opposite Annie. She was well-wrapped up against the cold and foggy weather, but she swiftly divested herself of her outer garments, except for her large and stylish hat. Her energy seemed to fill the space all around her, just as it had before her illness.

Annie ordered tea and scones, and then turned to Janey to say how enormously pleased she was to see her looking so buoyant.

Her friend interrupted her. 'Don't keep me in suspense, Annie. Was he nice or not? Hot? Brainy? Good enough for Alice? *Tell* me!'

So she did.

'Well, his wife sounds a total bitch,' Janey announced as she poured herself a second cup of tea.

'I'm sure she's not. I mean, as Tony said, if he had never met Alice, he might have had a pleasant and companionable marriage. He wasn't frogmarched into matrimony. But he was obviously naïve and inexperienced in relationships, just like Alice. Actually, something Prue said last night kept coming to mind today. She said that if she could go back in time and advise her younger self, she would tell her to get out more, and that's just what I used to wish for Ally. I'm sure I've said to you repeatedly that I wished she had a man in her life … I wished she had more fun …'

'Yeah, well,' Janey's voice took on a sardonic tone. 'You have to be careful what you wish for. Do you think I'm getting fat?' Without waiting for an answer she helped herself to a second scone, split it open and covered it in raspberry jam and cream.

Annie shook her head. 'No, I think you're just catching up after months of being poorly, and far, far too thin.'

'That's all right then, particularly because it looks like I might have a new telly job. Imagine – after all this time!'

'What is it?'

'I can't tell you, in case I jinx it. You know me, I'm nervous till I've signed anything, but I have you to thank for it. It's come through your lovely young producer from the Channel 4 programme. She recommended me. Good, eh?'

'Very!'

Looking at Janey's hat, Annie wondered how soon the television job would start. She poured more tea for them both and then, as casually as she could, asked for a progress report on her friend's hair.

'Oh, I'm completely bald now and the wig itches. So it's easier just to wear hats.'

Annie reached for her friend's hand. 'I'm sorry.'

'Don't be! I'm alive, I'm doing well. I've probably only got one more round of chemo to go. I've got career plans. And if the telly thing becomes definite, I'll invest in a really *expensive* wig. It'll be fine!'

Annie laughed, her heart full of gladness for the positivity that was Janey. 'And what about Miguel?'

Janey rolled her eyes. 'I think that the generation gap is beginning to widen. For one thing, he *hated* Southwold. My idea of long walks, watching the stormy waves, afternoons in chintzy tea shops and lots of reading didn't appeal to him one bit. Even the lovely Adnams pubs failed to hit the spot.' She sighed. 'He was grumpy the whole week.'

'Maybe you should have gone somewhere warmer.'

Janey shook her head. 'I don't agree. I've been thinking – and I've decided that if we're going to stay together he needs to understand what's important to me, and that includes pottering about in the UK. More importantly, he just doesn't get how I feel about London. I keep remembering how, when I was a kid, I used to watch old films on the telly on Sunday afternoons. My favourite was *Passport to Pimlico*. And when I moved from Hertfordshire to London and found that there really *was* a place called Pimlico, I was thrilled! Then, years later, when I could actually afford to buy a flat there, I thought I'd died and gone to heaven. I still think it was my greatest achievement!' Janey laughed, but Annie could see from the set of her jaw just how serious she was.

Annie smiled at her friend. 'This city has been your most enduring love affair.'

'Exactly! So, I won't be moving. By the way, what are you doing for Christmas?'

'Christmas?'

'Yes, Christmas! You know. It happens every year!'

'I haven't thought.'

'Well, it's a month today.'

Annie frowned. 'Gosh! I suppose it is.'

'Look, you old tart, what I'm trying to ask you – not very subtly – is if I can spend it with you?'

'Of course you can. I … I need to start thinking … My dad obviously won't come this year. I ought to see him but, well, maybe Boxing Day. And Lucy said, ages ago, she was bringing Jean-Pierre. I don't know about Alice. Perhaps I should have a drinks party on Christmas Eve like I used to in the "Edward-Era". Anyway, yes please *do* come. Will you bring Miguel?'

'No. He's going home to Spain. And his mother won't be happy if I turn up as there's some senorita she's been wanting him to marry since he was four. But I'd love to come to you. Could you bear it?'

Annie reached across and gave her friend a huge hug.

Janey looked quite pink for a moment and slightly tearful. It was unlike her to be emotional.

'I can't tell you how much I'd love it,' Annie reassured her.

Janey smiled. 'Lovely. Well, better go – do you mind? Got a piece to write.' And so saying she pulled on her various layers of outdoor clothing, kissed Annie on both cheeks, and was gone.

Christmas … just a month away …

Still thinking about it, Annie wandered up to the counter to pay the bill and then made her way to the luggage room, where she collected her overnight bag and started to trundle it to the exit.

'Sorry,' she apologised, as she almost collided with an elegant woman in a beaded gold dress, who was talking animatedly to her male companion.

275

Their eyes met. 'Dr Kaur!'

Jaspal hesitated before giving the man a little push and suggesting he went into the bar without her. The two women stood facing each other, awkwardly. Neither of them spoke.

Despite feeling suddenly middle-aged and distinctly provincial beside the striking younger woman, Annie recognised that it was up to her to take charge.

'You look wonderful,' she said as she grasped Jaspal's hand and led her to a seated area. 'And, very much more on top of things than your husband.'

Jaspal nodded. 'He said he was seeing you. Did he tell you that I tricked him into marriage?'

'Not at all! That's absolutely not how he presented it. Obviously, he's in the wrong, so is Alice, but I've no doubt that they're very remorseful that they've hurt people. And, of course, they're devastated at being apart.'

'Mmmn. Even so, I bet that now you know the whole story you've got less sympathy for me than you had. Still, I think we might have made a good team, had your daughter not come on the scene. What are we to do? That's the point.'

'What *can* you do? You have a small son. Presumably, you want to co-parent him and stay married?'

Jaspal gave a little shudder as if she was cold. 'I thought so, but I'm beginning to realise that Tony and I can never get back what we used to have. Interestingly, my parents – whom I'd assumed would tell me I must lie in the bed I'd made for myself – have said no such thing. So ...' She took a deep breath and stood up. 'Sorry. I have a dinner with colleagues.'

Annie rose to her feet too. 'And I must catch my train.'

Jaspal's expression softened. 'I know you're sorry for me. But you don't have to be.'

A number of young doctors, dressed for an evening function, crowded in through the main door to the building, bringing in a blast of freezing air with them. They were quick to notice Jaspal.

One of them detached himself from the others and tried to drag her away from Annie. 'Come on. This is drinking time!'

Jaspal looked somewhat apologetic, but allowed herself to be swallowed up by the good-natured group. Annie gave a little wave but knew that the younger woman had not seen it.

On the train home, she finally tapped out the text message she had been composing all day.

Dear Alice. I met Tony. I can see why you love him, and also how you would be good together. He wants me to tell you that I'm not cross with you. I'm happy to do that. When I first heard, I admit that I was disappointed in you because you have always been so fair and decent. But I've heard the whole story now. I know you don't want my advice, and to tell you the truth, I have none to offer. All I can say is that if you and Tony and Jaspal can work this out so that you and Tony can be together, then I will be overjoyed for you. Much love, Mum. x

Would she really be 'overjoyed', she wondered as she put her mobile away in her bag? She breathed deeply and then pressed the fingers of both hands on to her forehead and massaged it for a moment in a bid to soothe the headache that had been nagging at her for most of the day. It was difficult to work out exactly what she did feel.

Opening the *Evening Standard*, she skim-read the news, and then rooted around in her handbag for a ballpoint so that she could tackle the Codeword. Most unusually, she failed to make any headway with it.

The train was crowded with commuters even though it was past eight o'clock. Most were wearing large headphones and appeared to be absorbed in their laptops or tablets – watching TV programmes or films or playing games. The only noise came from a nearby passenger who was loudly – and very irritatingly – discussing a business deal on her mobile phone.

As the train slowed down for its first stop, the young man sitting opposite her raced to the door, opened it, and stepped on to the platform, waving wildly. He jumped back into the train and was quickly joined by a pretty fair-haired woman who fell through the doorway, giggling, before reaching up on tiptoe to kiss him.

He seated her beside him and helped her remove her coat. Then, from his bag, he pulled a sandwich which they shared. They were wearing matching wedding rings. Perhaps they were newly-weds; they seemed so delighted with each other, and they could hardly be sitting closer together. There was only one way this particular evening was going to end for them, Annie decided, feeling a smidgeon of envy.

She tried not to stare, but somehow they seemed, in her imagination, to take on the personae of Alice and Tony – listening to each other's account of the day, planning their evening, desperate to get naked together, and brimful with joy at simply being on the same planet as each other at the same time.

She felt a pang of yearning for Jonathan; if only his orientation were different and he could be attracted to her. Greg had shown her that she was capable of great passion, and Henry had demonstrated that she could enjoy sex in a less frenetic and friendly way. But what she craved now was to have love, desire, friendship and companionship, all served up in the shape of one special individual.

She had never had that mix of delights with Edward. She was never going to have it with Jonathan. And maybe she would run out of time and never, ever find it.

The young pair were leaning against each other now, with their eyes closed. They looked comfortable and complete.

Would Jaspal, she asked herself, ever decide that she wanted to end her marriage? Had she perhaps begun to think that way? She was not only clever, but obviously popular. Life with Tony, as he had become, could not be any fun. She was a beautiful woman and certain to attract more admirers. Surely, it was not impossible that she might find someone new.

Remembering her own mother, Annie mulled over the question of whether an uneasy marriage was a suitable place in which to bring up a child.

Her phone vibrated, interrupting her deliberations.

'Darling!' It was Arabella, who told her that her television hospital drama was going to be screened in the new year, and that she had to go to Bristol to do a last-minute sound recording for it, sometime before Christmas.

'And, talking of Christmas,' Arabella went on, 'Martin and I are going to his constituency house for the holiday – which is a bit daunting for me. But as the divorce is nearly through, it's time I met people there. So, are you doing your drinks thingy that you always used to do, because we could come to it on our way to Norfolk?'

'You're the second person today to ask me about Christmas.'

'Well, it is the twenty-fifth of November!'

'That's what she said too! OK – I *will* have a party, on the 24th. I'm not sure I'll know what to say to your beloved though. I've never met a …' She lowered her voice, '… Home Secretary before!'

'Oh, you'll be fine. He's a pussycat. But one thing that always goes down well is to tell him he looks like Nigel Havers. He loves that. Ooh, now, the other thing is this; while I'm in Bristol, I'm going to find Alice.'

'No! Arabella, I don't think …'

'Annie, I'm not asking you, I'm telling you. Someone needs to sit down and talk to her, and if I'm going to be in the same city, I figure it should be me. I don't think she'll be hard to find. Chances are her locum shifts are at the Bristol Royal Infirmary. I've had a look on Google. I don't think there's anywhere else she *could* be. She's my niece, and I love her. I worry sometimes that I may have tended to favour Lucy because she's so easy to get on with. But I really feel for Alice and this is something I can do. I'll let you know how I get on and I'll see you at Christmas. Can't wait!'

The following morning, Annie was sorting the post in the reception area of the health centre – wondering, at the same time, what she should buy her daughters this year. Now that she had begun to focus on Christmas, she realised that everyone seemed to be talking about it. She was vaguely aware that Carole was drawing up the holiday roster and that her receptionist colleague seemed to be compiling a guest list for a party.

She felt her phone throb in her pocket.

The call was from Marianne. 'Annie, I'm thinking about Christmas.'

'You too? Everyone seems to be at it this morning!'

Marianne laughed. 'I wondered what your plans were with Duncan, and whether you'd mind if I visited him on Christmas morning? You know, in all the years we've been together, I've never seen him on the day itself. He's always been with you. But I don't want to butt in …'

Annie interrupted her. 'That would be perfect, but won't your husband miss you? It must be a vicar's busiest day of the year.'

'That's the point really.' There was a hint of sadness in the other woman's voice. 'It's service after service after service. I don't think he ever gives me a thought till he walks through the front door about three in the afternoon, ravenous, and exhausted.'

'Oh … Well, do visit Dad. That will help me, actually. I'll go on Boxing Day.'

'Thanks, Annie. Sorry to interrupt. I expect you're working.'

'Yes, better go.'

She gathered up the sorted post, put it on Carole's desk, and was about to leave when she realised that her practice manager and the other receptionist were still talking about parties. Carole was saying: 'Of course, Dr Margaret will probably have strong ideas about who should be there.'

'What was that about Margaret?' she asked. 'Did I miss something when I was in London?'

'Oh …' Carole looked up. 'Yeah – Gareth met her in the street yesterday, and he came back and said we ought to have a proper send-off for her. So I rang to find out if she'd like a farewell party, and she would. So that's one more thing we've got to organise in this department.'

'When is it?'

'On the nineteenth. Of course none of us has got anything else to do!'

'Are we inviting any of her patients?'

'Absolutely not!' Carole was emphatic. 'Let's keep it simple. Just us, plus some of the doctors she knows from Addenbrooke's and other general practices. And maybe a couple of the physios she used to refer people to.'

Annie nodded. 'OK, look – if you'll do the invites and get the place looking reasonable, I'll order the food from Waitrose, and ask Gareth and Jonathan to organise the drinks.'

'*Would* you? That would be a help. I think Gareth just thought it would all miraculously happen.'

Annie laughed as she headed off to start her surgery. She washed her hands thoroughly and was just about to call in her first patient when Carole rushed into the consulting room.

'Sorry – I've got Dr Margaret on the phone. She's the bloody limit. She now wants to know if a party would cost as much as …' Carole looked down at a scribble on a bit of paper, '… a pair of Meindl Burma walking boots and if it would, she'd sooner have them instead!'

Annie quickly tapped the brand name into Google. 'Here we go … They're about £170. Oh what the hell … tell the old bat that she can have shoes as well as a party. It'll be such a relief to get rid of her. Don't tell her *that* of course!'

The staff room had never looked so tidy. The sagging sofas had been removed, the table at the far end was covered in Christmas paper, and on it stood bottles of Merlot and Prosecco, elderflower pressé and sparkling water. Most of the canapés had been eaten, but there was still plenty of Christmas cake and Stollen.

The party crowd was thinning out as people began to drift away, but as yet there was no sign of the guest of honour. However, her Meindl Burma shoes were on a plinth, which Gareth had brought in for a joke, placed in the centre of the room for all to admire.

'That was a masterstroke,' Annie murmured to Jonathan, nodding towards them. 'It's like when Roy Hattersley failed to turn up for *Have I Got News for You* and they replaced him with a tub of lard!'

Jonathan grinned. 'Will she deign to look in at all, do you think? It's a bit bizarre, even for her, not to turn up for her leaving do.'

'Who knows? She might still come. She's only an hour and a half late!'

Annie surveyed the room. Everyone seemed to be drinking, laughing and chatting. Many of the guests – and staff – had imbibed freely. Carole in particular had become quite loud in the last half hour. Annie exchanged amused glances with Gareth as they both watched her drape herself around a young doctor who occasionally did locums for them.

'I think,' Annie murmured to Jonathan, 'that I've now talked to every single guest, so I feel my duty's done.'

'Mine too. Let's sit down.' He indicated two empty chairs at the far end of the room. She followed his gaze and walked towards them.

He glanced at her glass. 'Do you want more elderflower?'

She shook her head. 'There's only so much one can have before it seems rather sickly.'

'I know. It's usually me drinking it, but I decided to leave my car here tonight and have wine for a change. I thought booze would fortify me for dealing with Mad Margaret!'

'Have another one then,' Annie jumped up and reached for a half-empty bottle. 'I suppose Gareth won't be driving either?'

'Definitely not. Anyway, I'm pretty sure he plans to make a night of it. I think he's off clubbing later.'

'Oh! Are you going too?'

She noticed that he looked slightly bewildered. 'Me? No.'

'You're still happy together though aren't you? You always seem to be getting on brilliantly. I hope it's … you know … nice for you …'

'To have a lodger you mean?'

'Uh … yes. But, I mean, well … you and Gareth are … together aren't you?'

'*Together*?' Jonathan stared at her. 'I don't … Oh! Annie … You don't mean that you think that Gareth and I are in a relationship?'

'Um …'

'*Me*, of all people? How could you have thought that?'

'All sorts of reasons.' She could feel herself blushing. 'I mean you were so keen to redecorate your house for him. Then that day he fell off the ladder, you were in a terrible state – ashen-faced.'

'I'm not surprised. I owned the most rickety wooden stepladder in the world, which I should have thrown out years ago, and I thought I'd killed him. But I'm not gay. I can't believe you would think … not that I've got anything against … oh heavens. In actual fact, for ages, I've been trying to tell you …'

'Dr Williams! Where's Dr Williams?' Carole's teenage daughter who was helping out for the afternoon was rushing around the room trying to find him.

'No! Not now,' Jonathan groaned under his breath, before reluctantly putting up his hand to indicate where he was.

'There's a call for you,' the girl said. 'Urgent.'

'All calls are supposed to be switched through to the out-of-hours service.'

'It's personal, Doctor – your nephew.'

Jonathan threw Annie an apologetically despairing glance before disappearing out of the room.

He isn't gay. He *really* isn't gay. He is … not … gay.

Annie's heart was thumping in her chest. What had he meant when he had said that there was something he had been trying to tell her for ages?

She topped up her glass with sparkling water and gave into an impulse to eat a sizeable slice of Christmas cake, but after that, Jonathan still had not returned. What on earth was going on with that nephew of his?

She meandered over to where Gareth was standing. Perhaps she could glean something from him. He was recounting a complicated joke, so she stood on the edge of his circle, watching him. Suddenly, she felt a pull at her elbow.

'Annie,' Jonathan said. 'I'm going to have to go. I've got a taxi coming. Can you walk with me to the main door so we can talk while I wait for it? Oliver's taken his awful girlfriend to Jamaica. *This* time of year! Must be costing him a fortune, which he hasn't got.'

'I'm so sorry.' She tried to soothe him. 'But maybe they'll sort things out once and for all.'

He sighed heavily. 'They're getting *married*! On the beach. The day after tomorrow.'

'Oh, my God.'

'I know. I've got a travel agent trying to find me a flight. I've got to get there somehow. Maybe I can talk him out of it. But if not, well, I should be at his wedding. I'm the nearest thing to a parent that he has.'

'Of course you must go. Gareth and I will cover for you. And you could stay on and have a lovely Caribbean holiday,' she suggested brightly, trying hard to stem a sense of crushing disappointment. She wanted him here. She wanted to find out …

'No,' he contradicted her. 'I'll come straight back, assuming I can get a flight. I want to be here and I want to come to your party on Christmas Eve.'

Feeling hopeful, but also unsure, she asked, 'You know that day in the staff room, when you were talking about me helping with your interior decoration, what were you trying to say? I thought

284

you were telling me that you and Gareth were in a relationship.'

'I realise that now. And it's all my fault. I was a bit like a youth in a chemist shop who really wants condoms, but who keeps coming home with combs!'

Annie giggled, and her heart seemed to give a little jump in her chest.

'Gareth was living in pretty dismal and noisy accommodation,' he explained. 'So I invited him to lodge in my house – to give him some company and also to support him while he explored his … well … you know … inclinations.'

'That was very nice of you,' she beamed at him.

He shrugged. 'Anyway, I think it's worked. He's recently met someone.'

Annie felt her smile widen. 'How marvellous. But later, when Gareth asked me if I understood about what you'd been trying to tell me … about feelings … I assumed he meant about you and him. So, what was that about?'

A taxi slewed to a halt outside. Jonathan opened the door as the driver jumped out of his cab and ran towards him. 'Dr Williams!' he barked.

'Yes,' Jonathan answered. 'But I need a moment. I have to tell this lady something.'

'Sorry, got to get on, mate!' The driver was not in a mood to be delayed. He walked back to his car and jumped in. 'I've got another three jobs to be done in the next half an hour. The city's practically gridlocked. I'm running so late …'

The two doctors walked towards the taxi. 'I'll come back as soon as I can,' murmured Jonathan. Quickly, he leaned over and gave her a light kiss on her right cheek; then he climbed into the cab and opened the window before pulling the door shut. The driver revved the engine impatiently, almost drowning Jonathan's words. 'We'll talk … soon …'

She nodded, and raised her own voice, 'And will you tell me then what Gareth meant?'

As the driver executed a speedy three-point turn with much screeching of brakes, Jonathan leaned out of the window. The taxi hovered at the entrance of their small car park, the cabbie edging forward impatiently, eager to join the passing stream of traffic. She saw another motorist give way. Jonathan was shouting to her, as the vehicle turned into the road: 'Gareth was just checking whether …'

But he had disappeared – along with the end of his sentence.

Chapter Fifteen

Annie padded into her sitting room, shut the door behind her and sank into a sofa, nursing a mug of strong tea. The daylight was long gone on this crisp and cold Christmas Eve, but the twinkling lights on the tree provided a sliver of illumination.

She had done a morning surgery, and then come home to prepare for her party. Now all that needed to happen was for Sue and Maggie – two local women who ran a small catering business – to come and serve drinks and food to the guests, who should start arriving in about an hour.

Last year, she had had no inclination to host her annual gathering. In fact the whole of Christmas had been a dilute affair, what with her father's vagueness and her own misery. But this year, she was excited; excited but apprehensive.

She had not been in touch with Jonathan during his absence, though she was aware that his plane had been scheduled to arrive at Heathrow earlier. It could, of course, have been delayed. Then there was the journey from London to Cambridge to contend with. Doubtless, he would be exhausted. There had to be a strong possibility that he would not turn up.

Still, Alice was coming. And that was more than she would have dared to hope for a few weeks ago.

Everything seemed to have moved on because of Arabella. Whatever she had said when she had gone to Bristol and sought out Alice, had persuaded Alice to stop hiding away, and to return to London and talk to Jaspal, who had been surprisingly civil to her.

After that meeting, Alice had phoned Annie. 'I was so nervous, Mum. But Jaspal was OK – though she obviously thinks I'm terribly ordinary, and can't understand what Tony sees in me.'

'I'm sure that's not true.'

'You're biased! Trust me, she thought I was seriously unimpressive. Still, she's so stunning, isn't she? I'd met her once before, but I'd forgotten how gorgeous she is. Tony always said that she was only interested in work, not men. But she kind of looks like she's up for new adventures now.'

Ten days later, Alice had rung again to say that Jaspal had packed up Tony's belongings and demanded that he leave their house.

As far as Annie knew, no agreement had been reached about divorce, or about access to baby Bahir. Personally, she could not understand how Tony could have moved from the family home without first ensuring that he would be able to see his son, but she had kept those views to herself.

Annie finished her tea, and then sat, savouring the silence and inhaling the fragrance of the Christmas tree. She loved seasonal smells ... satsumas, turkey, mulled wine ...

'Mum!'

The sitting room lights flashed on. Annie jumped.

'What were you doing in the dark? You're not getting all morbid are you?'

Annie reached out an arm and hugged Lucy to her. 'Not at all. I was only catching my breath for a few minutes. I'm about to get ready. Is this you just getting up? It's way past six ...'

'Yeah.' Lucy glanced down at her pyjamas with a shrug of embarrassment. 'Sorry. I think last night when we arrived I said I would help today.'

Annie grinned. 'I didn't take you seriously! I'm sure that you and Jean-Pierre were exhausted after your journey back from Paris.'

Lucy laughed. 'Yeah. God, the whole world seemed to be on that Eurostar! And then the train to Cambridge was, like, so crowded, we had to stand all the way back. Of course, we then had lots of sex in the night, so we're even more knackered now! Did you hear us?'

'I tried not to! Where's lover boy now?'

'In the shower. He'll be down soon. Mum, is Auntie Bella really bringing the Home Secretary tonight?'

'Of course. He'll be marrying into the family soon.'

'Cool! You don't, like, mind about me and Alice and our boyfriends going to stay with Dad tonight, do you? We'll be back after tomorrow's lunch.'

Annie paused before answering. 'If I'm honest, I *partly* mind. But he's your father. Of course you want to see him, and he wants to see you …' The doorbell rang. She sprang to her feet. 'Oh, no …'

Lucy pushed her towards the stairs. 'Go and get ready,' she urged. 'I'll deal with everything.'

Annie tried to object. 'Darling, you're still in your pyjamas.'

'I'm quite decent. Go!'

Lucy waited till her mother had run up the stairs, and then threw open the front door.

From the landing, Annie could hear her daughter chatting to Sue and Maggie, who had been helping at parties since the girls were small.

She ran the bath, and was about to get into it when there was another ring at the bell.

'Janey!' She heard Lucy shriek.

Annie ran out to the landing and leant over the bannister. 'I'm in my bathroom. Come and talk to me.'

Janey went to pick up her suitcase but Lucy stopped her.

'Go on up. I'll bring your case.'

As Annie lowered herself into the water, Janey appeared in the bathroom doorway. Blowing a kiss in her friend's direction, she sat down on the lid of the lavatory, but did not remove her coat or hat, or gloves.

289

'You look great.' Annie hoped her tone sounded convincing because she felt quite alarmed by how tired Janey looked.

'I don't. I look exhausted. But I'm OK.'

'I meant to tell you, Prue and her husband are coming – they're doing a detour on their way to Aldeburgh. That won't be embarrassing for you will it?'

'Why should it be?'

'Well, her being your doctor.'

Janey pursed her lips. 'Not a problem. Maybe she's worried that I'll corner her and bang on about my treatment!'

'I'm sure she knows you better than that.' Annie smiled. 'I'm so glad you're here.'

'Me too. But would you mind if I put my feet up before meeting the madding crowd?' She stood up and stretched.

'No. Good idea. You're in the spare room as usual.'

'Thanks. By the way ...' Janey stopped at the bathroom door, took off a glove and flashed her left hand in Annie's direction.

'What? Oh! No ring!'

'I've dis-engaged myself from Miguel. He went home for Christmas at the end of last week, and I found I loved having the place to myself again. And then I did some thinking, and some sums. I'm sure he loved me in his way, but he also saw me as his financial provider. To be honest, I was pissed off with that. Also, the passion was dwindling, and he was so moody. So, I texted to say it was over. He didn't seem that surprised!'

Annie clambered out of her bath and grabbed a towel. 'I would hug you but I'm too wet.'

'I'll take it as read,' laughed Janey.

'Maybe you should follow Arabella's example and go for an older bloke next time.'

'Not sure there'll *be* a next time!' Janey yawned. 'Right, I'm going to have that kip. I'm sure I'll enjoy the party once I'm rested and tarted up.'

Half an hour later, hair and make-up done, Annie ran downstairs, dressed in her new red party frock and matching heels.

In the kitchen, the delectable Jean-Pierre – resplendent in a vivid turquoise shirt and black harem trousers – was opening a bottle of champagne. Lucy, who was wearing more of a pelmet than a skirt, plus an off-the-shoulder glittery top, was leaning against him with a look of lustful admiration in her eyes.

Jean-Pierre started as he noticed Annie, then smiled and walked towards her to plant a kiss on each cheek.

Annie beamed at him. Maybe she even blushed a little. It was just as well that the boy did not resemble his father. Her romantic memories of Greg – and of her abandoned behaviour with him in Biarritz – were fond, but distant. And she was happy to keep them that way.

The bell rang again. Lucy patted Jean-Pierre's bottom as she ran past him to open the front door.

Annie heard her say, 'You must be my mum's friend Prue.'

Eager to see what Prue's husband was like, Annie rushed to greet them. Prue was swathed in a dramatic, floor-length plum-coloured kaftan. In contrast, Alan – who was shorter and stockier – wore ancient corduroy trousers and a threadbare tweed jacket.

Annie encouraged the couple into her sitting room and watched as Prue accepted a glass of champagne from Lucy, while Alan took a glass of sparkling water before putting an arm around his wife. Despite the difference in their appearances they were obviously a great fit as a couple.

The next hour was crazy. The doorbell rang every minute or so and a mix of neighbours, friends and colleagues crowded in. Jean-Pierre mingled with the guests, languidly proffering a cham-pagne top-up to anyone who wanted one. Annie observed Carole eyeing his rear view, and laughed, as the doorbell rang again.

'Darling!' Arabella cried before flinging herself at Annie. 'What fun! Thanks for inviting us.' She stepped to one side to reveal the chuckling Home Secretary. 'This is Martin ...' she announced with passionate pride. He reached for Annie's hand and kissed it. 'Oh, I forgot the flowers ...' he muttered, and sprinted back out of the front door. Annie followed, with Arabella. There was a Jaguar parked by the pavement beyond the short drive. Its interior light was on.

'Is he a bodyguard?' Annie nodded towards the figure in the car.

'No! Just a driver. Well, I think …' Arabella dropped her voice to a stage whisper. 'Actually, you've got me wondering now.'

Annie giggled. 'This is all a bit unbelievable isn't it? I don't suppose he wants to come in and have a drink?'

'Well he might, but he can't! I think we should just pretend he's not there.'

'Dear Madam, for you!' Martin was back, carrying a huge bouquet.

Annie glanced at Arabella's radiant face and then turned back to Martin. 'Has anyone ever said that you look like Nigel Havers?'

'All the time! Good old Nigel – known him forever. Funny thing; since I became Home Secretary he tells me that sometimes people ask him if he's *me*!' Martin's booming laugh echoed down the quiet village street.

At that moment, Lucy emerged from the front door and threw her arms round first Arabella, and then Martin. She giggled as she led them inside.

Annie was about to join them when a taxi drew up and three men emerged from it.

'Annie! You look wonderful!' Gareth strode towards her then steered her towards the light spilling from the open front door. 'And even more splendid, now that I can see you properly – fabulous, isn't she, Jonathan?'

Jonathan nodded. 'Yes … lovely.'

Annie stared at Jonathan, aware that her pulse was beating loudly in her ears. 'And you look very dashing,' she breathed.

He did. Perhaps Gareth had given him some style tips. He was wearing an emerald green velvet smoking jacket, a white shirt open at the neck, and beautifully-cut black trousers that emphasised his fit, athletic build.

292

Jonathan beamed. Then he leant over and kissed her on both cheeks. She put her hand on his velvet sleeve. It felt good there. She looked at him from under her eyelashes, suddenly shy.

'And this …' Gareth was gesturing to the third man, 'is my lover! Tim, come and say "Hello" to your hostess … God I love being gay! This time last year, I was in Caerphilly, agonising about coming out. Now, look at me!'

Annie gave the young man a quick hug. 'How do you put up with him, Tim? Come and have a drink.'

Sue and Maggie descended on the newcomers, moving them into the sitting room and offering drinks and canapés.

Annie was keen to follow, and to continue the conversation she and Jonathan had been trying to have when he left for Jamaica, but she felt she should check on Janey first. She had just planted one foot on the stairs when the doorbell rang again.

'Rupert!' Annie had not expected Diana's husband to attend. 'How lovely – are you well?'

The new arrival, looking much more like one of the country's top civil servants than he had a couple of months previously, drew himself up to his full height. 'Pretty good. Actually, we've …'

'Rupert! Where've you been hiding?' A female neighbour, recently divorced, swooped on him and dragged him into the sitting room with a predatory look in her eye.

'I think she's barking up the wrong tree there,' muttered Annie as Lucy floated past.

'What?'

'Tell you another time. Have you seen Janey?'

'Not since she arrived.'

Annie ran up the stairs and gently knocked at the door of the spare room.

'Come in, you old tart.'

'Wow.' Annie was genuinely taken aback by her friend's transformation.

'Do I look better?'

'I'll say. The best I've seen you since before you got ill.'

'Even though I'm bald!'

'Well, you look terrific in that turban thing. You've got great bones. Now, if I wore that, I'd look puddingy and sad. Love the dress too.'

'It's Biba.'

Annie hugged her. 'Terrific.'

'Thanks. I've been sitting here, willing myself to go down and meet everyone, but I'm a bit anxious.'

'I'm sure you are, but you're going to be by far the most fascinating woman in the room. Come on.'

Janey stood up and sprayed the air around her with a perfume that smelt exotic and spicy, then she walked into its cloud. 'Right! How about a sizeable drink?'

She walked ahead of Annie as they made their way down the stairs. As she reached the open door of the sitting room, Janey glanced back, winked, then took a deep breath and launched herself into the throng.

'I'm Janey!' she declared. Immediately, a crowd gathered around her. Lucy gave her a flute of champagne. Carole, who knew her from parties in the past, hugged her. And Jonathan abandoned Gareth and Tim and introduced himself. He looked very taken with her, Annie noticed.

Lucy moved away to monitor whether other guests had someone to talk to, and had been offered food and drink.

She was all grown up, Annie thought proudly. And she had become kinder, and more aware of others. People had always gravitated to her because of her bubbly personality and her easiness on the eye, but now there was another dimension. Annie had always thought that it was Alice who was the more caring of the two girls. But Lucy had developed a genuine warmth and concern for people – not least for her own sister, which had been a big surprise to Annie. She was a rounded individual now; a fine young woman.

Martin's guffaw interrupted her musings. He and Rupert were chatting in very animated fashion. Arabella always said that Westminster and Whitehall were 'twin villages' so probably they already knew each other. Annie moved nearer, smiling at various guests as she edged her way through them.

'I've had a spot of marital disharmony, as you may have heard,' Martin was saying. 'Like measles … Lot of it about!'

Both men laughed and held out their glasses as Jean-Pierre ambled into their orbit proffering a bottle of Veuve Clicquot.

'Hell to pay with the PM, of course,' Martin continued. 'Bad enough to be dumping the Memsahib after almost four decades, but to take up with your son's live-in girlfriend … and an actress to boot …'

'Tricky,' agreed Rupert, nodding.

'So, what about you, Roopy? You got *yourself* in a bit of a scrape didn't you? No longer found the divine Diana quite the ticket?'

'Something of that nature,' Rupert's voice was low. 'It's all resolved now. Diana's got someone new. I've got … my own arrangements. I'm retiring from the civil service next year, and probably going to leave Cambridge. Considering the Cotswolds, actually. Both of our sons live in Oxfordshire and it would be good to be near them and their growing families. Plan is to tokenly stay married. But do our own thing, as they say these days.'

Where was Diana, Annie wondered? Surely she would not stay away because Rupert was here? Not when it appeared that they had reached an amicable understanding.

As if on cue, the doorbell rang and there was Colin with her friend. They both looked cheerfully flushed. But then Annie did a double-take. Portly, shambling old Colin had turned into a lean and toned Adonis.

'What have you done to him?' Annie laughed as she drew Diana into the kitchen, while Colin headed for the crowded sitting room.

'He took up running to spend more time with me, and now he's keener than I am.'

'You look marvellous too.' Diana's silvery-grey bob had been allowed to grow, and her hair was now prettily swept up into a loose bun. And instead of her customary smart black dress, she was wearing lilac.

Diana giggled. 'Thanks. It's all down to Colin. He's fantastic!'

'Hang on a second …'

Annie looked across the kitchen to where Sue and Maggie, who both knew Diana and Rupert, were standing over the oven checking on its contents.

'Most people are here now, I think,' Annie called to them. 'And the sitting room is absolutely heaving. Do you want to move some guests into the dining room and start serving hot food?'

The women swiftly donned oven gloves and carried a couple of steaming dishes out of the kitchen.

Annie pressed a drink into Diana's hands. 'OK, go on.'

'Thanks … that might have been embarrassing. I hadn't realised they were there. And I'm so taken with Colin that I know I'm not as discreet as usual. Actually, once Rupert came on over here, and we had the house to ourselves, we had a little "quickie". Never fails. It's just explosive for me. Hopefully for him too.'

Annie put her arms round Diana. 'He's certainly never looked better. So, I gather Rupert might move to the Cotswolds.'

'How did you know?'

'I heard him talking to the Home Secretary!'

'Ah, of course. Martin's in lust with your former sister-in-law isn't he? He and Rupert went to the same school. It's such a mafia! Anyway, Rupert's retiring. Meanwhile, Colin is keen to get out of the health service. So, we're actually thinking of all living together in one big house!'

'Gosh! How um … civilised.'

Diana grinned. 'That's one way of putting it. Somewhere near Oxford would be perfect for family things as well as being not too far from Rupert's dominatrix! Colin's happy to move and start a new life. So am I. I haven't missed my physiotherapy business one bit while I've been in Scotland, so maybe it's time just to live a little!' Diana's eyes sparkled with some knowledge or memory that she chose not to share.

'All sounds good.'

'Yes. Mind you, I've put my foot down and said that though I don't mind cooking occasionally, we'll need to have a housekeeper. I've no intention of cleaning up after two men! I'll be lustfully attached to one of them, and officially married to the other. God knows what the neighbours will think! But hopefully it'll work. We're all off to Oxfordshire in the morning to try and explain it to our two sons.'

Annie hugged her friend. 'Go and rescue poor Colin before my newly-divorced and somewhat desperate neighbour lurches at him.'

In the dining room, Sue and Maggie were serving ginger and lime chicken with rice, and vegetarian moussaka. Annie quickly scanned the line of guests waiting for food, hoping that somehow Alice might have arrived without her having noticed. But there was no sign of her.

Back in the hall, Lucy approached her, glass in hand. 'Are you all right, Mum? You haven't had a drink yet; here you go.'

'Thanks, pet. I was just wondering if Alice is really going to come.'

'Of course she is. Tony had to operate all day. They're probably caught in traffic.' She broke off as Jean-Pierre appeared behind her, slipping an arm round her waist and nuzzling the back of her neck.

Annie left them to it. She was very pleased with Lucy and loved her to distraction, but that did not heal the hole made by Alice's absence. She was not in the mood for alcohol, but she was thirsty so she went to the kitchen for a glass of water.

Passing Lucy on her way back to the sitting room, she noticed that her daughter was on her mobile, looking rather tense, and that Jean-Pierre was stroking her arm.

Jonathan caught her eye as she entered the sitting room. He was still standing close to Janey, who was recounting stories from her days on breakfast television. Annie walked round the corner of the L-shaped room and saw Prue practically pinned to the wall by the recently-divorced neighbour, who was in garrulous mode about her ex-husband. Her friend had a faraway look in her eye. How long had she been trapped?

Annie swooped on the two of them, put her arm around the divorced neighbour's waist and guided her through the other guests and out into the hall.

'I so want to catch up with your news later,' she claimed. 'But first you must get some food. There are lots of doctors here – and they're like locusts. There'll be nothing left if you don't get in there.'

The woman looked nonplussed, but did what she was told and headed for the dining queue.

Jonathan was still with Janey when she returned to the sitting room. She really wanted to talk to him herself. But as he seemed to be engrossed in her friend's current story, she wandered around various groups of guests, encouraging them to think about eating, and indicating where the food was.

'Annie!' Jonathan reached out an arm to catch her, and turned his back on Janey. 'How are you?'

'Really, really well. What happened in Jamaica?'

'Well, quite a development. I got there just in time. The beach party was in full swing – and then it turned out that the marriage couldn't go ahead after all!'

'What! Why?'

'Well, apparently, the couple have to send copies of various official documents in advance, which my nephew had done. But they also have to take their *original* birth certificates, to Jamaica with them – and Oliver's girlfriend had forgotten hers. So, it was all off, much to my relief!'

'Amazing!'

Jonathan moved nearer her, and – in a conspiratorial whisper – asked, 'Could you ... I mean ... did you hear what I was shouting to you from the taxi the other day?'

'Sorry, no. Was it important?' Why had she said that? It sounded rude. 'I mean, do you want to tell me now?'

He nodded. 'I do, but you're busy with ...'

'Mum! Have you got a moment?' Lucy's voice from outside the sitting room was unusually shrill.

Annie reluctantly backed away from Jonathan, and headed into the hall. Ahead of her, Lucy was striding towards the kitchen, clearly expecting her mother to follow.

'What is it?'

Lucy slumped into a chair and burst into tears. Jean-Pierre stood beside her, looking worried and hopping from one leg to the other.

'It's Dad. Or rather that fucking Suzie.'

'What?'

'He phoned. He doesn't want me and Alice to go there tonight. He says Suzie's tired.'

'Well, she is eight months pregnant.'

'It's not about that. She likes to keep Dad to herself. I'm sure she wishes he didn't have us.'

'But I thought you were going there to sleep, and then have the morning and lunch with them tomorrow. It all sounded very, um, jolly.'

'Well, to be honest, I kind of talked Dad into that. He says Suzie wants some peace and quiet – and for it to be just the two of them because obviously next year they'll be parents. God I hate her.'

'Sweetie, don't be upset ...'

'He says we can all, like, go round tomorrow and have tea. Big deal. I mean, he hasn't even met Jean-Pierre yet.'

'Darling, I'm sorry. And Alice will be too if she ever gets here.'

'I don't think she'll mind, to be honest. Her theory is that Dad just pays us off all the time – sends us big cheques and so on – in the hope that we won't trouble him much. He's so under the thumb of that bitch.'

Annie was surprised to find that Lucy's criticism of the woman she had once considered a rival no longer thrilled her. Perhaps I'm growing more mature about her at last, she thought.

She took Lucy's hand and pulled her up from the chair so that they were standing facing each other. Then she cuddled her daughter for a moment. Stepping back, she smiled at Jean-Pierre and saw his stricken expression relax.

'Well, one good thing,' she said brightly, 'I can now have you here tonight, *and* for lunch tomorrow – which will be really nice for me!'

Lucy dried her eyes. 'Yeah. That'll be great.' She slipped her arms around Jean-Pierre's waist. 'Cheer me up, babe,' she whispered.

He grinned as he took her hand and led her from the room. The next moment, Annie could hear the sound of two people running up the stairs.

Annie poured herself a glass of sparkling water, then, suddenly tired, she leant against the draining board.

When I was at my most miserable, she remembered, this is where I used to stand and gobble ice cream. She surveyed the kitchen, which was a mess of silver foil and trays, discarded glasses and half-empty champagne bottles. Suddenly, her thoughts drifted to her father. He had loved celebrations. A wave of unhappiness swept over her at the thought of him tucked up in his lonely bed in the nursing home – his 'party days' behind him.

Had this evening's gathering really been such a good idea? It had been a lot of work and she had had no chance to speak to Jonathan properly. And if Alice didn't come …

'Annie!' It was Jonathan. 'Annie, what's wrong?'

'Why should anything be wrong?' she asked in as merry a voice as she could muster.

'I don't know,' he murmured. 'That's why I'm asking.'

'I thought you were looking after Janey …'

He seemed puzzled at her tone.

'… she's very good company,' Annie went on.

'She is,' Jonathan agreed, evenly. 'But she's fine. There are other people with her. I've been looking for *you*. Are you all right?'

Annie felt her eyes well up at his kindness. She absolutely must not cry, and yet tears started rolling down her cheek. She sniffed and turned away, but Jonathan was too quick for her.

He pressed a paper napkin into her hands. 'Annie, please tell me what's wrong.'

Annie wiped her eyes, and then shrugged. 'Oh, I'm probably just tired. I was thinking about my father in his nursing home. I've always spent Christmas with him till now. I *will* see him on Boxing Day, but I really miss him. Also, I was so hoping that my daughter Alice would come, and it doesn't seem very likely that she will now.'

'Christmas isn't always easy, is it?' Jonathan was looking down at her with such genuine concern in his eyes that it almost took her breath away.

She smiled at him. He smiled back. Then she put her hand on his left sleeve and stroked the velvet of his jacket. His face moved towards hers. He looked into her eyes and …

'Mum!'

Annie and Jonathan jumped apart.

'Alice!'

Her daughter, resembling a tiny radiant pixie, stood in the kitchen doorway.

Annie held out her arms and Alice burst into tears and ran into them. She hugged her mother tightly.

'I promised myself I wouldn't cry, Mum,' wailed Alice as she sobbed in Annie's arms. 'But I can't help it.'

Suddenly both women looked around at a movement in the doorway.

Tony, tall, nervous and slightly fidgety was watching them both.

'You know Tony.' Alice's voice warbled as she reached out her hand to pull him to her. Watching them together, Annie stopped trying to hold back her tears, and let them flow.

'And this,' Annie beckoned Jonathan into the group, 'is Jonathan. My ... colleague from the practice.'

Tony and Jonathan nodded at each other before swinging into action – producing more paper napkins to mop up the women's tears, and finding an unopened bottle of champagne.

'Where do you keep the glasses?' asked Tony.

Annie sniffed. 'I think all the proper ones are in the sitting room. Just use tumblers.'

So he did, pouring generous amounts into each one and emptying the bottle.

'Happy Christmas!' they cried in unison. Annie took a sip, then another, and suddenly she felt festive.

Tony and Alice recounted their Christmas Eve travel difficulties – finishing each other's sentences and laughing. Jonathan joined in about his overcrowded train from London to Cambridge. Annie looked on, delighted with everyone and content just to listen.

Suddenly, she remembered that she was supposed to be hosting a party. 'I must go and circulate ... but I'd better pop upstairs first and check I don't look too much of a fright.'

She paused in the doorway and turned back to smile at Jonathan. 'Thank you,' she mouthed at him.

His face lit up. Really, he was a very, very attractive – and good – man.

In her bedroom, she reapplied her lipstick and wiped away some teary flecks of mascara. As she gazed into the mirror, she could see that Alice had come into the room behind her.

'Are you all right, poppet?'

Alice nodded. 'I am so happy ... even though I don't know what's going to happen.'

'Will Jaspal give Tony a divorce?'

'Oh yes. She wants a fresh start now. In fact, she's been invited to apply for a job at the Mayo Clinic in Rochester, Minnesota. She's very impressive. I don't think she used to realise it.'

'If she goes, what will happen about their little boy?'

Alice peered into the mirror before helping herself to her mother's eye make-up remover and then reapplying her mascara. She looked so young, and so innocent – despite all the drama of the past few months. 'I don't know. I suppose Tony could visit a couple of times a year … Nothing's sorted … I know it's a mess. But we're just so, so happy that we're together.'

'That's good. I'd better go back down. Are you OK?'

'I'm fine, Mum, except, I'm dreading having to go to Dad's. I hate Suzie. I've *tried* to like her …'

'Oh, I forgot. You don't know. It's all off. Apparently, Suzie's tired. You don't have to go till tomorrow teatime.'

'Really?' Alice's eyes shone as if she had just won a lottery prize. 'Great. I can start enjoying Christmas. Wait till I tell Tony. We can go to the pub later now. They always have an extension on Christmas Eve and lots of old friends will probably be home for the holiday.'

She ran out of the bedroom ahead of Annie and jumped down the stairs two at a time.

The dining room was full of people enjoying themselves. Most of them had chosen to sit at the main table to eat properly with knives and forks. Gareth was recounting some risqué story to Martin and Rupert. Diana and Arabella were laughing hysterically at something Colin had just said. The recently-divorced neighbour was on her own outside the French windows, having obviously opened them so that she could go out and have a cigarette. Annie would have liked to tell her that she did not allow smoking anywhere, even in the garden, but she thought that the poor woman probably needed some comfort.

Reassured that everyone was being fed, Annie walked back along the hall in the hope of finding Jonathan and continuing their conversation. Instead, she bumped into Prue as she emerged from the downstairs cloakroom. 'Oh, Annie,' she said. 'Do you mind if we go? It's been lovely …'

Annie hugged the woman who had become so important to her in the past few months. 'Drive carefully. Are your stepsons coming to you?'

'Yes, tomorrow,' Prue answered happily. 'By the way, I just saw a small, darker-haired version of you with an adoring guy glued to her hip. I take it she's Alice?'

Annie nodded vigorously. 'Would you like to meet her?'

'Another time. But I'm so glad … you know …'

'Well, it's not what I would have wanted for her, a divorced man with a tiny child, but …'

'It'll probably end up OK. Don't worry. Alan!' Prue yelled at her husband who was just inside the sitting room talking to Jonathan. 'We have to go; things to do before tomorrow.'

'Of course, my angel!' He sprinted to her side and then winked at Annie. 'What it is to be married to such a capable woman!'

Prue gave him an affectionate nudge with her elbow. They both laughed, and headed for the door.

'Happy Christmas,' Annie called after them.

Passing the kitchen, she stopped for a moment to watch as Alice sat talking earnestly to Tony. He was stroking her hair.

This is too private and too lovely, Annie thought as she moved on to the sitting room.

Janey, who had been talking to an elderly neighbour, suddenly saw her.

'There you are! I've been looking for you,' she hissed. 'Jonathan is *divine*.'

Annie blushed. 'You think so?'

'I do. How could you ever have thought he was gay? No wonder you weren't interested in the internet dating I kept nagging you to do. And it's obvious that he's mad about you.'

'I don't know what you mean.'

'I was talking to him for ages, trying to fascinate him with the story of my eventful life, and all he wanted to do was ask about you.'

Suddenly, Annie felt tears stinging her eyes again. 'I'm getting far too emotional tonight – I don't know what's wrong with me.'

'Well, I do! This has been your "come-back" year after your divorce. And you've had Alice's trauma to deal with. And Arabella's. And Diana's. And mine. No wonder you're like a limp rag.'

'How charmingly you put it!'

Janey laughed. 'It's my trade, innit? I have a way with words! Talking of which, I'm going to enjoy work much more now that young Miguel is out of the picture, and I no longer have to keep him in the manner to which he longed to become accustomed. I'm not going to do rubbish jobs for very little dosh. I'm going to pick and choose – and do the kind of stuff I love and am good at. The telly thing, by the way, is now definite. I'm going to be the agony aunt on a new relationships show on Channel 5!'

'Congratulations!'

'Thanks. Now, go and get cosy with Jonathan. Trust me, Annie. Just as I now know that I'm better having the odd one-night stand but generally being on my own, I know you should settle down. And you'll never get a better man for you than that doctor of yours.'

'Are you sure you want to be on your own?' Annie pressed her.

'Totally. Listen, I know the odds with my illness. I know I'm doing OK, but that I'm not out of the woods.'

'I don't think …'

Janey planted her hand firmly on Annie's arm. 'Please don't say anything comforting. Obviously, I hope things will go well, but they may not. And so, whatever time I've got, I'm going to spend it as I want to. And I'm going to stop chasing something I've never been good at – namely live-in relationships!'

There was a sudden rush of chatter as Colin and Diana and Arabella appeared in the doorway.

'You can't possibly go to the local church,' Diana was insisting in response to a guest's suggestion of Midnight Mass at St James's. 'It's too ghastly for words – all "happy-clappy". Come with us to St Mary's in the city. I've booked three taxis.'

305

Before long, she had marshalled Rupert and various neighbours into two of the cars and sent them on their way. Then, just before joining Colin in the third cab, she rushed back into the hall to hug Annie.

'I'll be in touch as soon as we get back from Oxford,' Diana said. 'What are you up to in the next few days?'

'Oh, you know – Christmassy things.'

'I hope they include the dishy doctor.'

Annie smiled but said nothing.

'Annie!' Arabella joined her at the front door. 'You don't mind if we go to the Midnight Mass too, do you? Afterwards, we'll head off to Norfolk. It's so marvellous having a driver – especially after a skinful of bubbly!'

Annie shut the door behind them all. The house was much emptier and quieter now. Perhaps she might get Jonathan to herself for a minute.

'Mum,' Alice appeared and put her arms round her mother. 'Is it all right if we go to the pub now? Where on earth is Lucy, by the way?'

'I'll give you three guesses.'

Alice giggled, and called up the stairs, 'Lucy, stop doing what everyone knows you're doing and come down immediately. I want you and Jean-Pierre to come with us to the pub.'

With the girls gone, Annie wandered back into the messy kitchen and found Janey sitting at the table.

'Are you OK?' Annie asked gently.

'It's been a bit of a performance, really. I'm tired now.'

'Of course you are. Do you want to go to bed?'

'I think I should help you clear up first.'

'Sue and Maggie will do it. They've already started on the dining room.'

'Well, if you're sure …'

'I'm sure. Come on.'

Together, and slowly, they climbed the stairs. Janey had obviously run out of energy.

In the spare room, as Janey was undressing, Annie heard a car draw up outside. She walked to the window and saw that it was a taxi. Gareth and Tim were walking towards it, but was there someone already inside? It looked like it. Could Jonathan have gone too? Surely not, but maybe he was exhausted after his flight. They could, after all, talk another day.

She forced herself to chat while Janey creamed off her make-up and then put on a pair of fleecy pyjamas. Should she tell her how much she had wanted to have some time with Jonathan, but that he had gone home? No. Her friend's eyelids were already closing, so she helped her into bed and left her to sleep.

Downstairs, Sue and Maggie had almost finished cleaning the kitchen. The chaos of a few hours ago had gone.

Annie paid them and added a generous tip.

'Oh, you don't need …'

'I do,' said Annie firmly. 'I had no idea how tonight would go. It's the first party since Edward left. I couldn't have done it without you.'

In the dining room, various people from the village had gathered together and were talking about local issues, as if they were at a rather boozy Neighbourhood Watch meeting. The newly-divorced woman was sitting, forlornly sipping a glass of red wine. Occasionally, she said something at an elderly male neighbour, who, as he was asleep, did not reply.

The man from two doors down was walking around the table in that upright, careful way deployed by individuals who know that they are drunk. He picked up someone's discarded white wine and, with enormous concentration, poured it into his own drink. The wine stained rosé as it combined with the red in his glass.

'Haven't you had enough?' snapped his weary wife. 'I wouldn't mind going now.' She sighed before turning back to a couple who were arguing about house prices.

I'd like them all to leave, Annie thought, as she shut the dining room door behind her and walked down the hall.

She glanced into the sitting room. It appeared to be empty. Maybe she should have a cup of coffee to keep herself awake till the girls came home and the neighbours finally departed.

While the kettle boiled, she laid the kitchen table for breakfast, pleased that she would have her daughters and their men – as well as Janey – for company on Christmas morning. She made coffee and then wandered through to the sitting room with the idea that she might put some music on and sit by the tree.

But then she saw him, at the far end of the room, stretched out, sleeping. He looked familiar and comfortable – and absolutely wonderful. 'Jonathan,' she whispered.

He woke, and his face broke into an expansive smile. Then he jumped up and pulled another armchair alongside his.

'I'm very glad you're still here. I thought you'd gone with Gareth and Tim.'

'Annie!' His tone was amused but admonishing. 'As if I'd have left without saying goodbye or wishing you a happy Christmas.'

She settled herself in the deep armchair as he sank back into his own seat.

'I wondered,' he turned to her, 'whether you'd like me to come with you to see your father on Boxing Day?'

'Gosh! That would be so nice, but, presumably you've got plans for the holiday. Do you want coffee, by the way?'

Jonathan shook his head. 'No, no coffee thanks. As for plans, to tell you the truth they're rather fluid and flexible and might, to some extent, depend on you.'

Suddenly nervous, Annie looked at her new red shoes. Did he mean what she thought he meant? Could he possibly want to spend Christmas with her? Perhaps she had misunderstood. She heard herself say, 'Can I get you anything else then, if you don't want coffee? A drink? Some water? What would you like?'

Jonathan leapt from his seat, and pulled Annie out of her chair, then with a firm arm around her waist, he hurried her to the middle of the room till they were standing beneath a sprig of mistletoe. He pulled her to him, and kissed her.

Eventually, he stepped back and looked into her eyes. '*That's* what I'd like! I've been longing to do that all evening. And you can throw me out now if you're offended – but after more than a decade of longing, I finally decided to seize the initiative!'

Somewhere inside her, a balloon of tension burst.

'I've been aching to tell you for ever that I have feelings for you … that I've had them for years, since long before your husband left. I kept quiet, obviously, while you were married. I used to get a sense you weren't happy and that maybe you might leave him. But then he left *you*, and you were sad when he went, so I didn't say anything. Then in late spring, when you were looking much happier, I got cold feet. Then I started confiding in Gareth, and he told me I needed to be bolder. So, after you came back from Biarritz, I managed to take you out when we'd been to the ophthalmic meeting – the day you weren't well. It was wonderful. I had plans to tell you how I felt then, but your friend Diana turned up. And every time I tried to say anything I got it wrong. *Spectacularly* wrong. And then you went off for a break to Suffolk. And when you popped in a few weeks later I was so shocked at seeing you, I mucked everything up again. And then I went to Florence with my nephew, and when I came back, the more I looked at you, the more I thought you were indifferent to me. It was only last week at the party that I began to hope … So now, I'm finally trying once and for all to tell you that I love you, Annie. I don't know if you could ever – might ever – feel the same? I shouldn't think so for a minute, but, could I just hope and wait?'

Annie felt as though her body had turned into millions of fizzing champagne bubbles. He loved her. He must do. He had never, ever, said so much at one time in all the years she had known him.

One of his arms was still around her waist but he looked unsure.

'You don't have to wait, Jonathan,' she reassured him, staring fondly into his eyes. 'I love you too. I have done for months.'

'You do? That's marvellous. But why?'

'Why?' She burst out laughing.

Just then a raucous voice outside the window started to sing 'Silent Night'. This was followed by hoots of laughter.

She put her arms around his neck and pulled him close. 'There are lots of reasons – but unfortunately my daughters are about to stagger in from the pub, so I'll list them later. However, a very important one, which I've only just discovered, is that you're the most amazing kisser.'

They could hear the front door opening and the sounds of four noisy revellers jostling into the hall.

'Really?' His eyes danced with delight.

She continued to hold on to him tightly.

'Yes, really,' she murmured. 'So, please will you do it again?'

About the Author

Christine Webber originally trained as an opera singer but had to rethink her career plans when her voice professor told her: 'Your voice is OK, but your legs are very much better!'

Musical theatre beckoned. There was some success. But not much.

In 1979, she became a news presenter for Anglia TV. At last she had found something she enjoyed that other people thought she was good at. It was such a happy relief that she stayed for 12 years. Towards the end of that period *In Honour Bound*, her first novel, was published.

After leaving Anglia Television, she became an agony aunt for various publications including *TV Times, Best, Dare* and *BBC Parenting*. And she wrote a relationship advice column for *The Scotsman* and one for *Woman*, called Sexplanations. She also regularly broadcast advice on *Trisha, The Good Sex Guide … Late* and from the BBC's *Breakfast* sofa.

During her 'problem page' years, she decided to train as a psycho-therapist. This led to her starting a small practice in Harley Street, which she still has.

Christine has written twelve non-fiction books including *How to Mend a Broken Heart* and *Get the Happiness Habit.* But finally, she has returned to her original love of writing fiction with *Who'd Have Thought It?*

She says: 'Mid-life women are fascinating. Having explored their hopes, fears, insecurities and options in my 2010 guide for female baby boomers, *Too Young to Get Old*, I thought it would be an absorbing challenge to fictionalise what I had learned. This book is the result.'

Book Club Questions

1. How much did the book reflect your life or that of friends or colleagues?

2. Which character did you most closely identify with?

3. Do you share Annie's belief that mid-life is much more topsy-turvy than you would once have imagined it to be?

4. Do you feel that Annie would have left Edward eventually, had he not found love elsewhere? What would it have taken to make her walk away?

5. How much of the talk about friendship in mid-life rings true for you?

6. How easy is it to make friends as you grow older?

7. What happens when people you had thought of as 'mates for life' begin to disappoint or anger you?

8. How daunting is it to learn a whole set of new rules and etiquette when you return to dating, after a long period of having been in a stable relationship?

9. Have you ever found secrets about a parent who has died or whose home you are clearing, after they've become too ill to live there? How did you deal with this and what was the impact on you?

10. What are the biggest challenges people face when they find love – and want to be together – at a time when their family thinks they should be winding down and buying a rocking chair?